Working the Dead

The tenth Otto Fischer Novel

Jim McDermott

Copyright Jim McDermott, 2021
All rights reserved

Abbreviations and acronyms used in the text

BfV – *Bundesamt für Verfassunsschutz*: Federal Office for the Protection of the Constitution, German domestic security agency

BND – *Bundesnachrichtendienst*: Federal counter-intelligence service of West Germany (from 1956; formerly the Gehlen Organization (or 'Org')

CIA – *Central Intelligence Agency*: US foreign intelligence service

DDR – *Deutsche Demokratische Republik*: German Democratic Republic, or East Germany

GRU - *Glavnoye Razvedyvatel'noye Upravleniye*: Soviet military intelligence directorate

KGB - *Komitet Gosudarstvennoy Bezopasnosti:* state security agency of the Soviet Union, formed in 1954 by the amalgamation of former domestic (MVD) and foreign (MGB) security agencies

Komsomol — *Kommunisticheskiy Soyuz Molodyozh*: Soviet political youth organization

MfS - *Ministerium für Staatssicherheit*: East German Ministry for State Security; known colloquially as **Stasi**

MGB - *Ministerstvo Gosudarstvennoy Bezopasnosti SSSR*: Ministry for State Security, counter-intelligence successor organization (from March 1946) to the former **NKGB**, and part-forerunner of **KGB**

SIS – *Secret Intelligence Service*: British counter-intelligence service; known also as MI6

Stasi – see **MfS** above

Bremen, 29 June 1961

The Pastor finished his reading and looked up. A few eyes were upon him, but the majority examined knees immediately below them, or searched the architecture for clues as to what was very old or very new, or, if they belonged to one of the few mourners not weighed by the occasion, a particularly striking hat. The pause, at first merely sufficient to the sentiments just expressed, began to drag a little, but only one member of the congregation – a large, gnarled man on the front row – noticed this, and probably because he was the cause of it. Eventually, reluctantly, the Pastor nodded at him and vacated the pulpit. The man stood, limped forward, took his place and spoke without notes.

'Otto Fischer was my friend, though we didn't know each other as children, or even as comrades in arms. We met as war invalids, useful for nothing except taking news of military disasters and working it into something only half-crap (the Pastor winced slightly at this). I don't know whether it was us being in the same boat that first made me think of him as a mate, but I soon felt that he was more than that.'

The big man examined his audience, all of whose attention was upon him now.

'Otto was a decent man, in a world where decency doesn't get you far. He was clever too, but he didn't wear it like a hat. It came up on you so gradually that you thought yourself stupid for missing it, when really it was him just not wanting to be noticed. He had the least need for admiration of anyone I've ever known. Peace was all he ever really looked for – the peace of being allowed to live in peace. He only got it late in life, and even then it didn't quite work out. He had a plot of land in a place where memories wouldn't press too hard, and a good woman too; but the soil wasn't as rich as it needed to be, and what he'd imagined might grow into love never quite did. Eventually, she married someone else, but they remained good friends. While he was on his land he worked for the effort's sake, and made just enough to keep house. I went out there once, to stay with him, and we laughed about a lot of stuff that hadn't seemed funny the first time around. It seemed to me that he was as content as I'd ever known him; but he died alone, and I can't forgive myself for that.'

The pause that followed allowed a few handkerchiefs to be flushed from pockets and purses. The speaker swallowed twice, not trusting himself to continue until the lump had subsided.

'The coroner said that Otto's heart gave up. He must have sensed that *something* was coming, because recently he'd sold his property and moved into a hotel in the town nearby. At the time he didn't mention any of that – at least, not to his old friends. I wish that he had. He might have come back to Germany. Kristin and me would have given him a home, and I know a lot of you would have done the same, whatever General Gehlen thought about it (the Pastor, interested suddenly, sat up). But that was our friend Otto – he never liked to put upon folk, and now he can't.'

A sob interrupted whatever the big man was going to say next. He took the interruption gratefully, rubbed an eye with a fist and went back to his pew without another word. The woman sitting next to him squeezed his arm, which was as much as was needed to breach the dam. The Pastor said something more, a form of words too familiar and expected to be given much attention, and then the casket was carried outside, to the hearse that would carry it to Riensberger Friedhof and a plot next to the grave of Maria-Therese Fischer, the deceased's second wife.

The nave of Sancti Martini, one of Bremen's oldest, most-bombed churches, emptied slowly, the congregation following the casket from the front pews. Only the big, limping man remained in his seat, an envelope in hand, waiting until the business could be done tastefully. When everyone else had filed out, he rose, shook the Pastor's hand and offered the donation.

'For the renovations, or whatever.'

'Thank you.' The Pastor managed to keep the pain from his voice as he repossessed his half-crushed extremity. 'What was that about Gehlen?'

'Otto was a wanted man.'

'Really? What did he do?'

The big man considered this for a moment, his eyes on the plain stone floor.

'It's hard to say. He got up people's noses a lot. They thought they could work him, but it never turned out well. Germany wasn't safe for him – it's why he moved abroad.'

The Pastor's face must have asked the obvious question. The big man shook his head. 'He wasn't one of those. He served as honourably as anyone could in that war, a front-line man. It ended for him outside Moscow. They gave him the Knight's Cross, did you know?'

'I didn't.'

'Yeah, a proper hero, for all the good it did him. Well, thank you. Do you need a lift to the friedhof?'

1

Three hours later, following a *leichenschmaus* held at a small restaurant nearby, a number of the mourners – the families Holleman, Branssler and Hoeschler, and an unaccompanied young man, Jonas Kleiber - were gathered at a substantial villa off the Schwachhauser Ring, the home of Adolf 'Earl' Kuhn, one of the city's leading businessmen. Two girls in maids' uniforms were passing among them with trays of finger-food and filled wine glasses while the host (a balding, generously-proportioned man in his mid-30s) warmed his rear on the unnecessary but cheerful log-fire behind him and dabbed his eyes with a folded napkin. In one of the room's deeper armchairs, the big man with the artificial leg examined something in his fist.

'What's this?'

'It's an olive, Freddie. You *must* have seen one before.'

Freddie Holleman frowned at the skewered item. 'I can't recall, though I've tasted the oil, obviously. Do you have a lot of olives in Frankfurt, Gerd?'

'It's like the south of Italy, mate – we can't move for them.'

Gerd Branssler's wife sniffed and jabbed him with an elbow. 'Don't be silly.'

'Sorry, sweetheart. Not the time or place.' Branssler looked around, addressing himself to everyone in the room. 'He didn't say *anything*? Anything at all?'

Holleman shook his head. 'The last for me was a letter, back in February. It was just farming and house repairs, like always. Rolf?'

Rolf Hoeschler, a sleek, well-manicured gentleman, shrugged slightly. 'Sometime last year, the same thing. He sent some money for a christening present, and begged us not to let our grandchild be named Otto.'

His wife, Mila, smiled sadly. 'We wouldn't have. It's not ideal, for a girl.'

Earl Kuhn moved slightly, to give the benefit of the fire to the rest of the room. 'The latest I had was a Christmas card, and a request that I send out some records he couldn't find in Portugal. He tried to pay for them, but I didn't bank the cheque.'

'Jazz?'

Kuhn's company, *West Side Records*, was Northern Germany's foremost distributor of recorded jazz music (its stock of other genres confined to a small selection of Broadway musicals and home-grown *schicksalmusik* for the elderly and over-nostalgic). The proprietor snorted.

'Otto? He'd sooner have listened to Goebbels. No, it was classical – I'd heard of Beethoven, but the rest ...'

His voice trailed off, and he swallowed hard. Though he hadn't seen Otto Fischer for some years, his affection for the man had been born in a desperate place and time, and was as enduring and painful as love of family. His sorrow was further teased by wife Alisz, who had hardly known the deceased but had been crying since she left the church. Kuhn was not the sort of husband who could be unmoved by such anguish.

All eyes (except Alisz's, which were too full to focus) turned to Jonas Kleiber. He was examining the depths of his wine glass, and for a moment didn't noticed the attention. When he did, he twitched slightly.

'No, I didn't hear anything that made me worry he wasn't well. He telephoned me a few months ago – from Porto, I think. He wanted me to find him something in German or English, on grape-fungus. He said that everything was *alright*, when I asked.'

Greta Branssler nodded firmly. 'It must have been very quick, then. A blessing.'

A polite murmur of agreement belied the doubtful cast to many faces. A true blessing would have been no heart attack, but despite the room's generous scattering of atheists no-one cared to challenge what might turn out to have been God's Will.

'Poor Otto.' Holleman slumped in his armchair. 'He survived the Ivans God knows how many times, and Gehlen's mob, and several sods who paid to have him Offed, and the shittiest luck that any man ever endured, only for a weak clock to wipe him out, just like that.'

The flick of his thumb and fingers set off Alisz once more, and Kuhn put down his glass so that he could deploy the full hug. Everyone else sighed, or nodded, or contemplated the terrible inscrutability of the universe.

'Was the casket sealed in Portugal, Father?'

Ulrich Holleman was too young to bear the silence of mourning for long, but he regretted the question before it was fully out. Several sharp intakes of breath confirmed his poor judgement.

'Yeah. It took a couple of days to get his body down to Porto. Then, it ran up against the sort of bureaucracy that dictatorships love. Zofia and her husband tried and failed to find refrigeration in the town while they waited for the right papers, and by the time it arrived he'd started to smell like Barbarossa at Antioch, apparently.'

The ladies winced. Gerd Branssler glared at Holleman, who not only mistook his meaning but seemed a little pleased with himself.

'It's the only bit of school history I remember - how the vinegar they filled him with didn't take.'

It was a measure of her embarrassment that Mila Hoeschler – who, in her own right, was almost certainly the wealthiest person in the room - interrupted with a question in whose answer she had not the slightest interest.

'Is there a will?'

Jonas Kleiber looked around and coughed.

'He sent me a copy a while ago, for safe-keeping. There are no living relatives except a nephew he only ever saw once, at the font. A third of everything goes to him, the rest to Zofia. There are a few personal things he wanted Freddie to have.'

As there was nothing to say to any of this, no-one tried. The hired girls did their best to interest the guests in more wine and *zucherkuchen*, but appetites had become as stunted as the conversation. In the hush that followed, the Kuhn parlour's fixtures and fittings received an unusual degree of attention.

Their host felt the silence keenly. He searched for some pleasant memory of his dead friend that he might share, but Holleman's official encomium had done such justice to the subject already that anything he offered would be a poor, thin thing.

'I wish ...' he paused, trying to put a tail on the thought; ' ... that he could have had a happier life. I mean, more *normal*.'

Holleman sighed. 'I wish he'd got out of Berlin before he did.'

Gerd Branssler – like Holleman, Berlin born, bred and fled – nodded. 'There's too much bad memory in that place.'

'Too much unfinished business.'

Almost every head nodded. The Kuhns and Jonas Kleiber weren't native Berliners; all the others were but had long since departed their *heimats*, prodded by the city's seemingly eternal role as a rag-doll gripped between two powerful sets of jaws. Even the Hoeschlers, whose fortune was built upon the rents from dozens of Berlin properties, had gradually sold up and moved their business to Munich, where the Americans would have a chance at least to defend local real-estate against a communist tide. It was universally accepted that Otto Fischer had done the sensible thing, even if it had come late, and required the threat of KGB assassins to prise him from his adopted city.

Having broached the elusive quality of happiness, Kuhn gave a little play to his sentimental nature.

'Do you ever wonder what it would have been like, if Otto hadn't ever been in the world?'

Branssler snorted. 'They've done that one already, with Jimmy Stewart.'

'I mean, just for us. If I hadn't met him it would have ended for me in Stettin, back in '46. I was squatting in a filthy cellar with a pile of hot money, an arsenal I'd pinched from Third Panzer Army and no idea how to get out of the city alive. It was Otto who found a way for us both.' Kuhn turned and touched an urn that stood on the mantelpiece. 'And my dog, bless her.'

Gerd Branssler rubbed his bald pate. 'I got him into trouble with Gehlen's lot, but that was to help Freddie. He got us all out of it, didn't he?'

Holleman nodded. 'He helped me hide the twins from the Reich (Ulrich blushed slightly, perhaps recalling his youthful enthusiasm for the *Hitler Jugend*), and he helped us again on the day of the Uprising, when we crossed the Line. But then, I sprang him from Sachsenhausen. And I got him out of Berlin, three years ago.'

Kleiber regarded him critically. 'No, you didn't.'

'Well, I was company for him, wasn't I? A wise voice, when he needed it?'

Those who knew Holleman managed not to gape incredulously. As the greatest beneficiary of Fischer's keen mind and appalling luck he bore a weight of guilt that needed talking out of itself occasionally.

Rolf Hoeschler studied his glass for a few moments, and spoke slowly. 'We met in a ditch, in Crete. Later, I saved his life under a bridge in Tiergarten, but he more than repaid that debt. Mila and me, we'd probably have been blackmailed into poverty and then handed over to the Soviets if he hadn't thrown himself in the way.'

'Well, Otto didn't do anything for me.' Jonas Kleiber stood, handed his empty glass to one of the maids and checked his watch. 'But he's the best friend I ever had. I have to leave now - my flight's in an hour.'

Earl Kuhn glanced around the room. 'Do you need a lift to Neuenland?'

'No, I ordered a taxi when I landed. It should be ...'

The doorbell chimed, punctuating Kleiber's foresight. He shook hands with every one of the other mourners, offered a half-sincere invitation to put up visitors to London at a day's notice and departed quickly, before one or more of the women in the room thought to hug him. During the twenty-minute drive to the airport he tried not to let his mind wander towards time, transience and worms, but the day had made him feel old beyond his thirty years. Only the return flight to London raised his spirits slightly, and that was because the ordeal (he was an expert aerophobe) was milder than expected. The BEA Trident took off so powerfully that for once he didn't feel as if the engines were stalling halfway into its climb, and the 'plane seemed to begin its slow descent almost as soon as it had levelled off. Throughout, he remained calm enough to appreciate one of the stewardesses, a novel experience.

From London Airport he took a bus into the city. The rain that had threatened Bremen came down steadily here, but being an adopted Englishman he hardly noticed. At Westminster he was tempted to break his journey and telephone his girlfriend, but at this time of the evening the call would almost certainly be taken by her mother (a Cerberus, particularly when a German suitor hovered). He comforted himself with the thought that the day's sad passages weren't the best preparation for a romantic interlude, and Gloria always insisted upon a degree of romancing.

His flat – a neat, two-bedroomed accommodation above a bakery in Kennington – smelled, as usual, of the product, which whetted his appetite.

Fortunately, his foresight had extended to ordering an evening meal a day in advance, so rather than have his bath immediately he turned on the kitchenette radio and waited for his delivery.

As always, the main news was anglocentric. The English Church had acquired a new Archbishop of Canterbury the previous day, so platitudes about spiritual renewal were strewn thickly. Three weeks old now, the stripped bones of the Duke of Kent's marriage to Katharine Worsley were being picked at still, though nothing new could be made of them. Kleiber had filed a syndicated story about it with major German newspapers, comparing the massive interest that any royal wedding excited in this latter-day Ruritania to the local reaction to the death of Carl Jung ('who's he?'), a contrast that must have pleased someone, as the fee for it was wired less than two days later. The big story from abroad was Adolf Eichmann taking the stand in Tel Aviv to begin his defence (a straightforward piece on British newspapers' reporting of the trial had been his only, circumspect contribution to the story, as no German media wanted the thing put up in lights). Otherwise, the two US deserters' killing spree across America, ending with their capture a fortnight earlier, continued to bring up the occasional body for the edification of crime desks everywhere.

The last of the football results (matches involving quaintly-named Scottish teams) were being recited when the downstairs buzzer announced the arrival of his much-anticipated Italian supper. He opened his front door and hurriedly set his tiny table in the time it took the delivery man to ascend the stairs. He turned, and was about to offer some glib but flattering remark about his love of the cuisine when he noticed the newspaper wrappings.

'Oh, Christ! Not fish and chips?'

Otto Fischer shrugged apologetically. 'I have to try the legend, while I'm here.'

?

'I'd like to see the First Secretary as soon as possible, please.'

A.S. Shevchenko offered General Zarubin his bleariest face. 'May I ask what it's about, Comrade?'

Put like that, the question was perfectly proper. It was only the inflection's hint of *what the fuck could you possibly want now?* that suggested the man had less than a lively enthusiasm for exposing his boss to yet another nagging.

'It's regarding further thoughts I've had on the Vienna Summit.'

Nikita Khrushchev's personal assistant was nodding wearily before *Vienna* reached open air.

'Perhaps they could be presented to the forthcoming Collegium meeting?'

And have them rendered as bland as milk-soup? 'The matter's too urgent to wait until then, Andrei Stepanovich.'

'Then you might speak directly to Comrade Gromyko. I can ask whether he's at the Ministry today?'

'Again, I would prefer that the First Secretary heard this in my own words.'

Without further comment, Shevchenko reached for his office diary and opened it. A frown, a sigh and a hopeless shake of the head put Zarubin on notice that he was going to be grievously disappointed.

'Tuesday, 9.15am? Ten minutes only, I'm afraid.'

'But today is Thursday.'

Insolently, Shevchenko made a point of examining his desk calendar. 'So it is, Comrade General. I wish I could be more helpful.'

On his way back to his office, Zarubin forced himself to smile at everyone he passed, including secretarial staff he wouldn't normally have noticed. No-one in the Kremlin gave greater scrutiny to reputations than those who had the clearest, furthest view from below, and he was beginning to fear that his own might be attracting more than the occasional upward glance. It was the one truly egalitarian feature of their system, that everyone had the opportunity to go all the way, both ways.

His own secretary, Levin, was waiting with the day's briefing papers. Usually, these came from embassies and KGB stations in countries where Soviet and American interests met forehead-to-forehead, with an occasional plum that some ambitious fellow had managed to blackmail or buy from a compromised CIA or SIS field-operative. Everyone was trying a little harder at the moment, having had a stick pushed up their fundaments following the arrest of KGB's star double-agent, George Blake, two months earlier. Unfortunately, extraordinary efforts often produced extraordinarily bad data, and much of Zarubin's energy had been wasted lately on testing, challenging or bluntly contradicting what too many members of the Foreign Affairs Collegium desperately wished to believe.

'He said no, then?'

Levin tried to look sympathetic, but the smile couldn't be entirely smothered. He had predicted disappointment, and the cast to Zarubin's face confirmed his prognosis.

'He said next Tuesday, which is as much as to say no.'

'You must have expected it. They think you're a Cassandra.'

'Cassandra's predictions were invariably correct.'

'An unforgivable offence.'

Levin's native common sense should have tamed his imprudence, but invariably it turned up without whip and chair. Zarubin had employed him for a number of years now, and had yet to decide whether his wantonly unvarnished opinions reflected a warped moral courage or rank idiocy. He was often entertained by them, but a dangerous sport had to be played carefully.

His secretary was right, of course. Prescience was laudable if it served the policies of powerful men, but waiting until their porridge was in the bowl and then pissing in it was a doubtful strategy. Unfortunately, circumstances demanded that the effort be made. For several months now, the First Secretary's (already-exuberant) self-belief had been bolstered by a series of disastrous decisions on the part of the new Kennedy Administration. In normal times, Blake's exposure would have been an occasion for drawing in horns a little, but it had coincided with the gloriously inept Bay of Pigs incursion, an enormous propaganda coup that had required not the slightest investment of resources from Moscow. Then, just three weeks ago, Khrushchev and Kennedy had met at their Vienna Summit, where the American President had performed so weakly that he might as usefully have signed the concluding declaration in advance and left the details to the Soviet delegation. For a man of Khrushchev's temperament, this degree of political success was as intoxicating as it was unfamiliar, and he was behaving exactly as a drunkard would.

Zarubin's principal role was to advise on the American Government's motives and intentions. The task of keeping the First Secretary's mood swings within a narrow band fell to him more than anyone else, therefore, because it was precisely upon this ground that they were likely to be most pronounced. In 1958, Khrushchev had threatened to sign a peace treaty with the DDR and recognize it as a sovereign state, thus rendering the Allied presence in West Berlin untenable. He had then done nothing about it. More than two years later, he repeated the threat, and this time put a date on its consummation – December, 1961. The Americans and British had continued to keep their heads, however, and prospects of getting them out of Berlin short of war had seemed distant, until Vienna.

Kennedy was a young man, and inexperienced in foreign policy matters. Perhaps he had been too eager to accommodate, and at best seemed uncertain about his country's future intentions in, and for, West Berlin. Khrushchev, like all practiced bullies, had pounced upon his hesitation, his ambiguities, and come away from their summit with a sense of things pouring his way. The bluffer had not been called out, and he had let the reprieve go to his head.

In Zarubin's opinion, this was not sensible behaviour. With titanic effort, the Soviet Union had closed the long-range bomber- and atomic ordnance-gap with the US over the previous three years, but despite or because of that. and the massive – and massively expensive - technical triumphs of Sputnik and Gagarin's space voyage. the nation was driving on a near-empty tank. Their ballistic missiles, so terrifying to the American Congress and public, had rudimentary guidance systems and a parlous under-provision of solid fuels. Worse, they had been built on the bellies of the Soviet people. Food riots had broken out in several cities earlier that year (an alleged impossibility in their model socialist society), while cattle had dropped dead in their fields for want of winter feed. Even where palpable achievements occurred, they had the effect of goading the enemy into superbly-financed response. Americans were a perennially anxious people but not cowardly (an uncomfortable combination), and for all his faults Stalin had understood how far they could be pushed profitably. His successor, always sensitive to how much weaker his own position was, gave his strongman persona far too much leash. Zarubin often had the urge to explain (precisely as if to a simpleton) that a good leader managed bad situations carefully and exploited good ones judiciously, but he knew that the effort would have been more of the same piss pouring into the same bowl. Khrushchev heard what he wanted to hear, and nothing more.

So, Zarubin was being avoided. A once-open door was now not only closed most days but guarded by Shevchenko, who had standing orders to allow him brief access somewhere between the Novosibirsk Girls' Choir and the Bulgarian Ambassador. Meanwhile, too many lickspittles were telling the First Secretary exactly what he wanted to hear – that the Americans were reeling; that Ulbricht's sealing of the internal border between East and West Berlin (a persistent demand since the start of the year) would be the final shove that ejected the Allies from the city; that, with Kennedy as President, the Soviet Union could be more assertive in Europe, Africa and the Caribbean without consequence. In his present mood, Khrushchev was listening to all of it, and ignoring Cassandra.

As usual, Levin was reading Zarubin's thoughts as if they were circulating on a neon display somewhere above his head.

'Let them make their own nooses, Comrade General. You've offered your opinions frankly, so you're on record.'

'I would be happy to do so, if the beneficiary of my wisdom wasn't Khrushchev himself. If or when I'm proved right he'll blame me for not talking down the wrong more convincingly. Not in so many words, of course - I'll just find myself heading a committee for the storage of atomic waste. With site visits, naturally. If he's really angry he might have me re-assigned to KGB, where a lot of grudges can be satisfied.'

Levin nodded slowly. 'They might *not* be wrong, though – about Kennedy.'

'They are. Even if the President's innocence persists, David Dean Rusk won't allow his State Department to continue to be played. He's probably been calling Kennedy a horse's ass since Vienna, and to his face. What worries me most is that, like all weaklings, the young man will over-compensate when he realises that he's been taken for a *rube*.'

'A what?'

'It's an Americanism – something similar to *derevenshchina*.'

'Ah. I like that – it's almost onomatopoeic.'

'I'm gratified that you think so.'

'So, what will you do? If the First Secretary won't listen?'

'What indeed? The brilliant solution would be to conceive a course correction that's sufficiently subtle as not to disturb our Captain.'

'A nautical metaphor. Delightful.'

Being almost inured to Levin's insolence, Zarubin didn't rise to it. His *brilliant solution* held its own problem, which was that subtlety was largely wasted upon Khrushchev - he either missed the point entirely or pretended that he had. When circumstances were unfavourable he might listen to something that offered a chance of better, but with a diplomatic triumph fresh in mind Cassandra would be screaming her dark prophecies into a void.

This would require a great deal of thought, and Zarubin feared that time was pressing. Though he had as yet committed to nothing, the First Secretary couldn't continue to stall Walter Ulbricht - and now, with Kennedy's unwitting assistance, he might not wish to. The DDR was bleeding citizens, many of them highly educated and trained, pouring into and finding a welcome home in Europe's most dynamic economy. The national border was sealed, but Berlin remained a vast, almost risk-free escape-tunnel to the West, and Ulbricht was tiring of *wait a while longer*, of Khrushchev's glibness, of the jokes made at his expense and of the threats, thrown at the Americans, that hadn't been followed through. The man was as reliable an ally as anyone with three hundred thousand Soviet troops on his soil could possibly be, but the bonds had been loosening since Stalin's death. Giving him his Berlin wall would re-cement them, at little apparent cost.

The peace treaty was coming in December, if Khrushchev's latest promise could be trusted. It was now almost July, which gave Zarubin a month or two at most to find a defusing mechanism before inertia took over and led to a confrontation that no-one could win but the Soviet Union could most definitely lose.

'What about a nice cup of tea?'

Zarubin regarded his secretary coldly. 'I could have had you shot, three years ago. Perhaps I *should* have.'

'Yes, Comrade General. I'm grateful that you chose not to. We had a profitable outcome, did we not?'

'Which is why you're here still, as irritating as head-lice in clogs. Don't think yourself immortal.'

'Of course not. Shall I bring hot water?'

3

'Why aren't you dead, Otto?'

'I *am* dead, Jonas. There's a piece of paper that says so, and it's stamped. And now I'm buried, too.'

'Then why are you wandering restlessly among us?'

'This really is delicious. Haddock, is it?'

'You never know. It's haddock-shaped, at least.'

'And I never would have thought of putting vinegar on potatoes. Cabbage, obviously, but not fried potatoes.'

The corpse ate its rations with apparent relish, and when it had finished it began to pick at the remnants that Kleiber, finding himself not nearly as hungry as he'd imagined, had pushed away.

'Mmm!'

'Oh, come on, Otto! What the hell are you doing, upsetting us all?'

A hand paused halfway to its destination and dropped. Fischer glanced around and found what he was looking for.

'Can we have a drink? Something strong?'

A half-empty bottle of French brandy stood on a small tray on the sideboard, flanked by two glasses. Kleiber brought them to table and poured almost to the brim.

'Well?'

Fischer took a sip and looked up. 'I can't return to Germany.'

'I know. It's why you became Portuguese.'

'But I *have* to return to Germany.'

'Why?'

'I can't tell you.'

'Alright. Why are you here, in London?'

'I need your help with something.'

'Money?'

'No, I have plenty, though you might change some of it for the British stuff, if you would. I need to speak to someone, and you can help me find him.'

'Who?'

'I don't have a name.'

Kleiber breathed hard. 'Well, there are only seven million people in this city. It shouldn't be difficult. I assume Anonymous is *in* London, or need we be spreading the net?'

'No, he's definitely in London.' Fischer paused, and frowned. 'Unless he isn't, of course.'

'What in the name of Holy God are you talking about?'

'He *works* in London. But what if he's on … what do the English call it?'

'Holiday? Leave?'

'Yes, those.'

'You didn't bother to check, before you left Portugal?'

'How could I? I don't know the man.'

The giant hands pressing against Kleiber's temples put a little more effort into it. He waited, hoping that not asking questions might elicit something more useful. Fischer picked up his glass, took another sip and turned slightly in his chair to examine the terrain. It was dominated by a feminine pink and cream striped wallpaper, most of which still clung to the walls. A small tiled fireplace, standing out from symmetrical alcoves, hosted a smaller gas fire with a coin-fed meter to the side. Two ragged leather armchairs flanked it sufficiently closely to scorch shins during the winter months, while the tenant's wanderlust was teased by a bucolic scene (tree-line, threatening skies, cottages and a horse and cart taking on a river lengthways) hanging over the mantelpiece in a chipped gold frame. Everything bore the patina of long service, and for anyone who had spent the post-war years in Berlin the whole was an oasis of shabby comfort.

'Constable.'

'What?'

Kleiber nodded towards the painting. 'The artist – John Constable. Not an original, naturally.'

Fischer stared at it for a few moments, his face betraying neither admiration nor disapproval – an enigmatic performance he'd maintained since the previous evening, when he had arrived with as much notice and impact as descending ordnance. Since then, not-so-polite enquiries regarding his corporeal condition, his purpose in England and the monstrous deception of his closest friends had been parried deftly or merely ignored. Too bewildered even to feel relief at the prospect of Otto Fischer upright, breathing and as uncomely as ever, Kleiber had managed to seize only the briefest initiative when he mentioned – blurted - that the funeral had yet to take place, and that he would be flying to Bremen the following morning to bury a man who plainly wasn't in the mood for it.

That had seemed to trouble Fischer, but only for a moment. He had nodded, taken another pained sip of American-style powdered coffee and stressed that nothing was to be said to anyone, not even Freddie Holleman (as if Kleiber could possibly have found the nerve to fling such a grenade into a group of mourners); that he was to behave in all ways as he would if the body in the casket was that of Otto Henry Fischer, late of Stettin, Berlin and a half-fertile hillside in northern Portugal.

Whether he'd achieved this masterful deception Kleiber couldn't say, but no-one had reacted suspiciously to his few contributions to the sad musings, or to his demeanour (he'd been as jumpy as a bomb-defuser all that day). In any case, no-one's mind could be clear enough at a funeral to notice nuances (much less dissect them), so for the moment at least none of them could suspect that Otto Fischer had done a Lazarus …

The thought jolted something in Kleiber's mind. He'd noticed it the previous evening but hadn't said anything – not least because it would have been starkly inappropriate. There was something quite different, and slightly startling, about the deceased object.

'You're looking very *well*, Otto.'

'I'm tanned.'

'No, it's more than that.'

'The farming life, then - it either kills you or reminds you where your muscles live.' Fischer raised his mutilated right arm, the elbow bent to form a right-angle. 'Even this useless thing's proved not to be, quite. It's mad, but at sixty-three I'm probably healthier than I've been since my school days. Which doesn't put me among the elite, obviously.'

'It's more the pity that you're dead, then.'

Fischer smiled but didn't rise to the bait.

Kleiber sighed. 'Alright. How can I help you find this man?'

'I just need an address.'

'For what?'

'The British Library, Manuscripts Department.'

'That's it? Why come to me, then? Why didn't you just hail a taxi at the airport and tell the driver where to go?'

'Because I didn't arrive by 'plane. I came into the Port of London on a merchant ship – the fortified wines express. And if I'd asked directions from a taxi driver, he wouldn't then have put me up for the night. Or several.'

'Several?'

'As much as a week, perhaps? If you don't mind?'

'Of course not. You'll be in the cot-bed, though.'

'It's very comfortable, thank you. I'm used to much worse.'

'A farmer couldn't afford a decent mattress?'

'He couldn't find one. The Portuguese seem to enjoy pain - it must be their flagellant tradition.'

'Can I ask what you're going to say or do when you find your British Library man?'

'You can ask, but I can't tell you, so put your busy mind at rest. There's no story here, I promise.'

'I was being a friend, not a journalist. I'm worried. Trouble finds you the way flies find turds.'

'That was the old Fischer. I'm just a retired man of the soil, doing ...'

'What? *What* are you doing?'

Fischer smiled again. 'I should go to bed. May I have a cup of that foul coffee to take with me?'

4

'Have you been *done* yet, Roger?'

There it was. For almost an hour now, Greville Pearce had been trying to get his most whimsical expression noticed, the usual prelude to what he liked to think of as one of his witty thrusts. The latter arrived, finally, with all the spontaneity of a West End denouement, garlanded by the obligatory world-weary drawl. Pearce didn't believe that there was a line of dialogue yet conceived that couldn't be improved by a drawl.

Roger Broadsmith didn't find Greville Pearce amenable. It was a cross he might have been more willing to bear, did he and the cross not share a tiny office. They had been desk-mates for almost a year now, since Pearce's arrival from SIS's Baltic Section. It was testament to the value placed upon his work that he had remained there for a half-decade following the catastrophic failure of Operation *Jungle* and the death or imprisonment of almost every one of the section's field-agents. Whilst attaching no fault to him for that debacle, Upstairs had considered it more prudent to hand him the mop and bucket than offer fresh pastures.

Yet here he was, translated from Queen Anne's Gate to 54 Broadway, gracing the 'Franz-Josef' Section (so nicknamed because its remit covered much of what, formerly, had been ruled from Imperial Vienna) with his urbane presence, wit and very little industry. He was clever enough when he made the effort, but as a rule he much preferred to let the old school tie do the heavy lifting (though a persistent rumour had it that the livery belonged to Crawley Secondary). In the meantime, Broadsmith was obliged to shift his own work while bearing the brunt of languid silences, bored sighs and attempts to recruit his attention for the latest sprankle.

He had found it best to surrender judiciously - to be the butt for the space of a single exchange, after which, vanity satisfied, Pearce usually allowed his attention to wander off in the direction of another cigarette, or lunch, or his bookmaker on Victoria Street. Today's was an easy thrust to counter, the reference being in no way obscure despite Pearce's effort to make it so. Everyone had been *done* over the past eight weeks, from the lavatory cleaners to Dickie White himself (the latter, presumably, by Her Majesty or God). It had been the inescapable consequence of George Bloody Blake's extramural activities, now revealed to the world – and, more importantly, to the CIA, who were as much inclined to share data with SIS as they were with KGB (if the one were not merely a convenient means of doing the other). Losing the Americans' cooperation would be at least as damaging to British interests as Blake's betrayals, so it had been determined that the stables had not only to be cleaned but shown to be so. In Broadsmith's case – and he assumed it had been the same for every other case officer - all contacts, local agents and communications to and from the same had been pored over, and any gaps or discrepancies waved in his face and explanations demanded. Fortunately, the former had been minor and the latter convincing. It also eased the process that Broadsmith hadn't left any evidence of awkward juvenile political beliefs for posterity to fling back in his face (as a schoolboy, he had toyed with the idea of joining the International Brigades, but his mother, shrewdly construing the posters hanging in his bedroom, had confiscated his savings book). Pronounced *clean* two weeks earlier, he had thought the matter closed, until Pearce decided to Have a Go.

'Yes, Greville. I've been done.'

'And who did you?'

That was out of bounds, but a hard stare seemed to do little to dissuade the interrogator. Broadsmith, not usually a cruel man, applied the dagger.

'Harold Shergold and some fellow I didn't know – MI5, probably.'

Pearce's face dropped comically. To be debriefed – however rigorously – by Acting Controller Sovbloc himself, the man currently leading the British team in the debriefings of HERO, was no light matter. It suggested that Broadsmith was regarded as important enough to be tested to an extreme, whereas Pearce himself – as everyone knew – had been called into some nobody's office to be gently quizzed on such searing topics as whether he preferred cricket to football or had ever holidayed east of the Curtain. No-one cared to be too suspicious about Pearce's loyalties, and it must have wounded to the bone.

'Shergy grilled you?'

As the question was superfluous, Broadsmith didn't bother even to nod. He returned to the report he was writing, a difficult piece, that, to get right, required a great deal of not having to listen to Greville Pearce. For almost two years, SIS had been running a minor official in the Hungarian Trade Ministry, someone who had supplied a steady stream of gossip regarding more senior figures in Kádár's Government. That he was able – and willing - to do so was a consequence of his predilection for other men, something he wished to keep from his wife, his employers and the Security Services. Unfortunately for his British handlers, the Hungarians had seen fit to decriminalize homosexuality earlier that year, and while the condition had yet to become remotely acceptable in their society, Broadsmith could sense a loosening of the ties that bound their agent to his second job. To complicate matters, a drinking problem that had helped to facilitate SIS's original approach seemed to have worsened in recent months (a common reaction to the stress of maintaining two faces to the world), and the quality of information they were receiving had suffered accordingly. It was time to cast an asset loose, but in such a way as to leave no trace of the anchor chain.

The ideal solution would be a shake of the hand, a hearty thanks for services rendered and best wishes for the future, but their profession allowed little opportunity for conventional goodbyes. Failing that, a careless elbow that sent the man onto the tracks of the Budapest Metro would do quite satisfactorily, but SIS maintained no special operations unit in Eastern Europe (and in any case, tragic mishaps were regarded as options of last resort, mainly because they were notoriously difficult to bring off convincingly). A third, implausible resolution would be for their man to break the link cleanly by begging to be excused any further commitment. To do so, however, he would need to walk away also from his traitor's remuneration - which, though modest, represented a hefty slice of what provided for his comfortable lifestyle. Very few of those whose clandestine work was not founded upon principle could make that sacrifice. Typically, they demanded more, not less – a final, substantial payment to ease the financial pain of separation. Broadsmith knew perfectly well what Budgets would say to anything he might suggest in that regard.

So, what to do? Broadsmith could go with tradition, which was to delay a difficult decision in the fond hope that carelessness, a random swerve of fortune or, in this case, hardening arteries would render it either unnecessary or a matter for his successor. Given that the intelligencer's work relied upon people and circumstances that were anything but reliable, only striking bugger-ups tended to blot a record (and even those could be partially excused by an unexpected burst of enemy competence). It was why men such as Greville Pearce could build a pension on doing very little that shone or even found its way into the Other Matters section of SIS's annual report to Whitehall. Their line-managers were frustrated men, distracted by their civilian responsibilities and a longing for a proper war; it was too easy to satisfy expectations of the bread-and-butter work they were obliged to oversee.

Broadsmith couldn't tread that amenable path, unfortunately. An elusive quality, vaguely located between diligence and an inability to tread water, made him uncomfortable with just clocking in and out. His ten years with the Service had coincided with its greatest humiliations – Jungle, Gold, the outing of Burgess, Maclean and now Blake, the deep suspicion that at least one more traitor sat comfortably within their midst, doing harm still – for which an assiduous man would feel a weight of reflected responsibility. What had been a lean and successful wartime organization had bloated into an ambulant mass of self-inflicted wounds, an embarrassment to itself and

Allies who had once looked to SIS as a benchmark. There were a few good men here – Shergold and White would have graced any Agency – but the majority advanced or maintained altitude mostly on the strength of their regimental connections. A bloody fool could see that radical change was needed, and it had to extend much further than the blast-radius of George Blake. Until that wondrous event occurred, Broadsmith had only the thin moral consolation of doing a job to the best of his average abilities.

An hour's fruitless navigation of his Hungarian problem did nothing to resolve it, so he pushed it to one side and turned to that week's 'G' notices. Devised originally as a means of flagging names and events between sections in the hope of sharing relevant memories or experiences, they had been severely culled recently (no operations officer wanted his field-agents betrayed by another's bad apple), to the point at which they offered little that couldn't be gleaned from staff meetings. Broadsmith applied himself, however, reading everything carefully and finding nothing either that interested him or, more importantly, to which he could contribute. The fact was that, despite their internal ructions and upheavals, most of the sections dealing with Warsaw Pact countries had very little going on at the moment. In Czechoslovakia and Yugoslavia, low-level intelligence gathering continued, obviously, but the most interesting developments of the year so far could be observed any Saturday afternoon on the local terraces. It was the same with Romania and Bulgaria, and even Hungary had settled into a sullen stupor following her uprising and its crushing, half a decade earlier. Poland was a special case, not to be discussed (though it was the common gossip at 54 Broadway that it had been one of SIS's Polish moles who had outed Blake), leaving only the Soviet Union and East Germany to carry the load for international disharmony and overt confrontation.

The big news was about Berlin, as it almost always was, and to Broadsmith's lasting regret the city's great affairs were nothing to do with him. It was the only place on Earth where the protagonists faced each other at punching distance – where a rough parity of resources and hinterland allowed the closest thing to a fair fight that any intelligencer might hope for. True, the Allies were losing that game, and had been for some years now. *Stasi*'s penetration of West German institutions was legendarily adept, and KGB – thanks largely to Blake – had been two steps ahead of SIS and CIA since 1952. Even so, a man couldn't be in that fight without feeling that he was playing a part in the central struggle of the age, rather than colluding in a seedy, backroom exploitation of broken misfits.

Broadsmith felt that collusion more keenly for not being part of the wartime generation that had seen its enemy at killing range. He had been recruited directly from university, his youthful vanity caressed by the unsolicited approach and an interview in a room off Gower Street at which opaque references to unseen battlefields had been made by men who had seen and done things they weren't ever going to admit to. None of them had been so indelicate as to mention the salary, much less the sordid, everyday work - the harvest of professional embitterments, emotional instabilities, sexual deviances and financial necessities, compiled and curated by men in ties and shirt sleeve-bands, their paperwork salaciously punctuated by the sort of photography that, out on the street, would have earned its peddlers prosecution under the Obscene Publications Act. What would he have said to them, had he known? Would a career in banking or chartered accountancy (the heart's longing of his parents) have been more satisfying, or merely less wear and tear upon a man's sense of self?

He recognized his mood for what it was – a product of one of *those* days. Pearce had been the immediate trigger, but he had added to a missed breakfast, a brutally protracted commute from Brent Cross and the unseasonable weather, all of which irritants applied themselves to the dolour that his thirty-ninth birthday had brought on the previous week. Though not usually sensitive about his age, the inevitable audit - a father lost to lung cancer and a fiancée wandered off in the direction of a wealthier, prettier, younger man - had made his latest year seem more lost than acquired. It was at such times that other prospects and vistas pulled with untypical force, but the nature of his work precluded any option of uprooting and trying something new. After the Blake debacle, his employers might just assume the worst and put a cautionary bullet through his head as he dropped his resignation letter on the desk.

His head was still playing with the idea of a struggling artist's life in Pont-Aven when his immediate manager, Stanislav Dawidowski, wandered into their tiny workplace. Stan was a genial fellow, always happy to waste as much time wagging his chin as didn't get him noticed, but today the set of his face didn't encourage idle chatter. He ignored Pearce and tossed his head at Broadsmith.

'Do you have a moment, Roger?'

'I have several, Stan. What can I do for you?'

'It isn't me, actually. Harold Shergold wonders if you might pop upstairs to see him at your earliest.'

Which meant immediately. Without bothering to look, Broadsmith could sense the grin spreading on Pearce's face. Apparently, at least one recent cleansing hadn't taken.

5

'And what's the purpose of your research?'

She smiled and raised her eyebrows, making it sound like innocent curiosity - a neat way to deflect the fact that she understood hardly a word of the letter of recommendation. Fischer returned the smile, and offered his best Portuguese accent.

'My dissertation examines the effect of the Union of Crowns on Anglo-Portuguese trade in the later sixteenth-century.'

'Oh. It must have stopped, mustn't it?'

'One might think so, but no. Of course, there was no *official* trade after 1580.'

'And you're with ...' she glanced at the letterhead; '... the University of Porto?'

'Yes. Professor António Simas is my sponsor.'

'Lovely.' She picked up a pen and counter-signed the form that Fischer had completed. 'Your reader's card will be ready in a few minutes – it will get you into both Manuscripts and the main Reading Room. It's issued for six months in the first instance, but you can renew it without further interviews. Have you visited the Library before?'

'It's my first time.'

'Here's a guide – it isn't very good, so please ask an archivist or librarian if you have any problems. Do you have references for what you need?'

'Yes, thank you.'

'Good luck, then.'

Fischer left the building (the British Library or British Museum - it seemed to be both, confusingly) and sat for half an hour in a nearby cafe, taking his time with another coffee-type beverage. He returned to find his reader's card waiting for him. Consulting the rudimentary map supplied by the friendly young lady, he located Manuscripts without difficulty, filled in a request slip and placed it into the shallow cardboard box that sat on the archivist's desk. He'd been told that supplying documents could take up to twenty minutes, so he perused the wall of books that lined the room, extracted a volume – *Acts of the Privy Council, 1581 – 1582*, and took it to the desk whose number he'd written on the slip. It was the correct period, and therefore something he would be interested in, were his purpose remotely to do with what he'd claimed. In any case, he'd recognized the English word 'privy', and, as a quasi-expert in the drainage system of southwest Berlin, was fascinated to discover that, almost four hundred years earlier, the British had a standing committee for sewage standards.

It took only a few moments to discover his error, but the discussions and decisions of the Kingdom's greatest men were sufficiently interesting for him to polish his English vocabulary until the expected shadow fell upon the page. A middle-aged gentleman held his order slip; he was smiling apologetically, as if there were a problem that might be his fault.

'I'm sorry, but the reference is incorrect.'

'Oh. Is it?'

'Cotton MSS, Otho E XV; f. 42.'

'That's right.'

'I'm afraid the Otho E collection contains only fourteen sub-fonds. There isn't a fifteenth. '

'Ah, this is my mistake. I'll look again. Thank you.'

The archivist returned to his desk and whatever his duties entailed. Fischer went back to the *Acts*, glancing up occasionally to confirm that the man was on duty still. When a woman took his place almost an hour later he stood, went to the desk and put the request slip back into the box.

A few minutes later, the *Acts* were darkened once more.

'Excuse me?'

'Yes?'

'This is wrong. There *is* no Otto E XV.'

'There isn't? That is very stupid of me.'

Calculating that he had time for lunch before the next shift-change, Fischer paid a second visit to the nearby cafe, and, misunderstanding the hand-scrawled menu on the wall, ordered a fish-paste sandwich. The large mug of strong tea that followed was hardly enough to kill the memory of it, so he broke with the tradition of his adult lifetime and ordered dessert - a currant scone. When it was finished so was he, in every sense. He returned to the Library feeling the pull of gravity far more keenly than earlier.

To his dismay, the original, male archivist was on shift once more, so he sat down at his table and gave the *Acts* more attention. By now he could probably speak on his alleged subject for several minutes without betraying himself (the Queen's Privy Councillors seem to have been every bit as exercised by the Union of Crowns as any Portuguese patriot), so in a way his day was being only half-wasted.

When he looked up again, an unfamiliar woman was sitting at the desk. He stood, went across and placed his slip into the box once more. This time, he had hardly returned to the sixteenth century before she was beside him.

'This isn't right. You must mean Otho E XIII, f. 42.'

'Yes. What is it that I asked for?'

She placed the slip in front of him and went back to her desk without another word. He picked it up. On the reverse side, *Sorrento's, 4.30pm* was scribbled in pencil. His heart sank. Having sampled the establishment's coffee, tea and fish-paste he hadn't intended ever to return.

He was there five minutes early, warming his hands – but not his stomach – with something called Ovaltine. It came in a mug whose handle, not being pierced, gave precious little purchase and allowed the full heat of the beverage to be transmitted to one's fingertips (design-flaws to rank with the entirety of the Messerschmitt ME 210, if Freddie Holleman's memory could be trusted). He was attempting to puzzle this out when she sat down at his tiny table.

His *man* was a women, then - late 50s, squat, dressed in the cliched, sensible mode of career-librarians everywhere. She seemed slightly breathless but her eyes were bright, and in his mind's-eye he conjured an entire traitor's story - recruited long ago (perhaps even at university), almost certainly an idealist, a willing joiner of the fight against fascism at a time when the West was looking the other way, a patently ordinary woman, patiently counting off the years, awaiting a particular, peculiar error: *Otho E, XV; f. 42*.

He realized that he was being examined every bit as minutely as she. His face surprised her; she must have expected one that could pass through crowds unnoticed, not a circus exhibit that drew them. After a few moments she broke their mutual gaze, performed the obligatory left-and-right glance and leaned forward.

'What do I call you?'

'Olavo Guzman.' It was the name on his reader's card. There was no point in making things unnecessarily complicated – the lady was required only to provide a single piece of information and then forget everything about him.

'I'm Mabel de Vries. I assumed you'd be, well, Slavic.'

'It was thought that a more direct approach from our friends might be observed. The British are unusually sensitive at the moment.'

'Because of Comrade Blake?'

Fischer winced. 'It would be better not to mention his name. And *comrade* will only get you noticed. I'll refer to him – if at all – as Mr Johnson. However, you've brought us to the matter in hand.'

'*He's* the matter?'

'The organization, not the man. We need a name, of someone who can be trusted.'

'To do what? You said it yourself – they're very sensitive right now, so any attempt to recruit ...'

'Not that - in fact, quite the reverse. We need to identify an officer who can be relied upon not to mistake an approach.'

Puzzled, she frowned at the table. 'Why would we do that?'

'I can't be specific, obviously. We need to establish a mode of communication – a reliable means of transmitting information when circumstances demand that it *be* transmitted.'

Her brow cleared. 'You mean *mis*information?'

'If you like. But we don't want our motives to be suspected, which is why we prefer to go in through the front door, so to … how do you say it?'

'Speak. So to *speak*.'

'Yes. The approach will be open, or as open as such a thing can be. We want the organization to feel that it can examine a presented possibility, rather than suspect that we're playing games, or perhaps looking to replace … Johnson.'

'So, someone who won't panic at first touch.'

The half of Fischer's mouth that could move freely beamed, and for the first time she flinched slightly.

'Yes! A senior man would be best, but that may not be possible. How good is your knowledge of the personnel in SIS?'

'I worked at Broadway for eight years.'

'You did? Then why …?'

'The outing of some of our friends made it ... difficult for me, so it seemed wiser to change career. A few new faces have wandered in since I left, but most of them are long-term inmates. Still, I'll need to think about it. How much time do I have?'

'A day, two at most – this is urgent.'

'Alright.' She pushed back the chair and reached for her large, canvas bag. 'Don't come back to the Library. There's a pub - the *Lamb*, on Lamb's Conduit Street. I'll meet you there tomorrow, after work, yes?'

'I'll find it.'

'You have an A to Z?'

He lifted his tattered copy from a pocket. She nodded and smiled. 'Bring some flowers. It'll make it look like you're a suitor.'

'No-one will think much of your preferences in men.'

'You look like a war hero. And middle-aged, unmarried women don't tend to wait for the handsome ones. Oh! I don't mean …'

Fischer waved the hand that held the A to Z. 'That's alright. I was once quite pretty – at least, my mother thought so. It's while since I've cared about that.'

When she had gone, he worried – about his English (which wasn't very fluent), but more so about whether he'd said the last without disguising his true accent. She hadn't seemed to notice – or, perhaps, care. It couldn't be that she expected the entire truth, even from one of her own. Paranoia had its own rules, and made its own excuses.

To familiarize himself with the terrain and his street-guide, he walked back to Vauxhall via Trafalgar Square and Whitehall, crossing the bridge beside the Gothic fantasy that housed the alleged Mother of Parliaments (he imagined the Athenians had something to say about that). It was a route that bustled with every type of civic activity, a symptom of an old city's organic growth that contrasted nicely the compartmentalism of planned capitals such as Berlin. Shops, museums and buildings of state were thrown together almost haphazardly, and pavement hawkers plied their shabby wares within a few steps of the home of the Prime Minister. About a hundred metres south of a plaque that identified the execution site of King Charles I, he found and entered a pub. He stayed for half an hour, drinking a dark beer, hoping – and failing - to sense some patina of great historical events (though the interior's decor came from some prior geological period). That failure was only partly compensated by the damage done to his lungs by the establishment's other patrons.

By the time he stepped on to the South Bank he had formed a superficial but pleasing opinion of London. It was visibly dirty, smelled much too interesting, the air was only half-breathable and the layout conformed to no logical urban plan; but, despite its vastness, there was a homely feel to the warren of streets that made him think of it more as a dense cluster of villages, keeping company around a broad, filthy river. A few years earlier, soon after he'd arrived here, Kleiber had claimed to find the place more *gemütlich* than Berlin, and Fischer could see now what he meant. No city was an easy place to be alone, but this one did its best not to intimidate.

That was his second mistake of the day. The Privy Council thing had been a simple error of translation, but for a man - even a dead man - in his present situation to assume that he was *alone* was unforgivably slack.

6

'Cuba.'

KGB Chairman Shelepin sighed. His deputy, V. Y. Semichastny, was a friend, a protege, a son almost; but he was a persistent bastard also. He sat at the other side of the large desk, a blue briefing file open on his knee, and before he had even opened his mouth Shelepin might have risked a month's salary on the first word to emerge. It wouldn't have been so much a wager as a sound investment.

'No.'

'It's inevitable.'

'Of course it is, and desirable also. But we don't make the suggestion.'

'I know ...'

'We *don't* make the suggestion, because we've been told, categorically, that KGB are no longer in the business of attempting to set foreign policy. You'll recall that Comrade Serov had different ideas about his role?'

'Yes.'

'And look at him now, a *far-neighbour* at Khodynka, reporting to the General Staff rather than to Khrushchev directly. If we want something to happen in Cuba, we make a very subtle approach to Minister Gromyko, whose business it is – and even then, we wait to hear his opinion first.'

Semichastny nodded. He could have recited this conversation from memory. When, three years earlier, Serov was demoted to the Directorship of GRU, Khrushchev had made it clear to his successor that he wanted no more KGB noses in Soviet foreign policy. Since then, their organization had complied faithfully, confining itself to intelligence-gathering and counter-intelligence operations. However, for a young man Semichastny was unusually sensitive to time - particularly its briefest standard division, the moment – and found it difficult to play any sort of waiting game. He looked down at his file, reordering his thoughts, and then tried a flank attack.

'Leonov has sent another analysis ...'

'Of course he has - he's persistent, and I respect him for that. But Comrade Mikoyan's perception of Cuban affairs differs from his, and the First Secretary always listens to his old friend. The meeting with Castro in the Harlem hotel was intended merely to embarrass the Americans – it was not *any* sort of commitment. Khrushchev remains convinced that the Americans won't allow a communist regime to put down roots in the Caribbean. The Bay of Pigs was a stupid, amateurish attempt to achieve a result cheaply, but a full-scale invasion will follow – at least, he's convinced himself that it will, and we're not allowed to say differently until we're proved right by events. Now, move on.'

Semichastny breathed deeply and turned a page in his folder

'Berlin.'

'As if I didn't know you were going to say that.'

'Ulbricht wants his wall.'

'And pigs want potatoes.'

'I mean, he's made another approach to the First Secretary.'

'You mean he's pestered him again?'

'Yes.'

'I know. He was told that the Central Committee has no objection, as before.'

'I think he wants explicit agreement, to show solidarity.'

'Well, KGB can't do anything to help with that. Anyway, didn't he get implicit approval from that idiot Kennedy?'

'*And* he wants joint military exercises within the DDR to coincide with the move – to give a strong hint to the Allies.'

'Khrushchev won't agree to that. If he's averse to having Soviet foreign policy run from this building, he's doubly so about it being dictated from the *Neues Stadthaus*.'

'Of course. This was merely for your information.'

'I consider myself informed. Is there anything else?'

Semichastny placed his file on the seat next to him, took out his cigarette case and offered it across the desk. 'Only gossip.'

'The meat of our business, finally.'

'I've heard that General Zarubin is being less well received these days.'

'Excellent. Presumably, the First Secretary is tired of hearing the very worst construction upon every trend and event?'

'Shevchenko tells me that he calls him *Azrael*, to his face.'

'Ha! You're a cure for rainy days, Vladimir Yefimovich.'

'Can we use this?'

'Yes, by doing and saying nothing. Serov overplayed his hand with regard to Comrade Zarubin, so any advantage we attempt to secure at the General's expense will be seen as vengeful and suspected accordingly. If the man's digging his own grave, let him be.'

Semichastny nodded. Again, he could have recited the received wisdom. Any information regarding Zarubin was of interest to KGB, but the organization had buried the legacy of Beria and Serov and did things differently these days. If a neat, blameless means of crushing the man presented itself it would of course be snatched at; failing that, the strategy was to observe, contain and cast reasonable doubt upon his work. Eventually, a misstep would occur, or events would leave the General exposed. He was a man whose power base consisted of the goodwill of one man, their First Secretary, and it appeared to be a depreciating asset.

'There's something else, and it's not unconnected to Zarubin.'

Shelepin took a long drag on his cigarette. He was looking out of his window, down onto Dzerzhinsky Square, a hint that he was losing interest in this briefing. He was a polite man, however, and made the effort.

'What is it?'

Three years ago, the Berlin *Rezidentura* identified a West Berliner as being one of his former – or, perhaps, current – contacts. The man's name was Fischer.'

'I read the file - the fellow with the burned face, yes?'

'He got out of Berlin, apparently, though *how* isn't clear. After that, we had conflicting intelligence. There was an alleged sighting in Switzerland, but it wasn't corroborated. We put out a standard request through our western European network, and a few weeks after that a PCF friend in Bordeaux reported that someone answering this man's remarkable description had departed the port on a steamer bound for Portugal. Again, we were unable to confirm it.'

'Well, if he *is* in Portugal, he's lost. We don't have a single man in the country.'

'No, but there are a few good socialists there still, keeping their heads well down. A comrade in Lisbon suggested that a vessel from Bordeaux would likely be bound for Leixões in the first instance, and that a number of dockers in the port could be trusted to pass on word.'

'Did they?'

'No. If Fischer came into Leixões, he did it discreetly. No-one answering his description was noticed.'

'How disappointing.'

'Perhaps not. Surprisingly, Portuguese dockers have good memories, and they're not entirely illiterate. One of them has passed on word to our Bordeaux Consulate that a local Porto daily newspaper ...' Semichastny opened the file next to him and glanced down; '... the *Jornal de Notícias*, recently carried a death announcement, of one Otto Henry Fischer, late of the city of Guimarães.'

Shelepin looked engaged suddenly. 'Oh, that's fortunate. I might pass on the news to Zarubin, to see how he reacts.'

'I haven't finished. Our docker kept his eye on the Press, and a few days later a coroner reported that our German friend had been betrayed by a weak heart. The notice stated that the body would be returning to Germany, to be buried next to the deceased's second wife. I checked on that. The funeral took place three days ago.'

'I doubt the General will regret that he didn't send flowers.'

'He may be regretting anything, Comrade Chairman.'

'What do you mean?'

'Our friend in Leixöes reported that the Porto Coroner's Office has long been known as a place where findings can be bought in advance - apparently, local shipping companies prefer to avoid paying compensation to sailors' families for their little mishaps at sea, and the local administration obliges them. So, he went to the trouble of tracking down the casket. It was carried out of his port last week on a Bremerhaven-bound ship, but not before he and a comrade managed to unscrew its lid and peer inside.'

Shelepin was fully upright now, the cigarette forgotten. 'Go on.'

'An elderly gentleman, quite dead, with no obvious signs of foul play. In fact, he seems to have benefitted from some world-class surgery, as his face was entirely untroubled by war damage.'

'They had the right box?'

'I'm almost certain of it.'

'Explain.'

'Because a face that most definitely hasn't been repaired departed the same port, London-bound, two days later – in the dark, and again, very discreetly. *That* has been corroborated.'

'Get on to this, Vladimir Yefimovich. If there a chance that he's still Zarubin's ...'

'Our Bordeaux Consulate man has anticipated us. He informed our London station before Moscow, even. They managed to pick him up at the Port of London – literally, one of ours got there as he came down the gangplank. Eyes have been on him ever since, and we'll be getting daily reports. It may all be nothing, of course – just another fascist refugee who's sick of being homesick. On the other hand, it may be a great deal.'

Back in his own office, Semichastny congratulated himself on a successful day's briefing. It wasn't often that Chairman Shelepin let his satisfaction show so openly. He was a reserved man who kept his thoughts carefully corralled, the best sort of intelligence chief; so the smile and the slapped table were as much as a pat on the back and a hearty handshake. As someone who owed a great deal to Shelepin's patronage and encouragement, Semichastny never allowed himself to take for granted what most other KGB men couldn't ever hope to obtain. He worked longer hours than a gulag inmate, pushed his subordinates hard and never allowed wishful thinking to fill the gaps that even the best data left open. He was precise, methodical, committed to the Organization and entirely deserving of his swift rise to its penultimate rank, whatever his relationship to the Chairman. Above all, he had made no enemies among those political men who could bring a career to a halt more effectively than a side-stepping wall, a blessing which made what he was doing now seem all the more irresponsible.

When it began he had been sure of himself, but the questions had risen as the path became clearer. Which was worse – to tell a series of small truths, or the one, big lie? Which carried the greater risk – to keep an operation wholly off the books, or to attempt to deflect attention by bringing it partially into the light? Which was the least sensible option – to take a step when none was necessary, or to leap forward in the hope that a fence could be leapt before the dog's teeth found one's arse?

7

'What's this?'

Kleiber screwed up his face and thought for a moment.

'Billy Fury - *Halfway to Paradise*. Do you like it?'

Fischer shook his head. 'It's awful.'

'I know. The British will never have their own 'sound'. Everything is either a bad copy of what young, greasy-haired Americans are doing, or sentimental love ballads, or some big-band jazz'y thing. They have even fewer original thoughts about modern music than we Germans.'

'They have some good classical composers.'

'Do they? You wouldn't know it. The British despise anything that smacks of intellectualism – they think it's an attempt to patronize them, or a French plot. You might hear something on the *Third Programme*, but even then it's usually the classical 'pops'.'

'How can you live here?'

'Oh, come on, Otto, there's more to life than music. Their beer's not at all bad, and the local girls are a willing species.'

'I don't drink the first, and I'd have no chance with the second.'

'Well, you're only here for the week, aren't you? Pretend to be an anthropologist, observing native customs. Write a paper, when you get home.' Kleiber peered meaningfully at his friend. 'Wherever that will be.'

'You're right, of course. I'll just enjoy the novelty. What should I see, as a tourist?'

'Not what tourists see - except the Tower, that's marvellous. Walk along the river, the south side, from Westminster to Bermondsey. It'll take you an hour each way, and you'll get a real feel for London.'

'If I have time, then.'

'Why wouldn't you? What else will you be doing?'

'Stop it, Jonas. This is very good, by the way.'

'Thank you. It's called cottage pie. Gloria gave me the recipe.'

'Your English girlfriend?'

'Almost. When she's in the mood she can suck the tongue out of my head, but I haven't managed to scale the inner walls yet. She's saving herself.'

'For the wedding night?'

'For safety's sake. Her mother would throw her onto a pyre if a cock got too close.'

'Perhaps you should point it at the mother, then.'

A small quantity of cottage pie sprayed the table between them. Jonas dabbed at his eyes with a napkin.

'I *have* missed you, Otto. You should have visited more often - for holidays, when you were alive.'

'Farmers don't get time off. Whenever the notion of leisure started to nibble my ear something would happen - a rockslide, or grape pestilence. Eventually, I realised that there was at least one hour missing from every day'

'Didn't you enjoy the life, then?'

Fischer rubbed his nose. 'I don't know. For a long time I told myself that it was worthy, and it *was* as peaceful as anything I've ever known. But you need a head and heart for the soil, and mine weren't quite there.'

'They longed for the mean streets?'

'Is that a quote?'

'Probably.'

'No, then. They just accepted that whatever might content them lies somewhere else, well camouflaged still.'

'So, you're looking for it here, now?'

Fischer stood, reached across the table and took both empty plates. 'This is business, of a kind. Shall I make coffee?'

It was as close as Kleiber had come to worming something out of his friend, and his journalist's instincts couldn't leave it at that. In any case, it wasn't as though they were talking about real coffee.

'Your woman, Zofia – was the farming life why she left?'

'That's a *very* personal question, Jonas.'

'Friends worry for friends.'

Fischer sighed, placed the stacked plates back on the table and sat down.

'Sometimes you can't make something work, even with the will. There was some love there I think, but not the right love, and not enough of it. Eventually we stopped trying, and it became easier. We have – we *had* – a neighbour, Felipe, an elderly widower who married and bred late. His estate's substantial, and profitable, but the son and heir badly needs to grow up. He isn't a wrong type - just too many false friends and too much money in his wallet. So his father, knowing our situation, came to us with a proposition. He offered Zofia a wedding ring, a comfortable life and no obligation to share a marital bed, so that when he died his heir would have a few years' grace to become a man before he could inherit everything. In return, she was promised a good settlement, and Felipe urged a very generous price on us for our property. We couldn't think of a sensible reason to say no.'

'You didn't mind losing her?'

'I didn't lose her, really. After the wedding I dined at their home at least twice every week, borrowed half his library and drank half his cellar. Apart from the sex – which had stopped in any case – everything was easier than before. I moved into a warm, comfortable suite in Guimarães' best hotel, explored the lands I'd seen from my house but never been able to visit, and even managed a walking tour of Alto Minho.'

'That's a place, is it?'

'A region. And *that* is enough of my recent history. Coffee?'

'You're not going to go back, are you? I mean, when you said you had to return to Germany, you meant *return*, didn't you?'

'I don't know. Nothing's certain.'

'Except that it's going to be dangerous.'

'I really can't say, Jonas. I don't mean to be mysterious, but asking me the same question forty different ways isn't going to work. If everything goes well, at the end of it I'll be able to make choices about what comes next. If not, then *next* won't matter.'

'Oh, shit.'

'Forget what I've said. I'm going to meet someone in a pub tomorrow, so I'll need to practice. Do you have a preference nearby?'

'A *local*, Otto. That's what the British say.'

'A local, then?'

'Yeah, the *White Bear,* a five-minute walk. It's a bit rough but the beer's good. And they have real coffee sometimes.'

'Then we can rinse down Gloria's delightful cottage pie.'

Two hours later, they returned to the flat. Without taking off his jacket, Kleiber sat down at his typewriter and for several minutes attempted to move his piece on the death of Ernest Hemingway - about which he felt he should write something memorable - beyond its first, unsatisfactory paragraph. Eventually, his beer-dulled senses, and the sounds coming from the tiny bathroom, where Fischer was vomiting up his own portion (a foolhardy, three-pint beginner's assault on Guinness), conspired to end the effort.

Below his journalist's window, on the corner of Alberta Street and Penton Place, a man approached another and begged a light. The samaritan obliged and then departed, leaving the other fellow leaning against the lamp post he'd previously been warming. On Newington Butts he hailed a taxi, and, twenty minutes later, paid off his ride on Kensington Palace Gardens, opposite the Soviet Embassy. When the taxi moved away he crossed the road and entered the security gate without being required to show his pass. A few minutes later he was sat in front of his own typewriter, constructing a report that had nothing to do with Ernest Hemingway.

8

When Levin heard the news a number of uncomfortable considerations queued for his attention.

His first reaction – and he was gratified that it *was* the first – was concern for his employer, a man who hadn't been under any obligation to take on a troublesome, disrespectful cripple as his personal assistant, nor to keep him on once those failings became obvious. Following hard on the tail of that noble thought, a more self-interested stab reminded him he was as likely to find alternative employment in the Kremlin Palace as he was to hear Leonid Brezhnev tell a joke, at which his concern sharpened considerably. The news was word of mouth at the moment, both vague and unreliable, so it wasn't clear how badly General Zarubin had been injured – or, indeed, if he breathed still.

There was a solid rumour, at least, of a car-crash - that Zarubin had been a passenger in the vehicle, and that his driver was dead. The vehicle was a ZIL-110, a heavy limousine with a herd's worth of well-padded leather that would absorb a great deal of shock. What it didn't have – what no Soviet domestic vehicle possessed – was any form of belt or restraint that might prevent a man from continuing his journey once the machine around him came to a catastrophic halt. All of which told Boris Levin that his own wellbeing presently dangled by a frayed thread.

A few telephone calls later, the situation had become slightly less foggy. The General had been dragged from the car alive and rushed to the Central Clinical Hospital at Kuntsevo. Of course he had - it was a facility reserved for the communist state's allegedly non-existent elite (the *Kremlin Clinic*, as it was universally, and cynically, known). There, he would get the best attention that money couldn't buy, from doctors who certainly had been bought. If he could be saved, he would be - *if*, of course, he was meant to be.

A stomach-emptying thought, but Levin couldn't let it go. Zarubin had survived the previous KGB Chairman's best efforts to erase him, yet could anyone really walk away from that sort of battle? Ivan Serov had lost, decisively, but three years on he headed GRU and had a division's worth of assassins at the other end of his telephone receiver. And even if he had the sense not to pursue a vendetta that could restore nothing to him, there were plenty of people in Dzerzhinsky Square still who had enough reason to want Zarubin dead, or at least removed.

If the adverb could apply to anything to do with the Kremlin's internal politics, Zarubin would *normally* be safe from such thrusts; but his power sat on a thin base, and lately, that base had been crumbling at the edges. An advisor whose advice wasn't heeded was of less utility than a jammed magazine, and someone had to have noticed. A wise enemy might think any move against Zarubin premature as yet, but Levin by no means underestimated the imbecility of some middle-ranking KGB men. Though Chairman Shelepin's reforms had been vigorous he was only three years into the job, and his organization was a home still to a large number of former NKVD types whose game-strategies ran only to shooting, poisoning or denouncing their opponents. Or doing things to automobiles, perhaps.

How did one sabotage a car? Levin neither owned nor understood the inner parts of the device, but something so complicate undoubtedly had many areas that were vulnerable to interference. He imagined that loosening all the bolts holding its four wheels onto the axles might do the business, though it was likely the driver would sense something was amiss before the fatal moment, and forewarned assassinations tended to be failed ones. In any case, it had to be some failure that occurred at speed, allowing no time or opportunity for correction – a sufficient speed to ensure that the unlucky occupants had no chance of survival. His dull, anxious mind couldn't conceive a sure means of achieving that end.

It did, however, recall a name – Vasily Papazian, an Armenian mechanic, working in the Kremlin's Special Purpose Garage, who owed him more than one favour. During Levin's brief time as secretary to a housing allocation committee he had arranged to get the man, his wife and infant child out of a crowded *kommunalka* and into a two-room apartment – and, furthermore, had waived the tiny bribe he'd been offered. A year later, when he was warming a seat in the Kremlin, Papazian had asked to whom a more substantial gratuity might be directed, to get a good mechanic onto the Garage's vacancy waiting list. A good word from Levin had ensured an interview and job offer within four months. It would be a small repayment now, to enlighten his benefactor as to all the ways a car could be messed with to make sabotage look like an innocent mishap …

Idiot, Boris. If an SPG vehicle had crashed as a result of mechanical failure then every man working in the Garage would be under suspicion of incompetence at least, and possibly sedition. No doubt they were being questioned closely at that moment about why something as obviously wrong as a corroded brake cable could possibly be allowed to pass inspection. Until it all went away, Papazian was no more likely to talk than a costive monk, particularly about *that* car.

For several hours, Levin's head moved in tightening circles, letting slip only the worst possibilities for himself and his boss. He picked up important briefing papers, misread their content and put them in the wrong order; he tried and failed to arrange Zarubin's diary for the next week (what was the point, if the man might be dead by sunset?); he took three 'phone calls regarding upcoming committee meetings and afterwards couldn't recall which of them belonged to which time and day. Had he drunk a bottle of Purveyance Board vodka – the roughest, cheapest variety – he might have made a better job of his job.

The torment was interrupted at 11.30am, when a despatch rider brought him a sealed envelope. Inside was a brief note – *Come to Kuntsevo, immediately. Z.* - and a Ninth Directorate pass authorizing the same. It had been signed by under-secretary V.S. Akvilev personally, a heartening hint that, as yet at least, the General's influence hadn't plummeted into the same ditch as his ZIL. Quickly, Levin placed a few items in his briefcase, locked his desk drawer, and, after briefly considering his chances of requisitioning an official car from the Garage, picked up his walking stick.

He queued with the masses at a halt on Ulitsa Il'inka, and when he boarded an already-crowded bus, five people – including a girl in a Young Pioneers uniform – stood to offer him a seat. At Krylatskoye he changed to a direct service to the hospital (for staff and ancillary workers, naturally; their patients invariably arrived by ambulance, limousine, military helicopter or gentle, officially-authorized breeze). At its main gate on Marshala Timoshenko Ulitsa, he showed his pass to the guards (also Ninth Directorate, and armed to repulse an extended family of black bears), who, gratifyingly, came to attention when they read the name on it. Not usually one to push his luck with anyone other than Zarubin, Levin nevertheless took advantage of this show of respect. Leaning heavily on his stick, he asked if some means of conveying him the considerable distance to the main hospital building might be arranged, and within three minutes he was being assisted into a GAZ-69 by a *soldat*, as tenderly as if he'd been the young man's grandfather.

A nurse at reception gave him the best news of the day so far. General Zarubin was not in surgery, nor post-operative intensive care; he was merely under observation, though she stressed that he was in considerable pain and therefore should not be disturbed unduly (as if it had been Levin's idea to come here to pester his boss). He promised to be as brief as possible, and meant it.

Zarubin was in a room of his own, propped up in his bed by a pneumatic lift. His head and midriff were swathed in bandages, and his ghostly complexion suggested that the nurse hadn't been lying about the pain. When he saw his secretary he raised a hand, winced, and gestured him in.

Levin, possibly because of his own, life-long experience of pain and discomfort, found it difficult to sympathize with the suffering of others. He gave his face what he imagined to be a caring cast and sighed.

'Does it hurt, Comrade General?'

'Not the head, fortunately. My broken ribs make up for that, though.'

'Perhaps you were lucky?'

'More so than Kozlov. He went through the windscreen like a bullet, straight into a tree.'

'Was it sabotage?' Out before he could consider the implication of asking it, Levin wished that he'd thought of something more discreet. It was entirely possible that rooms allocated to important men were monitored carefully for slips of distracted tongues.

'It seems not. As we came off the Garden Ring the car's brakes failed to operate.'

Even Levin's limited understanding of mechanics encompassed the importance of brakes. He frowned.

'Could someone have drained the hydraulic fluid?'

'Had they done so we would have noticed at the bottom of my street – Kozlov would have, certainly. The investigators looked at it, of course, as soon as I gave them my recollection of events. The cable is corroded, not cut through.'

'Oh.' Levin sincerely hoped that the car hadn't been on Vasily Papazian's docket, otherwise the least of his worries would be finding new employment. Still, it was a relief that blind chance could be blamed for anything to do with Zarubin, a man for whom an uneventful day was an affront.

The General stared down at his secretary's right hand. 'Why have you brought a briefcase?'

'I thought you might want some paperwork, if you weren't too poorly.'

'I can take off a day, under the circumstances.'

'And ...'

'What?'

'I cleared out the yellow box, just in case things *were* what they seemed.'

There was no yellow box in either man's office. The term was their code for a large cash contingency (in high-denomination Swiss francs) that lived, usually, in a small but almost bomb-proof safe behind a bookcase opposite Zarubin's desk. Concealed by a set of volumes containing successive iterations of the Soviet Civil Code, it was unlikely to be discovered before the Kremlin itself was re-modelled or torn down.

Zarubin gaped. '*All* of it?'

'I thought it best, given that you might need to ...'

'How did you get here?'

'By bus. By two buses, actually.'

'Mother of God!'

'I know, I know. What can I say? I feared that they'd moved against you.'

They was too wide a constituency to give a name to, but any one of the very many people who felt that Zarubin was owed some grief would have regarded a secret Swiss hoard as manna from a place they weren't supposed to believe in. Levin, they would have shot out of hand just to free their own to count it, but his boss would have been given – might still get - the full show-trial, followed by thirty years' work-camp experience somewhere east and north of where ice doesn't bother to melt in summer.

Zarubin breathed deeply, several times, and stared up at the heavily-piped ceiling. When he spoke it was as close to a whisper as could be heard at his bedside 'I'll arrange for you to get a lift back to the Kremlin. Go straight in, and don't speak to anyone until it's back where it belongs. If anyone asks you the time of day in a corridor, tell them to make an appointment.'

Carefully, he touched his bandaged head, gave Levin another glare for good measure, sighed and gestured to the bedside table. 'Those are from the First Secretary, by the way. A pleasant thought.'

Levin sniffed. 'Chrysanthemums are funeral flowers.'

'I doubt that his many talents run to floral etiquette. They came promptly – that's the important thing. And look, he wrote a note.'

Levin picked it up and read it. Khrushchev wrote as he spoke – like he was sat on a log, passing the time with a fellow *muzhik*. His hopes for a speedy recovery read more like he blamed the patient for willing his car into a tree, and he stressed that Zarubin should try to be less of a cock next time. Actually, it was very reassuring. Men in the process of falling from favour didn't get the informal, teasing touch, usually.

Reverently, Levin replaced the note next to its vase. 'So, this wasn't someone coming for you.'

'No, but the result is much the same. I can't be here *and* at the First Secretary's side, telling him that his situation briefings from other sources ... don't *fully* cover all the necessary considerations.'

That was perhaps the most flattering assessment of KGB intelligence that Levin had ever heard slip from Zarubin's mouth, but he didn't rise to it. 'You think he'll be pressed about the Berlin ... situation?'

'Undoubtedly. KGB and MfS have a very close relationship still, so if *Stasi* are being pushed hard by Ulbricht to do their bit to raise his wall – and they are – then their most direct way to Comrade Khrushchev is through Shelepin. Obviously, the Chairman's aware of the nuances, but I fear he won't stress the need for caution and letting the Americans continue to fashion their own noose. The word of the day – the week – will be seize the opportunity while it's presenting itself. And yes, I know that's seven or eight words.'

Levin swallowed the retort and closed his mouth. A nurse appeared in the doorway and paused, raising a glass teacup in the manner of a question. Zarubin nodded.

'With lemon, please. The thing is, Levin, this whole business feels like something that will go its own way the moment it starts rolling. Ulbricht puts up his wall – well, it'll be a fence to begin with, no doubt, and done at night so that the Allies can't react until it's staring at them. What will they do, then, though? Until the First Secretary signs his peace treaty with the DDR, the Potsdam Agreement continues to give the Americans and British the right to send patrols into East Berlin. I suspect that their first reaction will be to find any number of reasons to do so. Do we block the checkpoints, or wave them through? If the latter, will Ulbricht continue to be quiescent, or construct a little confrontation that we can't control?

'In the meantime, the Allies will almost certainly reinforce their Berlin garrisons substantially – not because they have any chance of defending their half of the city should it come to a fight, but to increase traffic provocatively on their air, rail and road routes through the DDR. This, too, will invite a response that may swiftly pass beyond the point of pulling back. We'll then find ourselves in the uncomfortable position of hoping that the Allies keep their heads – in other words, we'll have surrendered the initiative for no obvious advantage.'

Levin assumed that it was Zarubin's present disarray that was making him repeat, almost word for word, the meat of what he'd been fretting about for weeks now. He was about to say something to that effect when his boss put a finger to his lips and then pointed it at the ceiling, and immediately the whole monologue made sense. *If* the room was wired, Zarubin had just danced around Khrushchev's infuriatingly efficient personal secretary and put his case directly to the Man - or at least, onto a Ninth Directorate report than he'd almost certainly demand to see. KGB would see it too, of course, but nothing in it either slapped their face or would tempt them to take the very risky step of making it less than verbatim as it passed through Dzerzhinsky Square on its way to the Kremlin.

Levin's grudging surge of admiration was tinged with more than a little anxiety. If Zarubin was convinced that KGB was listening, perhaps he didn't want them to know that *he* believed (or knew) that the brake cable hadn't just corroded – in which case who could say what was up or down, this way or that? The arm that wrapped the briefcase to his body tightened. With almost ninety thousand Swiss francs warming his chest, the urge to find either a nearby dustbin or a pilot willing to fly into Finnish airspace pressed strongly.

Zarubin noticed the reflex spasm. 'You seem uncomfortable, Boris Petrovich. Are you concerned for my state of health, or your job?'

'Both, naturally.'

'Don't worry - unless they find a concussion I should be released within forty-eight hours. And if it comes to the worst, I know that V.S. Stepanov of the State Committee Secretariat would be happy to take you from my dead hands. He thinks very highly of your industry.'

'Really? That's … pleasing.'

At the moment, the prospect of a safe, uncontroversial career preparing briefings for Ministerial Committees pulled at Levin like Calliope singing from her rock, but it might have seemed ungracious to say as much. He filed the information for future use and cleared his throat.

'I'd prefer to remain in my present situation, Comrade General.'

General Zarubin smiled broadly, which, framed by an ashen complexion, gave him the appearance of a tickled ghost.

'Of course you would. What other work could be nearly as diverting?'

9

Mabel deVries was wearing a smear of lipstick, which would have caused Fischer some anxiety, had he not already been briefed as to the pretended nature of their assignation. He stood as she approached, offering the potted rose he had bought at a stall in Leather Lane on his way to the *Lamb*. A woman, sitting with two men at a nearby table, noticed and smiled sentimentally.

'That's very nice, thank you. I'll put it on my kitchen window. Half of bitter, please.'

He went to the bar and ordered two, ignoring the strong protest from his hangover. When he returned and sat down next to her she put a hand on his. He glanced around, desperately searching for a cue.

'This is a comfortable place.'

'It's very old. Charles Dickens drank here, apparently.'

'Did he? Well, well.'

Fischer had never been fluent at small talk, and the little squeeze she gave his hand – he hoped earnestly that it was reflexive rather than a statement of intent - deterred him from practicing further. He leaned a little closer to her.

'Do you have a name for me?'

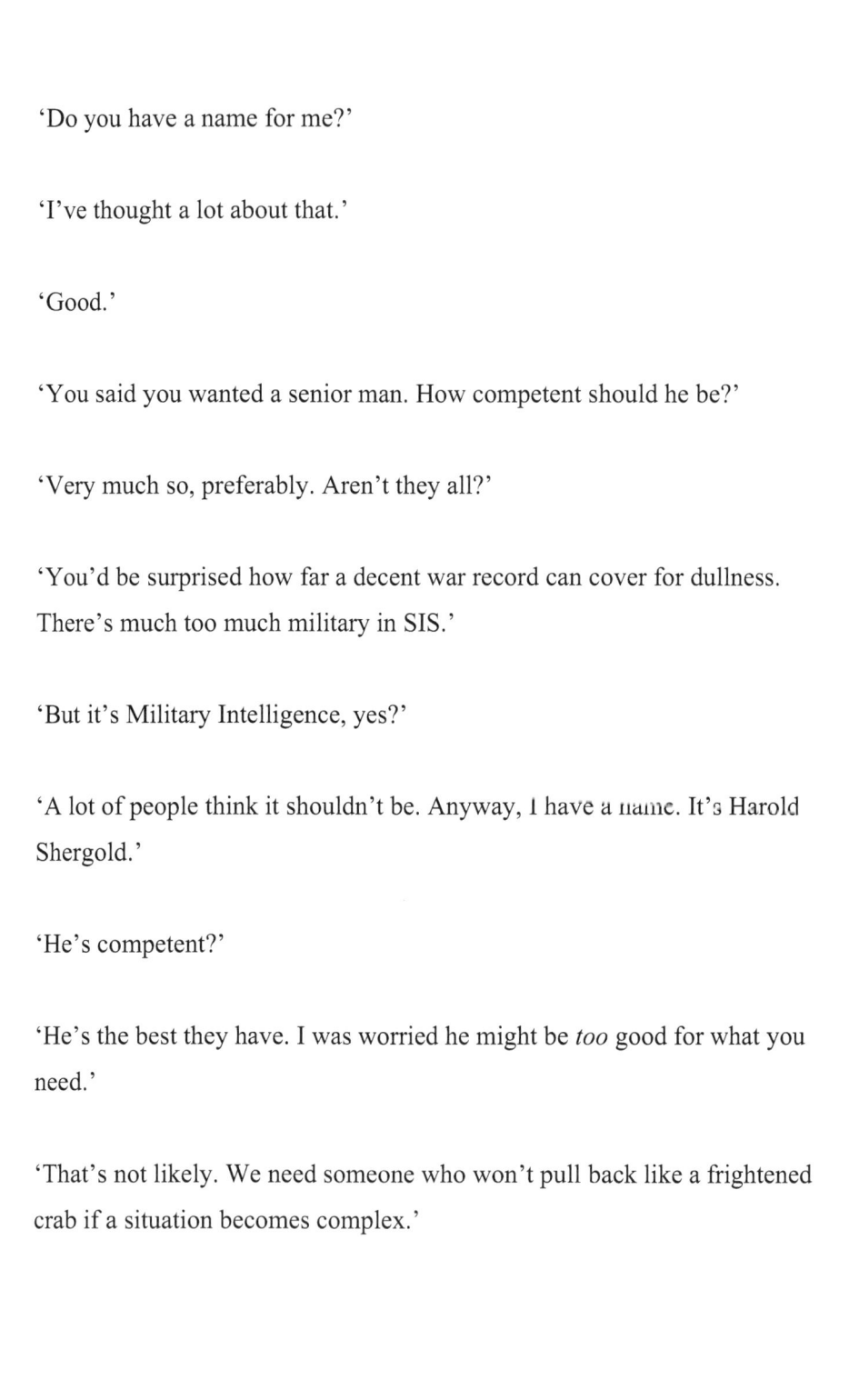

'I've thought a lot about that.'

'Good.'

'You said you wanted a senior man. How competent should he be?'

'Very much so, preferably. Aren't they all?'

'You'd be surprised how far a decent war record can cover for dullness. There's much too much military in SIS.'

'But it's Military Intelligence, yes?'

'A lot of people think it shouldn't be. Anyway, I have a name. It's Harold Shergold.'

'He's competent?'

'He's the best they have. I was worried he might be *too* good for what you need.'

'That's not likely. We need someone who won't pull back like a frightened crab if a situation becomes complex.'

'Harold won't do that. He enjoys complexities. I heard that it was him who broke Blake – I mean, Johnson. But won't that tell against him with ,,, our friends?'

Fischer gave the pub another admiring scan to ensure that no ears were turned their way. 'They won't take it to heart - it's the man's job, after all. He's good with his fists, then?'

She laughed, an attractive noise. 'Harold? He wouldn't know *how* to hit a man, much less hurt him. He has the knack of making people want to tell him things. It's a strange quality.'

Fischer wasn't sure what a *knack* was, but the rest sounded very satisfactory. He took a sip of his beer and felt his stomach turn.

'You've done well, thank you. I imagine they'll be pleased.'

'Don't they know about Harold already?'

'I couldn't say. If they do, I doubt it's as more than a name. For obvious reasons, their intelligence efforts been directed far more towards field agents and their local contacts, rather than home staff.'

He had no idea if this was true, but to his mind it sounded entirely plausible. Satisfied, she nodded and finally took her hand from his.

'Do you need anything else from me?'

'No – at least, not for the moment. I can't say when they'll contact you again.'

She shook her head. 'It's difficult, waiting without any idea of when or how I might be useful. I *want* to be of use.'

'Of course you do. I'm sure they realise that.'

That was the enduring trouble with idealism – it wanted to be tested, to be tempered in flames, but it was far more likely to be consumed by a purpose it wouldn't ever see, much less understand. He almost felt sorry for her, but memories of what fervour could do were too fresh, and raw. She was going to be disappointed, one way or the other, and he couldn't feel too guilty about the part he'd play in that process.

They sat for a few minutes longer, the conversation limited to polite observations about London, the weather and the recent royal wedding (curiously, Mabel was enthusiastic about the spectacle of monarchy, despite her Marxist-Leninist convictions). When it had staggered to an awkward halt she stood, thanked him for the drink, picked up her infant shrub and departed without looking back. Fischer, glancing around, received a sympathetic grimace from the lady who's noticed their tryst earlier. He smiled and shrugged, trying hard not to look relieved.

Harold Shergold. If the man had been placed in charge of George Blake's interrogation (and Fischer had only the lady's word for it), his employers must hold him in high regard. The approach required some thought. It couldn't be done without raising some suspicion as to motives, naturally -

one didn't wave a flag of truce, wade across no-man's-land and then ask for that day's racing results, or invite the enemy to supper at mother's. They would know that some advantage was being sought, even if they couldn't discern it at first prod. The trick, then, would be to convince a wary man that the benefit accruing to their enemy was fully revealed and likely to be reciprocal, and at the moment Fischer hadn't the first idea of how that might be done.

Looking back over his staggered experience of espionage – the brief association with the Gehlen Org, his protracted immersion into what he'd imagined to be KGB's penetration of West Berlin politics and the very real KGB operation to silence him thereafter - he could draw only one conclusion with which he was reasonably comfortable: that he wasn't very good at any of it. He had no strong ideological convictions, no need either for dirty money or filthy women - nor, most importantly, any strong urge to be casting sideways glances for the rest of his life. He fitted the intelligencer's profile as much as he did a pimp's, and felt as easy in the one life as he imagined he would the other.

His return route to Kennington may have been influenced by his self-flaying mood, because it took in almost every monument to rectitude – or at least, the lip-service paid to it - that London could offer. In short order, he passed through Gray's Inn, Lincoln's Inn and the Temple, letting the history wash over him, the bustle of powdered wigs enchant him and the pretensions of 'Honourable Societies' of lawyers raise the day's first genuine smile. At the bottom of Middle Temple Lane he turned left, crossed Blackfriars Bridge and attempted half of the (mostly) riverside walk that had been recommended to him. He enjoyed it enough to promise himself another day to complete its eastern section (where the *real* history lay, according to Kleiber), but then recalled that Otto Fischer the holiday-maker was a pleasant, impossible fiction.

He let himself into the flat with the key he had been loaned and found a note on the table. Apparently, his optimistic young friend was going to make another attempt upon Gloria's defensive perimeter that evening and wasn't expecting to return early. Rather than give his head the space and time to work further upon his mood, Fischer washed, changed his shirt and went out again, walking south and west into as yet unknown territory, using Battersea power station's dead-cow legs as his Pole Star.

He ate his supper at place called Izzy's Fish Bar, an unadventurous yet welcome second-helping of haddock and chips, with smashed peas that looked and tasted very much like *erbsenbrei*. Despite the establishment's tiled walls, plain white laminated tables and morgue-bright lighting, it felt curiously homely. He was surrounded by families, yet his singular face got only the occasional, swiftly diverted glance (a legacy, he assumed, of the long-familiar damage wrought upon their young pilots by the Battle for England). For a while he allowed himself to drift, idly wondering what might distinguish a Jewish fish and chip restaurant from its gentile competition (he'd ask Kleiber, if he remembered), while slowly sipping from a heroically-proportioned mug. Wisely, he had chosen tea rather than coffee with his (excellent) meal, though it came strong enough to scour barnacles from a hull. He must have pulled a face at first sip, because a man facing him two tables away did the same, then grinned and raised his own mug in salutation.

He really didn't want to like these people. The span of his coming betrayals couldn't be measured as yet, and the mass of guilt he bore already was quite sufficient. So, he watched this clutch of cheerful folk enjoying their innocent pleasures and reminded himself that the British may have tended to shoot fewer of their prisoners out of hand than either the Soviets or Americans, but they had flattened German cities as enthusiastically as they had indiscriminately. The thought helped, a little.

He took a roundabout route back to the flat and got lost, twice, in the dark. When finally he found his way home (having asked directions from one of London's famously obliging 'Bobbies') Kleiber was waiting, glass in hand, propping himself on the mantelpiece and scanning his Constable landscape for enemy movements. When the door opened he turned and beamed.

'Otto! How was your secret day?'

'Much as I expected. I assume you haven't broken Gloria's resistance?'

'No! She manoeuvres like a fish - I got a hand on her thigh during the intermission and I swear she was three seats away before I had time to squeeze.'

'Intermission?'

'*La Dolce Vita*. I hoped it might give her ideas.'

'It didn't, obviously.'

'Not so you'd notice. Never mind.'

'You didn't used to be this philosophical about girls, Jonas.'

'Renate taught me that it was mad to care too much.'

Renate, Fischer's former shop assistant, had been Jonas Kleiber's first great love. Her distant, frigid nature had lured him onto the rocks, and once there, her belatedly-discovered preference for girls had made the stranding a brutal, salutary ordeal. At the time, Fischer had wondered whether his young friend might make some drastic, destructive gesture in the vain hope of making her want him. Instead, a previously unsuspected core of resilience and common sense had sent him out into the world - where, apparently, he had learned to roll with the amorous punches.

Fischer never, ever, gave advice about women, but it seemed a moment to say something on the matter of wooing (he had, after all, been the instrument by which Renate and Kleiber had met, so a fatherly interest couldn't offend).

'She may never let you get close enough. Or, one day, without you having done the least thing to deserve it, her *no* could become an enthusiastic *yes*. They're an unreadable species.'

Kleiber was nodding before the final sentence was fully out. 'It's a mystery, for sure. What are you doing tomorrow?'

'Trying to see someone – or at least, to get a message through.'

'And it would be pointless for me to ask what it might be?'

'It's an invitation, that's all. Nothing that will get me into trouble.'

Kleiber took another sip of his brandy and contemplated a point where the wall met the ceiling and a small portion of wallpaper had started its long journey towards the floor.

'So, you fake your own death, tell no-one about it, uproot yourself from what was to be your last stop on this Earth – having, by the way, already palmed off your girlfriend to another fellow and sold the farm – and come to England on a secret mission that isn't, allegedly, going to get you into trouble. As if you've ever done anything that hasn't dropped you in the shit. Then, you're going back to Germany for a visit at least and possibly more, a place where two intelligence agencies - and Willy Brandt too, according to Freddie Holleman - want very much to wrap their fingers around your throat and squeeze. Unless you've found a way to profit from skipping through a mine-field, none of this will be remotely to your benefit. Which makes me realize that I shouldn't be asking questions at all.'

'Well, we can agree on that, at ...'

'Because I'm not qualified. It's a head-doctor you need, to explore what's gone very wrong with the inner Otto.'

10

'You're certain we didn't do it?'

'I've asked everyone who might have had the thought. No-one admitted to anything, even when I made it seem as if I was pleased about what's happened. We must assume that brake cables can fail, sometimes.'

Chairman Shelepin sat back in his chair. 'Extraordinary. At an innocent stroke we could have been rid of the largest thorn in our collective fundament. I've sent my best wishes, of course. And grapes. Grapes are appropriate, I believe?'

Deputy Chairman Semichastny nodded. 'I'm surprised you found some.'

'I called the Yeliseyevsky, but they didn't have any. I didn't want to waste more time, so I asked the US Embassy if they could spare a small bunch.'

'You're joking?'

Shelepin never joked. He looked blankly at his subordinate. 'Really, they were very happy to oblige. I received a parcel less than an hour later, and had it sent straight on to Kuntsevo. Do you know what the biggest mystery is, Vladimir Yefimovich?'

'That he survived a high-speed crash with only a few broken ribs?'

'That he had a ZIL for his personal use. Of course, that's what saved him the damn things are built like a T55. But a mere General, even if he *is* the First Secretary's pet dog, shouldn't have been issued with a ZIL.'

'He wasn't, as such. When your predecessor was pushed across to GRU, Comrade Khrushchev played one of his little jokes on him. He told Serov that he'd be issued with a new model ZIL-111, which must have pleased him as much as he could be pleased at the time. But then the First Secretary had his old vehicle, a Zil-110, allocated to his nemesis Zarubin. That would have hurt, I expect, particularly as every other senior member of the General Staff has to make do with a *Chaika*.'

Shelepin stared pointedly at his subordinate. '*I* have to make do with a *Chaika*.'

'You've never cared for superficial tokens of status, Comrade Chairman.'

'No, but it would be pleasant to be allowed to demonstrate the fact. How will General Zarubin interpret this?'

'Interpret?'

'His brake cable failed. Will he believe the report or assume that we – that someone - helped it along?'

Semichastny pursed his lips. 'We've never attempted death by mechanical failure - he almost certainly knows that. There are too many variables that one couldn't begin to control, and it seems to me that brakes would be particularly problematic. The moment at which failure should occur could hardly be determined without having some explosive device trigger the event, which would of course leave clear evidence. Merely cutting the cable would drain the hydraulic system more or less immediately, so the target would be likely to pull off, attempt to slow at the first necessity – perhaps a parking garage exit – fail, and hit a wall or other vehicle at little more than walking speed. Personally, I'd be far more comfortable having a sniper with a clear shot at that same junction and not leave anything to chance.'

'*That* certainly wouldn't look like an accident.'

'An odourless poison, then - in grapes, perhaps?'

Shelepin smiled. 'If only I'd thought of that earlier. There's another possibility. The First Secretary has been cooling towards Zarubin recently, but he has a famously sentimental nature. Wouldn't an injury – serious but not fatal – have the effect of rekindling his affection? Might that prospect have tempted the spurned suitor?'

'That would raise even more problems than an assassination attempt. How does one accurately calibrate *serious but not fatal*? The vehicle's driver died, emphatically. General Zarubin was halted in his own trajectory only by an open briefcase, which jammed into the front seat and broke several of his ribs. What if one of them had turned and penetrated his heart? It happens, apparently. I can't think that this was other than a blameless incident.'

'A hard thing to accept, in our profession.'

'Still, as it falls out, he may gain some advantage from this. Khrushchev will make a show of paying more attention to him – at least, until he becomes a less pitiable prospect.'

'And what will he be hearing?'

'It will be mostly about not underestimating the Americans, as usual - particularly with respect to Berlin, given Comrade Ulbricht's inability to allow sleeping dogs their peace and quiet.'

'His fucking wall.'

Exasperated, Semichastny shook his head. 'It's too ironic. He's pushing MfS to push *us* to persuade Khrushchev to agree to it. On the other side, Zarubin's telling the First Secretary to press the brakes – ha, forgive me! – and leave things as they are, at least until we get a better view of how the Kennedy Administration shapes itself. And, if allowed their own opinion, MfS would concur heartily. They don't *want* a wall.'

'Of course they don't. The inner Berlin border is their flood point, where hordes of *Stasi* infiltrators cross to the west with the defecting masses, undetected and undetectable. If a wall goes up the exodus slows to a trickle of tunnellers, balloonists and the occasional pole-vaulter, each of whom can be rounded up and screened by BfV at their leisure. But Ulbricht isn't interested in the counter-intelligence perspective; it's his nose-diving economy – and the humiliation of a fleeing intelligentsia - that's giving him insomnia.'

'Are *we* agnostic still, about a wall?'

'To the extent that it would give General Zarubin an aneurism, we're enthusiastically for it. Otherwise, I tend to side with MfS. It will hinder their operations - and, by the way, hand the Allies a solid propaganda victory. *Look at the Communist Model*, they'll say: *so desirable and successful that its beneficiaries need to be caged like chickens.*'

'That leaves the question – what *is* our position, if asked?'

'We'll put Comrade Ulbricht's case as convincingly as a shrug will allow, and then beg to be excused. In any case, it's a moot point. Now that Gromyko's becoming enthusiastic for the wall, Khrushchev will follow and then we can all nod and say yes, we think it's a wonderful idea. In the meantime, you might send a personal note to Zarubin, hoping for his swift recovery. As I say, I've sent one already, but a show of unanimity from us would look gracious. And who knows? With luck, he'll be allergic to paper. Now, the other thing?'

'Other thing?'

'This half-faced walking corpse who might or might not be one of Zarubin's men. What's he been doing in London?'

'So far, acting like a tourist – or, perhaps, a scholar. He spent a day in the British Library, met a lady for a drink in a pub and is staying with an old acquaintance, a journalist.'

Shelepin pulled a face. 'I don't like journalists. And I'm beginning not to like this Fischer. I tried to get a better picture of what he was doing three years ago, in Berlin.'

Semichastny felt his stomach tighten. Anything that the Chairman wished to know he should have put through his deputy. He tried to smile casually. 'What can I tell you?'

'Probably very little. According to the Berlin *Rezidentura* the Resident himself put a surveillance team on to the man, but further details are lacking. Which, of course, is strange.'

'They must have reported.'

'You would have thought so, but there's nothing filed. Nor do we have the names of those who carried out the surveillance, which is stranger still.'

'Why don't you just ask the Resident? Oh! Sorry ...'

The question had been entirely disingenuous. Upon replacing Ivan Serov as Head of KGB, Shelepin had very quickly come to regard their erstwhile Berlin Resident, A.M Korotkov, as a problem. He didn't like the man's loud, brash style, but more than that, he regarded him as one of the more dangerous members of the old NKVD clique that he was flushing slowly from KGB. For three years now, he had been trying to manoeuvre the man out of his post and into retirement, and only eight days earlier had succeeded, though by default. He had summoned Korotkov to Moscow to criticize his recent performance in detail, and, following that uncomfortable meeting, the Berlin Resident had met his old boss Serov for a game of tennis (no doubt to fully apprise him of Shelepin's slurs). In the changing rooms immediately afterwards, Korotkov had suffered a massive heart attack and died, a development so remarkably convenient for Shelepin that he had asked the same questions then as he did today about General Zarubin. In their world, rivals and outright enemies just didn't drop dead or crash into trees when it was required of them, yet Serov himself had attested to the fact that Korotkov had seemed unwell during their game, and even complained - to Khrushchev - that his old friend had been overworked by Shelepin. He had intended the accusation to wound; it had merely absolved.

Semichastny watched his Chairman's face carefully. His interest in this business needed to go away, quickly. What had happened in Berlin three years earlier had been carefully buried by Korotkov, and for good reason. If Shelepin discovered that they had lost two field agents (one dead, the other fled) during that operation, he would have any number of questions for his deputy, the least of which would be about Otto Fischer. Their relationship was built upon absolute trust, a trust that Semichastny had willingly set out to side-step. If everything went as it should, the fact of his subterfuge would be regarded as a minor detail, even by Shelepin himself. If it didn't, there would soon be a vacancy at close to the very highest level of KGB, and probably as a result of another convenient accident.

Shelepin was tapping his fingers on the desk, as he almost always did when circling a decision. He was a cautious, thoughtful player, loath to move a piece without having all the permutations before him. He didn't like gaps, blanks, spaces where information should be or lack of good reason for the same. Most of all, he detested risks that couldn't be measured precisely, end to end. The old KGB had buried inconvenient failures, either beneath the bodies of those who had done the failing or the ones who had been scapegoated for it; but Shelepin had worked to end that tradition, and in bringing a degree of accountability to their work he had exposed himself to consequence. A man who put himself at risk didn't walk happily into places that weren't brightly lit.

The tapping stopped abruptly.

'Allow very little slack on this, Vladimir Yefimovich. Assume that someone who fakes his own death has good cause to do so, and is almost certainly of concern to us. If he strays so much as a step off the open path, be ready to put my mind entirely at ease. In the meantime, have a look at the gap in our Berlin *Rezidentura*'s filing system, and try to determine why it occurred. I'll do the same, from the other end.'

'The other end?'

Shelepin's mouth twisted as if it were sucking lemon peel. 'Given the choice, I'd rather join the New Year's Day swim across the Neva; but a conversation with GRU Director Serov may be productive.'

Roger Broadsmith spent half a morning trying to decide whether he was pleased or troubled by what he'd heard from Harold Shergold. His first reaction had been relief, of course. Having expected a reprise of the 'Blake' interrogation regarding his past, his work and political beliefs, the actual matter at hand had been nothing to do with R.D.G. Broadsmith *per se*, but rather how he might stretch his legs for Queen and Country.

It was the *stretching* that gave him food for thought. He was being offered what he'd wanted for many months now, or at least what he'd persuaded himself that he wanted. To be lifted on wings of departmental reorganization – from monitoring a regime where the burning issue was how to push as far along the road to capitalism as wouldn't disturb the men in tanks, to one where most of the tanks were likely to converge - was an unexpected and gratifying offer. The disappointment had come with the detail. He had hoped for Berlin, but he was being offered Bonn. He had imagined himself as a protagonist, seated at one side of a board, manoeuvring against a shadowy State Security counterpart. Instead, he was being pushed to accept a seat in the audience – a liaison role with BfV, West Germany's Federal Office for the Protection of the Constitution, their version of MI5.

Clearly, it was his near-fluent German language skills that had recommended him rather than his as-yet untested gifts for diplomacy, but the offer was a flattering one. He would be the very first SIS officer to work directly with any German intelligence service, given the cold distance that the British had maintained from General Gehlen's BND for more than a decade now. Even the humiliations of Burgess, Maclean and now Blake couldn't tempt the top floor at 54 Broadway to contemplate a reconciliation with a man they regarded - with good cause - as an enthusiastic recruiter of former Nazis (a predilection about which the Americans were far more forgiving). But with the CIA increasingly reluctant to open their hearts and files to their embarrassed British cousins, SIS needed alternative access to front-line intelligence, and BfV, for all their own embarrassments – *Vulkan*, Otto John – knew more about *Stasi* operations in the West than anyone else.

He had no personal ties or commitments to keep him in London, and the posting could be a fascinating challenge. His only fear was that, in accepting it, he would be placing himself on the inside track to a future career so far from field-work that he'd need to read Graham Greene novels to catch up. Working for SIS, he was no less a civil servant than if he'd been with the National Assistance Board, yet running field agents made it feel like something else. A job permanently trawling through paperwork generated by other men would give him a severe case of the Cardigans.

Should he be flattered that they had chosen him? Shergold had tried not to overstate it, but there were far more ways that a fellow could bugger up than shine. He was told that he would need to be reserved yet approachable, confident in what he was doing yet deferential enough not to bruise German feelings - above all, he was to create a strong impression that SIS were not the set of superannuated asses that their recent form might suggest. As the list of required talents grew, Broadsmith had suggested that this was perhaps a job for a more senior member of his organization, to which Shergy had smiled rather sadly and told him – far more bluntly than was his habit – that no-one Upstairs wanted it. Half of them had liberated some foul place in Northern Germany back in '45 and couldn't yet bring themselves to think of the race as human. The others were far too comfortable in their present cocoons - sipping tea, briefing politicians and planning the deployment of their looming pensions. It was a remarkably frank admission from a senior man to a case officer, and Broadsmith almost believed him, but it was equally likely that the preliminary work on both sides was to be done by personnel who weren't allowed near their organizations' most precious jewels.

His last question should have been his first, but he'd been distracted by the offer.

'Why isn't our Berlin Station handling it?'

'Bad history – Blake's, mainly, given that he used to be one of them. Since the Otto John affair, Gehlen's been trying trying to absorb BfV into his BND, so they're a little twitchy about offering him any further ammunition. And negotiating a direct relationship with London gives the thing a wider political dimension that Gehlen will find hard to nobble.

'Now, we estimate that you'll need to be there for three to six months, to get a basic working relationship going. You'll assure them that we'll give full access to materials in areas upon which we can agree to share intelligence. That will be overstating it a little, but I've agreed with Dicky that we'll show the right spirit when deciding what can and can't be released. Obviously, you won't be involved directly in such decisions.'

Obviously. Shergold had dismissed him with a breezy request that he make a decision within twenty-four hours, as if they'd been discussing an office move to the Queen Annes Gate building around the corner. That was alright, though. The offer hadn't really been presented as such, not when his future career with SIS would otherwise constitute a one-man backwater, like Greville Pearce's. His present casework would be reassigned, never to return – a ten-year accretion of expertise given up for some other field officer's benefit, and in Bonn he would be the new child at school, not knowing where anything was, how anything was done. That was the worst of it. A sunnier view was that his would be the first steps into new territory - into a job that required little more than being an amiable conduit for other men's dealings while taking care not to jab his elbows into any ribs. And at the end of it, even Harold Shergold might have to defer to his judgement on dealings with the Germans.

This happier perspective put him into a lighter mood. If he was to be allowed little initiative he could hardly be held accountable for other men's missteps, while the warm rays of a successful outcome would scatter indiscriminately. By lunchtime he'd decided to give his answer, but when he went up to the fourth floor he was told that Shergold was with the Americans, a form of words which everyone at Broadway now took to mean that HERO was having yet another conversation with his new friends.

Broadsmith's decision was buttressed that afternoon when his room-mate came back from the bookies with new cash, a hint of spirits on his breath and a winsome mood that made any thinking work impossible. From now on his days would be Pearce-free – why hadn't that occurred to him immediately? It was a substantially greater perquisite than the dislocation allowance and modest bump in salary that Shergy had hinted at – more, even, than the opportunity to see new and slightly exotic places that his forebears had done their best to raze. And even if the man's abject uselessness didn't get him transferred to a decoding cellar in the meantime, surely Broadsmith's post-Bonn career wasn't likely to be disfigured by vistas of Greville, picking his teeth with a paper-knife or nose with a little finger?

He typed a short note, thanking Shergold for the opportunity and expressing his pleasure in accepting, put it on the man's desk and clocked out early that afternoon. Walking across St James' Park, he allowed himself pleasing daydreams of a plush office in Bonn, a welcoming handshake from Hubbert Schrübbers himself and the undeserved respect that seconded intelligencers could bank until familiarity wiped the slate. He even speculated upon the potential for romance, in a country currently suffering both a parlous shortage of menfolk and an unrealistically glamorous view of secretive Englishmen (thanks to the sterling work of Mr Fleming). It must have put a smile on his face, because he received several in return as he approached Admiralty Arch.

The bus journey to Brent Cross seemed less tedious than usual, and he suspected that this had little to do with the sunshine. Before returning to his bedsit he called in at his landlady's, explained the situation (a private school, teaching English to the children of wealthy Germans) and begged to be allowed to give flexible notice. She was a decent old thing, usually, but he got a pinched, sideways look and a sigh, which he took to mean that she'd long since spent his deposit and would have to raid the mattress to refund him. He stayed for a cup of tea, and cheered her slightly with a promise to write occasionally with tales of the Hun.

At home, he collected his post from his elderly neighbour (though his door had a letter-box he had sealed it when first he moved in, and in return for having her week's shopping done each Saturday, Miss Ellis was happy to act as his postmistress). There was yet another invitation to subscribe to *The Reader's Digest*, a new Rediffusion television rental card, a form confirming that his 1961 census documents had been received late yet would incur no penalty and a solitary letter, the handwriting upon which drove almost all the day's other matters from mind.

His ex-fiancee had realised her mistake – that she had treated him very badly, and that George Betterman was not, in fact, any kind of better man. Though she had no right to expect his forgiveness, could she hope that he might see her again, and perhaps that they could still be more than friends?

He sat down and thought about it for a great while, before deciding that the cruellest cut would be kindness – the sort that lets a person down so gently that their mistake inflates itself enormously, puts on a top hat and chases them relentlessly. It was cheap and unworthy, of course, but he intended ensure that the ghost of Roger Broadsmith haunted Amelia Harcourt-Duff until George Betterman improved considerably or some other fellow came along to take up duties.

The day couldn't have closed on a better note, and Broadsmith would have opened the bottle of claret he'd been saving for morale purposes, had not a single knotty matter remained front and centre. What would his other masters think of the Bonn posting? Would they regard it as a squandering of a painstakingly cultivated asset at the heart of British foreign intelligence, or as an unexpected, suspicion-free insertion into West Germany's domestic equivalent – their principal enemy? He wouldn't be blamed for any of it, obviously - an agent went wherever he was posted, they understood that. Even so, Broadsmith would have rested a little easier knowing whether Herr Markus Wolf was going to chew off a chair leg or send for champagne when he heard the news.

Harold Shergold had 'borrowed' a couple of MI5 men for his little jaunt out of the office. It was highly unlikely that the Other Side would stage anything on London's streets in broad daylight, but nerves being what they presently were, prudence demanded that precautions be taken – indeed, over-taken - when a meeting outdoors was not at one's own suggestion.

The popular assumption was that British Intelligence maintained a core of iron-hearted assassins. It didn't, of course. For practical business, MI5 had access to a number of ad hoc resources, ranging from mildly psychopathic criminal types (for off-the-book matters) to former and present Special Services men. Brian and Micky were the latter, both familiar to Shergold from previous baby-sitting jobs, whose long-term secondment to Leconfield House allowed them to be made available to SIS at very little notice.

As a courtesy, Shergold had apprised his MI5 counterpart of this meeting (in the broadest terms), and promised to pass on a copy of his report to the IS Liaison Committee. In the meantime, he asked Brian to cover one end of the alley and Micky the other, far enough from anything that might need not to be overheard but close enough to do the business with the Browning HP that each of them carried, should it be necessary.

You'll recognize me. A little cryptic, perhaps, but the clouds parted when he saw the man. He was propping himself on one of the hotel's dustbins, pretending to read the *Daily Herald,* and it wasn't until he looked up and half-turned that the right-hand side of his face revealed its awful glory. Shergold's first thought was shrapnel, but the discoloration suggested burns. A former tank man, perhaps, or pilot, and almost certainly someone who hadn't seen the war fully out.

They shook hands (a gesture whose absurdity their profession had yet to excise), and Shergold forced himself not to look down at the further damage he had gripped a little too robustly.

'Shergold.'

'Fischer.'

German – eastern, probably Pomeranian (Shergold had a particularly acute ear for middle European accents), and likely, therefore, to be MfS. He nodded, but withheld a smile.

'Tell me something to make the rest of what you say credible.'

The half-brow furrowed slightly and then cleared. 'Meetings were held in London between SIS and CIA on four consecutive days from 15 December 1953, to discuss preparations for the operation known to the CIA as *Gold* and to you as *Stopwatch*. Your side brought nine representatives, the Americans five. George Blake was present at all of them.'

Shergold hadn't been one of the British team and would need to check the numbers, but he recalled the dates and the rest sounded plausible. He nodded.

'You have a proposal.'

Fischer glanced both ways down the alley, gauging the distance between ears. 'Yes.'

'Who is *you*, precisely? MfS?'

'Not them.'

'KGB?'

'No. Nor SB, StB, DSS or KDS - or CID, for that matter.'

Shergold smiled. 'I hadn't quite mistaken you for Chinese. But if none of those, who?'

'It would be better to think of this as a ... *political* approach, not intelligence.'

'Then why are you speaking to me?'

'Because you won't consider the politics of it. I didn't want to be chased away before being heard.'

'Alright. What are you offering, and what do you want?'

'Information, and nothing.'

'Wonderful. Christmas has come early.'

'These are my instructions. Information on certain matters will be passed to you, via a mechanism to be agreed upon. Obviously, you can take your time confirming its accuracy, or reject it if there's any doubt. The persons making this offer asks for nothing in return, though it's hoped that, eventually, you may rec ...'

'Reciprocate.'

'Yes, thank you. Reciprocate, if you feel that circumstances indicate it may be useful – to both sides.'

Both sides. Shergold stared at the hotel's kitchen door, willing it to stay closed. *Eventually* had made his heart quick-step. Someone wanted a channel, a conduit, to people they shouldn't ever be talking to. Half the fourth floor at 54 Broadway could spend a month in a locked room considering the implications, and come up with a dozen answers – a trap, a gift, a would-be traitor to his own, a lunatic, a looming change of political leadership, a ....

Joke, perhaps. When in doubt, doubt; but the *what ifs* kept coming, even to someone as immune to wishful thinking as Harold Taplin Shergold. If this were a genuine approach, a single foot in a door wouldn't necessarily lead to anything, but it might allow a little light upon something not previously seen. It couldn't be ignored – that was the only certainty he could pin at present.

He turned back to Hermes the damaged Messenger. 'I don't expect you to tell me *who*, but from *where* is this coming?'

'Moscow. But, as I say, not Dzerzhinsky Square.'

'The Aquarium?'

'No.'

Christ. If it wasn't KGB or GRU, then there was only one possibility. Fischer had said that his was a *political* approach, but Shergold had assumed he had been referring to its intended recipient, not the source. If this - whatever *this* was – originated in Red Square, God alone knew who would have to get involved in assessing the data. It would make the effort that went into *Stopwatch* look like arrangements for the annual office lunch.

He went over, around and through it in his head, while the man Fischer waited patiently. The damage made it difficult to parse his expression, but Shergold didn't sense any anxiety, which was unusual. Whatever his relationship to the person or persons making this offer, he must have known that it risked being seen as a ploy, a means of sowing disinformation. That didn't seem to worry him, though, so Shergold drew out the pause, pulling his pipe and tobacco from a coat pocket, slowly filling the one from the other and taking his time lighting it, and all the while keeping his eye on the kitchen door as if deep in thought, weighing a yes or no.

Fischer waited patiently, not twitching or glancing at the armed men who might so very easily rid SIS of a potential looming problem. Eventually, the Englishman tapped the pipe on a railing and nodded.

'Will we be dealing with you?'

'For a while at least, yes. But not here. Somewhere I might feel a little less lit up – and of course, where my contact can get documents to me without exposing himself.'

'Which would be …?'

'The Federal Republic, your choice of location.'

'You have no suggestion?'

'I only know Bremen, but that's American territory.'

'Bonn, then.'

Fischer smiled. 'I'm told it's a very pleasant place.'

'When will we next hear from you?'

'Shall we say, in a week? That will give me time to arrange a few matters - and you also. I don't suppose you keep a presence in Bonn?'

'Not at the moment, but by the time you're ready we will. How will you contact us?'

Fischer shrugged. 'By telephone, if you give me a number.'

Shergold removed a card from his wallet. 'Our direct line is monitored, as you'd expect. This is my home number. If I'm not there and a woman answers, ask if you're speaking to Anael. It's my wife's middle name - she'll make sure that I get any message quickly. I'd be grateful if you didn't share this with anyone.'

'Of course. May I go now?'

'You needn't ask my permission.'

'I thought your men might shoot me, if I didn't.'

'They won't do that unless my time's being wasted. *Is* my time being wasted?'

'No.'

'Well, then. Goodbye.'

13

Jonas Kleiber stared at the blank sheet of paper in front of him. It was begging to be filled with typed characters – ideally, in an order that would entice German commissioning editors to pay his rent, food and beer expenses for another week. He had an idea for a piece on the ongoing clash between Graham Hill and Wolfgang von Trips for the Formula One World Championship (von Trips' win at Aintree the previous day had been a particularly pleasing slap to British faces), but as hard as he tried to smell the scorched rubber and gasoline, nothing memorable came to mind.

He blamed the Unquiet Dead. How could inspiration bloom when a ghoulish apparition was trampling the buds? The week's stay had stretched to nine days now, and Kleiber was not a single clue closer to understanding the situation, much less getting a sense of how far the shit would splash (as shit surely must) when Fischer did what he needed to do. In the meantime, work wasn't being done, and the pressure of keeping a great secret – though he didn't know what the damn thing *was* – had the headache ticking along like a well-wound clock.

Did a friend deserve such treatment? He'd asked himself that a lot, and its self-pitying echo had been a small comfort in the small hours. After all he'd done for the man – giving him a (virtually) rent-free home after his shop burned down, and forgiving him for having brought the fatally beautiful Renate into his life – he might have expected more than a shake of the head and the finger to the lips he'd been given whenever he tried to prise off the lid. *Of course* Otto would say that he'd be safer not knowing - it's what he *always* said. Kleiber was left wondering (also as always) how safe any man could be who didn't have the first idea of what was going on around him.

He hadn't faked his own death for no big reason. *That* was sound enough to be repeated almost as much as the self-pitying stuff. You'd have to owe serious money, or be needing a gun to point elsewhere, or hoping to distract a man whose daughter you'd stuffed up, and of those possibilities (there might be more, but Kleiber wasn't a practiced desperado) only one could apply to Otto Fischer. He was in shooting trouble again – *yet* again – and almost certainly, it wasn't a Portuguese wine-making cooperative that was doing the chasing.

He didn't bother with the next question – if not them, then who? It took a rare talent to antagonize both sides of a yawning ideological divide, but his friend had managed it handsomely. Soviets and Americans, both sorts of Germans and the Poles, too – who *wouldn't* want a clear shot at the man?

Kleiber stared at the blank page in front of him. *And why the hell was Formula One a 'sport' anyway?* Whoever had the best car won, as long as he drove like a would-be suicide. Two years earlier, he had been taken to Brand's Hatch as the guest of a fellow journalist, to watch the Kentish 100. The spectacle – if it could be called such – had given him a migraine, courtesy of the noise and a neck twist brought on by trying to follow individual vehicles as they tore past him. The ordeal had seemed to last a half-lifetime, yet the action (so to speak) comprised forty-two momentary slices of wondering which of the blurs was in the lead. He'd seen more exciting ...

Why hadn't Otto come to London and done whatever he needed to do without bothering anyone? Oblivious to the truth, Kleiber could be mourning already - a straightforward process requiring that he recall the deceased through warm, misty glass and entertain regrets about how he hadn't done or said things that he could never have thought to do or say anyway. And, in the meantime, the sympathy that grieving brings out in the feminine psyche might have made the final breach in Gloria's defences.

The thought of that particular breach cheered Kleiber only briefly. He was sensitive enough to be aware of his shallowness, but the fact was that almost five months' investment of time, money and sundry professions of tender feelings - and then more money - had generated next to no return. He had been told that he was *a nice boy* (discouraging), and *sweet* (she might have said that to a brother), and, worst of all, how much she *treasured their friendship* (which was as much as to tell him that he needn't bother bringing along his penis to their dates). In the face of all that, his imperishable sexual optimism had climbed out onto a high ledge and was waiting for the shove.

Bloody Otto. As he couldn't be mourned it was reasonable that he be blamed instead, for adding sour sauce to Kleiber's present woes. He had been a Londoner for almost five years now, and the other-worldly magic had faded to a sort of normality – which, like all normals, comprised a pallet of greys. Had some wonderful scoop come his way recently, or Gloria relented and handed him her hymen, *normal* might have been accommodated or even passed unnoticed; but over the past few months, routine had settled like an old carpet, undisturbed by even momentary triumphs. Had he needed to work to eat he might have put his head down and forced himself through this dolor, but even if the commissions dried up entirely there was always his German bank account, still largely bloated by what Herr Grabner, his mentor and former editor, had bequeathed to him, to keep him both well fed *and* bored.

Ironically, he'd been thinking of calling Otto and asking if he might visit for a few weeks, to shake off the blue passages and discover what kept the Portuguese in Portugal, when news of his friend's demise made the trip unfeasible (or at least a little inappropriate). So, here he was, still in his monochromatic, chaste rut, further burdened by fears for what his undead friend was up to, and he *still* couldn't name the difference between Formula Fucking One and Two.

To ease the coiled spring he decided to leave the glamorous world of motor racing briefly and attend to the domestic stuff. There was enough beer in his kitchen but his unwanted guest was a wine man, so a trip to the off-license was both necessary and an opportunity to flush a head. Halfway into his jacket and a quarter-way down the stairs he recalled that he lacked bread, butter and tea also. The local Premier could supply all of these, but Kleiber didn't see the point of living above a bakery and not taking advantage of it. He turned left at the bottom of the stairs, left again, and joined a queue of three customers.

Maxwell's was one of the few bakeries in that part of London to offer fresh French bread, and probably the only one to follow an authentic recipe (courtesy of a grateful fellow-baker whose Caen premises somehow hadn't been atomized either by the RAF or the Middlesex Regiment (Bertrand Maxwell's former unit) seventeen years earlier. Given that Kleiber was now officially defined as a 'continental', he thought it only right to do the continental thing, and he did it so consistently that the proprietor was wrapping a baguette for him as he reached the glass counter.

'Hello, Bert.'

'Alright, Jonas? Where's yer gorgeous friend?'

'Having his eyelashes done. What's the news?'

'Mavis has gone to see her mother in Lowestoft. I don't expect the *Berlin Times* will bid for that.'

'*Morgenpost*. And no, I shouldn't think so.'

'Anyway, you're a journalist - you're supposed to tell *me* the news, aren't you?'

'Not for free, I'm not. What's the difference between Formula One and Two?'

'Loudness, I expect. One and fourpence please, mate.'

Bert took the exact change and was allocating each coin to its correct slot in his till drawer when something occurred to him. 'Oh.'

'What is it?'

'Someone might be interested in you.'

'How's that?'

The baker nodded at his front window. 'Alfred was getting the ovens going about three o'clock the other morning, and he noticed some bloke standing on the corner opposite. He was there again today, and hadn't shifted by five. We don't owe money to anyone, so I wondered if *you'd* robbed a bank or something.'

Kleiber tried to smile, but it felt like the onset of the seizure that Otto Fischer had been doing his best to induce for almost ten years now. He excused himself, left the premises and almost ran back upstairs to his flat. He'd tucked the slip of paper into his desk drawer the previous week, and to his great relief it hadn't since managed to relocate itself as so many other important things did. He took it downstairs, re-entered Maxwell's Family Bakers (est. 1884) and waited impatiently while an old lady finished declaring her list of ailments, and, with exquisite care, packed a small white sliced into her basket.

Kleiber opened the door, almost kicked her out into the street and returned to the counter.

'Bert, may I use your 'phone, please? It's important, and I'll get the operator to tell me what it costs.'

'Where's it to?'

'Germany.'

'Ok. As long as it's not the Luftwaffe.'

Kleiber gave him the rictus once more and went into the back of the shop, to the tiny cubicle designated as office space. With a visibly shaking finger he dialled the operator, asked to place an international call and gave her the number.

It rang twelve times before someone picked up. He might have replaced the receiver in the meantime, but his panic had metastasized to a form of paralysis. When he heard a voice it took a considerable effort for him to retain consciousness.

'Hello? This is Jonas Kleiber, calling from London. Yes, very well, thank you. I need to tell you something, but it's in strict confidence. And you have to promise not to be angry.'

14

'Levin!'

A thud, creak and clumsy shuffle identified Zarubin's secretary in motion as clearly as ocelli would a peacock feather. No doubt a mumbled curse would have reinforced the evidence, had the door between them not been closed.

The head, appearing around it, confirmed the diagnosis.

'Comrade General?'

'It's like the fucking Tsytsin Gardens in here. Get rid of it all.'

'Yes, Comrade General. Don't you like flowers?'

'In sensible quantities, possibly. This is mad. And couldn't you have put them in vases?'

Dozens of bouquets, mainly of roses, lay on almost every surface in Zarubin's office. His desk (fortunately cleared of paperwork) was particularly burdened, its leather inlay already ruined by the pool of water gathered upon it.

'I did, over there.'

On the deep windowsill, a half-field's yield of flowers had been stuffed into large glass jar without trimming or any attempt at arrangement.

'You couldn't borrow more?'

'Not without a requisition order. Which I'm not authorized to sign.'

'Well, send the live ones down to the typing room, with my compliments. And get someone to dry out this place while I try to make an appointment with the First Secretary.'

Zarubin's head was bandaged still, so his brusque manner gave him the air of a brigade commander organizing a hasty withdrawal. Since leaving his apartment at daybreak he had experienced several momentary bouts of dizziness (which he wasn't going to admit to), and every time he forgot not to breathe deeply his ribs reminded him of his error. If things weren't as they presently were he would have been happy to take a fortnight's leave, but this was not a time to leave free space between bad advice and his boss's ears. His three days in hospital might already have created that space, but he was hoping that the remarkable circumstances of his accident had caused KGB to pause while it tried to work out whether one of their own was responsible. It was the one great disadvantage of their trade - that duplicity could wind back upon itself endlessly, leaving no clear view of anything.

He made his way tenderly through the Kremlin complex, gratified to note that the numerous security personnel who usually complicated that journey did their best not to inconvenience him. One of them, a major who was nodding him through even before he saw his pass, went so far as to wish him a speedy recovery, which suggested that at least some elements of Ninth Directorate bore him no ill-will for his past sins (unless they wanted him out and about once more in order to have the clear head-shot). He told the man that it was nothing, a minor mishap, but didn't dare risk a shrug.

A waiting room stood to the side of Shevchenko's office, which in turn protected the First Secretary from the importunities of access-seekers. Zarubin knew better than to try to shove his way past the lesser supplicants (Shevchenko had the use of an inegalitarian, four-room apartment with a fine view of Christ the Saviour, but he was careful to treat peasants and General Staff with equal contempt), so he gave his name to an appointments receptionist and took a seat. He appeared to be in a queue of just three men, but as he reached for a copy of that morning's *Izvestia* the door opened and the two highest ranking officers in KGB stepped in.

Well, this is embarrassing.

Shelepin notice him immediately, smiled broadly and came to take the adjacent seat, but his deputy Semichastny started visibly, as if Banquo's ghost had nudge his elbow and asked for the asparagus. He recovered himself quickly, though, found a neutral expression and followed his boss.

Shelepin patted Zarubin's shoulder tenderly. 'We were worried for you, Sergei Aleksandrovich. And poor Kozlov! He was my driver for more than two years, did you know? I've sent condolences to the family, naturally.'

Zarubin believed him. Shelapin's predecessor Serov was an animal, but the current KGB Chairman could have been mistaken for one of his western counterparts – a clubbable team-leader, happy to have his subordinates' talents recognized and to keep his far subordinates in hope of the same. It *would* have been a mistake, of course; the man had degrees in philosophy and history, and was said to write poetry in his leisure hours; but he'd also been one of Stalin's favourites, and when a wet operation was needed he would sign the authorization unblinkingly. He was also an enthusiastic proponent of arming liberation movements in places where the quality of life was already deathly. Only that month, he had single-handedly convinced the Central Committee to send more armaments to their African clients than 1st Ukrainian Front had deployed in the battle for Berlin. Whether they arrived would depend upon how well his principal opponent in the Kremlin – one Sergei Aleksandrovich Zarubin - could argue the alternative case for export credits to the legitimate regimes, to wean them from their growing American infatuations.

'Thank you for your concern, Aleksandr Nikolayevich. The grapes were very welcome.' Zarubin turned to Semichastny. 'And your flowers, Vladimir Yefimovich.'

Semichastny was composed now, and managed a smile. 'I didn't send flowers, General. Mine was the bottle of brandy.'

'Then it was doubly welcome. You'll forgive me if I wait for my head to stop throbbing before I open it?'

'Of course. That's a quite heroic bandage – the wound must be substantial.'

'Not at all – a large bruise.'

Shelepin patted Zarubin's hand. 'Don't be brave. A bruised head can mean a lot of things, so you must take care of yourself. Have a consultation with Kandel at Burdenko – he can tell you if there's any danger of complications.'

The patient was touched, but he couldn't help wondering if the KGB Chairman was hoping for a lengthy rest-cure, preferably at a facility where mind-dulling drugs could be administered regularly. Under the circumstances, he decided that the damaged ribs might heal better if they weren't mentioned at all.

'I'll certainly do that. Have you an appointment with Comrade Khrushchev this morning?'

'We do, yes.'

'May I ask why you're meeting with him?'

Shelepin gave him the weary, we-all-have-to-go-through-this tilt of the head.

'Administrative matters, unfortunately. We're as accountable for our budgets as the Metro Expansion Committee.'

It was beyond plausible that the KGB's number one *and* two men needed to be present to talk finances with a man who famously couldn't give a damn for what things – a haircut, a nuclear bomber – cost. Zarubin might have felt insulted that such little effort was being made to deceive him, but then, there were far less courteous ways of being told to mind one's own fucking business.

So, it was probably about Berlin, or perhaps Cuba. Had it been Africa the Chairman might have told him so, or at least made some oblique reference to his recent foreign policy triumph. If it was Cuba, Zarubin had nothing to say as yet, because Khrushchev himself couldn't come to a view on how far he could support the *Revolución*. For the moment at least, Berlin was the only ground upon which both Dzerzhinsky Square and the small office of Major General Zarubin had urgent thoughts.

Zarubin acknowledged the lie with a knowing nod (a slow, careful nod) and turned his attention to the fingernails on his left hand. Why had Semichastny reacted that way? He couldn't have been surprised to see signs of life if he'd sent a bottle of brandy – corpses tended to have little use for spirits other than as embalming fluid – but there had been a palpable missed heartbeat when the otherwise pleasing prospect confronted him. And why had Shelapin not reacted in a similar manner? What did the one know that the other didn't?

Random elements abounded in the universe, any of which might explain the discrepancy, but Zarubin didn't allow himself to believe in *random* despite having just survived a supremely indifferent catastrophe. He recalled what he knew of Semichastny. A Komsomol man (weren't they all, these days?), he had served on the Ukrainian Front during the Patriotic War but somehow managed to get himself discharged, without decorations, as early as 1943, to return to university. A few years later he'd been appointed Second Secretary in the Azerbaijan Communist Party – which, unusually, didn't seem to have been punishment for anything – before being brought back to Moscow and placed at the right hand of his long-time patron Shelepin, whom he was generally expected to replace when the older man moved upwards. A bright, seemingly amiable young fellow who looked more like an aspiring American politician than a Soviet apparatchik, he was said to be ideologically conservative, with no known agenda beyond continuing the modernizing process within KGB. The sum of it wasn't anything that should have caused the hairs on Zarubin's very stiff neck to come to attention, but he placed a deep trust in them and whatever got them going.

The two men who had arrived earlier had been seen and swiftly disappointed by Shevchenko, who appeared at the door and nodded at Shelepin. The Chairman and his deputy stood, exchanged pleasantries with Zarubin and pointed themselves at the First Secretary's office. Only then did Shevchenko notice who remained in the waiting room, and barely kept his eyes from the ceiling.

'Come in please, Comrade.'

There was a very small opportunity here, and Zarubin intended not to squander it. He took a seat opposite Khrushchev's secretary, rubbed his head gingerly and let a small but affecting groan ventilate the space between them. Shevchenko's eyes narrowed.

'I hope you haven't discharged yourself prematurely from the Central Clinic, Comrade General. A head wound's not to be underestimated.'

Zarubin sighed. 'I know, Andrei Stepanovich. I was told that it was *probably* alright to return to work, but I have to say that this has knocked some of the wind from me. I need to ask the First Secretary about some rest leave, if he can spare me.'

That almost raised a smile. Shevchenko opened the diary, frowned at it, drew a line through an entry and looked up.

'Three o'clock, this afternoon?'

'That's *very* convenient, yes. Might I have a glass of water, please?'

While Shevchenko was at the water fountain, Zarubin turned the diary and glanced down. The scored-through name was V.V. Kuznetsov, which both flattered him and almost ruined the day. It was quite something, to be given precedence over Foreign Minister Gromyko's immediate subordinate – or at least, it would have been, if it hadn't spoken to how keenly Shevchenko (and, possibly, his boss Khrushchev) wanted him out of the Kremlin Palace.

15

'Do you have a gun, Otto?'

'Of course not. Why would I?'

'You're almost certainly going to get shot at – why wouldn't you?'

Fischer looked to either side of him. On a crowded Liverpool Street platform they were unlikely to be overheard, but the subject matter invited attention.

'Jonas, I don't intend to look for the sort of people who might want to shoot me. I'll be a tortoise, I promise.'

'You never *intend* to look for them. The trouble is, they find you. Have you got your Portuguese passport?'

'Of course.'

'Enough Dutch money?'

'No, I have dollars. I'll exchange some at Hoek, if I need to.'

'Do you have something to read on the ferry?'

'Jonas ...'

'Only the crossing can be deadly boring. Get a magazine at Harwich – practice your English.'

'Yes, mother.'

'And don't pay too much for sex. If they even sniff dollars they'll double the price.'

Fischer laughed. 'I'll be spending very, very little on sex.'

'Where are you going from Hoek?'

'I'll get a train at Rotterdam.'

'To ...?'

'Germany, via Eindhoven and Venlo I think.'

'For Christ's sake, Otto! *Where* in Germany?'

'There's no point in me telling you. You can't do anything with it, and knowing won't make you any happier. You're a worrier, Jonas.'

'Well, I've the right friend for that, haven't I?'

The previous evening, Fischer had planned to get Kleiber drunk enough to be distracted at their parting by a raging hangover. Unfortunately, youth had proved resilient. It was the older man who was feeling the pain today, and dreading rough seas. His minor consolation was that the culprit had been pale ale rather than Guinness, the difference being roughly that between a punch to the back of the head and decapitation.

Along the platform, a guard's whistle threw together a number of lovers, taking their reluctant farewells. Fischer put his case onto the boat-train, turned and held out his hand. Glumly, Kleiber took it.

'You'll call, won't you? Just to let me know you're not lying in a ditch somewhere?'

'In a few days, I promise.'

Two hours and twelve minutes later, the boat-train pulled into Parkeston Quay. Fischer's head, having brightened at roughly the same rate that clouds had cleared over the Suffolk countryside, was further eased by the discovery that the train station was accurately named, and closely abutted the quayside. His ferry, the *MS Koningin Wilhelmina*, was already moored directly opposite the platform, and barely two minutes after stepping out of the train he was handing his ticket to a crew member at the foot of the gangway.

The ship looked almost new, a low-raked vessel that seemed to be moving even while tied up. He found a cafe in second-class (shuttered while docked), took a seat and only then recalled Kleiber's warning about the tedium of the crossing. A brief trawl of the tables and benches landed no more than a well-thumbed copy of that morning's *Algemeen Daghlad*, the briefest examination of which confirmed that German and Dutch were not such similar languages as to prevent the onset of another headache. He resigned himself to eight hours' contemplation of the North Sea's grey majesty, and space for every fearful possibility he'd allowed to crawl into his recent dreams.

The cafe area had begun to fill up when the seat opposite was taken without any polite preamble, by a slim young man in a tweed jacket, hair brylcreemed in the standard Cambridge undergraduate style. He staring intently into Fischer's face but didn't seem to be disturbed by its unusual geography. After a few moments he nodded, leaned forward and held out a hand. The grip was light but calloused, a hand familiar with physical work. Or throats.

'Your report?'

The Cambridge diagnosis crumbled immediately. He spoke in German, two words only, but the long, rolled 'o's were a signature that Fischer's Eastern Front experience allowed him to place somewhere north of Smolensk and south of Petrograd.

'I met my contact three days ago.'

'Yes, we know. The name?'

'Harold Shergold. Apparently, he's ...'

'We've heard of him – a good choice, probably. He's agreed to consider this further?'

'I think so. I'm going to Bonn, where I'll meet his representative in a few days' time. In the meantime I have his home number; that will be how we arrange things, initially.'

'Please give it to me.'

The man had pulled a pen and slip of paper from a pocket. When nothing was said he looked up, surprised.

'We won't use it, naturally. It's a piece of information, to add to the little we have.'

Fischer recited the number from memory. He said nothing about using Mrs Shergold's middle name – but then, he hadn't been asked. As he watched the man write a thought occurred.

'Why have you waited until I'm almost out of England?'

That got a thin smile. 'We didn't want you pointing me out to anyone - your friend, for instance.'

'He doesn't know anything. Nor does anyone else.'

'It worried us that you'd allowed your resurrection to become known.'

'I couldn't see any other way to do this. England is a strange country to me.'

'The qualification is superfluous.'

'Still, I found it pleasant enough.'

The other man gave the room a lazy, unfocused up, down and around, as any bored passenger might. When he spoke again he was pretending to watch a thirsty queue coalesce as the counter shutter opened.

'Where in Bonn are you staying?'

'I don't know, as yet. It's another place that's strange to me.'

'Take this number. Call it the moment you have accommodation. We have people in the city, of course, but we need to be careful - our cousins regard it as home territory, even if it isn't. We don't want to *step on toes*, as the English say.'

'MfS don't know about this?'

That earned Fischer a tired, *why are even asking* glance. He could have guessed that it would be breath wasted, but a man who knows nothing loses nothing by trying. It was why he asked the next question, and with the same expectations.

'And the other thing?'

The eyes came back from the cafe counter and fixed on Fischer's. 'We have an agreement.'

'That tells me nothing. You haven't ..?'

'Concern yourself only to what you've committed yourself. If you do, all else will be fine.'

'I'm sure you say that sometimes without meaning it.'

The young man nodded. 'It's necessary, *sometimes*. But what we would gain by not keeping our agreement? All we want is what we've asked. We have no interest in collateral causes.'

Causes in which certain organizations had no interest were as likely to be cauterized for neatness' sake as they were to be permitted to wander away in peace, but with an effort Fischer kept his lips together. The man was a messenger, not a negotiator.

A steward wandered over to explain that there was no waitress service, as if the queue wasn't quite a sufficient hint. Fischer's companion gave him a broad smile, told him that they were waiting only for the line to shorten and asked where he might find the nearest toilet. With that information, he stood and waited until they were alone once more before.

'Do you have enough money?'

'Yes, for a week or two, at least.'

'You may be required for longer than that. If you need more, let us know when you call that number – we'll set up a local bank account, and place funds there. Goodbye.'

The Russian picked up his student's satchel and pointed himself in the direction indicated by the steward. Fischer watched him go, thinking about the novelty of being on a Soviet payroll. It was an unexpected offer, a hand outstretched when he might need it - and, if things went very wrong, a convenient trail of hard evidence for them to throw Gehlen's way and save the price of a bullet. He decided to follow his father's advice, and be very careful with what he had in his wallet.

The prospect of almost eight more hours in an increasingly smoke-filled cafe didn't appeal to his delicate constitution, so he went up to the main deck and stood on the leeward side, letting the breeze do its work. The day had stayed fine, and the waves weren't substantial enough to test whatever pale ale remained in his system. After a while, he found his balance and allowed himself the slight smugness of all lubbers who don't feel the worst of what they feared. Though he had grown up in a Usedom fishing village this was only his third sea voyage; the second, a fortnight earlier, had crossed a glass-smooth Biscay – a blessed contrast to his *Fallschirmjäger* regiment's withdrawal from Crete in April, 1941, when the Mediterranean had done its best to finish off what the Kiwis started.

He watched the sea for a great while, idly speculating upon a world in which *Operation Sealion* had proceeded (he and his comrades were to have been flown over this water, to secure radar stations and provide useful practice for Home Guard machine-gunners), and, perhaps, a *Barbarossa* that would have gone ahead in '42 but at a better time of year. Could he have survived all of that, and seen a Third German Empire? It seem unlikely, but different Otto's lives were never far from mind these days. It might have been age, or the leisure that an absence of farming opens up.

A better distraction was what the sea-breeze was doing to skirts along the deck, but his heart hadn't been fully into that matter since Zofia departed and he'd been obliged to come to terms with the end of his sparse romantic career. Still, he regarded a few pairs of legs in the way that a goat does a fat acorn on the other side of a sturdy fence – enduringly tempting, untouchable.

Which brought him drifting back to the unpleasant *now*. A man in his position might have thought himself a pawn, but every piece on a chess board knew how it could move and what it could do. He didn't enjoy those advantages. He was rather an object in a darkened cellar, being kicked between unseen players whose rules adapted as the game proceeded. Only once before, when General Zarubin had forced him into Berlin politics and then Willy Brandt's office, had he felt this impotent, and even then he'd at least been able to see the edges of his treacheries. This time he was adrift, without agency or initiative – hell, without knowing when and where the game ended. Only the *how* was visible, and even then he couldn't believe what he'd been told.

The ferry reached Hoek ten minutes ahead of schedule. As he set foot upon the European mainland once more, Fischer felt a great urge to go as far and as aimlessly as would remove him from any possibility of discovery. Yet the consequences of flight – even of delay - had been explained with brutal clarity, and the chains that bound him to other men's causes were every bit as weighty as those that Herr Marley had forged of his own free will.

Though Chairman Shelepin had flown in and out of Khodynka airfield several times, he had never visited the Aquarium before now - but then, his military career had been both fleeting and almost entirely conventional. GRU recruited predominantly from their own still, and *own* meant Red Army.

Director Ivan Serov had been NKVD and then KGB, but he had always taken care to maintain close links with GRU – not that he could have helped it in the post-war period, when every other week saw some new attempt either to amalgamate or separate the functions of military- and counter-intelligence. When it came to the push after Stalin's death, GRU had backed him strongly against his boss, Beria, and helped send the old monster to his deserved grave. When Serov in turn was toppled, there had been a home waiting for him at Khodynka, even if every man and his dog knew it to be a demotion, a humiliation.

That had been three years ago, and since then his successor Shelepin had seen him only at official functions (though each had been punctilious in sending the other such scraps of intelligence that impacted their respective kingdoms). He was aware that Serov blamed him for Resident Korotkov's premature death, but an unassisted heart-attack – particularly one triggered by the would-be avenger's strenuous tennis game - wasn't something to which a lasting grudge could be pinned. Still, he wasn't looking forward to this interview.

He had been surprised by the readiness with which Director Serov had agreed to it. One might have expected to be dangled for a while, to be made to feel the supplicant – or, if something were suspected, to be interrogated by official correspondence before any air was shared. Yet the request not only met with immediate agreement but also a range of dates and times from which the KGB Chairman might make a choice most convenient to himself. To Shelepin's knowledge, the only choice Serov preferred to extend was the quick bullet (for a full confession) or a slow beating followed by the same.

He was met by a colonel before he had the chance to give his name at reception, and saluted smartly. To his astonishment, the stringent security checks for which GRU were famous – and which all visitors to the Aquarium were obliged to endure, normally – were waived. He was escorted without delay through a series of corridors to a lift, which took the two men to the fifth floor and opened directly into a large office in which one man, dressed in the uniform of a Major-General, sat behind an ample desk. He looked up, jumped to his feet, and repeated the salute (which, if anything, was even more text-book than the first). Without a word, Shelepin was pointed at the room's only other door. He strode briskly towards it, twisted the handle and stepped through, trusting his trajectory not to pass into open space and the car-park far below.

It *was* open, in a way. Though GRU were technically subordinate to KGB when their spheres of operation collided, this was not reflected in the relative accommodations of the organizations' Heads. Shelepin's office was hardly spartan, but this was a four-wall-enclosed consolation for a disappointed career. If Khrushchev's was more lavishly appointed it was only because he'd pilfered a great number of its fittings from Beria's, back in '53 (before Malenkov and Molotov had thought to do the same), and even then its area was more modest than this. Taking a deep breath, the KGB Chairman began his trek towards the most substantial of three tanker-desks scattered about the room.

Ivan Serov waited until his successor was almost upon him before rising from his leather chair. He smiled affably, the face he offered equally to distinguished colleagues, professional rivals and men whose bones he was about to break. The handshake was too robust, but Shelepin didn't flinch. He took a seat.

Tea arrived with a *soldat*, who poured for both men and retreated without giving either a glance. Serov put five lumps of sugar into his cup and offered the bowl.

'This is a pleasant thought, Aleksandr Nikolayevich. We *far-neighbours* don't get to see many of our Muscovite colleagues.'

Shelepin snorted. 'It's a strange convention. Khodynka's, what, nine kilometres from Red Square?'

'Yes, but it's how it *feels* that matters. You KGB don't need to catch a bus to speak to our masters.'

Serov probably hadn't noticed a bus since his schooldays, much less caught one; but as he'd once sat at Shelepin's desk, with a view of the

Bolshoi (if not quite the Kremlin), his resentful tone was understandable. Still, it was those days that the present KGB Chairman wished to discuss, and he had at least provided the opening.

'Boris Aleksandrovich, do you recall an operation conducted by a KGB surveillance unit in Berlin, three years ago?'

Serov pursed his lips. 'There were many. Can you be specific?'

'The operation concerned a German national, living in the south of the city – in Lichterfelde, to be precise. His name was Otto ...'

'The mutilation?'

'His face is badly burned, yes.'

Serov's face darkened. 'He was that bastard Zarubin's man. I mean, he was a professional acquaintance of our valued colleague.'

'*Bastard* will do for me. May I ask why the surveillance took place?'

'Don't the files tell you?'

'There are no files – that's to say, they appear to have been redacted quite out of existence.'

'Who did that?'

'We're not sure, but Korotkov looks the likeliest culprit. It would have needed his authorization, unless someone at the *Rezidentura* was entirely rogue – which I doubt.'

'You never liked him, did you?'

'You and I had differing ideas about his value, but I don't wish to slur his memory – only to fill in what I can.'

Serov gave the window his attention for a while. He could hardly have relished aiding his successor at the cost of his deceased friend's reputation; but this was KGB business and the man was still KGB to the core, even if he now wore a different uniform. Besides, if there was any chance that this was something to do with his nemesis …

Shelepin waited patiently. Eventually, the Director brought his gaze back into the room.

'I made a mistake with Zarubin. I imagined that I'd have time to choose my ground before moving against him, but he'd already laid out his own. The Berlin operation was a feeler. We knew that this German had been one of his men years earlier, but we'd lost sight of him since. Korotkov seemed to think he might be important – that he could lead us to other men in Berlin whom the General was running. I told him to take a look, but not to move too soon in case we flushed Zarubin before everything was in place. After that, I was quite happy for Korotkov to interrogate the man, but I wanted him dead as soon as he'd been squeezed.'

'He got out of Berlin, though. How was that possible, with eyes on him?'

'He had help from somewhere, obviously, but I don't know what went wrong with the surveillance. Korotkov seemed a little evasive; I was about to press him about it when ...'

When General Zarubin went to Khrushchev with some form of poison from Serov's past, and had him booted out of the Lubyanka. Shelepin interrupted before self-pity became something more.

'There was a rumour that two field-officers we lost around that time were involved in the operation. Do you know if that's the case?'

'No. By definition, if it's no more than a rumour then you're right - Korotkov or someone else suppressed any record of it. All I know is that the morning I ... received word of my transfer to Khodynka, the surveillance team was being pulled out. If I had thought anything about it – and I was distracted, of course – it would have been to assume that they had snatched the objective. Why they didn't, and how the man got out of Berlin, are questions that can't now be asked of Korotkov.'

'He supervised the operation personally?'

'Yes, give that Zarubin might have been involved – though we can't now say for certain he was. I recall that the Resident was assisted by Berlin's then-Third Directorate Chief, Bolkov,'

'Shit.'

'I know. Suicides are the most inconsiderate people. Still, a cancer diagnosis will do that, won't it?'

From what he'd heard, it sounded to Shelepin that a major arse-covering operation had been undertaken back in '58, though the reason for it was now buried with Korotkov and Bolkov. Which meant that the mysterious Otto Henry Fischer remained just that, unless …

'Korotkov didn't discuss *anything* about the German with you?'

'Only that another German national, also known to Zarubin, was snatched from the street by our people and interrogated. He had – what was the other one's name?'

'Fischer.'

'He was found to have Fischer's name and address on his person. Unfortunately, I'd leaned on Korotkov to come up with some early answers, so the questioning was rather too robust. The man died before he talked.'

Shelepin leaned forward. 'I know this happened three years ago, but can you recall if you made a judgment about the potential link between Fischer and Zarubin, based on what you knew?'

Serov sighed and took a sip from his tea. The question was a little obtuse, but as the man was being unexpectedly obliging Shelepin didn't want to waste the moment.

'I can't say that I did, which I would now regard as indicating that I *assumed* the link to be moribund. But at the time we were trying to snatch up all of Zarubin's agents or associates in Berlin, so the question of their precise connection – as it stood in 1958 - was irrelevant. I wanted the man dead as soon as we had all the intelligence he could give us.' Serov looked pointedly at his guest. 'As you should now, I would suggest.'

Slowly, Shelepin nodded. A potential exposure was no less a threat than one whose surface area could be mapped precisely. He reached into the small bag he'd brought with him, extracted a bottle of *Stolichnaya* and held it out.

'For the cold wind that blows through Khodynka.'

Serov seemed touched. For a man who used to sweep up entire department stores' supplies of delicacies during his many foreign visits, his re-induction to the Red Army must have felt like an ongoing punishment drill.

'Ah, thank you, Aleksandr Nikolayevich. I can't say where that wind comes from, but I know very well where it goes. Don't forget where your old comrade lives these days.'

On his way back to Dzerzhinsky Square, Shelepin tried to read his daily briefing papers, but the matter of Otto Fischer – a likely inconsequence that had stolen almost half a day from his precious schedule - wouldn't lie easy. Earlier that morning, Semichastny had almost insisted upon accompanying his boss to Khodynka, to the point at which Shelepin had been obliged to insist that he remain at the Lubyanka, to deal with whatever slight matters might press upon KGB's second-in-command. The man knew that Serov detested him - he was young, well educated, with hardly a military career to speak of; in other words, a template of the detested new intake making pensioners of the war's heroic NKVD cadres (men who had shot almost as many of their own troops in the back as the Germans had managed from the front). To have taken him to the Aquarium would have been to seal Serov's mouth as if with duct tape, and he must have been perfectly aware of it. Why had he wanted to risk that, if only to hear first-hand about Fischer what Shelepin could have told him anyway? Or was it rather that he had wished to end a conversation before it began?

Had Semichastny merely kept his mouth shut, Shelepin would have returned from Khodynka and readily repeated to him every thin scrap that Serov had offered, but now he wasn't so sure. He needed to think about it, but he had no idea what *it* involved. His whole knowledge of this Fischer business came from his deputy, so what he knew might not be worth knowing. On the other hand, there was nothing unusual in his being barely-informed. A man responsible for the world's largest intelligence service didn't need – and certainly didn't want – to be kept abreast of every less-than-pressing issue. Had Otto Fischer not at some point been associated with Zarubin he would have mattered less than a mayfly's fart, which made Semichastny's briefing on the man's Portuguese exile and its apparent conclusion both proportionate and appropriate. Perhaps his desire to be present at the meeting with Serov reflected only an attempt to relieve his boss of the burden of giving the business more attention than it deserved.

By the time that his car pulled up outside the Lubyanka, Shelepin had almost convinced the small worm wriggling in his belly that there was nothing more to this. He wasn't satisfied, however, that what he knew of Otto Henry Fischer was enough to make that judgment. Perhaps he would press Semichastny to reveal a little more of what *he* knew, or perhaps he would insist upon having sight of the field-reports on Fischer's recent movements. The latter would be so unusual as to elicit some reaction, which might in turn give him a better idea of whether he should be more, or less, concerned than he presently was. He trusted his protege – at least, he trusted him not to betray his patron or knowingly compromise KGB's interests. He wasn't so sure, however, that he entirely trusted his judgement on anything to do – or *possibly* to do – with Sergei Aleksandrovich Zarubin. The man had a knack of making his enemies think themselves cleverer than he, and Shelepin had no intention of adding himself to their number. It was comforting to recall that he had a only single friend in the Kremlin (though its most powerful occupant), but that wasn't necessarily a fatal weakness. He might turn out to be like Mikoyan - discounted by innumerable rivals over the years and regimes, yet able to deflect light itself.

The only point upon which he had any certainty at the moment was that Serov's advice had been sound. Whatever Fischer was, whatever his present relationship to Zarubin, he was better out of the world than in it. Shelepin was not a callous man, but nor could he permit unnecessary exposures for no promise of return. He couldn't see how KGB might benefit from allowing this thing to play out further, not unless the German possessed some piece of information that might prove fatal to his friend in the Kremlin, and that was highly unlikely. Zarubin had defected to the Americans and then been allowed to return. He had wormed his way into the present leadership's affections by providing the bullet that felled Beria. It had turned out to be a false bullet, but that hadn't mattered – it had done the job, neatly. In Khrushchev's eyes the man had proved his loyalty, and that was sufficient to absolve past sins. It was just possible that Fischer possessed a photograph of Zarubin standing over the First Secretary's dead mother with a gun in one hand and his cock in the other, but failing that it could be assumed that his future value to KGB was negligible.

He would tell Semichastny to authorize and supervise the man's removal. He deserved a little inconvenience for having caused his patron to lose both time and composure, but at least the task was straightforward. Ongoing surveillance always ran a risk of discovery, with its attendant complications. An erasure was straightforward, requiring only that the operative have a steady hand, a clear view and the sense to make it look like a criminal act, rather than a mundane piece of house-keeping.

'Ruschestrasse isn't happy.'

Roger Broadsmith tried to seem relaxed, but despite the magnificent setting this was something that could become an interrogation very quickly. He lifted a hand, palm upward, acknowledging the point.

'What choice did I have? If I'd turned it down they would have put me in a back office – probably personnel, or logistics. What use would I have been to you then?'

The argument was irrefutable, but it would be refuted anyway. *Stasi* had a world-view that dealt with inconveniences the way that an oil tanker deals with dinghies in its path. The organization's record of success (in stark contrast to that of the nation it served) was almost unblemished in recent years, marked by the simultaneous smashing of domestic dissent and the broad penetration of West German institutions and society, to the point at which the meaning of a secret whispered in a Bonn corridor could be stripped and analyzed in Ruschestrasse before the breath on the ear cooled. With that legacy, a certain immoveable logic couldn't, or wouldn't, accept the possibility that Roger Broadsmith did not have a choice in this matter.

His handler, a man he knew only as *Cuttlefish*, conveyed that sense in the cold stare that answered the question. Presumably, it was thought that the brilliance of the coup that had acquired an MfS agent inside SIS - and

Broadsmith was the first and only such - was not to be blunted by how management at 54 Broadway might decide to juggle its resources. In the six years since he had been recruited he hadn't managed to pass on much that would compromise his country's security, but the long game could accommodate a slow start. The occasional dead-drop, containing little more than interdepartmental gossip and the mundane detail of fishing-espionage, had seemed to satisfy them so far. Perhaps they were nervous of asking anything that ran the slightest risk of exposing him before the one, golden, as-yet unforeseeable opportunity arose. Or perhaps having him *there*, at Broadway, was the triumph in itself. Intelligence agencies enjoyed coups almost as much for their own sake as any benefit they might bring – otherwise, why MfS hadn't offered him to KGB before now? Infiltrating SIS wasn't one of their core objectives (even he knew that), but to the Soviets it was as good as a back-door into Langley, or had been.

He was paid, a little, for his treachery. Unlike Blake he wasn't in for the sake of principle; unlike either Burgess or Maclean he wasn't a hopeless drunk looking for the cash to feed a habit (in fact, he had such little interest in money that he wasn't sure he'd walk away if MfS's Broadsmith budget dried up entirely). He didn't feel out of place, alienated or uncomfortable in his own society, and if he had any opinion on the capitalist system it wasn't one that bothered him, much less boiled his blood. Yet for all that he hadn't needed to be coerced. An approach had been made during a brief holiday in Bavaria, from men who knew who he was (had it been Blake who'd pointed the finger?); he'd considered and then agreed to their proposal with as little agonizing as he might have chosen a tie. If anything, he had been mildly flattered, and not a little amused. Only later had he considered the obvious, bloody dangers of being someone else's man in the one place it might be feared or expected, and by then it was too late to excuse himself.

Even now, with everyone at Broadway searching for further traitors, he couldn't summon the necessary, sensible anxiety to run, hide or defect. It wasn't courage, and he hoped it wasn't crass stupidity. Perhaps it was a symptom of the half-a-step-out detachment that had arrived sometime during puberty and forgotten to depart with the bad skin and odorous feet. One first needed a sense of belonging, to fear the loss of what gave it substance.

He understood perfectly well why MfS didn't want him transferred to Bonn. They had any number of men here already, native Germans who were far better placed than he to worm out what the Federals didn't want wormed. How could an *ausländer* occupy already well-filled skin, and why would he try?

He had only one answer to that, but it wasn't unconvincing. He picked up the bag that sat between them on the park bench, pulled out his sandwiches and offered one to *Cuttlefish*.

'Ham and cheese.'

His handler's pursed lips eloquently refused the offer. He was irritated, impatient, and had no way of easing either condition. Their English coup was here already, an ambulant *fait accompli*, and his middle-European sensibilities weren't comfortable with surprises, much less improvisation. He squirmed slightly, shifting as if to put distance between himself and an uncomfortable reality. Broadsmith took a small bite of his sandwich, and (despite the memory of his mother's iron rules on table manners) spoke while trying to negotiate its passage.

'To date, what I've been able to give you hasn't been much. If what I'm doing here really is intended to open a working relationship with BfV, London will have to provide Bonn with intelligence as an act of good faith, and I'll be the messenger – at least, until things get off the ground. Wouldn't you like to have a first sight of what I bring?'

'It may not be anything of direct interest to MfS.'

'But it almost certainly will be to KGB, and any good turn you can do for them isn't going to hurt, is it? And what about the data that BfV send to London in return? *That's* going to be of interest.'

'We'll almost certainly have it already.'

'But then you'll know that Broadway has it too.'

Knowing what the enemy knew was not a small matter. *Cuttlefish* shrugged to avoid acknowledging it and took another long pull on his foul cigarette. It was ruining the taste of Broadsmith's lunch, but he wasn't going to admit it. He waved what remained of his sandwich at the view.

'This is a very pretty place.'

They sat on a bench in Rheinaue Park, three kilometres south of central Bonn, overlooking the river and Oberkassel beyond. Though Broadsmith had yet to have his first meeting with the BfV people he had thought it wiser not to be seen in the company of an Interior Ministry official (it was all he knew about *Cuttlefish*). Even if the other man's true loyalties were entirely unsuspected, it wasn't wise to commence a delicate mission facing questions.

'Is it? I've been here too long to notice any more.'

The cigarette, flicked expertly from between thumb and forefinger, almost reached the water's edge. *Cuttlefish* stood, glanced around casually.

'Where are you staying?'

'A small hotel in Auerberg. It's basic, but convenient for BfV's Bonn office.'

'Which is in my building. I wonder why is it that you're not meeting them at their Köln headquarters?'

'I'm not sure. Perhaps they don't want Gehlen sniffing out this business. I'm sure he has his men in BfV.'

Cuttlefish smiled, an unconvincing effort. 'Not as many as we do - but some, certainly. Let's meet here again, next time.'

'Alright. Should I use the same number to contact you?'

'Yes, but speak German always. You have a good accent, not like an Englishman.'

'Thank you.'

Broadsmith waited five minutes after *Cuttlefish* departed, finishing his sandwiches and watching a large coal-barge pushing its way against the flow. Then, he walked north, following the Rhine along Stresemannufer, past the Bundeshaus (*why did parliamentarians always feel the need to ruin a river view?* he wondered) and into Bonn's oldest quarter, where he found a cafe whose outside tables overlooked the Bonner Münster. Three-quarters of the seating area was empty, the fourth jammed with customers jostling elbows between their tiny tables. Pleased to discover that German waiters could be as bloody-minded as their British cousins, he took a seat, ordered a coffee and removed the letter from his breast pocket.

He was to present himself at the Interior Ministry on Graurheindorferstrasse at nine-thirty the following morning, and ask for Herr Waldmann, whose precise role within BfV hadn't been made clear. As far as he knew, all of the organization's dirty-handed work was run from Cologne, so it seemed likely that if Waldman was stationed in Bonn it was to keep in with the politicians - a committee type, the sort one saw endlessly at meetings but whose remit shifted with the weather. Broadsmith didn't know whether the man had the authority to negotiate anything – like his English counterpart, he may have been no more than an errand boy, a dictaphone into which more important men stated their terms. What they would discuss at their first meeting was no more apparent;

Broadsmith had been given a portfolio of warm words and blurred half-promises to be deployed at his discretion, the purpose of which was to encourage the Germans to take a further step forward. Most probably, Waldman would turn up with something similar, in which case the meeting might proceed like an awkward dance in which each party was attempting, half-arsedly, to take the lead.

He couldn't see why someone more senior, with greater authority to negotiate a relationship, hadn't been sent in his place. One might almost suppose that Broadway's intention was to give the appearance of wanting to move closer to BfV without actually having to do so. In fact, the more Broadsmith thought about that possibility, the more feasible it became. For every decision made within SIS there seemed to be an equally resistant force applying the brakes - some people called it *balance*, but it looked and sounded much more like the reluctant shuffle of an organization that regarded all possible futures as mined ground.

He could hardly complain. He was himself torn between an instinct to do his job well and a capricious urge to do harm, and in a way his ambiguous brief relieved him – for the present, at least - of any ability to indulge the latter compulsion. Almost certainly, he had oversold himself to *Cuttlefish*. He might be able to tell the man that SIS and BfV had agreed to work more closely together, but the real, damaging intelligence would need to be signed off and passed between more exalted ranks than his own. It was a comforting thought, which made him suspect that the taint of the *reluctant shuffle* he affected to despise had passed into his own bloodstream during his years at Broadway.

Two coffees later he left money on the table and put himself in a queue at the corner of Münsterplatz. A fifteen-minute bus journey carried him almost to his hotel's front door. At reception he asked for his key and any messages. The latter was answered by a hand falling upon his shoulder, at which he almost parted company with the floor.

'Sorry, Roger. I should have said something.'

As mild, greying and nondescript as a retired sheep, Harold Shergold shouldn't have been the trigger for an infarction, but Broadsmith needed several moments to catch his breath and more to order his scattered thoughts. Naturally, the first of them was that he had been discovered, but Shergold was no sadist, so unless he was deploying the same sort of bonhomie that had snared George Blake the smile must have meant something else. But what else? HERO's debriefings were still occupying every waking moment of the joint CIA-SIS committee in London (a thought that, suddenly and incongruously, gave Broadsmith a plausible reason why it was he who had been seconded to Bonn), and it made no sense for Shergold to absent himself from where GRU's secrets were currently being spilled.

'Do you think we might have some tea?'

A small hospitality area in front of reception hosted two tiny tables. Shergold sat at one while Broadsmith spoke to the desk manager. Tea came less than five minutes later, ready-poured in mugs, interrupting a conversation that had been confined to the blandest pleasantries about the journey from England and the quality of Bonn's older architecture.

Shergold offered a mildly disapproving frown to the space a teapot should have occupied. It deepened slightly when he took his first sip.

A lowly case-officer had no right to demand the great man's business, but Broadsmith's nerves had frayed badly enough for the proprieties to go hang. He was trying to find a casual form of words to begin the interrogation when Shergold placed his mug on the table (with a certain force that hinted at an opinion) and looked up.

'You're surprised to see me?'

'Puzzled, rather. Have I done something wrong? Or not done something correctly?'

'You haven't been here long enough to do *anything*, Roger. Your brief has expanded a little, and I wanted to discuss it personally.'

'You could have recalled me to London for that, surely?'

'It's important that you're here, not there. You'll be meeting someone in the next few days.'

'Another BfV man?'

'Not quite. He'll be bringing something - I don't know what, precisely. I want you to accept it on my behalf.'

'Of course. Is it …?'

'And you're to *gauge* the man, as far as possible. If he asks for something, it's to be referred back to me for discussion. Tell him that, and watch for a reaction. If he decides to talk, listen.'

Talk needed no explanation. It was a symptom of their work's dislocations that some men, sometimes, couldn't leave it at hello, thank you and goodbye. One could hardly hope for a heart-to-heart, but even an attempt at polite conversation could offer a glimpse of some preoccupation or priority. It was less a science than a lunge into fog, but a sensitive antenna occasionally picked up things. Shergold was the ranking expert in nuances, of course, and Broadsmith was more than a little flattered to be invited to the game. He nodded, looked thoughtful, as might a man who knew exactly what was required.

'The thing is, Roger, this might be a punt, so for the moment it's to be left off the books. If it becomes known generally in London there'll be someone who pushes for us to take it on – to show the Americans that we're still on our feet, even after Blake. We can't risk that and have it go badly, so I arranged for our first steps to be taken far from where they might be noticed.'

'A punt? From …?'

'I'm not quite sure. We've been told Moscow - but not, apparently, KGB or GRU. *That* raises all kinds of questions, obviously.'

'Another HERO?'

'No. This comes formally, from someone who wishes there to be a channel, however flimsy, between distant parties.'

'How will we arrange this?'

'He'll call me, at my home. I'll suggest a meeting place ....?'

'Somewhere discreet, I assume.'

'But public. We don't want to risk your being shot in the head, do we?'

'*Café Rosamund*, then, in Münsterplatz.'

'Lovely.' Shergold stood and offered his hand.

'How will I recognize him?'

The older man smiled. 'That won't be a problem. He has a severely burned face. He gave his name as Otto Fischer, so I suppose that's how he'll introduce himself. Try not to flinch, won't you?'

'Levin, what do you think of Semichastny?'

'Eh?'

'KGB Chairman Shelepin's deputy. What's your opinion?'

Zarubin's secretary glanced around nervously, as if the walls of his office were leaning in to catch every word.

'It's not for me to have one.'

'Do try '

'He's ... an exemplary servant of the People. A good communist, worthy of the trust that ....'

'Oh, come on, Levin. I haven't wired the room.'

'You don't *know* that.'

Zarubin sighed. 'Alright. To your knowledge, has he shown any unusual interest in our work recently?'

Levin swallowed hard. The question was no less dangerous than the others, given his employer's history with KGB.

'Define unusual.'

'Less or more than ordinary.'

'Chairman Shelepin gets a stamped copy of all memoranda written by yourself for the attention of the First Secretary and members of the Central Committee or Council of Ministers. I assume Comrade Semichastny sees them as a matter of routine.'

Stamped copies were of material considered too sensitive to be photo-copied at will. Levin addressed each individually and franked it - with a red stamp bearing Zarubin's name - to indicate that it was one of a very few circulated 'originals'.

'That would definitely be ordinary. Anything else?'

'No. Well, just one other thing.'

'Shall I implore you to tell me, or might I hope you'll volunteer it?'

'The Vienna Summit.'

'What about it?'

'The day after you circulated your thoughts ...'

'My first thoughts?'

'No, the second ones – your detailed analysis. Once they were distributed he came to see me.'

'Where was I?'

'It was the weekend you were invited to Pitsunda.'

Two weeks after returning from the Summit, Khrushchev had summoned to his Black Sea *dacha* a number of the most senior men in the Praesidium to discuss his triumph. Zarubin hadn't been on the list, but he used up the dregs of Mikoyan's goodwill to get a seat next to him on that 'plane.

'What did he want?'

'A personal, stamped copy of your memorandum. He said that he didn't want to breach protocol by photocopying Shelepin's, but he'd read it and realised what a fine, thorough piece it was and intended to refer to it often.'

'And you provided one?'

'I didn't think of refusing. I would have mentioned it, but when you called from Pitsunda to dictate your copious *third* thoughts it slipped my mind. You'll recall that I was told to drop everything, including sleep?'

'I wonder why he came for it personally, rather than telephone and have it couriered across to Dzerzhinsky Square?'

Levin thought about that for a few moments. 'He may have been in the Kremlin already, and thought it more convenient to pop in. If he wasn't, and needed to send a courier, I would have had the man sign for it. And someone in the Lubyanka would have needed to do the same, upon receipt.'

'Yes, they would. Well, try to remember, next time.'

'Remember?'

'Not to forget.'

'Oh. Yes.'

Zarubin returned to his own office. He couldn't recall the last time KGB had wanted more than a single copy of a report he'd prepared, though it may have happened. There was nothing amiss with the request. KGB were above all an information-gathering and -analyzing organization, and if they couldn't be trusted with sensitive material, who could? Certainly, he fully agreed with Semichastny's judgement of his paper – it *was* a fine, thorough piece (though neither as fine or thorough as its successor, dictated over the telephone to an extremely irritated Levin), which would enhance any reader's understanding of what advantages and exposures derived from John F. Kennedy's feeble performance in Vienna. He would have given the matter no further thought, had his neck hairs not already put him on notice that V.Y. Semichastny might well be playing games on S.A. Zarubin's board.

A further cause for anxiety was that he didn't *know* the man yet. Semichastny had returned from his Azerbaijani exile to take up the deputy chairmanship of KGB only four months earlier. It was no secret that his boss Shelepin was on his way to the Council of Ministers at some nearing point, so the new man might be wanting to strengthen his claim to the soon-to-be emptying seat. A brilliant counter-intelligence coup that secured advanced western technology or destroyed an enemy's field network would doubtless do the job, but one's opponents rarely performed to order. A marked improvement in KGB's foreign intelligence analysis would also push his arse closer to the upholstery, but that was a longer-term process and it had far to travel (which is why Zarubin still had a job in the Kremlin despite the consistently unpleasing opinions with which he dampened the First Secretary's moods). A third option – and one that perhaps tempted with its relative simplicity – would be to make KGB look good by blackening the opposition.

How would he do it, though? Success would require that Zarubin offer an opening – a chink through which the spear's tip might be thrust. He had no intention of being so amenable, however. What might well have ruined him – his reverse defection bringing 'evidence' of Lavrenty Beria's approach to the Americans - had long since been discovered, examined, and, following the gentleman's execution, forgiven. Nothing about it could now be resurrected to allow Semichastny a second shot. KGB also bore a grudge still for the effective disposal of Shelepin's predecessor, Serov, but the latter's stained history precluded any attempt to pin blame solely upon Zarubin (much as he might deserve it). So what did that leave?

He had been careful. For the past three years he had resisted any temptation to reactivate his small Berlin network of former NKGB agents (not least because any slip in that respect would earn the poor bastards a midnight swim in the Spree) or otherwise to set up any sort of competition with KGB's field work. He had taken pains not to contradict KGB intelligence directly, or to suggest that whoever was interpreting it needed a modicum of sense kicking into their fundaments. His demeanour towards his professional rivals was at all times so pleasant and accommodating that rumours about his sexuality had circulated briefly (to the Kremlin typing pool's great delight), while the other flank – the Praesidium and Council of Ministers – he cosseted with a regular supply of unasked-for briefing papers that made the recipients feel more relevant to looming policy decisions than they were or possibly could be. In effect, he had neutralized his enemies by giving them no more grounds for his disposal than their sincere desire to encompass it.

But this was Moscow, where political gravity defied rational physics. Their system was defined by collectivist principles, but at its apex sat Nikita Khrushchev - a man whose temperament couldn't have allowed a grudging half-fuck for its steady, deliberative methods. It might take only a bad breakfast, or a toothache, or perhaps him finding Nina Petrovna in a Kremlin cupboard with one of her security men (an unlikely, unlovely prospect) for an approach by Semichastny, even without substantially damning evidence, to undo eight years' careful manoeuvring and have Zarubin re-assigned to the noisome end of Hell - or worse, Novosibirsk.

He took a key from a desk drawer and with it opened another. From a neatly-ordered hanging file he drew his copy of what Levin would now immortalize as his Second Thoughts on the Vienna Summit. It occupied some eight pages and took a little while to read carefully, but at its conclusion he was no closer to seeing the trap. It *was* a good report – comprehensive, even-handed (he'd taken pains to put the case that he knew KGB would eventually think of putting themselves, before dismissing it) and cautious to a fault. King Solomon could have written the thing and not managed to placate more egos, nor made a better case for the only sensible course of action – which was no action at all. If anything self-harming was hiding between the lines, Zarubin couldn't find it.

It was his Third Thoughts on Vienna that gave him more concern. At Pitsunda, Kosygin, Gromyko and Brezhnev had argued that the Americans should be pushed hard while Kennedy was still trying to locate the White House washrooms. Mikoyan had tried to knock down their logic, but Khrushchev (in Zarubin's hearing) had joked that if his old friend were given the keys to a sweet shop he'd consult a dentist, a dietician and his mother before proceeding. It had been a friendly enough exchange, but Zarubin hadn't been any more fooled by the First Secretary's flippancy than Mikoyan himself. It was how he always gave notice that his patience was wearing thin – that a decision was brewing, based upon what his stomach was telling him.

It had sent Zarubin hurrying back to his room, to make a telephone call to his over-pressed secretary in Moscow and dictate a new paper that was intended to quash any glib assumptions that Washington would play to Moscow's expectations. Given that he and Mikoyan had by far the greatest personal experience of America and Americans, and knowing that the other man would support him robustly, he worded his opinions more forthrightly than was his habit. Twice, Levin had interrupted the flow to ask if he was *quite sure* that he wanted to equate confidence with complacency (or even idiocy), but Zarubin hadn't been in a mood to listen to good advice. When it was done he'd had it read back to him, changed nothing and asked for it to be telefaxed directly to the dacha's communications room, where he had it copied for distribution.

He made no new friends that day, for sure. Brezhnev in particular had used his already expressive eyebrows to indicate what he thought of the paper; but its principal argument – that any miscalculation which pushed the Americans to the barricades couldn't be walked back without risking profound humiliation - had applied the brake, at least temporarily. There had been several men in the room willing to confront Kennedy as soon as possible, but none were remotely interested in personally examining the view from a high ledge. The gathering had broken up without a decision being made.

Shelepin had been present, naturally. He had listened to everything, offered nothing and taken away his copy of Zarubin's latest paper without commenting upon its content. As ever, he had been polite but unreadable, and on past form his eventual contribution to the argument – if any – would be offered too discreetly to trace back to its owner. Compared to Ivan Serov, whose opinions were proclaimed in much the same manner as Moses delivered the Commandments, he was a sphinx, and Zarubin both admired and feared his ability to scatter no clues on his way to an objective. The man was competition, but how much of an enemy also was impossible to gauge.

So, the same day that his deputy was asking Levin for a personal copy of the relatively bland Second Thoughts, Shelepin himself was flying back to Moscow with the more combustible Third. Nothing could be read into that – it had been Zarubin, after all, who had decided that a new version was needed, and that the KGB Chairman should read it. Why then should a coincidence that wasn't actually a 'coincidence' worry him? Was it because Semichastny had taken the opportunity to make his request to Levin when the report's author was far away, and probably preoccupied?

The question flushed out the other possibility, and Zarubin didn't know how to make a start on *that* one. What if it hadn't been *his* absence from Moscow that had given Semichastny his opportunity, but Shelepin's? It was forbidden to copy red-stamped documents, but he didn't believe for a moment that KGB didn't ignore regulations when it suited them. If Semichastny had wanted his own copy of the Second Thoughts he could have asked his boss and taken the thing to the photocopier without even a knowing wink to speed him on his way. He would have *needed* to ask, though, and then Shelepin would have known – ergo, KGB's second-in-command was playing some game in which even the referee wasn't being invited to participate. Ostensibly, the prospect of a civil war within KGB wasn't an unpleasant one, particularly if it diverted both men's attention from the First Secretary's Special Advisor on American Affairs; but if it in some way conscripted the latter's name, red stamp, reputation and testicles, the rules and purpose needed to be understood, very quickly.

Zarubin could deal with the blows that came front-on. He had good eyesight, and he was never at such repose that he couldn't shift, sideways or backwards, with very little notice. But the trajectory of shrapnel from other men's wars couldn't be anticipated, nor ducked. The cold ground was full of men who had been caught indiscriminately (or perhaps as a useful, collateral bonus to the main event), and they could be recognized as such by the half-surprised cast to their rotting faces. He had no intention of being half- or wholly surprised, but then no-one ever did. Something might be coming, and he had no way of knowing what, or when, or from which direction. What could he do to ready himself for that?

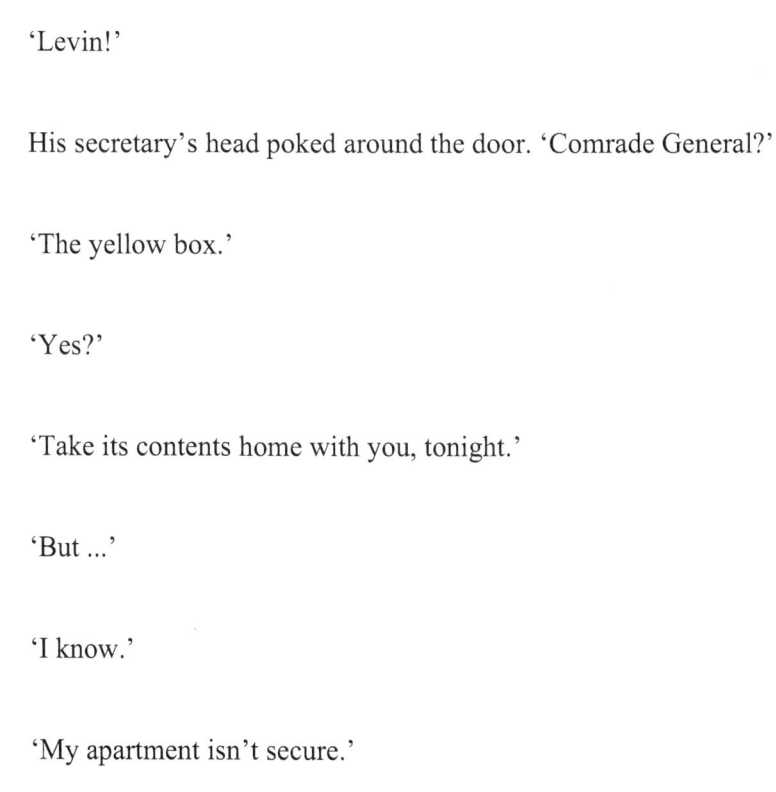

'Levin!'

His secretary's head poked around the door. 'Comrade General?'

'The yellow box.'

'Yes?'

'Take its contents home with you, tonight.'

'But ...'

'I know.'

'My apartment isn't secure.'

'How many times have you been burgled?'

'Never.'

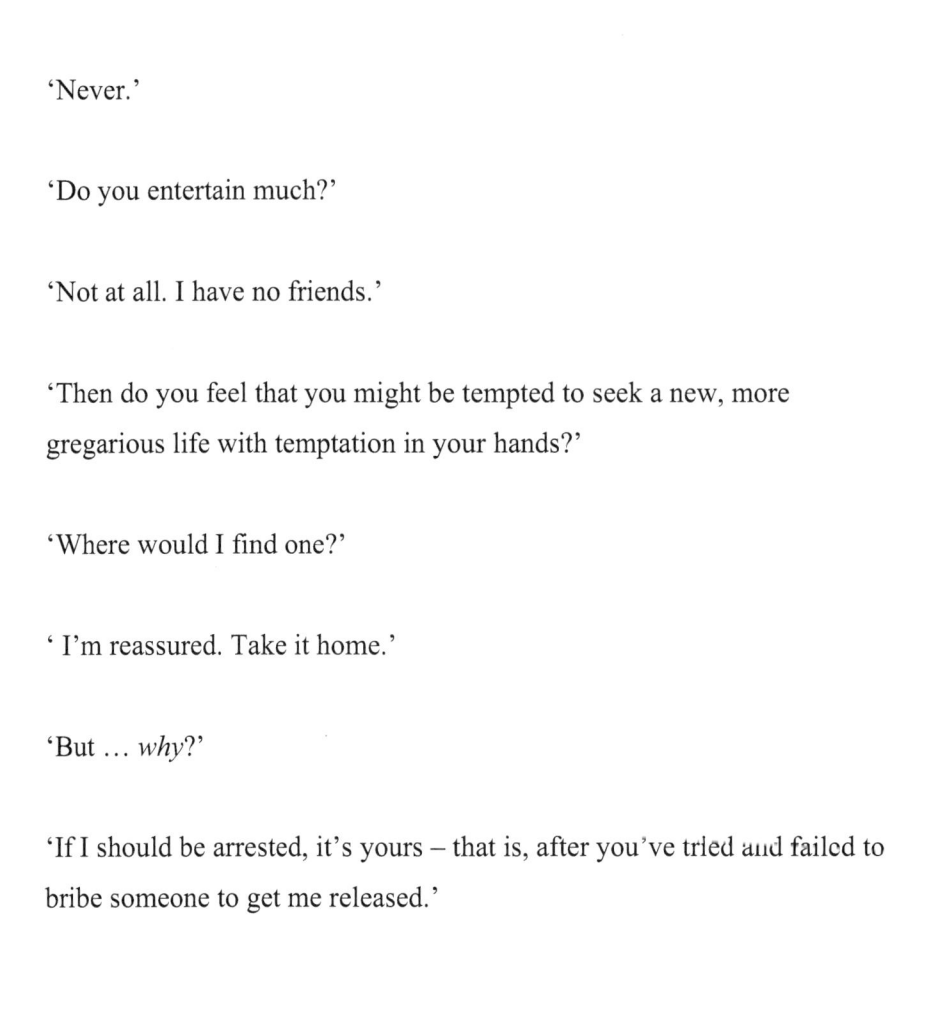

'Do you entertain much?'

'Not at all. I have no friends.'

'Then do you feel that you might be tempted to seek a new, more gregarious life with temptation in your hands?'

'Where would I find one?'

' I'm reassured. Take it home.'

'But … *why*?'

'If I should be arrested, it's yours – that is, after you've tried and failed to bribe someone to get me released.'

19

Fischer hadn't been told *not* to open the envelope, which he took to be permission of sorts. The thing was written in English – good English – and addressed to Mr Harold Shergold. That personal touch made him wonder what else they were trying to achieve. *To whom it may concern* would have done the job just as well. Did they want to compromise the man, impress him with their understanding of Broadway personnel or merely underline their sincerity?

It wasn't his business; still, he wondered about the subject matter. Why would KGB assume that SIS were interested in Soviet arms shipments to rebels in Congo's Katanga Province, when it was the Belgians and Mobutu's mob who'd be getting shot at? It surely wasn't something they'd be too concerned …

But Katanga abutted Northern Rhodesia, which SIS cared very much about. So, was this business worth flagging Soviet foreign policy to the enemy? Even if the information was unsound, surely it would be wiser not to invite the British to strengthen their troubled colony's border – or the Americans to increase arms shipments to *their* friends in that ugly war by proxy?

It's the Why that matters, not the What. After re-reading the note for the third time, Fischer replaced it in the envelope. It had arrived at his hotel's reception during the night, brought by a messenger-boy from another hotel, so someone had brushed away his tracks very effectively. It had found its way into the hands of yet another messenger, a delivery boy named OttoFischer, but that raised the old question once more – why him? Why had someone gone to the trouble of placing him in a vise if a series of simple handovers was the sum of it? A stranger, stopped in the street and offered fifty deutschmarks, would have done the job gladly and walked away thereafter, ignorant, innocent and untraceable. The next time they could have found someone else, and the next. Putting a name and the same, unforgettable face to the end-point of each transaction was asking for attention. It made no sense, unless …

Unless was what he had been trying to avoid, but it pressed too hard to ignore. Of course they would use Otto Fischer – it was the two birds, one stone principle. They could hardly expect him not to guess, and they probably didn't care. They knew that he wouldn't run, wouldn't hide, wouldn't throw himself on the mercy of the Federals or the British. He could be trusted to do everything in whatever way suited them best.

Roger Broadsmith. He *sounded* English to the bone, and Fischer's first mental image of the man had him in cricket whites, fending off a shot (is that what they called a flung ball?) without shaking loose the pipe from his mouth. Nonsense, of course. An effective intelligencer in the field would be notable only for his never-still glances, the slight hunch to the shoulders that subliminally tried to make the entire object slightly smaller, the odour of too many days since body and clothes were laundered. He couldn't imagine the British were any different. Shergold himself certainly hadn't shaken any preconceptions during their brief meeting.

His wife had sounded pleasant enough on the telephone. She spoke as if to a local voluntary worker arranging to pick up unwanted bric a brac rather than an enemy foot-soldier approaching a truce line, and the message had been passed on instantly. He was still in his hotel's telephone kiosk when Shergold had called back to give a name, meeting place and nothing else - not even goodbye, which suggested that he had called from where ears might be twitching. Fischer could hardly fault him for that. If he had been in the man's shoes he would be stepping equally gingerly towards this arrangement.

He tucked the envelope into his jacket pocket and took another mouthful of *kartoffelpuffer*. As much as he had come to love Portuguese peasant food, a German breakfast was like an angel's breath on his palate. In the three days since his return he had wolfed his way through a village's rations and savoured almost every mouthful (the exception being a leathery slice of *apfelkuchen* from a railway buffet, immediately offered to the pigeons that waited patiently outside). It seemed that his stomach was supplying the body's entire yearning for the old country.

The hotel's night-manager-cum-porter-cum-breakfast waiter refilled his coffee cup without being prompted and left a complementary edition of that morning's *General-Anzeiger* at his elbow. The establishment wouldn't ever earn a fourth star, but Fischer couldn't fault a thing about it. His room had a view, its bed was soft without deforming his spine, the breakfasts were heroic and the few staff pleasant enough to offer conversation even to guests who weren't likely to be substantial tippers. Did he ever expect to return to Bonn there would be no reason to seek alternative arrangements.

He dropped a single lump of sugar into his coffee and stirred it. The arms shipment was intended to be intercepted. No doubt its contents had been packed away carefully at some time following the Japanese collapse in Manchuria and forgotten ever since; the next shipment – the one they *wouldn't* flag to SIS – was more likely to be of munitions that might actually kill an enemy rather than the men that discharged them.

Fischer's Second Law of Espionage – One can be too cynical, but it can hardly hurt. He drank to the dregs of his cup and half-turned.

'Armin?'

The waiter returned to the table. 'More coffee, Herr Fischer?'

'No, thank you. Where might I find Münsterplatz?'

Armin scratched his cheek. Though Fischer had been acquainted with the man's habits for only three days, he recognized the gesture as the prelude to some witticism, delivered stone-faced.

'Surrounding the largest church in Bonn?

'Ha. From here, though?

'Turn right out of the front door, left into Vivatsgasse and follow it to the end. Six minutes' walk at most – you'll see the spire long before you reach it'

'Thank you. I'm to meet someone at the *Café Rosamund*.'

'It's slightly to your left-hand as you enter the Platz, in the far corner. A big, busy place, very popular with tourists and politicals.'

The look on Armin's face as he said the last suggested that he didn't think much of either demographic, but then his own establishment probably saw a great deal of both. Fischer had claimed to be in the city on business when he signed in. His paucity of luggage added weight to this, and no-one had pressed him further. He had reverted to his real name, papers and accent and therefore was on record as being in Germany once more, but he'd had neither time not contacts to organize new documents before he left Portugal. It was a small risk at most; he couldn't imagine that, three years on from his personal Flight into Egypt, Herod (that is, Willy Brandt or General Gehlen) was scanning the data-horizon still. Only the people most likely to want to kill him knew that he was back – in fact, had *sent* him back.

The only local interrogation he'd suffered to date had been from Armin himself, whose own war-record (France, North Africa, *Kriegsgefangenenlager* Kempton Park) had so palpably under-matched Fischer's that the full story had been demanded. Since then the service had been exemplary, if too often accompanied by knowing looks - or, in the case of Jeri, the young room-maid, moist eyes.

The hotel was inexpensive, but he had no idea how long he'd be required to remain in Bonn. Business trips weren't open-ended, so if he stayed into a second or third week his wallet might thin down and awkward questions be asked. Fortunately, this was now a seat of Government, so things didn't move nearly as quickly here as elsewhere. He had with him his only suit (a grey item), shirt (white) and tie (also grey), and could credibly pass as one of the countless applicants for the sort of bloated official contract whose overruns were underwritten by the uncomplaining taxpayer - a small, industrious cog in the great, mechanism that kept the Deutschmark stable, Germans in work and a resurgent National Socialism at bay.

It was pleasant thought, but it drove a nail into the reality of his situation. He could play at Normal, and that was as close as he ever came. It was a state, a condition, a wraith; it stood on every street corner and squatted in almost every home and workplace, yet he had somehow evaded its every lunge during his epic quest to find and occupy the latrine's edge. Portuguese exile had seemed like escape, the game finally won; but it had been an interlude, a cruel vacation from which he'd gained only a tan, better muscles and irreparably damaged fingernails (at least KGB could threaten nothing more in that department), and what he'd lost from it far outweighed those small gifts. He was back in play holding a pair of twos, with a mirror directly behind him.

His meeting wasn't for almost two hours yet, so Otto Fischer the pretend businessman might play the tourist for a while. He hadn't been able to find a printed guide to Bonn, but he had Armin's directions to its oldest church. The scents of centuries and candles were calming things, props for a better frame of mind – hell, if there was incense too he might make his rendezvous in a state of near-intoxication. Not being quite sober struck him as a very sensible way to conduct matters best suited to cellars.

He folded and pocketed his unread *General-Anzeiger*, gave his room-key to Armin and stepped out on to Sternstrasse. The Rhine had brought sea-air with it, and the clear day held enough coldness still to have flushed out the worst of his gloom by the time he found Münsterplatz. The surrounding buildings showed little bomb damage now, despite having been hammered by the Americans only seventeen years earlier, and the great basilica's thousand-year-old west end impressed even Fischer's agnostic sensibilities. He entered, passed about a third of the way down the nave and sat in a pew.

Several gaggles of schoolchildren and tourists meandered through the church, their attention directed by guides to this or that historical oddity, while he tried to lay out the possibilities in his head. It was possible that he was being followed by his employers, but in such a crowded city his chances of making the culprits were next to zero, and he didn't intend to try. SIS might also be reluctant to lose him once he made contact with Broadsmith – that is, if Gehlen or BfV didn't object to foreign intelligencers wandering through their pastures. Perhaps they had been informed already by the British as a matter of professional courtesy, and had their own men waiting to monitor his every future step. The sum of it was that Otto Fischer might be about to attract more attention than a circus act – one in which the audience came together at the end to shoot it out and catch him in the cross-fire. Again, there was little he could do about that.

Would SIS be convinced that Moscow's approach was worth exploring rather than cauterizing? Their recent embarrassments had been exposed publicly, so a potential new one was going to be looked at twelve ways before they pulled the ribbon from the gift. He was no cleverer than they, so it was likely they'd spot it for what it was – effectively worthless. Perhaps they didn't care; perhaps a discreet channel to Moscow was worth having for itself, a means of allowing each side to step back from stupid decisions.

He thought about that for a while, surprised that he could conceive a degree of rational thinking in their manichaean world, and decided that it was unlikely. No-one would do this without discerning some advantage to be had, even if they were mistaken. Moscow had baited a line, the British were hoping to snatch the worm without swallowing the hook, and that was all.

'I think you dropped this outside, Herr Fischer.'

His *General-Anzeiger* was handed to him, which seemed to answer the question as to whether he was being followed. But when he looked up, Jeri the maid stood over him, her uniform mostly hidden by a coat. A string of rosary beads were wrapped around her other wrist, which dealt with his second question (he recalled a silver crucifix that broke the plainness of her white blouse, which he had assumed to be jewellery when clearly it was something more).

'That's very kind of you, Jeri. I hadn't missed it.'

She regarded him hesitantly and then sat down in the pew at his side.

'You're a Catholic?'

'Lutheran, on paper at least. But I love old churches, for their peace.'

She looked around. 'It isn't very peaceful in summer. The tourists outnumber the congregation – except on Sunday mornings, when they don't want to get caught and have to sit through a Mass.'

Fischer smiled. 'It's not a pious age. It's good that old places still interest us, though. Do you remember the war?'

'No. I wasn't even a year old when it ended.'

Christ. Has it been that long?

'Everything was smashed up back then, so seeing it restored does us good. It makes us feel that we're moving on, to something better than it was.'

She considered this, the beads moving between her fingers. He thought for a moment she might be praying, but the frown said otherwise.

'*Is* it better, though? They have atom bombs, and missiles, and more soldiers than ever there were in peacetime before now. Half the world hates the other half, because everyone thinks that everyone else is either absolutely right or absolutely wrong.'

Surprised, he considered her profile. He didn't imagine there were many teenagers – particularly devout ones - who could pin the problem so precisely. It couldn't be an easy burden to bear, having a ration of so many years to come yet knowing that it might well be snatched away prematurely. It was ridiculous to feel that he might have been lucky to be born when he was, given what shit had splashed since; but the century was hardly past its midpoint, and there was ample time yet for things to sour further.

He stood and leaned towards her, thinking for a moment that he might say something wise, or reassuring, but nothing came to his mind that could possibly ease hers as much as her faith and present surroundings. He patted her shoulder awkwardly, a succinct admission of failure.

He arrived at Café Rosamund barely a minute before the agreed time and took an outside table that almost touched the perimeter rope. The metal seat hadn't begun to warm beneath him when a thickly-set gentleman approached, his hand outstretched. The smile seemed genuine, but then so much that wasn't often did.

'Herr Fischer?'

'Good morning, Mr Broadsmith. Isn't it a beautiful day? I have something for you.'

Above all, this must be arranged with discretion, be regarded as an accident and investigated only minimally; there is no utility in making any more obvious statement that may, eventually, be used against KGB. Don't utilize First Directorate resources, or even inform them. I leave the method, details and organization in your hands, but lose Otto Fischer.

Deputy Chairman Semichastny read it through the first time with an empty, clear mind – a technique he'd perfected years earlier, to survive long meetings in hot Baku offices during which chain-smoking Azeris had done their best to avoid decisions on water purification, street lighting, ideological standards for schools and universities or when to break for lunch. The second time, he allowed himself to look for meaning behind the bland form of words.

Used against KGB – he meant Zarubin, naturally. If they gave the man a good enough reason to turn on his old adversaries he'd take any opportunity. What he knew couldn't be guessed at, but the man burrowed better than a badger, and years of grubbing must have brought up some fat worms. The organization couldn't risk having exposed what great men hadn't cared to know about when authorizing operations (though of course they'd use it all to fuel the pyre if examples needed to be made). When Zarubin was finally brought down, it had to be so swift and unanticipated that the funeral party was dispersing before his secrets could be dragged from their vault.

Why now? wasn't too difficult to guess at. Shelepin had been to see Ivan Serov, whose career, like Beria's before him, had been built upon the bodies of those who hadn't got around to being troublesome before the bullet found their cerebellum. Culling all real and possible enemies was not so much a strategy as an instinct; only once, three years earlier, had Serov failed to see a looming threat, and the consequences of that error had to be poisoning his soup still. There could be no doubt as to what his advice would have been, if asked.

Semichastny had wanted to be there, to put a slant on Serov's opinion before it made too deep an impression; but Shelepin had said no, and pushing would have made him ask questions that needed not to be asked. Now, he wished he'd taken time to find some plausible reason for his presence, and then pushed anyway. This was a direct order and couldn't be ignored. It was also unsigned (it had arrived in one of the security envelopes that only the Chairman used, but that fact wouldn't stand as any sort of evidence subsequently), so it was clear who would take the blame should things go wrong. Fortunately, absolute responsibility provided much leeway, and a careful approach could slow the process considerably. Done properly, it might not require that he change his plans even slightly.

He picked up his telephone receiver, dialled zero and asked for a secure line to Karlshorst. The man he spoke to there took the message and promised to transmit it immediately. The return call came within ten minutes:

No, but if necessary I can arrange continuous surveillance by withdrawing men temporarily from other assignments.

No, he has given no indication of resistance to what has been asked of him.

Yes, he has been instructed not to change his accommodation or leave Bonn without permission, or, if a change of circumstances is requested by SIS, not to leave without first calling a number at our Bonn Embassy. Please advise on the matter of surveillance.

It was entirely as Semichastny had expected, but it calmed him nonetheless. He had taken pains to shape this operation as a funnel with himself at the narrow end. No-one at Karlshorst was aware of it; no-one in Dzerzhinsky Square – other than Shelepin – had the slightest understanding of certain events that had taken place in Berlin three years earlier. Their only surviving attestor, Ivan Serov, had been discredited by association, and would not risk further damage by willfully throwing himself in front of the tank once more. Which left only the trigger itself.

It was impossible to judge a man precisely. KGB ran courses on psychology, as did CIA, SIS, BND and all other major intelligence agencies, but at best they identified markers on a possible course. Semichastny had recruited Fischer by the simplest, crudest method, and so far he was performing according to type. The task was by no means difficult - in fact, care had been taken to smooth his path, and nothing more was (or would be) required of him than what had been demanded. That wasn't to say that the man didn't suspect or fear worse to come, but Semichastny was determined not give him any of the usual nudges or reminders of what might happen if he failed to perform adequately. To any reasonable intelligence the consequences were perfectly clear, and the man didn't seem to be lacking that respect.

So, while Semichastny now half-regretted having half-informed his boss of half the story, the kill order didn't overly complicate matters. This was a low-risk process, capable of being terminated at short notice if the British didn't play, and with few potential exposures. The piece of paper in his hand gave him *de facto* control of every aspect of its winding-down (though of course, Shelepin had no idea that anything needed to be wound down), and he intended to follow his instructions precisely, fastidiously but extremely deliberately. After all, his aims - however masked - were precisely in step with Shelepin's. The only dislocation was upon the matter of timing.

Jonas Kleiber took the news with better grace than he had anticipated. He read the letter carefully, folded it and replaced it in the envelope, thinking to preserve it as one of those sad but important moments in a man's life that should be recalled in later years with a little poignancy and the comfort of a glass of decent wine. Then he tore it into small pieces, threw them into the grate and immediately cursed his impulsiveness. It was July, and he probably wasn't going to light a fire in the fucking thing for several months.

In his moment of triumph he'd suspected that things might change. For as long as the task had been beyond him, separating Gloria from her underwear had seemed a consummation much to be desired (he'd read that phrase somewhere, yet as apt as it was he couldn't place it precisely). He'd forgotten, though, that sex did strange things to some girls – particularly, to their feelings regarding the cock-wielding party. He recalled an English farmer's daughter, previously a virgin, who had thrown herself into the business so whole-heartedly and energetically that eventually his ravaged foreskin had obliged him to cry off the dry-stone walling detail that had got him out of his POW camp in the first place. Three months later, another young lady (a neighbour of the sexual athlete) had responded to his invasion of her premises with a self-loathing that found release only by her abject confession of the event to her father, and via him to the camp commandant. After that, Kleiber had found release for his own imprisoned energies only in the effort it took to clean the toilet blocks each day.

Gloria's reaction, set out almost grammatically over four neatly-written paragraphs, was one of hurt, confusion and betrayal. That surprised Kleiber a little, because on the evening of their coupling she had thrown herself at him like a puppy at a butcher's half-open door, and used him rigorously. He suspected that her subsequent reassessment was not so much on a point of conscience as carelessness – that she had not pushed the offending underwear sufficiently deeply into the laundry basket, and that, consequently, Mother knew.

He had met the lady on just one occasion, and almost lost extremities to the iciness that filled the space between them. By way of introduction, she had gone straight to the point: Gloria was meant – in fact, created - for a chartered accountant, or an actuary, or a solicitor, and in all cases an English specimen of the profession. Welsh wouldn't do; Scottish was unthinkable; a German was … well, what came to one's dreams after a heavy cheese supper. Kleiber's courteous demeanour, his polite enquires after the matriarchal health, the effort he put into seeming interested in her vile collection of Capo de Monte figurines – all broke like waves upon the wall of Batroun. A silent gnomic figure, sitting in an armchair near the fire (probably the father), gave him what he took to be a slightly despairing look, and this had halted his nervous babbling long enough for Gloria to mention something – the cinema, a tea-dance perhaps – that had extracted them both from her presence. He hadn't attempted since to renew the acquaintance, and now never would.

That must have accounted for at least part of his sense of relief, but he wondered whether Gloria's own expectations, subtly but insistently hinted at, might also be moving him to something short of tears. Wisely, he had never revealed the true state of his finances to her, but even a struggling hack's intermittent rewards had given her ambitions for detachment (house), cultural improvement (foreign holidays) and belonging (bridge and golf clubs), to which she would contribute elegance, the necessary social graces and nothing so vulgar as paid work to help keep the invoices cowed.

He didn't have enough experience of family life (his father died early, his mother struggled horribly) to know if this was the way of things, but it had gradually come to him that his were expected to be the lifting biceps in their relationship. That wasn't an entirely unpleasant prospect. A man who looked after his woman was a proper man, after all; German society was at least as conventional in that respect, and Kleiber had no urge or motive to overthrow the teutonic model of marriage. But, he asked himself, wasn't this supposed to be at least the threshold of the Modern Age? Weren't old assumptions of what people were and were expected to be being challenged by the earth-moving dislocations of the past two decades?

Apparently not – at least, not in W4. A life with Gloria would have required that he set aside any aspirations for a life other than on two straight rails that disappeared inexorably towards lemon sweaters, drinks parties, microscopically-small talk ('I expect you don't have gin in Germany?') and an eventual reservation with a view at Kensal Green cemetery. And then there would be the children …

On the whole, he couldn't say that this counted as one of his bad days. He had been spurned brutally, but the world had donned its veil once more, and mysteries were yet to be discovered beneath it. He reminded himself that what he had long sought had, like so many yearnings, turned out to be a little underwhelming - that Gloria, sinning, had been all enthusiasm and too little art, and art (in sin) was important to him. He could do much better, he told himself, and it sounded good in his head.

Trying not to feel too *chipper* (as some of his local friends might have put it), he began a piece on the recent travails of the British motorcycle industry, a subject guaranteed to coax a rare sense of *schadenfreude* from his readership (whose own marques had been largely obliterated or handed to British companies – to ruin at their leisure – as war reparations). He already had a provocative title ('Sixty to Naught in Two Years'), the necessary statistics from the Board of Trade's Press Office and a handsome advance from *Bild*, so his usual thrashings-about in the creative marsh could be foregone. Three thousand words were required, and with a tailwind he could be done by the end of the following day.

He had flung down almost four hundred of them, summarizing the industry's wonderful production and sales figures for 1959 (but with a sly reminder of the 1930s designs that had achieved them), when a heavy shave-and-a-haircut on his apartment door killed the flow. He opened it to trainee-baker Alfred, a pleasant boy whose genuine interest in Germany and most of the rest of Europe hadn't been formed by the view from a forward gun-bay. He nodded at Kleiber and hoiked a thumb over his shoulder.

'Telephone call for you, Jonas. Hurry up - it's international.'

They both took the stairs in double-time, swerved on the pavement outside and tip toed apologetically through the queue of customers in the shop. Master-baker Bert was in the back, holding the receiver, frowning *faux*-sternly.

'Should we be getting you an extension, Jonas?'

'Sorry, Bert. I wasn't expecting ….'

'Nah, go on. I think it's yer pretty friend.'

Otto, calling, was better than Otto dead, but the thought did nothing to slow Kleiber's pounding heart. If he was calling now there had to be a reason, and there were no good reasons in the Fischer Firmament. He was in a telephone box somewhere in a desperate part of Berlin, slouched down, hoping that the men with guns hadn't …

'Hello? Jonas? Are you there?'

'Yes.'

'Oh. Good. I left some money with you.'

'You did.'

'At least your memory's not fuddled. Could you send it to me, please? I'm staying a little longer than I'd hoped. Do a currency exchange first, and then a wire transfer. Take the fees for both from what you send – I don't want you to bear the expense.'

'Er, yes, alright. Are *you* alright, Otto?'

'I'm fine. Why shouldn't I be?'

'I was worried. You said that you'd call.'

'I *am* calling, aren't I? Everything's fine. The weather's lovely here. How is it in England?'

'You're not interested in weather, Otto, not since your artillery days.'

'I was making conversation. Do you have a pen?'

'Why?'

'To make a note of where the wire transfer's going.'

'Right.' Kleiber found pen and paper on Bert's untidy 'desk' (a small occasional table tucked into a corner where it couldn't impeded the dough-proving process) and nodded. Then, realising that a nod wouldn't do, cleared his throat.

'Ready.'

'It's *Landhaus Europa*, Sternstrasse 49, Bonn. Your operator will give you the telephone number and exchange for the transfer.'

'Bonn? What are you doing in Bonn?'

'The same as I would in any other German town, which is to say Don't Ask.'

'Otto …'

'Breath wasted, Jonas. I'll call again in a few days' time. Don't worry, I really am fine. Goodbye.'

The line went dead. Kleiber stared at the receiver for a moment, dialled the operator and asked for the Bonn number. He wrote it down, went over each digit a second time with the pen and then drew an ornate frame around the whole, carefully putting off the moment when he would have to make a decision - no, a *Decision*. As long as it hadn't been likely to arise it had seemed a small, distant thing, but he was now in possession of facts which shoved it to the fore. If he went one way he would be betraying Otto; if he went the other he would have taken a half-step, jumped back and risked being made ridiculous; if he did nothing at all …

What a wonderful prospect. In Kleiber's opinion, sitting-on-hands was almost never a bad option. It allowed a fellow to convince himself that he was weighing a matter carefully, as all matters should be weighed, and the bigger the matter the more necessary the weighing – that was obvious, surely? Anything less would be impulsive, even …. he thought about it for a few moments ...

Precipitous.

Well, he certainly didn't want to be *that*. In any case, he had a money transfer to arrange, and if he managed that quickly and efficiently he'd feel better about putting off the other thing. He couldn't be expected to do more at the moment, not in his fraught emotional state. It wasn't every day that a wonderful woman wrote herself out of a man's life, so an appropriate amount of grieving had to do its good work. Perhaps in three or four weeks' time he could return to the prospect of having to make a decision …

Fuck fuck fuck.

'Bert?'

'You want to make a call. And it's not to Lambeth?'

'Would you mind?'

'Nah. Just write down what it costs and we'll add it to the rent.'

A severed undersea cable or unusual meteorological conditions might have broken his resolution, but the connection was made promptly. The voice at the other end was loud, abrupt and impatient, which almost did the trick, too. Kleiber took a deep breath, said *sorry, Otto* to himself and abandoned the beautiful path of prevarication.

'It's me. I have an address now.'

'I hope your meeting went well, Herr Fischer?'

'Ah, you know, Armin. It's difficult to get people in Government to make up their minds, particularly when they're spending money.'

Armin rolled his eyes sympathetically. 'It isn't as if it's *theirs*, is it? Will you be eating in the hotel this evening?'

Until now, Fischer had taken his suppers in his room, not wishing to advertise his presence in Bonn more than was necessary. The first meeting with the British agent (a very straightforward transaction) had eased his mind, however, and the boredom of having very little else to do was beginning to press. He looked up at Armin, whose present role was that of breakfast waiter.

'Could you recommend a nice restaurant on the river? Nothing too expensive – I have to justify my receipts.'

Armin pursed his lips and gave some attention to the mural of Amalfi that adorned one wall of the dining room . '*Em Hoettche* is the best cheap restaurant in Bonn, but it isn't on the river. If you don't mind the exercise you can cross to the north bank and walk upstream to Limperich. There's a small place there called *Weinhaus Hahn*, with nice views from the terrace.'

'It sounds perfect. You've eaten there?'

'My wife's last birthday, six years ago.'

'Oh, I'm sorry.'

'It's alright, we never really got on. As I recall, the food was delicious. Tea or coffee this morning?'

Fischer took his time over breakfast, having no idea when, how or if he would be contacted to report on his meeting with Broadsmith. It wasn't as though he would have much to tell; the man had been pleasant, quite voluble in a forgettable way (a practiced talent, no doubt) and just the right side of politely curious about a stranger's war record. The entire encounter had taken less than fifteen minutes, and that was with the Englishman insisting upon buying them both a beer. No doubt he'd been told to gauge his new contact carefully, given that SIS had no other way of assessing what they were getting into, but it hadn't felt like any kind of interrogation. For the moment they were merely sparring, jabbing at arm's-length, wondering what kind of punch the other fellow had and whether he'd choose to use it.

There was nothing about this that seemed immediately threatening. If he could have forgotten how he'd been dragged back to Germany he might have been tempted to relax a little; but in every direction he could sense walls, and none of them were receding. He might play, or pretend to play – act the businessman or tourist, sample the local cuisine and architecture until belly and head were full of what was delightful but not quite necessary, and still he would be wearing an iron collar whose key sat in someone else's pocket. Bonn was a pleasant place, and his task was straightforward, but neither fact made this situation any better than it was.

'Armin?'

'Herr Fischer?'

'Has anyone been asking for me?'

The moment he spoke, Fischer wished that there were better ways of addressing a matter than by raising it. The question was innocent enough – any visiting businessman had both a home office and local contacts, and until the advent of some form of civilian field-telephone he would be obliged to ask for messages to be relayed via some convenient third party. But Armin sensed (or scented) something more than that, despite hearing the same or similar most days of his working life. His eyes narrowed, and he gave the two other tables that were presently occupied a cold glance.

'Like who, Boss?'

'Oh, anyone. I was expecting ...'

'I'll keep my eyes and ears open. What shall I say, if I'm asked?'

That was a good question, and it depended on who was doing the asking. He didn't want to give KGB any reason to think he was trying to avoid them, much less lose himself. By the same token, if SIS came calling and found reason to shy away, his Moscow string-pullers would doubtless think him the cause. He didn't want to desert or even mislead - just to be aware who had eyes upon him, and when.

'Tell them the truth, Armin. I'm not avoiding anyone. But if you could let me know I'd be grateful.'

'Of course. If old soldiers don't watch out for each other, who will?'

The neat forehead scar had reddened slightly. War veterans had wholly unreliable memories of the camaraderie of the Front Line, but Fischer had no intention of refusing covering fire, however modest. He nodded and frowned, confirming Armin's suspicions (whatever they were) and sealing the brotherly bond. More coffee was poured, and that day's *General-Anzeiger* placed carefully at his elbow.

Having no plans for the morning, Fischer picked it up and began with the headlines. There wasn't too much that was spectacular (a blessing, of course, to all but news-desks). The previous day, Greece had become an associate member of the EEC, seventeen people had died during a crash landing at Denver airport, and remarkably, a German newspaper was reporting the release from prison of Mildred Gillars, the American lady whose unattractive voice had been a much-beloved feature of the Reich's English-language broadcasts to GIs in the field. For a moment he wondered if she'd be offered German citizenship and a slot on *Westdeutscher Rundfunk*, but the prospect didn't seem to be worth a wager.

He remained on page 3 for a great while. A small column, almost surrounded by local news, was out of place, a misstep by the typesetters. It wasn't the dislocation that drew his eyes, however, nor kept them there, desperately trying to parse a different meaning from the words. The *MV Save* was – had been – a freight-liner out of Porto, carrying 549 crew and passengers and a cargo of fuel and munitions. On the morning of 9 July, off the mouth of the River Chinde, Mozambique, a series of explosions had torn her apart. She went down in shallow waters, but fewer than two hundred survivors – many of them burned horribly – had been found. As yet, the cause of the disaster was a matter of speculation, but Fischer couldn't think of anything but *them*, and what they might have done if handed an easy opportunity. He couldn't possibly know, but the sour, unbearable gut-feeling grew to a near-certainty that neither Zofia nor Felipe had been among those pulled alive from the water.

On the night he had sneaked out of Portugal she had told him at the last moment, hoping to keep the argument brief. He had time only to say that it was unnecessarily dangerous, that what he was doing should protect her; but even as he said it he realized that their decision had been made days earlier. She gave him the name of the ship and its destination in the thin hope that they might be able to arrange something at some future, unimaginable time, and told him how sorry she was that she couldn't have said something earlier. Her husband Felipe had been too nervous in the face of an unfamiliar threat, and insisted upon it. They had a house and land out there, a tropical investment, far from where they could be found by the men from Moscow.

He should have stayed at the quayside, missed his own sailing, argued until she surrendered and agreed to remain where she was safe; but he knew how pitiful the argument would have been. They had come to Portugal because it was supposed to be off-limits to the Soviets. Without an embassy, or consulate, or even third-party diplomatic representation, they lacked the infrastructure to operate clandestinely there without courting disaster. At least, that had been Fischer's theory: if KGB couldn't mount a secure operation there, one former agent turned rabbit wasn't and would never be worth the risk of trying. It was the *whole* reason they had chosen a hard farming life on a northern hillside and not an easier, warmer existence in Latin America, where their most onerous task would have been to dodge invitations to National Socialist pool-parties.

But they were saying their goodbyes on a dark, rain-drenched quayside in Leixões precisely because his brilliant theory been proved wrong, so he kept his mouth closed and hoped that he was equally wrong about what she was doing. How could he have known how swiftly and terribly he would prove to be right?

If you do this, we won't harm her. Had they lied from the start, or was the fact of her flight enough to absolve them of the commitment? Perhaps they'd assumed that he'd renege on their arrangement once he knew that she was out of reach, and decided to not risk losing them both. His task was not complicated, so they must have calculated that it would be done before he could hear of a minor disaster at the other side of the world. Who might have imagined that Bonn's parochial Press would run the story, and misplace it on page three?

He tried, very hard, to tell himself that not even KGB would use such a blunt, callous instrument to kill a lone traitor, but then the familiar thought returned to him: *two birds, one stone*. Portugal's grip on her African colonies had begun to loosen earlier that year, with a clutch of rebellions erupting in Angola – including that of the Soviet Union's client movement, the MPLA. It was entirely foreseeable that an arms vessel sailing from Porto to Mozambique would have called in at Luanda *en route*, to discharge some of her cargo for the hard-pressed local regime's use. No matter how quickly it was done, someone would have had the time, the opportunity, to get onboard and arrange matters so that a small stain could be erased *and* the Portuguese authorities in Mozambique be denied the means of pre-empting yet another liberation struggle.

Had the thing not formed in his own mind he might have dismissed it as paranoia. But circling it, poring over every conceivable calculation and stray happenstance, he couldn't believe that an unsecured container, or a stray spark, or a casually misdirected cigarette butt had managed to give them this perfect triumph.

The dining room had emptied by now, but he couldn't move. Since the moment, six months earlier, when he and Zofia had sat on the porch of their home and decided that affection wasn't reason enough to stay together, a dullness had laid upon him, deadening his emotions. He hadn't grieved, hadn't felt a sense of loss, even; when KGB found them, his only fear was for her, because by then he had taken up once more the state of resignation that had followed him for as long and as faithfully as a gun-dog, ready to spring forward when hope receded. Passively, he had accepted their terms, said goodbye to the last period of contentment he might ever expect, contrived his own death and placed himself into a sink of double dealing without allowing the slightest, self-preserving qualm to slow the process.

The dullness was gone now, flushed by a few lines of typescript. To be used without pity was one thing, but for her to be used pitilessly changed the rules – into what he couldn't know as yet, but something had to be exacted. He was one man, and a dead one at that. He couldn't take on KGB, even if the consequences of doing so were entirely acceptable to him. He knew none of their secrets, so the British would hardly welcome him as a not-quite defector. He didn't even have enough understanding of what he was doing to frustrate or even embarrass the plan itself - except, perhaps, on the one small, central point …

Armin, tidying the dining room, glanced occasionally at the guest who didn't seem to want breakfast to end. He wondered if it had been his comment about old soldiers that had upset Herr Fischer (because clearly, he *was* upset). Perhaps he shouldn't have said it. One could never tell how memories of conflict lay on a man's conscience. Armin himself had fought a little, manoeuvred a great deal, never offered a bad word or harm to a civilian and then spent a mostly comfortable, dragging term in a British camp, but he knew that others had done much more. Herr Fischer's war was written across him like a tattoo, yet even that might be just a broad summary, a hint that what fire or metal had done to his face a greater, darker thing had put upon his soul. Not that everything the Allies said about Germans could be true. Winners always blackened the name of those they hammered, if only to excuse their own excesses, and Armin couldn't believe that men in uniform had done the things that the newsreels had shown. He couldn't deny that there were far fewer Jews, Gypsies and queers in Germany than before the war, but that must have been the work of a few, bad men, and couldn't be put upon the nation as a whole.

Had Herr Fischer done anything like that? Armin's gut said no, and it wasn't often misled. Perhaps he had seen things, things not to be mentioned, and it was the weight of secrets that troubled him. Conscience was strange – it could forgive or erase the personal yet fill a man with regret for what he couldn't ever have altered. Armin's cousin had been in Ukraine in the first four months of 1942, and wouldn't speak, ever, of what he'd seen there, yet no-one who knew Udo would think that he might have done evil himself. A man could be hurt by sin without having done it.

Having examined, tried and absolved his man, Armin took off his apron, went to reception and told Volker to take his break. The young man had worked at the hotel for only three weeks, and was still keen to prove himself. While breakfast was being served he had tidied the front desk, re-stacked the What to Do in Bonn leaflets in their holder, lined up the pens in military formation and wiped every surface within reach. Armin, who took care to find fault with the boy, gave the area careful scrutiny but could find no further ammunition this morning.

Volker handed the safe keys to Armin and nodded towards the pigeon-holes.

'There's an envelope for Herr Fischer.'

Armin nodded as if it were a matter almost beneath notice, but when Volker had gone he found the object and examined the exterior carefully. Fischer's name was hand-written in small script; otherwise, there was no clue as to its origin (other than a tiny stamp - *Lederfabrik Denner GMBH* - on the end-crease, that confirmed at least its German manufacture). It had been moistened and sealed, so the contents couldn't be examined without the recipient knowing. Frustrated, Armin held it up to the nearest light. He was wasting his time, but having committed himself to Fischer's cause he felt a certain obligation to know more about his business – at least, that's how he bedded down his conscience. It was a point of pride that he didn't like to pry, usually.

Defeated, Armin took the envelope into the dining room and placed it at Fischer's side. He glanced at it but left it untouched, and though his ruined face was visible for a moment only, it dragged Armin's mind forcibly back to war and what it did to those who fought. It was a terrible thing, and by time he was captured he had almost become inured to it; but like most of his generation he had been brought up to believe certain things, and one of them was that men didn't – shouldn't - cry.

23

Roger Broadsmith experienced the sensation for several minutes before he recognized it as anxiety. For the first time that he could recall, a sense of situations closing in seized almost all of his attention, yet he couldn't put a finger upon any single event that had excited his nerves-endings. Had the spirits of his dead parents each occupied a shoulder, he might have imagined that his mother's stoicism had been hushed slightly, and his father's nervous temperament given greater rein.

It could hardly have been his meeting with BfV's representative, Herr Gunther Waldmann, that had ignited this disquiet. The man had listened to Broadsmith's rehearsed proposals without interruption, asked little, promised less and left as deep an impression of being as interested in this business as he was in his fingernails. They had agreed to meet again in two days' time, but for what purpose wasn't quite clear to the Englishman. Unless Cologne was playing out a line, hoping to catch something larger than the bait deserved, SIS appeared to be considerably more keen to extend this relationship than BfV. At least, that was the message he intended to convey to Harold Shergold.

So, what was bothering him? His other, East German employers weren't pressing him to take risks – in fact, they had seemed as indifferent to Broadway's initiative as Herr Waldmann. Having given *Cuttlefish* a brief report on the meeting, the man had neither asked further questions nor offered suggestions as to how the next one might go. It made Broadsmith wonder whether he and his BfV counterpart were from the same batch.

Cuttlefish had, however, perked up when Broadsmith mentioned Fischer and his mission. Though neither SIS nor Moscow had insisted that their meetings take place on West German soil – that had been Fischer himself, apparently - MfS regarded the Federal Republic as 'their' territory, and would expect to be kept apprised of any Soviet manoeuvres there. Of course, the sinned-against might well be sinners themselves – after all, Broadsmith worked out of London, which KGB regarded as *their* hunting ground, so perhaps Berlin and Moscow were keeping things from each other. Or perhaps everyone knew everything. That was another unfortunate thing about treason – one's handlers invariably sought to know all yet say nothing.

Perhaps his present uneasiness had its roots in how little he knew about his present task. At Broadway he had run his modest part of the Franz Josef Desk, pushing or pacifying informers and field-agents, writing the requisite number of reports about not very much (several of which he had passed on to Berlin, to whatever end he couldn't say) and taking all proper pains to ensure that no-one Upstairs ever asked what it was that Roger Broadsmith *did*, precisely? As an adventure it wouldn't have sold many copies, but there was much to be said for keeping the Intelligencer's life as mundane as possible. Translated to Bonn, however, he was no longer in sight of familiar shores. Everything he did was at someone else's direction; every move he made was judged upon criteria that weren't set down neatly in any training manual or performance review. So far, he couldn't say that he'd been asked to do anything that would stretch the merest aptitude, yet for all he knew he was as exposed as a bird on a washing line. People were looking through and around him, their attention on means and ends, accommodations or betrayals, any of which might send bullets flying at some point. He couldn't expect to survive them if he didn't when or from which direction they would come.

This business of Fischer, for instance. He had been told by Shergy to assess the man, but how did one do that, absent the conventional features that gave away what the mind behind was thinking? Of course, he'd been told what to expect, but words couldn't convey adequately what he'd seen. The prospect had unsettled him, and before he could full recall himself the other man's easy, almost laconic manner had added to the dislocation (strange, that someone who looked like *that* could be easy about anything). At the end of their conversation, Broadsmith still had no feel for whether they should be hopeful, suspicious or soiling themselves about Moscow's approach.

And that was another thing. Back at his hotel, he had telephoned Shergold and read to him the contents of the envelope. The Congo was a bloody mess at the moment, but he couldn't believe that the Soviets wanted to betray the rebels they'd supported for almost a year past. Why else would they give details of one of their own arms shipments, though? They must have known that SIS would pass it straight on to the Americans, and through them to Kasa-Vubu's people. If the intelligence was bad, what advantage could be gained by it, other than – very briefly – to embarrass the competition in a relative backwater?

It wasn't Broadsmith's job to parse it, obviously. Shergy would pore over the Soviets' motives and probably do or say nothing – waiting, as usual, for the other side to push its head a little further out of the shell. His detractors at Broadway sometimes joked that, if he'd been in charge, the British Expeditionary Force would still be making sand-castles at Dunkirk while he calculated every possible variant of von Rundstedt's next move; but they were the sort – often former SOE types who had crossed to SIS in 1945 - who believed that doing *something*, however ill-considered, was always the right policy. That attitude had survived every reverse and balls-up since the war, and continued to form square any time that worthwhile change was mooted. It was probably why SIS had never managed successfully to infiltrate a rival intelligence service – to its old guard, patience was both a vise and a vice.

Why Broadsmith should care, he couldn't say – he was, after all, in the pay of the Enemy, whose best interests were served by the Duffers remaining in post. Perhaps it was because his tidy mind appreciated that of another, and despised the allegedly-gifted amateurs who consistently misread the lessons of disaster. In any case, and despite his betrayals, he wasn't sure that he didn't want to stay at Broadway until the pension arrived, in which case there had to *be* an SIS still. It was ironic that he regarded Harold Shergold – the man who might very well expose him - as the only feasible future for the organization.

When Broadsmith had finished reading out the information supplied by Fischer, Shergy had hung up without comment. Following form, he would have put on his coat immediately and taken one or several of his rescue dogs for a walk, sharing with them his thoughts as they tumbled out. Even

Broadsmith could see that the man faced a simple but troublesome equation. The longer he kept this to himself the more exposed he would be; the more people who knew about it, the greater the chance of another hasty decision and yet another bugger-up. Moscow – some *part* of Moscow - knew what it was doing, but Harold Shergold did not. Until he did, any decision he made would leave him vulnerable. Perhaps that was the entire reason for their approach. Slipping a knife between the ribs of the man who brought down George Blake would be just the coup to push an enterprising schemer far up whatever the communists used for a greasy pole.

Broadsmith hoped it wasn't that, though. He liked Shergy, and God knew, there were few enough people at Broadway about whom he felt the same. But this was a war, wasn't it, and didn't the good ones get in the way of bullets just as efficiently as the bad? A man could look only to himself, and Broadsmith was beginning to think that he had fallen short in that respect.

As he saw it, his only sensible course was to play his three roles as passively as possible. Broadway wanted him to be nice to BfV, so he would smile every time Herr Waldmann scowled and offer some anodyne hope for their two organizations' future collaboration. Harold Shergold needed him as a conduit for the information being supped by their mysterious would-be friend in Moscow. That was easy enough – in fact, it would take a conscious effort to complicate matters, unless Otto Fischer chose to be something other than an equally compliant messenger. Which left his MfS handlers. He wondered now whether it had been wise to mention the Moscow initiative to *Cuttlefish*. If Berlin knew about it already he had nothing to fear; if they didn't, *Stasi* and KGB might find themselves having a family spat, and when the crockery began to fly Roger

Broadsmith's head could very well be in the way. Either way, he intended to pay more attention to the small, urgent voice in his head that told him his store of good luck may well have been squandered.

24

I should be flattered. He cares about me.

Zarubin had said it to himself too many times in the past hour for the words to have retained any meaning- in any case, it was probably shit. Khrushchev had a habit of bestowing his greatest love upon a man immediately before dispensing with his services. Stalin had done the same, though in his case it was to indulge a sadist's glee in tormenting others. For the present First Secretary, it was more a way of easing a bad conscience and indulging his pathetic need to be well thought of by everyone, even those he was flushing away.

One of the nicer suites at the Shaxtiori Hotel in Tskaltubo had been reserved for Zarubin. He would have been delighted, but for two things. Firstly, he hadn't asked for it; nor had it been offered beforehand, but presented rather as a delightful *fait accompli.* Secondly, he had been booked in for six weeks of five-star pampering at the Defence Ministry's private spa there, at God knows what cost to their budget. It was princely treatment - or would have been, if all the princes hadn't long since fled or been shot in cellars. The thing was, *no-one* went to Tskaltubo for six whole weeks unless he was dying, hiding from his enemies or getting the Soviet equivalent of the gold watch for services rendered and a happy retirement.

He had been in a car crash – a very serious one. Since then, the First Secretary had been more than solicitous about his condition, even to the point of coming personally to his office on two occasions to enquire as to his progress, sending more (and more) flowers and warning members of the Council of Ministers not to pester the poor man with unnecessary demands for position papers. Ostensibly, Zarubin was being as treated a favoured son, and had all been as it seemed he would have been most flattered. But it wasn't, and he wasn't, though the irony wasn't lost on him. As the moment of his defenestration approached, his reputation within the Kremlin had never been higher.

Cassandra's warnings were no longer required, apparently. He didn't doubt that his office would be here still when he returned from Georgia with puckered skin and the whiff of sulphur hovering like - and being mistaken for - a fart; but if Khrushchev still valued his advice there wasn't a chance he would allow his best advisor to wander off for six weeks while the Soviet Union and US stumbled towards an accidental confrontation. This was deliberate, a means of streamlining what was said and heard about the coming crisis.

Could he refuse to go, or at least postpone the pleasure for a few months? There were precedents. After the failed *putsch* against Khrushchev in '57, Georgy Malenkov been kicked out of the Politburo, but had fought like a rat in a sack thereafter to remain in Moscow, and it had taken the better part of three years to get him on a train to Kazakhstan and obscurity. His co-conspirator Kaganovich, a far more dangerous man, lost every post he enjoyed within Government yet lived within two kilometres of the Kremlin still, despite most of the Praesidium wanting several time-zones between him and their backs. A man could dig in his heels, even as power slipped away.

But these had been big men, and Zarubin was a minnow who owed his place in the pond entirely to the person who wanted him out. He counted Mikoyan as a friend, but even the Great Survivor himself couldn't – wouldn't – risk his own friendship with the First Secretary to no good purpose. And why should he? By Soviet standards, Zarubin was being offered a gentle slope down which to fling himself. Probably, he had a few years of steady employment ahead of him, producing opinions upon matters of great weight that might occasionally be read before finding their eternal resting place in the filing wen. He would keep his apartment (it was too small for a Minister and his family or mistress), retain his Armed Forces Club membership, continue to enjoy access to the House of Government's shops and cafes and generally live a life only half-dreamt of by the vast majority of his compatriots. If the cost of all that was merely the loss of access to one of Khrushchev's hairy ears, who could pity him?

Himself, obviously, and possibly Levin. One or two members of the Council of Ministers who were not only in the habit of wanting to hear his thoughts but sometimes asked before he'd had them – they, too, might wish that his words carried weight still. Otherwise, his name would fade quickly from memory, being one that no could longer opened doors or be dropped to any good effect. And would that be so bad? A soft semi-retirement was a relatively novel option for anyone who had climbed so many rungs of the Soviet ladder, and obscurity a small enough penalty for avoiding the firing post or the careful positioning above a cell-sluice. Really, when he thought about it …

Listen to yourself. He was attempting to find diamonds in pig-shit, the forlorn occupation of falling men everywhere. Obscurity was just that (however comfortable), and he wasn't yet forty-six years old. Three or four further decades filled only by reminiscences, vodka and committee work was an ugly prospect, relieved only by the possibility that someone in KGB would sense the protective shield falling from him and risk the head-shot they'd been longing to take. He didn't doubt that he'd hope for it, eventually.

The door opened quietly, but Zarubin sensed Levin's head, poking around it, before he looked up. The cast to his secretary's face suggested that the outer office had been parsing Khrushchev's generous gift in much the same way as the inner. It was only at times like this, when an unwanted career-shift looked more likely than not, that his carapace of insolent indifference showed its eggshell-thinness. He stood, half-in and out, wanting to ask the question, until Zarubin waved him in.

'What will you do, Comrade General?'

'Go to Tskaltubo. Have a good rest. I hear the weather is generally wonderful down there at this time of year, so plenty of swimming too, I expect.'

'They'll circle while you're gone.'

'And wire this office, no doubt. Watch your mouth.'

'I only ever say things I shouldn't to you.'

'I'm flattered.'

Levin's mouth opened and closed twice, but nothing emerged. Zarubin sighed.

'What?'

'Should I come with you? I mean, I assume you'll be working.'

'No. Stay here, and keep our yellow box safe.'

'What if they search my apartment?'

'No-one's interested in you, Levin. My worst enemies won't think that I'm so big a fool as to confide incriminating material or thoughts to my personal secretary.'

'But you do.'

'Then be pleased that we have dislocated their realities.'

Levin didn't *seem* pleased. He glanced to his left, to the bookcase behind which the yellow box usually resided. For four days now he had played landlord to a hoard of Swiss francs, the possession of which, if discovered, would earn him the opportunity to see an inconsiderable part of Siberia for a very considerable time. With his employer gone from Moscow, that sword would hover horribly. In a moment of cloudy thinking he had transferred the hoard from a drawer in his kitchen sideboard to his mattress, throwing up one more obstacle to an undisturbed night's sleep. The following morning he had moved it again, and then again several hours later. It was now taped to the underside of the piece of furniture in which it had first resided, and he was no more convinced that this wasn't the first place the police would examine than he had the others. The fact was that no conceivable corner of a two-room apartment might be safe from the attention of expert men - men who could now take all the time they needed without fear of interruption from a once-influential guardian in the Kremlin.

'You seem uneasy, Levin. Don't worry, I'm sure Tskaltubo will be very pleasant.'

'You have to *do* something about this!'

'Do? Should I thank the First Secretary, but decline the offer? Tell him that I have a clinical aversion to sharing steamy rooms with naked men? What might he say to that?'

'No, I mean ...' Levin stared hard at the floor for a few moments. '... do something clever, to stop them taking advantage of your absence.'

'Ah, that *would* be clever, but the only thing that occurs would be to take Khrushchev with me and have all his calls directed to the steam-room. No, Levin, we must accept our burden graciously and bear the consequences as they arrive.'

'You're being very calm about this. You know that Gromyko, Kosygin and the rest will push the First Secretary to face down the Americans, once you're no longer there to out-argue them.'

'Yes, but they were winning that fight already. You know Khrushchev's been avoiding me. I'm beginning to think that we need at least one propaganda disaster before I'll be heard once more. If they push him to agree to Ulbricht's wall in Berlin and the Allies don't leave he'll look weak, and he hates looking weak. If that happens, I shall come again in Glory.'

Levin regarded him doubtfully. 'He also hates people being right about things he's got wrong.'

'If I'm still *persona non grata* when it happens, I won't be around to be hated.'

'That's true. And you won't be able to give him the face.'

'Which face?'

'The one that tells him he's a dolt.'

'I don't do that, do I?'

'To *everyone*. It's your most dangerous habit.'

Zarubin looked down at the note from Khrushchev once more. Perhaps a stay at Tskaltubo wouldn't be quite the disaster he feared. He had milked his car accident down to the curds, but a minor relapse during his rest-cure might rekindle a little of the First Secretary's tenderness. The great man didn't enjoy being nagged - very well, let others take on the burden of stoking his irritation. The moment Zarubin departed for his spa break they'd be rushing to make appointments to shove forward their opinions. From past experience, the First Secretary would offer the counter-argument – in this case, for treading water and waiting for the Americans to make further mistakes. No no, they'd say, to do nothing would be an opportunity squandered. Don't listen to Zarubin, he's just another Kutusov, avoiding every next battle …

But Kutusov's had been the right strategy, and Napoleon had fled Russia with the shattered remnants of his once-Grande Armée. Even Khrushchev knew that, so Zarubin's arguments - absent Zarubin - might begin to appeal more than they had to date. At worst, his enemies in Moscow would find themselves wearing the nagger's hat and having their appointments pushed further and further back by the Keeper of the First Secretary's Serenity, A.S. Shevchenko.

Zarubin couldn't help but smile at that happy thought, which had the effect of deepening Levin's frown.

'I wouldn't have thought this a laughing matter, Comrade General.'

'You rarely think that anything *is*, Boris Petrovich. Is that a characteristic of you Novgorod folk?'

'Possibly. But a man with few friends and quite a few enemies shouldn't be seeing any funny side to his situation.'

'You're right, of course. The moment I arrive at my hotel I shall find a secure line, call this office and give you the number. I'll rely upon you to use your many contacts to get a feel for what's happening while I'm gone. We'll speak every day, naturally, and if my pampering excites further ideas on anything important I'll dictate a paper from Tskaltubo.'

Levin groaned. 'You change your mind about what you want to say every six seconds.'

Zarubin stood. 'Mine is an agile mind. Now, where at present is our yellow box?'

'Underneath the kitchen sideboard.'

'Dear God! Your building has a maintenance room, does it not?'

'Of course it has.'

'And when was the heating system last flushed?'

'Three weeks ago, its annual cleansing. They made the usual damn mess ….'

'Then we can be fairly certain that the cupboard containing the corrosion inhibitor chemicals won't be accessed in the near future. Wrap the money in waxed paper and then plastic; speak to someone here in Palace Maintenance who can supply a clean Cosmoline canister and put it in that. It shouldn't be too difficult for you to then conceal it among, and preferably behind, others of its kind.'

'That's … clever.'

'Yes, isn't it? I seem to be doing the thinking for most of central Moscow at the moment. Now, I'll be gone for six weeks.'

'It seems so.'

'Or perhaps not. One never knows what may happen in politics, and doubly so in the Soviet variety. While I'm gone – and sooner rather than later – contact our friend at Khodynka airfield and tell him that I might need to get back here at short notice. If so, he'll have the necessary paperwork in advance. That, of course, will be your task, Levin.'

'It always is. But what if KGB decide to drown you in your mud-bath?'

'Then you should apply to V.S. Stepanov at the State Committee Secretariat and take him up on his kind offer of employment. Or retire on your unexpected chemical inheritance.'

25

If I go in here, will I reach the North Sea?

The Rhine was too broad to rush itself, but its currents were strong. A body falling into its middle passage wouldn't reach sediment; it would be carried a long way downstream, and Fischer didn't know what, if any, obstacles lay in its path. The course of the river became tortuous as it approached Dusseldorf, and even if an inanimate object managed not to ground itself upon a bank in that neighbourhood, it would reach Netherlander territory soon afterward, and the Dutch were famous for buggering around with their watercourses. Still, if great barges could come upstream, why couldn't one small Otto Fischer go the other way?

It was almost dark on a fine July evening, and traffic across the recently-rebuilt Rheinbrücke was very light. He had dined at the small inn recommended by Armin, and couldn't recall when – or even if – he had eaten so well. Every mouthful had been a delight; every sip a reminder of how well Germans could *do* red wine when they made the effort. He had enjoyed himself immensely, and all the while, somewhere in Africa, what remained of her burned corpse was being torn at, ripped apart by delta creatures. He wondered how he could have kept that image out of mind, even for a moment.

It hadn't been for hunger's sake that he had dined out – only a need to escape his own head. Earlier, he had telephoned Felipe's house in Braga, giving in to the mad, thin hope that a change of mind had kept them safe. The maid who answered was very polite; she explained that neither Senhor Luz nor the Senhora could come to the 'phone at the moment as they were in Africa, but if he left a message she would be sure to relay it when they called. It was only later, as he moved blindly through the Old Town, surrounded by happy families enjoying the evening sunshine, that it occurred to him he had replaced the receiver without thanking her, or saying goodbye.

In his grief he couldn't bring his thoughts to a single point, and consider where to go from there. He wanted to return to Guimarães and rethink the decisions he had made, but that was impossible. He wanted revenge, yet would never know who it should be directed against. He wanted to frustrate the men who worked him, but had no idea how that might be achieved. He wanted to be free, and here in the darkness, on the Rheinbrücke, there was a readily available means of *being* free, right in front of him. All he had to do was move forward a pace, and then remember not to swim. It would be a good ending, an appropriate way of marking hers.

His small repertory of talents didn't extend to suicide, though. He had no doubt of his ability to clamber over the rail and step off the narrow ledge, but the bridge was too low for the fall and impact to knock him out, so the moment he hit the water his body would ignore what the mind insisted upon. He didn't know what it was – a clear-eyed view of the world, courage, resignation or despair – that allowed some people to carry through what the strongest human instinct fought against. He admired the iron will that it must require, and regretted that he hadn't tried harder to understand the impulse. If he had, he might have saved himself a deal of grief.

What else was there? He had lost his last tie to the final chance of a new life. The past was interred and unmarked – hell, he was dead to almost everyone who was more than a half-stranger. The present was a hanging moment, and when his half-done task was finished, so was he. He had tried to guess what they might do to him - entertained a small hope that their promises might be worth more than the air they expended upon them. But what they had done to *her* removed any doubt on that score.

An almost-full moon lit the surface of the bridge garishly, picking him out. If they decided they no longer needed him and finished it now, he wouldn't mind. In fact, it would be a neat conclusion - a last stray thread tied painlessly (if his executioner knew his business, and almost certainly he would). His friends would mourn a different death, but that hardly mattered. No doubt Jonas Kleiber would fret for a while, hoping against hope that his baker's telephone might ring; but he was young still, and young hurt mended easily. The right girl would take his mind from bad thoughts, and with luck she'd be English. Then, there'd be no chance of one of their boys starting life with the burden of *Otto*.

At the north end of the Rheinbrücke, partly hidden by the gloom between lamp posts, two large men watched the solitary figure leaning on the safety rail. They had followed him from the restaurant at a discreet distance, deploying long-familiar tricks to stay invisible in plain sight. Each carried a pistol, hidden in an under-arm sling; both kept half their attention on every possible direction from which a witness might stumble upon business that wasn't to be overlooked.

While their target had been pondering the surface of the great river they had shared a cigarette and given an impression of being engrossed in a discussion about nothing in particular. Twice, when he seemed to be emerging from his reverie, they had leaned over the rail and pretended to find the water as interesting as he (though God knew there was little enough in that black, hardly visible expanse to entertain the most ardent hydrographer). They were patient men - they had to be, because this sort of work could never proceed except at the target's pace, and this one didn't seem to need to be anywhere, urgently. When he moved again so would they, and eventually the right circumstances would allow them to conclude the exercise, unseen and undisturbed.

'What the fuck is he doing?'

'Not much. Watching fish. Working out if he left the right tip on the table.'

'We could rush him.'

'It's too far. He'd see us coming and run.'

'Yeah. We should close up, once he's in among people again.'

'That won't be for a while. He'll probably drop down into the park – it's the shortest way back into Bonn.'

'We could lose him there. It isn't well lit.'

'We know where he lives, don't we?'

'Yeah, but if he gets there this thing's going to drag into tomorrow. Here ...' The larger of the two large men pulled a coin from his pocket and placed it on the knuckle of his thumb. '... if it's the eagle we close up as soon as he moves again and take him in the park.'

'Alright. Well?'

'Shit.'

'What?'

'It went into the river.'

'Oh, for fuck's ...'

Fischer opened his eyes. Something had brought him back from guilt, hopelessness and the coast of East Africa, and he couldn't quite say what it was. He glanced to his right. At the other end of the bridge, two men seemed to be having an altercation. Perhaps it had been that, or just the breeze, whispering in his ear that he'd been indulging himself – that it was time to make up his mind about whether he'd stay here forever or just until he became an impediment to traffic. He turned, and made his legs move. A few moments later he was no longer directly above the river, so jumping over the rail now would leave a striking mess in the Rheinaue Park. The thought quite took away the romance of self-murder.

At the first stairs he came to he descended from the bridge road into the park. It was lit only occasionally, along the principal north-south paths, with large areas of darkness to negotiate between. What might lie in wait there didn't interest him, but the prospect of an hour's stumbling around didn't improve his already low mood. He paused, wondering how much longer the route back to his hotel might be if he stayed on the road above, and heard steps above him, descending, getting closer. Already in shadows cast by the metal staircase, he took three paces back and beneath it.

Two men filled the dim illumination between themselves and a path light several hundred metres ahead. Though little about them could be made out, Fischer could see that there *was* nothing little about them. Either could have lifted him off his feet, and probably thrown him into the nearest bushes. It was perfectly possible that they were two respectable citizens of Bonn, taking the air or returning home after an evening's entertainment; this route *was* the quickest back into the city from the bridge, so they had every reason to be moving in the same direction as he. Still, he had no intention of testing his luck. A few minutes earlier, a swift, neat execution had seemed an attractive way out of the morass; now, the prospect's imminence roused that small, inconvenient urge to stay in the world. He held his breath, hoping that neither man would find reason to turn around.

They paused at the foot of the stairs, their backs to him, facing the direction he'd intended to take. One of them whispered to the other, who shook his head and move sideways to improve his angle of sight. It removed the last of Fischer's doubts – they were looking for someone, and there had been no-one else on the bridge but himself. His still-dull mind could only will them forward - far enough to give him at least an outside chance of getting back up to the road and flagging down a passing vehicle.

A frustrated half-sigh broke the tension. 'Come on, or the sod will be back in Bonn before we reach the park gates.'

Fischer let go the breath he'd been holding for too long. The sound sent both men half into the air. They reeled around as he emerged from the shadows.

'Hello, lads.'

Freddie Holleman shook his head and raised a fist. For a moment, Fischer feared he might use it, but fifteen years of something heavier than mere friendship managed to weigh it down again.

'You .. fucking *clown*.'

'I know. I'm sorry.'

26

Chairman Shelepin finished the article and pushed the newspaper away. It had taken a while to read, his conversational English being much more accomplished than his familiarity with the Latin alphabet. He looked up at his deputy.

'Was it our friends in Luanda?'

Semichastny nodded. 'They're in contact with the Mozambique comrades, so when they discovered what the cargo was and where it was going they made the offer. As you can imagine, it was accepted eagerly.'

'And our agents in Luanda?'

'Not consulted. The MPLA knew that a thing like this would have to be agreed at a political level, so ...'

So they went ahead on their own initiative. Referring any decision back to Dzerzhinsky Square would have been time-consuming. It would have needed to go on to the Kremlin also, the decision sent back to the Lubyanka and finally to Luanda, and by then the ship would have long departed. In any case, they almost certainly guessed what Moscow's answer would have been.

Shelepin shook his head. 'How many dead?'

'More than three hundred. The ship went down in several pieces.'

'Mother of God. There's nothing that can be linked to us?'

'I spoke to Sakharovsky. Naturally, he turned First Directorate upside down when he heard about it. None of his people had any warning, so we're spotless. KGB had no part in this, not even by association.'

'But what a mess.'

'And pointless.The Portuguese can always re-supply their colonial forces, so I can't imagine what our friends were thinking, unless they took the opportunity simply because it was *there*. It isn't as though resistance to the regime in Mozambique is even organized, as yet. '

'I want a warning sent to the MPLA. Any more of this pan-African camaraderie nonsense, and we cut them off.'

'That isn't your decision, surely?'

Shelepin smiled. 'They don't know that. Every face-to-face contact they have with the Soviet Union is through KGB. Whatever happens in Angola is their business, tell them. Anywhere else, they consult us before doing *anything*. You can say that Comrades Sakharovsky, Shelepin *and* Khrushchev have been embarrassed by this.'

'They may not like it.'

'And? What will they do – go to the Chinese? Let's see them deliver the revolution with the expired munitions we sent to Mao fifteen years ago.'

Semichastny laughed. It hadn't been that amusing, but he wanted to seem at ease. He had hesitated to bring this to Shelepin because it involved Portugal, and …

'While we're discussing Portuguese matters, where are we with the removal of Herr Fischer?'

Shit. For a few moments the deputy Chairman pretended to search his file. This was a small matter still, and he wanted to keep it that way. A quick, rehearsed answer would be as much as an admission that it was at the forefront of his mind, which would place it in precisely the same place in his boss's head.

'It, ah ... oh, yes.' Semichastny looked up. 'The subject has travelled to the Federal Republic. We lost him briefly, but his ID papers were presented at a hotel in Bonn three days ago. We've had eyes on him since, and we're putting together a local wet team at the moment.'

Shelepin sat up abruptly. 'Bonn? What the hell's he doing there? Is he BND? BfV?'

'If he is, he's behaving very casually – using his own name, visiting the expected sights, dining out alone. It seems to be a vacation. Perhaps he has family or old friends nearby.'

'I've been giving this business further thought. It's …. unusual.' The KGB Chairman rubbed his temple with a thumb. 'A man who escapes decides to return – why? He was Zarubin's man at some point. Is he being brought back into the game.'

'Perhaps, if he needs money.'

'That doesn't seem likely. There'd have to be a great deal of it on offer, to tempt someone back into the fire, and I doubt that Zarubin has the contacts or means to provide anything substantial. And to what purpose? Three years ago, he and Serov were at each other's throats, but now? It isn't as though we're coming after him – in fact, I've deliberately made every show of kissing his hand. Even if he doubts my sincerity, he has no reason to risk the present peace by reactivating his old pawns – and in Germany, for God's sake! It doesn't make sense.'

As Semichastny wasn't supposed to know anything more about the business than Shelepin, it was an invitation to say nothing. His boss pulled a face, rubbed his temple more vigorously, sighed and looked down onto Dzerzhinsky Square. It was a bleak prospect, offering little in the way of inspiration to even the most monochromatic mind, but today it received long and close scrutiny. Minutes passed, and Semichastny spent them willing the other man to move on, to change the subject, to occupy his mind with something that wasn't becoming more trouble to its conceiver than it might be worth. Shelepin was a dogged thinker, though, and didn't let go of a thing until it had been chewed. Eventually, he looked up, and made a start on ruining Semichastny's day.

'What if ...?'

'Yes, Comrade Chairman?'

'This Fischer – what if he *isn't* being reactivated by Zarubin?'

'As I say, he may be on vacation ...'

'No, I mean, what if he's coming back to do harm to the man? He must know things, history that Zarubin would prefer to keep buried. If, as you suggest, he *has* run out of money, wouldn't a subtle threat to spill secrets offer the easiest means of curing the condition?'

Semichastny kept the groan down. Why had he offered a possibility that was now being snatched at? *Say little. Better still, say* nothing - he'd told himself this, over and over, but a conversation had begun and there was no way to kill it. He cleared his throat, and the noise sounded nervous even to his own ears.

'Is that likely? Wouldn't he fear that the General would just disappear him?'

'Which, perhaps, is why he's treading water in Bonn. I wonder if he's sent a message threatening something, and waits for an answer.'

'I doubt that we can determine that, one way or the other.'

Shelepin smiled. 'Unless we grabbed him? If I'm right – and, of course, I may not be – this Fischer may have something explosive that we can re-use against the General. If I'm wide of the mark, we can dispose of the man once we've reassured ourselves. Either way, tell the team you've assembled that their task has changed.'

For a few moments, Semichastny couldn't speak. When first he had mentioned the existence of Otto Fischer it had been to put himself on record, should some other KGB eyes register the man's movements, identify him and report back to Moscow. The risk had seemed slight, however, and he had not expected this to break soil, much less flower into catastrophic prominence. He had intended that Chairman Shelepin half-hear a name and promptly forget it, not blunder into an operation that needed a deft, delicate touch. If they seized Fischer, there was no possibility that the truth could be hidden, disguised or dressed as something other than a rogue initiative with an unmistakeable source. It was the one, cardinal disadvantage to Semichastny holding all the strings in this business – they led only to one hand.

'Well ...' Desperately, he searched for something anodyne yet more than moronic; '... that may present problems.'

'How so?'

'A snatch is always more difficult than a termination, even in neutral territory. The obvious relocation would be from the street to our embassy at Rolandseck, but the place is closely watched. It's also twenty kilometres from central Bonn, which puts the snatch team at risk of interception. We don't have a safe house in Bonn itself, unfortunately.'

'MfS do, surely? We can request squatting rights for a few days.'

'They'll want to know why we're grabbing a German national - particularly, why we didn't put it to Berlin first.'

'I'm sure we can come up with something to sooth their outrage. Why not that this man once worked for KGB? It may well be true.'

A damnably good point. Semichastny pretended to consult his file. Shelepin wasn't going to let go, which left only one option - to make this thing even more problematic than it presently was. That the further step was based (for the first time) on solid intelligence didn't make it any more palatable to the Deputy Chairman.

'There may be another problem.'

'Oh, Christ. What?'

'You told me to dig deeply on Fischer.'

'Yes. And?'

'I went as far as I could with old NKGB and MGB files, but I suspect that Zarubin did some cleaning before he was ousted. Certainly, a lot of what might be expected to form a history isn't there.'

'I know that.'

'So, I asked MfS what they had - specifically, on Otto Fischer, but also on operations involving Zarubin. He was our chief liaison with their predecessors, K-5, back then.'

'An excellent idea. Did they send anything?'

'Yes. Fischer was an associate – a friend, I think – of one of *VolksPolizei*'s senior men in Berlin, Kurt Beckendorp, who worked closely both with Zarubin and K-5. It seems that Fischer spent three years in one of our Special Camps- Sachsenhausen – for an offence that somehow hasn't been recorded. It was Beckendorp who got him out, just a few days after the DDR took over the camps from us.'

'That *is* a good friend. We need to have words with this Beckendorp, obviously. I'll speak to Berlin ...'

'Beckendorp defected, in 1953. On the day of the Uprising, in fact. MfS haven't since been able to track him down, so he may not be in the Federal Republic. And it's possible ...'

'Yes?'

'That his clean escape was at least partly due to Fischer.'

Shelepin sat back and blew out his cheeks. There was an obvious *so …*, but Semichastny wanted it to come from the other man's lips, not his. He was now as far out into the light as he intended ever to be, and needed the cover of a direct order – one that would allow him a little space to finish this business before it exploded in his hands.

His boss scratched his favourite temple and breathed deeply. 'So, MfS will want to get to Fischer as much as we do, if you give them the name.'

Which I have no intention of doing. 'I think that's very likely, yes.'

'Well, it can't be helped. I leave it to you. Speak to Markus Wolf directly, and emphasize that we only waited this long to contact MfS because we weren't – we aren't - certain that Fischer is active again.'

'The interrogation?'

'I don't mind. If MfS want to lead it, that's acceptable. Hell, we may even save the price of disposal, once the man's squeezed dry. You know how hard our budget's being pressed at the moment.'

Shelepin was smiling as their meeting concluded, but Semichastny regarded the pain building between his eyes as a more accurate symptom of where things stood. He'd been offered a little time – liaising with Berlin, and particularly with Marcus Wolf (a man supremely sensitive to jurisdiction), would throw back the schedule by several days at least. It was hardly ideal. He would much have preferred to lay a longer, more robust line of incriminating evidence, but if Herr Fischer could be used for just one more errand it would probably be sufficient to the purpose. After that, he intended to be present during every moment of the man's interrogation, in order to lead the questioning down the correct path. It would require careful judgment, but he comforted himself with the thought that once Fischer was dead, the evidentiary loop established couldn't be broken. KGB would have their triumph, Shelepin would be wafted up to the Council of Ministers and the question of his successor wouldn't detain them for more than a few moments.

27

'I'll kill him.'

'You can't, Freddie – he's dead already.'

'Gerd ...'

'But if there *is* a breath of life still, *I* want to finish him off.'

The object of the two men's affections sat at the other side of the table, one of only six in a small, shabby bar behind the Altes Rathaus. It was one of the few establishments in Bonn open still at 2am on a weekday morning, and served a particularly ferocious line in spirits. Fischer was clutching a half-empty glass of something alleged to be brandy, and intended not to deplete it further. Freddie Holleman and Gerd Branssler had drained their first at the counter, the second on the way to the table and had full glasses in front of them now. So far, they had managed to keep their voices low, but an explosion was imminent.

'*Why*, you cock?'

The answer had been rehearsed over the long trek from the Rheinaue Park, but Fischer didn't yet trust it to sound convincing enough to spare him from one or more punches. It had the strength of being true, and reasonable, and even a little flattering to their friendship, yet all that might mean nothing against the indisputable offence of his having let them mourn him. If he had been sat at their side of the table, he was fairly sure that he'd want to use his fists too.

'Because … I didn't want to put you where I might be going.'

'Which is?'

Fischer pointed downwards, a gesture that couldn't be misinterpreted. 'Anticipating the event seemed the best way of keeping you all out of the way. I suppose it was Jonas who told you?'

'Yeah. He was worried.'

'I didn't want him to be. I suppose I should have said a little about it – but then, he would have been more worried, not less.'

Gerd Branssler threw back his third in one gulp and replaced the glass on the table with surprising delicacy. 'Well, give it to us. *All* of it.'

'KGB found us. I mean, they found Zofia.'

'How?'

'I don't know. I'd assumed that Portugal was safe, but they got a note to me – a note, not a letter, so someone had to put it into the hands of the receptionist at the hotel in Guimarães where I'd set up home, after ...'

'After you and she broke up?'

'I suppose they wanted me to know how close they could come. I got the message. I went down to Porto and met someone - a Latvian, I think. He made an offer, that KGB would forget about her if I came back.'

'Back? For what?'

'To be a go-between. To pass intelligence from the Soviets to the British.'

'And they needed you for that?'

Tired, Fischer rubbed his face. He had turned the thing over until it wrapped itself like string, and all but one possible ending had turned out to be variations on a theme of more or less blind optimism. He hardly wanted to think of it, much less explain himself.

'I couldn't see why, at first. It was presented to me as a simple transaction, one that an idiot couldn't spoil. They have dozens of agents in Europe who could have done it, and with a far better understanding of why. So I thought that perhaps they needed someone who couldn't tell the enemy *why*, if he was compromised. But the business was too straightforward – it *seemed* too straightforward – to need any double-thinking about which knives might be going into which backs. I couldn't work it out, until I looked at it reverse-wise.'

Freddie Holleman - who had been staring into his glass as if trying to place the taste of his poison - looked up. 'What?'

'From the direction that starts with the assumption that it had to be *me*, and no-one else. Why would KGB go to the trouble of following me into hostile territory, do no more than threaten Zofia – whose crimes against them were so much greater than mine – and then offer a way to put it right, the slate wiped clean?'

'They'd need a good reason.'

'Of course they would. Yet the task they presented wouldn't pay off a bus ticket, much less Zofia's debt. She killed two of their own – including an NKVD legend.'

Holleman snorted. 'A legend they'd rather forget about.'

'But one they'd sooner have had drink himself decently to death. They don't appreciate assassinations of their own men, even monsters.'

Forgetting himself, Fischer took another sip of his brandy, winced and pushed it away. 'So, the price of Zofia being left alone seemed light – far too light, if all they wanted was what they asked. Unless, of course, it was for a reason I couldn't see.'

Gerd Branssler gave the eye to a couple of gentleman at a table nearby, whose own conversation had stopped. They returned the favour for a moment, then stood and left the bar. Holleman stared suspiciously at the largely-innocent door as it swung to and then turned back to Fischer.

'Do you know them?'

'No. I'm probably being followed, but I haven't noticed anyone.'

'You're out of practice.'

'I am, certainly. But if someone's on me, they're being very discreet. Unlike those two.'

'So, the reason? Did you find it?'

'Yes, and it told me a lot. The first piece of information I passed to an Englishman was a trifle – some arms shipment to Congolese rebels that Moscow didn't seem to mind being intercepted. The second arrived at my hotel this morning. It's also about the Congo, I think, but in Russian, and a longer piece. It seems to be a briefing paper. And it's signed.'

'Anyone we know?'

'Yes, an old friend - Zarubin.'

'Christ. He survived?'

'Apparently, though perhaps not for much longer.'

Holleman nodded. 'There shouldn't be a signature on stuff that's going to the enemy.'

'Unless it's to incriminate. Naturally, it answers the other question also – about what they intend for me.'

'It won't be a pension, will it?'

'KGB have wanted Zarubin gone for years now. If they're … what do the Americans say?'

'Setting him up?'

'Yes. They can't leave him with any defence, can they? A witness?'

'In fact, you're part of the proof against him.'

'I am. Zarubin's a traitor, and his instrument is an old comrade – one who's going to die, most unfortunately, in the process of bringing this into the light.'

'Very neat. So the price of not cacking Zofia is your arse.'

'They lied, though. Have you seen the newspapers today?'

'What about?'

Briefly – if only to keep his voice from breaking – Fischer told them about Zofia's flight to Africa, and the sinking of the MS *Save*. Both men's eyes widened, and Branssler's *fuck!* was too loud not to be heard by everyone in the bar. For a while, Freddie Holleman seemed incapable of speech (an unprecedented phenomenon). His lips moved, but the conversation was entirely with himself. Eventually, he leaned in towards Fischer.

'Are you sure, Otto? I worked with the bastards – and they *are* bastards – but even they wouldn't kill hundreds for the sake of one score settled. I mean, would they?'

'*Wouldn't* they? The ship was carrying munitions for the Portuguese administration in Mozambique, and the Soviets are now champions of every liberation movement in Africa they can find. So they had at least two good reasons for ...'

'I'm sorry, mate.' Gerd Branssler's massive, gnarled hand came down gently upon Fischer's. 'But there's no reason now to do what they want, is there? Go home, to Portugal – you'll have a chance there, it's your ground. Buy a few guns. If they come for you, blow the bastards to pieces.'

Holleman nodded. 'The Portuguese Government's fascist, yeah? You'll probably get a medal for it.'

Slowly, Fischer shook his head. 'I know I can't do anything to hurt these people, but if I just walked away they wouldn't have a choice. They'd have to keep coming at me – I'm the only solid proof of Zarubin's innocence, aren't I?'

'What will you do, then?'

'I don't know. Get word to the British that they're being played, I suppose. At least then there's a chance that the people in the Lubyanka will be found out, eventually.'

'You'll be dead in a minute.'

'How am I not dead already, Freddie? There's no way out of this. Every plan I had for a future depended upon them not having a strong enough motive to find me. But they *did* find me, and now I'm just about indispensable to their plan – if it's what I think it is. Any decision I make takes me one way.'

Branssler turned to wave over another round of drinks for the table. He brightened suddenly.

'Defect! To the British. Say you've been doing this under duress.'

'And what use would I be to them? I have no intelligence on anything. They'd laugh in my face and wish me the *best* of British.'

'What's that?'

'It means good luck. At least, that's what Jonas told me.'

'There have to be places where KGB can't follow you.'

'Where? The Nazis abandoned New Swabia, so we no longer have an Antarctic territory.'

'Don't be glib. Find yourself another nice little dictatorship, one that tortures communists. Even if KGB found you, they'd think hard before sending in agents who'd end up as dog food.'

'I can't think of one where living wouldn't be another sort of death. Portugal was bearable only because its fascism's a mild, apologetic strain. I couldn't settle where Franco, or Trujillo, or ...'

'He's dead.'

'Trujillo?'

'Someone pointed a machine-gun at him a couple of months back. Didn't you know?'

'I've been distracted. In any case, the Dominican Republic's only a short swim from Cuba, so ...'

'Oh. Yeah.'

'Running's not going to help. The only thing that might work ...'

Holleman slapped the table and beamed at Branssler. 'See? He's thought of something!'

'... is if Zarubin falls, finally and irreversibly, before they get to me. Then, they'd have no reason to tie this loose end.'

'How the hell would that happen?'

'It wouldn't, because I don't have friends in Moscow. It was a thought, that's all.'

The drinks arrived as the three men contemplated the small table's pitted wooden surface. Branssler picked up his glass, sighed, replaced it and waited for the bartender to retreat. He wasn't a man at ease with discretion, but he tried to keep his voice low.

'Fuck a dog's leg! Didn't the three of us make Gehlen's people dance? We should be able to hand the same to KGB.'

Fischer smiled. It was hard not to be raised by wild optimism, even seeing it for what it was.

'That was a long time ago, Gerd. Everything then was so shitwards that no-one really knew where or what was up or down. The mines are laid more closely these days. KGB have grown up and spread out massively - their foreign surveillance pot is probably greater than Gehlen's entire budget was, back then.'

'But ...' Holleman paused, putting his thoughts in order; '... they think they're dealing with one desperate idiot who has no clue what the story is. They don't know that you've worked it out already, that you know what it is they're doing. That means something, doesn't it?'

'Only if there was a way to use it, but I don't see how we can. Yes, I can tell the British to drop it and run, and then run myself. But what will that do? Zarubin will still be a target, Zofia will still be dead and I'd have to learn to live in a hollow log.'

'If you do nothing you're compost – that's for certain.'

'Yes, well ...'

'Me and Gerd have been thinking this out. Whatever we decide, the first thing is you come with us – tonight. We can move you around, keep you hidden, gain time to plan something.'

'You mean, make three refugees out of one?'

'Six eyes are better than two. Gerd?'

Branssler nodded. 'They aren't going to send a battalion after you, are they? You're not Trotsky. Me and Freddie can cover your back while we drag some brilliant idea out of its dark corner.'

Fischer shook his head. They were right, and wrong. He wouldn't be as vulnerable with two very large men - one police still, one ex-*kripo* – watching the horizons. If, however, KGB wanted him dead badly enough they'd find a way, and ensure that there were no surviving witnesses to the act. Both men were grandfathers, and had a great deal more to lose than he. He looked up.

'I didn't ask – is this a flying visit, or have you got somewhere to stay?'

'An old comrade from our Berlin beat days, he has a farm outside Lohmar. We put up with him the day before yesterday. It's only a fifteen-minute drive, but we can't hide you there.' Branssler pulled a face. 'His wife's ready to kill us already, on account of the catching up we did on the first night.'

Holleman grinned. 'We caught up to the floor, face-first.'

'Alright.' Fischer stood. 'You go back there tonight. I have to hand over this latest gift to the Englishman tomorrow. I won't say anything to him for now, but time – my time – is probably tightening.'

'You won't run?'

'If I can't run from them, Freddie, I can't see a reason to run from you. Except to save myself the earache, of course.'

'Don't be clever. I'm still thinking of killing you for being dead.'

'I promise I'll stay. Who else knows that you're here?'

'Just our wives. We agreed not the tell the children.'

'Kristen and Greta didn't mind you doing this?'

Holleman and Branssler looked at each other. 'They called you plenty of names. But they didn't think it was a thing that could be left alone.'

'They may change their minds about that. We'll meet tomorrow, at 3pm, in the basilica in Münsterplatz - it always seems to be busy, but there are spaces where we can't be overheard. You're both carrying, aren't you?'

Two hands moved instinctively, betraying the answer. Fischer shook his head. 'Leave them in the car, next time. If there's trouble and you get me arrested, no-one will have a use for me any more. But everyone will know where to find me.'

28

'I wonder if you *ever* relax, General.'

Zarubin tried to raise his head and turn it towards the gentleman who put this half-question, but the professional wrestler's thumbs were deep into the tissue at either side of his occipital bone, making any movement likely to sever his spinal cord. He kept his face on its padded rest, directly above the newspaper article he was trying to read.

'I'm easily bored when nothing occupies my attention, Comrade Third Minister. This is just a *little* work, to take my mind from the pain.'

The hint didn't ease the pressure on his neck, and Comrade Third Minister groaned slightly as his own torturer applied a little more brute force to a tender part. He had been at the spa for almost eight weeks, apparently, trying to have several years' over-indulgence of just about every socialist vice – fine food, tobacco, strong drink and the company of women who did not share his surname – sweated, beaten and floated out of his corpulent frame. To all of this he admitted cheerfully, by way of introducing himself to new arrivals. Zarubin had heard it all four days earlier, even before he'd had a chance to unpack his valise and admire the vista from his window. The Minister's suite was directly opposite his own, a mirror-image, though as a high-ranking official of the Defence Ministry (whose facility this was), his had the benefit of a lake-view, rather than the woodland his reluctant new friend was obliged to endure.

An amiable man, he appeared to have a dread of silence, and Zarubin had made a start on planning his own treatments so as to minimize the time they spent in each other's company. Complete success was impossible, though, and all meals being taken in the hotel's vast dining-room (during which searches of patients' rooms were made to seize contraband foodstuffs), there was ample opportunity to enjoy lengthy reminiscences about the War, departmental politics and the talents of one Valentina Federova, wife of a junior Ministry official. It was during a protracted description of her methods of entertaining up to three men simultaneously that Zarubin began to long for some – any - occasion short of nuclear conflict with the United States that might get him recalled urgently to Moscow.

This morning, however, his voluble would-be friend was somewhat subdued. The latest sweep of his suite had uncovered an emergency supply of Lindt & Sprüngli chocolate, and without its blood-sugar-raising qualities he struggled to keep any story moving beyond its natural span. The question he'd asked was uncharacteristic - it indicated interest in something other than himself, and implied a readiness to hear an answer - and Zarubin was so struck by this phenomenal event that he felt bound to offer a little more than his first, conversation-killing comment. He picked up the newspaper and waved it.

'The *New York Times* – Seymour Topping's article on the Vienna Summit. An interesting piece.'

'Ah. I don't read English. Is the gentleman pleased or dismayed by his President's performance?'

'Worried, I should say. A little comforted by the joint statement on Laos that they issued; much less so by the First Secretary holding out the possibility of war between our two great nations.'

'Hm. Well, war's a terrible thing, certainly.'

'Is it the Defence Ministry's opinion that we're ready for war?'

The Third Minister laughed. 'We're never *ready* for war. But neither are the Americans – and of course, they won't have all the time they need to prepare, as they have in previous wars. Oceans are no barrier to long-range bombers, or missiles. In an exchange, our far greater landmass and ability to exist on smaller resources will be a great advantage.'

The reference to previous wars surprised Zarubin. It was an obvious point yet he hadn't considered it. Had Khrushchev, though? Was his bullish mood partly based on an insane belief that an atomic war might possibly be survived? To Zarubin, the implied threat had seemed to be the same bluster with which the man habitually conducted foreign policy; but what if it had been more than that? What if the pain of several failed bluffs had worked on the man's ego to a point beyond prudence, and even rationality?

No-one yet knew how to calculate the effects of a war using atomic weapons. Enough warheads existed to make much of the planet a wasteland, yet the present generation of leaders had seen wastelands recover. The Soviet Union was by far the largest nation on Earth; its forests could - and did - hide places where men might expect not to be targets. The United States was much smaller, and, more importantly, its principal cities and industrial centres were clustered unwisely. Bombs falling on Moscow would remove the seat of an already fled government; a clutch falling around Baltimore – perhaps of the monster RDS-220s currently approaching testing phase - would lay waste to Washington and much of the hinterland that supplied New York, leaving government, finance and a large part of the East Coast's maritime supply chain smashed. It was an obscene, unthinkable calculation, but if Zarubin could make it, why not others close to Khrushchev? He might not seriously be considering going to war, but many politicians who suddenly found themselves in the middle of one could say the same. To accept a possibility, however theoretical, was to take a first, long step towards it – and the next conflict wouldn't be one that a backward step could halt or reverse.

Suddenly, Zarubin wanted to force himself upright, find a telephone and dictate another briefing paper to his secretary. Instead, he breathed deeply, slowly, and asked himself - who would care to read the thoughts of a man so far removed from the heart of things as to be wearing a bath towel at 10.30am? It was only a theory, after all. At Vienna, Khrushchev, blinded by his apparent success in cowing the callow President, may simply have allowed his mouth a little too much leeway (though the fact that his comment and Kennedy's response were reported was unfortunate). Perhaps he just wanted to see how the younger man reacted. Perhaps all their futures weren't hanging on anyone's whim, or pride.

'You seem very thoughtful, Comrade General. Is the article *that* interesting?'

'Oh, no. I was thinking about what might have piled up in my absence.'

'Ha! It's only been a few days. You need to get the knots out of your neck, not worry about the coal-face. It's what you're here for, isn't it?'

The Third Minister was correct, of course. Zarubin hadn't wanted to come to Tskaltubo, but it would be absurd not to take advantage of the excellent facilities. The food (though undoubtedly healthy) was excellent, vodka was not permitted anywhere on site but a modest amount of wine was provided at meal times, the various treatments were administered by professionals and the tennis courts, laid out only the previous year, wouldn't have disgraced Forest Hills. Any unasked-for exile was something to be endured, but the Soviet Union had far, far less agreeable alternatives to test a man's patience than this.

He pushed the newspaper on to the floor and allowed his tormentor to complete the separation of his vertebrae. He had telephoned Levin every day since his arrival, and heard nothing that should worry him. Even the hint of a threat would have exploded his secretary's fraught nerves, so the Yellow Box was almost certainly undiscovered still and KGB hadn't yet begun to test the perimeters. But then, why should they hurry whatever surprise they had in mind? He was going to be here for five weeks more, and Comrades Shelepin and Semichastny knew that. They were careful, methodical men, and all their plans were well-considered.

If they were planning something. The breathing exercises recommenced. Zarubin couldn't recall when, if ever, he'd felt as helpless as now. Even his first day at the Front in summer 1941, supervising an intelligence unit tasked with kidnapping German soldiers (to give Stalin some clue as to which vast part of the Red Army would next be encircled and shot to pieces), hadn't seemed quite as fraught with opportunities for extinction as his present situation. He was older now, with an older man's fear of losing what he'd managed to grab, but it wasn't just that. Perhaps he had stretched too far, and was seeing the chasm more clearly than before. He wondered now whether he should have tried harder to repair his burned bridges, or at least not lobbed so many stones from the opposite bank.

If onlys being the most sterile form of self-torture, he forced himself to think about lunch, though it required little consideration. A fixed menu was circulated to the inmates, or guests, each morning, presumably to whet or crush appetites. The offering was invariably a soup or fish course, followed by a meat dish dressed with salad. The Third Minister had made his low opinion of this regime quite clear (using a pleasingly wide vocabulary), but Zarubin, who ate to satisfaction rather than immobility, had been perfectly happy with the non-choices to date. A few more weeks of the regime might temper his enthusiasm; for that matter, a few more days of having nothing worthwhile to occupy his mind might make Valentina Federova's unusual tastes and abilities of more interest than presently they were.

Naturally, boredom was amplifying his anxieties. Had he been sat in his Kremlin office he would have surveyed the same ground with a more dispassionate eye, and not allowed every worst possibility a front seat in his head. In this Georgian paradise, time slowed and stretched to over-accommodate a man's yearning to get back into the world – a yearning that only increased as his back loosened, his skin and circulation improved and his belly retreated to its natural frontiers.

'Oh, God.'

'Did you say something, Comrade General?'

'Not really, no. Have you looked at today's activities schedule?'

The Third Minister waved a hand at his masseur, and the man retreated far enough for the patient to sit up.

'There's a presentation on the implementation of mass-scale prefabrication technologies to solve the housing crisis. That's immediately after lunch, in the ballroom. I'm told the subject is sufficiently exciting to stop healthy hearts.'

'So you'll be avoiding it?'

'Like syphilis. But there's also a small excursion into the woods above Tavshava, leaving at three. I might join it.'

'An excursion?'

'A deer-stalk. Will you come?'

As a boy, Zarubin had been dragged to the hunt often by his uncle, a man who believed firmly that humanity retained all of its primordial instincts. The theory was certainly correct with regard to himself, being in every sense a beast (many years later, his nephew had experienced no regret or revulsion when arranging his destruction). Animals, however, excited no sanguinary impulses in Zarubin. He ate and enjoyed meat as part of his natural diet, but he had never found the act of killing the beast to improve either its flavour or his digestion of the same. Nor did he believe that the heads of slain animals were suitable ornaments for a home, and if he wore a fur hat in winter it was because it did a better job of keeping his head warm than the alternatives. It was his opinion that, in their present age, Man the Hunter was as artificial a construct as Man the Cosmonaut or Stalin the Wise Father, and as much to be emulated.

On the other hand, he was horribly bored, over-anxious about matters he couldn't influence and afraid that becoming familiar with the challenges of mass-scale prefabrication technologies would prise a final finger off the cliff's edge. Under the circumstances, killing something could hardly dampen his mood.

'Yes, that would be delightful.'

It was during their second meeting that Roger Broadsmith was able to form an opinion regarding Otto Fischer. *Gauge the man*, he had been told, and he decided now that the man was nervous, or at least uneasy, about something. Two days earlier he had been relaxed, as if their business had been a trifling thing. Unless he was the sort of person who allowed a change in the weather to affect his mood, part of his, or *the*, situation had changed in some way.

Why it had changed was Harold Shergold's job to lose sleep about, but at least the observation would put a tick on Broadsmith's homework. As for Fischer's latest package, he had photographed its contents for *Cuttlefish* and sent the original on to London immediately thereafter. Moscow hadn't bothered to translate this one, and he didn't read Russian. It looked more substantial than its predecessor, so perhaps they were getting more serious.

He had also sent on to Broadway a note of his second meeting with BfV's Herr Waldmann, containing an offer from the gentleman. This, quite predictably, proposed that an inter-Service committee be formed to examine further the ways in which SIS and BfV could work together, and to what end. It went no further than that, but Broadsmith would happily have followed Cyril Pearce's example - had a bookie been willing to take the bet - and put his entire month's salary on a geological schedule of meetings, counter-meeting and meetings to summarize the progress of meetings being all that came from it. SIS would need to drag this bride to the altar – if not kicking and screaming, then definitely clutching at every pew she passed on the way.

Why are they bothering to try? Waldmann's indifference pushed the old question to the fore once more. Why the hell hadn't Broadway just swallowed their old distaste for General Gehlen and tried to form a working relationship with BND – a fellow foreign intelligence agency? All that BfV cared about was the Federal Republic's internal security – that, and not getting absorbed into BND. SIS had been compromised by the Soviets, BfV by the East Germans; where was the utility in two penetrated, humiliated organizations collaborating, unless it was to share the pain?

Yet again, he had to remind himself that he shouldn't care. His job was to *do* the job, however badly thought-out it appeared to be, and if BfV were wasting SIS's time he could hardly be condemned for it. He had taken the knee like a suitor, hinted at riches to be shared, played up the value that Broadway placed upon this relationship and given not the slightest hint that he regarded the business with no less indifference than Waldmann himself. Everything had been presented upon the silver salver, and if the Germans didn't like it they couldn't blame the waiter. As far as was in his power he had ensured that this would be an earnest, creditable failure, the sort that Englishmen regard almost as a kind of success.

Unless something was lurking, as yet unsaid by either side, the courtship wasn't going to drag out until the end of the month, much less the six suggested in his briefing. How had Shergold and Dickie White got it so wrong? They were astute men, not prone to seeing the world as they wished it might be, rather than it was. Broadsmith could hardly believe that they'd agreed to this pantomime, much less conceived it. But here he was - enjoying the scenery, practicing his German and achieving nothing.

His thoughts returned to Otto Fischer, the only interesting object on his present horizon. A declared enemy posing as a would-be friend, bearing gifts that didn't hold up to scrutiny, and now apparently disturbed by some matter. The best training couldn't allow a man into another's head, so Broadsmith applied himself to what it wasn't likely to be about. He could rule out guilt or remorse; Fischer's accent placed him as an East German, probably a Balt, so there could hardly be an ideological issue. Nor was it likely to be nerves. However insincere Moscow might be, they wouldn't have trusted this business to a novice, much less …

An unpleasant thought intruded forcibly. This was a German, working for Moscow – *someone* in Moscow – on German soil, and Broadsmith had told his *Stasi* handler about him. Had Berlin got on to the man already? Was Fischer good enough to know when he was being surveilled? Had they come so close as to speak to him?

Christ. MfS wouldn't dare harm a Soviet agent, but if Fischer was aware of their attention he would be wondering *how* they knew, and unless he was an idiot he could hardly fail to regard Roger Broadsmith as the leading suspect. What would he do with *that*?

The unfamiliar feeling returned, stronger and more well-defined than before. He tried to convince himself that KGB and MfS were close allies, so even if there was a jurisdictional issue neither would betray the other's agents. But when Shergold had put the obvious question, Fischer said that he was speaking, not for KGB, but 'Moscow'. God knew, there was nothing monolithic about Soviet politics - as mysterious as the Praesidium fondly imagined itself to be, even British Intelligence had been aware of much of the infighting after Stalin's death and again in '57. Whatever their motives, it was hardly inconceivable that someone in Red Square was playing a game without giving the nod to their KGB brethren (not least, to prevent them interfering). And, if that were the case, would they hesitate if *Stasi*'s only British agent needed to be sacrificed to protect their lead pawn?

The near-nonchalance that, for several years, had shaved the edges from Broadsmith's double-life felt more like crass stupidity now. How the hell could he have thought himself untouchable? If Moscow decided he had to be flushed out, it wouldn't require the expenditure of a single bullet. Broadway was convinced that Blake wasn't the final traitor on their payroll, so even an anonymous denunciation would meet willing ears, and what defence did he have? That his betrayals had been anodyne to date? That he was an oddity – a British intelligencer picked up almost accidentally by MfS, who hadn't since seemed to know quite what to do with him? At best it might half-convince them, and earn him a mere twenty-year tariff rather than Blake's forty.

A small core of panic had nested in his chest, and his eyes flitted around the office that BfV had given him for the duration of his stay in Bonn. It was the end room in an unfrequented corridor - heavily carpeted, acoustically-deadened – a place where, probably, he was expected to cause the least inconvenience to them by sleeping though his assignment. Until now he had appreciated its soporific, soothing charm, but stillness was a deadly illusion if things were happening behind and around him. His chest told him he had to do something, yet the urge came with no revelation as to what *something* might be. Should he attempt to silence Fischer? Run? Tell MfS that he had been blown, and might he come to spend the rest of his life somewhere east of the Curtain – at their expense, of course?

It might just be a bad tooth, for God's sake. With difficulty, he returned to the casual observation that had thrown him into this funk. A bad breakfast, a fled wife, haemorrhoids, new shoes, an ill-advised flutter on the horses - a man could be in a mood for a hundred reasons. It might even be that Fischer was in a funk of his own, having been recognized by BND or BfV, and wondering when he was going to be picked up. The possibilities, Broadsmith told himself, far outnumbered the nightmares.

His thinking became less cloudy as he grew calmer. There were options available to him. *Cuttlefish* could tell him whether word of Fischer's mission had been passed on to Berlin already and agents assigned to monitor him. It was possible, even likely, that Ruschestrasse would liaise with KGB, to put them on to whatever the hell was going on in Red Square. Even if Broadsmith himself was regarded as a low-value asset by MfS (and of absolutely no value by the mysterious players in Moscow), protocols mattered. Making waves for their own sake wasn't what intelligencers did.

He had asked Fischer when the next package was due, but received no answer. When one knows little, the temptation always is to assume that others knows more; but what if the German stood in similar darkness? He was, after all, acting the mirror-image of Broadsmith's passive messenger-boy, handling information about which he might have not the slightest understanding. Perhaps *that* was what troubled him, and not piles, or tight footwear, or fear than his contact had ratted on him.

If - *if* - they had that in common, there was an opportunity here. Shergy would no doubt urge it – to gain Fischer's empathy, if not quite his trust. Even if it shifted him only slightly, the man might say more than was strictly to the point and partly lift the present veil. That would help Broadway of course, but, more importantly, it would give Broadsmith a better idea of how close to discovery he had wandered.

30

'I have a plan.'

Surprised, both Fischer and Gerd Branssler turned in their pew to Holleman, who sat immediately behind them.

'We do a proper surveillance job, but on Otto. Sooner or later, someone from KGB's going to be coming after him. We take him, or them, use our fists and get them to tell us what the score is.'

Fischer sighed. 'Freddie, I'm almost sixty-four years old. You're fifty-nine, with just the one leg. So either creeping up on the bad men or running after them's going to be a challenge. Gerd's the hard man, but he's ...'

'Seventy, next year.'

'Which makes him a lot slower than he used to be, and probably stiffer.'

Branssler nodded ruefully. 'My shoulders hurt, most of the time. But I could still kick the face off a statue.'

'The men that KGB send after me won't be from their Methuselah Directorate. They'll be young, tough fellows, well-armed and looking in all directions at once. Your only chance will be for them to mistake you for their grandfathers and hesitate before shooting you.'

'We're not *that* old, you cheeky bast ...'

'In any case, we don't know when they'll be coming for me.'

'When you've passed on the final package.'

'Yes, but I doubt they'll warn me when that is.'

'We could ...'

'What?'

Branssler glanced around to check that the worshippers were at a discreet distance.

'Keep eyes on your hotel. The packages are always dropped at reception, yes? We follow whoever delivers the next one and get them that way.'

Reluctantly, Fischer gave it more than the single thought. The messenger might be an innocent, hired for two minutes' work; or very culpable, and clever enough to smell pursuit. His colleagues might be a team of two or three, looking for anyone showing an interest. Their orders could very well be to erase a tail immediately, before he could pass word back to Fischer, his SIS contact, BfV, BND, CIA or any passing logistician researching the incidence of packages dropped off at hotels in Bonn on any given day. All of that acknowledged, it was the closest to a plan they had yet conceived.

'One of you would need to stay well back, to cover the other.'

'Freddie's the slowest, so I'll be the rearmost eyes. And that way, he'll be more likely than me to get cacked.'

'Thanks, Gerd. What if he sprints away from me?'

'Then we'll know he isn't just some blameless cock they paid to do the errand. If you don't make any obvious effort to follow him you won't be noticed by his friends, and when he comes again with a package we can grab him inside the hotel.'

Holleman brightened. 'We can torture him in Otto's room.'

'The Management won't like that. What we could do – *if* we get that far – is to quieten him and wait for his mates to arrive. If they don't, then we'll know he's on his own. You can bring your car in behind the premises, and get him out of Bonn.'

The other two men nodded slowly, liking it. A movement at Fischer's extreme peripheral vision caught his attention, and he turned towards the nave. His young friend, Jeri the pious room-maid, was waving timorously in his direction. He returned the smile and half-raised his own hand, a gesture that caused two heads to follow.

'You dirty old sod! You haven't wasted any time.'

'She's about eighteen, Freddie, and not remotely aroused by decrepitude. She works at the hotel.'

'What's she doing here?'

'Thanking God for her drudge's life, I expect. She comes every day.'

'She's very sweet.'

'Should I tell Kristin you said that?'

'A man can look, can't he?'

Branssler had been regarding Jeri more thoughtfully than the lecherous Holleman. 'Is she a friend, then?'

'Sympathetic, I'd say. There's also the man who runs the hotel, Armin. I think he can be trusted not to say anything, if ...'

'Well, that's one direction covered, at least. Now, where can we put you, to solve this?'

'Put me?'

'When it's over. Will you return to Portugal?'

'How could it ever be over, Gerd?'

'Pretend that it might. Will you?'

'Why? There's nothing there now.'

'Paraguay, then. You could meet a nice *Bund Deutscher Mädel* breeder, and make lots of Aryan babies.'

'I think women are done with me, Freddie. And I'm certainly done with the Reich.'

'What about the US? It's big enough to get lost in. And if it's too noisy you can head north, to Canada. We'll visit - won't we?'

'If he wants us.'

'You're both thinking too optimistically. There are thirty possible endings to this story. Twenty-nine of them put me in a ditch, the other one relies upon KGB forgetting what it is they do best.'

Holleman shook his head. 'They're only men. And we're on home ground.'

'They're only *thousands* of men. And how could any German ground be *home*, in 1961?'

'Christ, Otto! We have a plan now, don't we?'

'We have what we hope will stop their first attempt to kill me. Do you think they'll be put off by that, or is there a chance they'll try again, harder?'

Branssler opened his mouth and closed it without speaking, which was sufficiently out of character for the other men to notice.

'What is it?'

'I get what you're saying, Otto, but ...'

'There's a but?'

'You seem more, well, *vergnügt* than yesterday.'

Holleman nodded. 'I was going to say that. Like you dropped a turd and picked up a pfennig. It's not much, but your mood's lighter than it was.'

'Not lighter. I had an idea a few days ago. It didn't seem practical, but the more I circle it the more hopeful it looks. With the help of you two cocks, it might have a chance. A very small chance.'

'Tell us, then.'

'Not yet. I want to find the holes, first.'

'Fuck your mother! We're not going to sit on our fat arses, waiting while you play the Moltke. Tell us what's in your head.'

Fischer regretted having said anything. That *hopeful* might be infinitesimal, or even illusory. It had nothing to recommend it other than that it appeared to be the only possibility left to him - a sole, not-quite-a-path out of the forest into which he'd been dragged. It relied upon a half-dozen happy circumstances converging at a point that wasn't out of reach, or heavily overlooked by KGB ordnance; above all, it required the complicity of someone who couldn't be influenced or even read. In sum, it was hardly worth the price of the headache it was giving him, much less the abuse his friends would …

Briefly, he outlined his thoughts to his friends. When he had finished, they regarded him carefully. Eventually, Branssler pulled a face and shrugged.

'Well, that would do it – if it worked.'

Holleman shook his head. 'You daft *muschi*! Gehlen himself couldn't arrange something like that, much less you – or us!'

'Of course he couldn't, because he wouldn't know where or how to begin - and if he did, he'd hit a wall the moment he started. But I do, and if we're lucky we can climb the thing, once it looms.'

'I don't see what advantage we could have, Otto.'

'We know the problem, Gerd. General Gehlen doesn't.'

Holleman's head was still moving from side to side. Usually, any idea that had little chance of success appealed to his impulsive nature, but this one had failed to gain hold.

'We'd need an army – *and* an air force.'

'Not if we're persuasive.'

'Who could be *that* persuasive?'

'Me, Freddie. It isn't as though I don't have a convincing argument.'

'Are you sure? About the argument?'

'Almost. We need to examine the next package carefully.'

'It may be in Russian.'

'You know a little, don't you?'

Holleman shrugged. 'I can make out names, but the grammar's beyond me.'

'That should be enough. Until then, we tread water.'

'So, do we grab the messenger or not?'

'Not yet, and perhaps not at all. If this works we may not need to go to war with KGB – at least, not from a direction they'd notice. But follow him, if you can.'

Branssler and Holleman grinned at each other. 'Like our beat days in Berlin, before Adolf spoiled everything.'

Fischer frowned. 'And try not to enjoy yourselves.'

If, in the old days, a Deputy Chairman of KGB had wished to speak to anyone in MfS, a peremptory summons would have had the man on a 'plane to Moscow within the hour. Now, of course, the organizations pretended to be more or less equal partners in the struggle against capitalist aggression (though KGB continued to maintain liaison officers in every MfS Directorate), so Semichastny had telephoned Markus Wolf and asked politely if he might fly to Berlin to consult on an urgent matter. It was no less a demand than anything his predecessors might have said, but the courtesies had to be observed.

Five hours later, the two men sat in an office in Ruschestrasse, sipping tea. They were well known to each other; Wolf had been an attache at the DDR's Moscow Embassy in the early 50s, at the same time that Semichastny was working with Shelepin at Komsomol headquarters, and two men of such similar age and expectations couldn't help but collide at the same, very few parties that the city's starved social calendar could offer.

Wolf had entered their game far earlier than Semichastny, and prospered. MfS's foreign intelligence department - *Hauptverwaltung Aüfklarung* – was almost entirely his creation, and though he reported to Minister Mielke, the latter was happy to ask few questions and play out as much line as his gifted subordinate required. Semichastny wished fervently that he enjoyed the same leeway within KGB, and never so much as at the moment.

'This is a pleasant surprise, Vladimir Yefimovich. I assume the weather's too oppressive in Moscow?'

'Actually, it's unseasonably mild. But Berlin in July is always a treat for me. How are Emmy and young Franz?'

'Doing very well, thank you. When are we going to see *you* dragged to the altar?'

'When I can spare a day to fall in love. Which won't be soon, I fear.'

They spoke in Russian, naturally. In 1934, when his Jewish communist father had fled the new regime in Germany with his family and few, faint hopes, Wolf had been only ten years old. The Soviet Union had taken in the boy, raised and educated him, shoved him in the right direction (that is, towards Comintern and away from the ultra-Marxist German émigré colony in Moscow) and made him the voice of German People's Radio, broadcasting propaganda into the Reich. With the coming of peace they had been almost sorry to see him go. Without doubt, he was regarded as 'one of us' - as trusted by the Lubyanka as he was at Ruschestrasse. It was why Chairman Shelepin had wanted the thing explained to him, and not merely handed down as a *dictat*.

Of course, what Semichastny was about to explain wasn't quite what his boss expected, and he squirmed slightly. There was always a chance that

Wolf would refuse point-blank to participate in such a wantonly off-the-books operation - or, worse, pick up the 'phone, ask Shelepin if he had any idea what his deputy was playing at and offer to arrest the man while he was sitting conveniently in front of him.

It's a timing issue – that's all. Semichastny cleared his throat.

'Markus, we've been monitoring a German national for some time now. He was involved in an unfortunate matter three years ago, and – at various times – in other, quite badly-documented operations that may or may not have compromised KGB interests.'

'A mysterious man.'

'Yes, and probably because someone took pains to make him so – him, or, more likely, the operations themselves. We don't believe that he *is* anyone, per se.'

'But you want him, because …?'

'He may be in contact still, and working with, his former principal.'

'Who *is* someone, I assume?'

The unpleasant moment had arrived, a little too quickly. Wolf was no kind of fool. The business would hardly require the attention or presence in Berlin of KGB's Deputy Director if this someone wasn't really *someone*, so Semichastny wasn't going to be able to throw out any sort of shit and then ask him to proceed. He would want to know who, and why, and how it was that *Stasi* were being dragged into this late, and at such short-notice.

'You'll have heard of General Zarubin?'

'The First Secretary's American specialist? Of course. In fact, I've met him several times.'

'I didn't know that.'

'A long time ago. I was covering the Nuremberg Trials for German People's Radio. He was NKGB, newly transferred from what he called the World's Arsehole – Stettin. I found him to be pleasant company, but I can see how KGB might think differently.'

'He *is* pleasant company – a very amusing man, and not at all vain about his achievements. But he's also an individualist, usually convinced that he knows more than anyone else.'

Wolf smiled faintly. 'I take it that his defection to the Americans still rankles in the Lubyanka?'

Semichastny shrugged. 'For some it's like an open wound, but time is gradually removing those who feel it the most. My own concern – and that of Comrade Shelepin – is that his opinions still carry greater weight than they should.'

Wolf nodded slowly. 'And this man you've tracked – he's abetting Zarubin in some way?'

'Almost certainly not. As far as I can ascertain, he and the General haven't been in contact since the man fled Berlin, in '58.'

'Then why …?'

Semichastny breathed deeply. 'A chance sliver of intelligence placed him in northern Portugal, living as a farmer. I managed to get a man to him.'

'Why isn't he dead, then?'

'I had a different idea. It seemed to me that his former association with Zarubin could be used.'

'To incriminate, you mean.'

'We believe that the General almost certainly assisted the man's escape from Berlin three years ago, shortly before he was to be apprehended, or possibly terminated, on the orders of Ivan Serov. During this mess, we lost two field officers, one of whom died. The other – a female - disappeared. Subsequently, we discovered that she was also living in northern Portugal.'

'Ah. So this operation will cauterize more than one wound.'

'If successful, yes. Zarubin will be implicated in the passing of intelligence to the British. His former associate will be arrested and disappeared.'

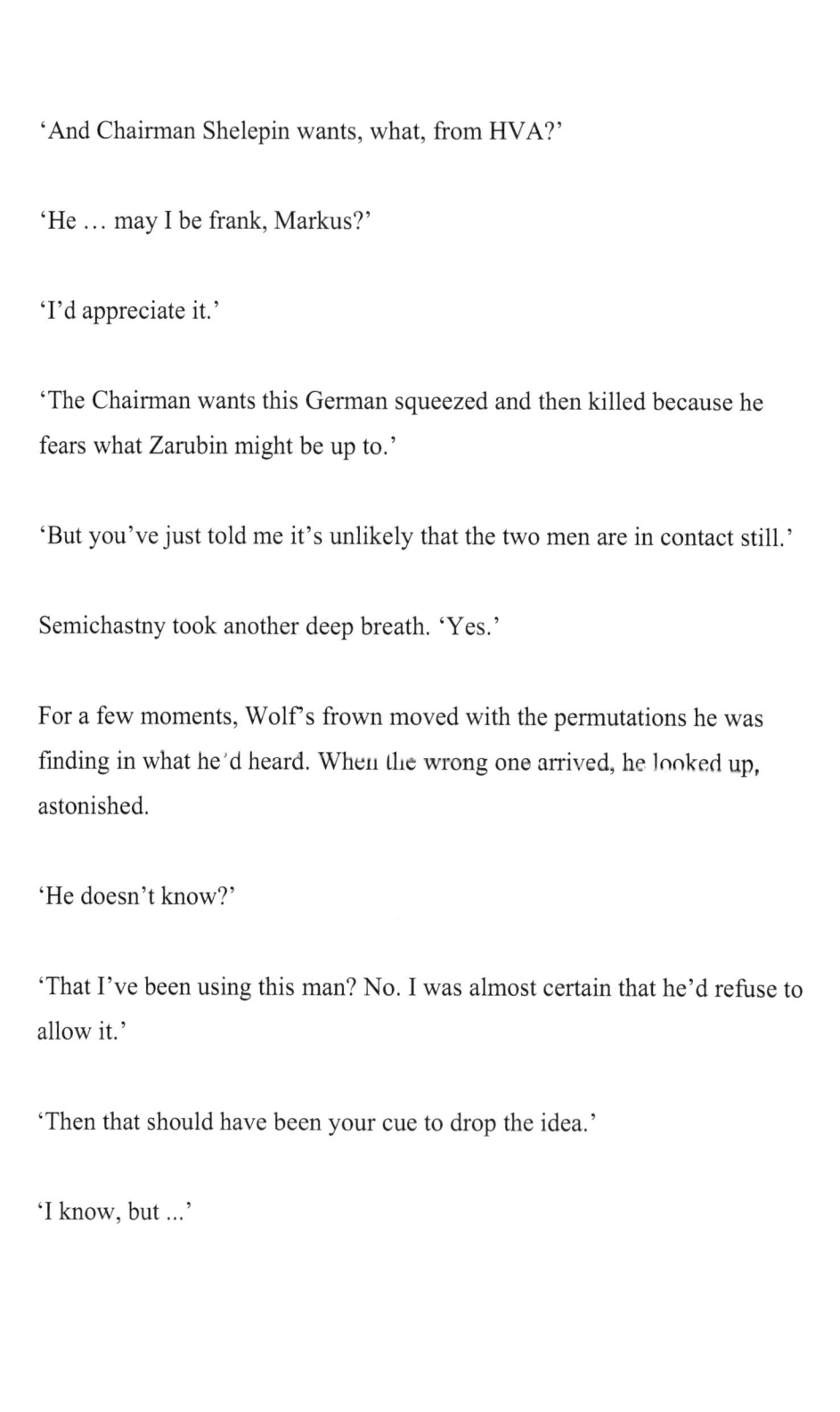

'And Chairman Shelepin wants, what, from HVA?'

'He … may I be frank, Markus?'

'I'd appreciate it.'

'The Chairman wants this German squeezed and then killed because he fears what Zarubin might be up to.'

'But you've just told me it's unlikely that the two men are in contact still.'

Semichastny took another deep breath. 'Yes.'

For a few moments, Wolf's frown moved with the permutations he was finding in what he'd heard. When the wrong one arrived, he looked up, astonished.

'He doesn't know?'

'That I've been using this man? No. I was almost certain that he'd refuse to allow it.'

'Then that should have been your cue to drop the idea.'

'I know, but …'

'But? What *buts* could there be? An unauthorized operation that involves one of the First Secretary's closest advisors? What were you thinking?'

'He's not that, exactly. Your point is well taken, Markus, but please, let me finish.'

The expression on Wolf's face suggested that this was a conversation he wanted entirely unsaid rather than pressed, but he sat back and waited.

'Chairman Shelepin has made a vigorous effort to move KGB away from the attitudes and practices of his predecessors. I think you'll agree that this was necessary?'

Wolf nodded.

'When he was first appointed, Comrade Khrushchev made it clear to him – explicit, even – that foreign policy in particular was solely within the purview of the Council of Ministers and the First Secretary himself. In future, the Lubyanka was not to regard itself as having a voice therein. Chairman Shelepin has obeyed that directive to the letter. KGB gathers, collates and presents intelligence that allows these parties to make decisions; it does not offer recommendations on what their decisions should be. Which, of course, is entirely correct.'

'I agree.'

'Good. Unfortunately, we have Zarubin. He, along with former KGB Chairman Serov, was instrumental in removing Beria and ensuring

Comrade Khrushchev's accession to the First Secretaryship. I assume you're aware of that?'

'We know the broad details. The specifics weren't ever committed to record, I believe.'

'No, they weren't. Subsequently, Serov's past became an embarrassment, but General Zarubin has continued to enjoy the trust and confidence of the First Secretary, even if his advice is not always welcomed unreservedly. Recently, he's found himself increasingly at odds with voices arguing for a more forceful policy towards American adventurism.'

'Those would be the voices of Gromyko, Kosygin and others, I expect.'

'And others, yes. We might also add Walter Ulbricht to the list.'

'Our Chairman doesn't make Kremlin policy.'

'No, but he influences it. The matter of sealing Berlin is coming to a head, I think?'

'It appears to be so, yes.'

'A wall will make things ... difficult for MfS, won't it?'

Wolf shrugged. 'Like KGB, MfS doesn't set policy. We merely implement those political decisions that fall within our area of responsibility.'

'But when political decisions are made – or influenced – by those outside the political process? What then?'

'You're speaking of Zarubin once more?'

'I don't suggest that he's necessarily a bad or damaging influence. In different times, his circumspection can be a valuable counter to more impulsive voices. But these are the times we have. In Berlin, the Caribbean and much of Africa, urgent decisions based upon partial or fragmentary data will need to be made in the coming months. Our First Secretary has many virtues, but his few vices include a tendency to move impulsively and then, strangely, to allow second thoughts prior to the manoeuvre's resolution. The latter quality is often complicated by Zarubin's input.'

'Alright.' Wolf sat forward. 'What, exactly, do you intend and want?'

'Assistance in taking Zarubin's German. He's currently in Bonn. His name ...'

'Is Otto Fischer – a half-faced gentleman.'

Astonished, Semichastny gaped at his MfS colleague. 'You ...?'

'A number of years ago we turned a junior SIS man. At the moment he's on a forlorn mission to liaise with BfV – and in Bonn, moreover. In fact, it was his controller in London who suggested that he be the one to deal with Fischer's approach – or *your* approach, I should say. He's been keeping us fully informed on the transfer of intelligence packages.'

'You didn't tell us that you had a man at Broadway.'

'I'm telling you now - as you're telling me *now* that you've been running an operation on West German territory. It seems we both forgot to follow protocol.'

Slowly, Semichastny nodded. He disliked hypocrisy, particularly in himself. In any case, Wolf's admission hinted that he was at least considering the proposal. He pressed gently on that good omen.

'Chairman Shelepin's only concern is to remove this Fischer. I fully concur, but I'd ask for three further days' grace in order to complete my operation. Would you …?'

'It would require that much time at least to organize a snatch team and safe house. Bonn – as you know – is sensitive for us. We have our people in almost every institution of the Federal Government, so the last thing we want is for some badly-executed mission to stir BND and BfV into any sort of industry. Shall we say four days?'

'That would be perfect, Markus. I'll leave all the arrangements to you.'

'Will you assist in interrogating him?'

'Yes. There are too many areas in our records that he and Zarubin appear to have had at least some part in blurring. After that ...'

'He goes into the Rhine. Unless you have another preference?'

'Whatever you decide. It's almost your country, after all.'

32

'*What?*'

Branssler and Holleman looked at each other sheepishly. The latter cleared his throat and repeated it.

'We lost him.'

'You silly bastards! How?'

Branssler groaned. 'He was a kid. Freddie got on to him as he left the hotel, and I followed about twenty metres to the rear. But then he started running.'

'He'd made you?'

'We don't think so. It's just one of those things that teenagers do. One moment he was walking, the next – *whoosh*. He went 'round the corner like a bird, and by the time we both got to it he was lost in the crowd.'

The three men sat on a bench in the Hofgarten Bonn, about a hundred metres from the *Akademisches Kunstmuseum*, a faded but grand edifice to which none of them had yet paid attention. It was a pleasant late afternoon, the tree-lined walk busy with promenading families who, even distracted by crying infants and melting ice-cream, would make excellent witnesses to an attempted abduction, or murder.

'A teenager?'

'Yeah. About seventeen.'

Fischer relaxed slightly. 'If he's that young then this was definitely an innocent errand. The KGB fellow probably stopped him in the street and offered a couple of deutschmarks to drop off the package at reception. Why didn't you come straight back and tell me?'

'We were going to, but Freddie had an idea.'

'Oh God. What?'

'To follow you instead.'

Fischer rubbed his face. 'Why would you do that?'

'To make sure that KGB haven't got eyes on you.'

'We couldn't discuss it beforehand?'

His friends regarded each other once more. 'We thought you'd be angry about us losing the kid, so we wanted to give you something useful.'

'And?'

Another meaningful look, another pause. 'They ... don't have eyes on you. They didn't this morning, anyway.'

'So, a marvellous day's work, then?'

'Well, you say that, but ...' Holleman's lugubrious expression lifted slightly; '... we made sure that you were clear, and then we kept on following you, all the way to the café. You didn't notice us, did you?'

'Don't feel too pleased with yourselves. I wasn't looking for unwelcome company.'

'You should have been. Anyway, we put ourselves where we wouldn't be seen, you ordered a coffee and then your British contact arrived.'

'Yes.'

'He talks a bit, doesn't he?'

'He did this morning. I was interrogated about everything except my shoe-size. It came across as politely disinterested conversation, obviously.'

'Is that what spies do?'

'I imagine his bosses back in London want him to get a feel for the go-between, the better to assess what this arrangement's really about.'

'What did you tell him?'

'Everything he wanted to know – my war record, what I've done since, how long it took me to recover from the visible damage, that I had been married but widowed and had no children. Everything except why I was doing this.'

'He didn't want to know that?'

'Of course he did. But he couldn't have trusted the answer, could he?'

'No.'

'You're both looking more pleased with yourselves than you've any right to, you idiots. What's happened?'

'When you shook hands and parted, we followed *him*.'

'Why?'

Holleman shrugged. 'Why not? He's part of your master plan, isn't he?'

'He will be.'

'Well, you might want to rethink that. He went to the park, by the river - the one where we found you the other night.'

'It's pleasant weather - why wouldn't he?'

'He met someone there, and showed him the stuff you'd handed over.'

'So, SIS has two agents in Bonn.'

'That's what we thought. After a few minutes, they parted company. My leg was shouting by then and I wanted to give it a rest, but Gerd said no, let's just see where these gentlemen are going. We took one each. Luckily, mine left the park at a gate where there's a small taxi rank. He got into the lead one, I went for the second.'

'Not *follow that cab*, surely?'

'Why not? Clichés are that for a reason. Gerd drew the wrong straw and had to trudge back into Bonn behind his guy. Which is a shame, really.'

'Why?'

'Because we ended up in the same place – a building on Graurheindorferstrasse, the Interior Ministry. I could have offered him – and the fellow he was following - a lift.'

'But ...' The sentence hadn't fully formed in Fischer's head when the implications struck him. If both men were SIS agents and guests of BfV why hadn't they spoken in the Ministry? If they'd wanted a discreet chat out of BfV's earshot they could have smoked a cigarette in the carpark. To have met several kilometres from the building in which they both worked meant that they didn't want to be seen together. So, one of them wasn't SIS. And if, by all the same logic, he wasn't BfV either ...

Freddie Holleman was scratching his cheek. 'You might need a new plan, Otto.'

'Or a different messenger.'

'Who would that be?'

'I'm not sure. But thanks for what you did.'

'Do you think this Brit's talking to KGB?'

'Why would I be passing on packages from KGB to the British Secret Service, for their man then to show the contents to KGB?'

'Oh. Yeah.'

'I can think of two possibilities – that this Broadsmith's also working with Gehlen's BND, which seems unlikely, or ...'

'Why unlikely?'

'Why would BND have penetrated SIS? They're on the same side.'

'It could be cousins, swapping intelligence for courtesy's sake.'

'With Broadsmith presently squatting in a BfV office? BND and BfV are two sides of the same Federal coin, but they detest each other. SIS seem to have some sort of association with BfV. If so, they''d be risking it by courting their enemies also – on German soil, at least. Once London has the package I passed to Broadsmith it would be far easier for them to pick up the 'phone, call Gehlen and pass on what they have.'

'What's the second option, then?'

'An ugly one. Broadsmith may be friends with our East German brethren.'

'*Stasi*? They'd either leave a Brit alone or pass him straight on to KGB, surely?'

'We don't *know* that they would. The man speaks perfect German – I wouldn't have said that he was an Englishman if I hadn't been expecting him. As long as his nation's occupying large parts of the northern Federal Republic they're the DDR's near enemy, so one of their own – particularly one with access to American intelligence also - is potentially useful. It's at least a possibility, so we have to assume the worst.'

'Alright. So, what now?'

'We wait for a response to the signal I've sent.'

'You've done it, then? Started the thing?'

'Two hours ago.'

'How long will it take?'

'I don't know. The signal's a tripwire, so hopefully we'll hear something quickly.'

'You mean before KGB decide to retire you?'

'Exactly that, yes.'

'And then?'

'I'm still at the stage of wondering whether there's going to be a *then*.'

The feeling must have been brewing quietly for some time, but on the ninth day of his exile, Zarubin realised that he was finding the experience less than entirely gruesome. It was a worrying thought, but not so much as the one that followed - the one that told him he worried too much.

There was some sort of learned paper yet to be written, that pondered the curious ways in which communism had managed to satisfy the human need for decadence. He wasn't thinking of the Soviet regime's loving preservation of every Fabergé egg or Romanov Palace it stumbled upon; more the slightly shame-faced provision of fripperies that allowed apparatchiks to reassure themselves that society's proper demarkations had survived Red October.

Here at the Hotel Shaxtiori, courtesy of the Defence Ministry, Zarubin had daily access to – no, was urged towards – an array of indulgences that would have kept an Astor contented, or at least reluctant to complain. He couldn't recall have eaten half as well during his American exile (even during the brief, pleasant interlude when he had provided cock-services for an heiress), and if the staff avoided the last degree of self-debasement to be found in the best western establishments, he suspected that a request for the use of their daughters wouldn't be refused, or even taken badly. It wasn't enough that a newly-opened jar of caviar sat upon one's table (whatever the meal); a lackey always took the trouble to inform the guest of its provenance, should a terrible suspicion have arisen that the product was mere hatchery dross. Similarly, every waiter was a part-time sommelier also, on hand constantly to reassure the increasingly relaxed customer that the decanted article (only *shampanskoye* was opened at the table) was something other than the domestic article. After several days' observation, he had almost convinced himself that the guest who unquestioningly accepted everything that was laid before him was somehow not playing to the rules.

If the victuals and deference pleased, the treatments made a man feel like a thoroughbred breeder. Zarubin had regarded his first few maulings as little less than violations, but he realised now that he'd needed a little time to develop the correct sense of over-entitlement. He had found that it helped if he thought of himself as a neo-Roman patrician rather than an almost-humble servant of the Soviet State - a man whose health and wellbeing were as much to the citizen's benefit as his own. Once this small psychological correction had been made, the pummellings, immersions, swathings and almost-gentle kneadings seemed more the necessary tools that aided the vast machinery of government. This was a necessary process of maintenance, not cream on an over-sugared cake.

Naturally, he wanted it to end. He had to be in Moscow, calming Khrushchev and guiding hot heads towards the ice-bucket before some wildly stupid idea struck them as their only option. The urge had definitely lost its edge, however. He'd begun to appreciate that the walls of Tskaltubo no more frustrated his efforts than those of the Kremlin Palace - that distance did no more to deny access to the First Secretary than did A.S. Fucking Shevchenko. The problem was not so much this gilded interlude as how and why it had come about. He had to accept that he was not regarded as the asset that once he had been, and that he would have to come at least partly to terms with his disappointments. Put another way, a long-game man in an age of strategic tic-tac-toe needed to learn to live with redundancy.

Everything now was about 'The Moment', and he had come to detest the concept. It made strategy the slave of a schedule, the common-sense pause a weak betrayal of resolve. He couldn't see why it always had to be *the* and not *a* moment - the Universe, after all, had provided not only more than the one item but enough to fill minutes, hours and decades, all of which might serve a successful purpose. Yet half the briefings that came out of Dzerzhinsky Square and Khodynka these days were built upon the one fatal premise – if not *now*, when? Why was it that those who considered action to be better than contemplation were so bound by the *now*?

More of them should come to Tskaltubo, he decided. The days here had loosed his own neck fibres and made him think more of what was important and what could be let slip. He had, for example, just about given hope of influencing a decision on whether to support Ulbricht's absurd Berlin barrier. The man wanted it, and Khrushchev had promised too much in the past and then backed down to do the same again. He didn't like to be worked by the German Premier, but he hated to look weak. It was probably going to happen, however superficial the benefits and severe the damage to communist prestige. *I'm on record, and perfectly happy to be resented for being right.*

The Caribbean was another matter. Mikoyan had returned from his US tour (well, from the United Nations Building to Harlem) convinced that the

Americans wouldn't permit Castro's regime to survive. Khrushchev trusted his old friend's judgment more than he ever had Zarubin's, but the potential prize – a Soviet version of Roosevelt's unsinkable British aircraft carrier, a mere 165 kilometres from the Florida coast - was too tempting to tuck away in the never-never box. Half the Politburo was having premature ejaculations at the prospect, and the First Secretary wasn't strong enough to crush their expectations. Unless the Americans moved quickly to make the question moot, Cuba was going to become an open sore.

As he had tried to explain to a deaf audience for a number of years now, Americans were different. The United States of America was a young, self-absorbed phenomenon, an early-teen with all the paradoxical complications that innocence brought. It was a nation that hadn't needed to come to terms with a world in which borders could dissolve under thousands of horses' hooves - or, latterly, tanks' tracks, and hadn't learned the necessary art of dealing with enemies other than by the most direct, final means. Their entire, brief history had been a succession of conflicts entered into with the intent of entirely expunging the competition – native Americans, the colonial British administration, that part of Mexico north of the Rio Grande and a feeble Spanish Empire whose crushing had been so easily achieved that even some of the more thoughtful victors had – much too late - been ashamed of their victory. It was a tradition of ensuring that no threat ever came close enough to disturbing the sleep of their *malyshkas*, and drove every aspect of their foreign policy, however much they pretended that it was built on moral foundations. They kept their enemies at a continental distance, or erased them.

So, they would regard their piling of hundreds of atomic bombs on Turkish soil as an entirely justifiable precautionary measure, and the appearance of a single one of the same upon Cuban territory as a dagger's thrust into the throat of freedom, liberty and that curious confection, the American Way of Life. *The* Moment would then truly have arrived, the one with the potential to make all future moments redundant. And what if, at that particular, memorable *moment*, Khrushchev wasn't allowed to play to his instincts and back down once more?

Where's Zarubin? he would cry out, much too late. *How the fuck could he have allowed this to get where it's got? Why wasn't I advised properly?* Even as the missiles passed each other in the stratosphere, the Soviet hierarchy would be pointing fingers still, trying to shove blame on to some other imminent pile of ashes. *He's still in exile, in Tskaltubo*, no-one would think to say, *pushing himself lower into the mud-bath, hoping it'll protect him from the nearest blast-radius*.

It was a strangely comforting fantasy, but Zarubin couldn't cheer himself on the back of a prospective atomic war. He took more satisfaction from the fact that, however briefly, he had managed to regain a state of semi-anxiety. He *should* be anxious, not wondering about the day's menus, or whether his favourite masseur, Georgi (a twelve-fingered, three-elbowed thug from Sochi), was on duty once more. They were living in momentous disturbing times, an age of uncertainty, upheaval and doubt, and the one great mind available to the Council of Ministers and First Secretary was presently pondering book puzzles, the view from its windows and whether its host body might ask the hotel's kitchens to repeat the venison recipe from two nights' earlier. It was tragic, historic folly, to so underutilize what they had

Am I being arrogant? He thought about that for several moments before he felt able to reassure himself. Modesty was a luxury he could indulge in retirement (if he wasn't there already); in the meantime, he was the only fire-blanket in a smoking kitchen, yet still folded neatly. A small momentum had established itself. In the Lubyanka, Shelepin and his First Directorate Chief, Sakharovsky; at Khodynka, the ever-willing Serov; in the Kremlin, Gromyko and Kosygin – all of them crediting the Americans with more of a strategy than they'd actually yet conceived, and a strategy demanded a counter. How much longer they'd tolerate Khrushchev's meandering approach to the unfought war was an open question. The 22nd Praesidium was due to be elected in the coming October, an opportunity for quelled voices to find a brief megaphone, and if the First Secretary wasn't on form he might find himself a mere moderator of immoderate intentions.

Zarubin could do nothing to head off that prospect from the sylvan glades of Tskaltubo. He couldn't write a briefing paper that anyone would read. He couldn't get on a 'plane, fly back to Moscow, thrust himself past Shevchenko and into Khrushchev's presence. He couldn't even ensure that the data which determined policy was being circulated to his office any more. All he had was a forlorn hope that the First Secretary would tire of being pushed towards The Moment and recall that a sobering voice was missing from his counsels. But to do that, the man would need to pause and think, and these were not among Khrushchev's more notable talents.

On his lap, *The Brothers Karamazov* (a loan from his new friend, the Third Minister) tried to engage Zarubin. The book lay open at pages 10 – 11, read many times but not absorbed. He had never really taken to Dostoevsky but appreciated that this was his fault, not Fyodor's, and was attempting to fill a gap in his cultural life. With only 691 pages remaining he was well on his way but feared he might not reach the denouement before some arse in Moscow flipped a coin badly and kicked off the War to End Species. By means which reflected poorly upon his integrity he had secured an illicit supply of a reasonable Bulgarian red wine from the kitchens, and was tempted now to open a bottle (with an equally illicit corkscrew), drown out his fears and attempt to return to meanderings of Imperial Russia. The present, however, pressed like an affectionate hog, so he made up his mind to dress for the outdoors and attempt to clear his head the wholesome way.

He was halfway into his walking trousers when a single knock on the door of his suite almost caused him to topple. He buttoned-up quickly and opened it. A young Red Army Captain saluted and deployed a frown.

'Comrade General, visitors are not allowed without prior agreement.'

Puzzled, Zarubin nodded. 'Quite right.'

Satisfied, the Captain stood back, saluted once more, turned his head, nodded it in the direction of the door and stepped to his left. From stage right, a thoroughly dishevelled Levin shuffled into view. Between his arms he clutched a briefcase to his chest, and Zarubin knew immediately, allowing no possibility of doubt, that it contained what had recently sat in a Cosmoline tin in a maintenance cupboard.

Weakly, Levin nodded. 'Good morning, Comrade General. May I come in, please?'

'How the Holy Hell …?'

'The papers you had me draw up, authorizing your early return flight to Moscow. I took a lift with the 'plane.'

'Why didn't you call first?'

'Because...' Levin swallowed, hard; '… there's been a deposit.'

For a moment, Zarubin had to search for the meaning, but then it came to him, hard.

'How much?'

'Ten deutschmarks.'

He had long been hoping not to hear that precise amount, for a very precise reason. It was a message, agreed upon years earlier, telling him that a stalk was on, and that one of two men (and probably both) were wearing the antlers.

'When?

'Yesterday. The depositor gave a contact telephone number, but no other details.'

Zarubin closed his eyes and thanked God, both for assiduous Swiss bankers and Boris Petrovich Levin's shattered nerves. There might still be time, if prudence, proper forms and circumspection were dropped into the ditch as he hurried by. He looked at his forlorn secretary, and reluctantly adjusted his thinking. As *they* hurried by.

'I just thought ...'

'Yes, you did the right thing, Levin. Is our pilot content to proceed?'

'I told him we were returning immediately to Moscow.'

'Again, that was the correct thing to do. Not accurate, but entirely correct. During your flight here, did you happen to ask him how his mother was, these days?'

'Yes, of course. He says very well, and thank you again.'

Zarubin breathed a little more easily. He had organized the very best hospital treatment for the old sow a number of years past, but feared that she might since have decided to die anyway. Her continuing good health was absolutely necessary to the moral debt he was about to call in. He picked up the telephone receiver and dialled 9.

'Yes, please send a meal to my room – nothing too healthy, it's for my secretary. And inform the Director that I've been summoned urgently to Moscow. By the First Secretary, if he asks. I'll need a car to the airfield, in an hour. Would you thank your staff for their excellent service, and let them know that I shall be returning in two or three days' time?'

As he replaced the receiver he noticed Levin's odd expression.

'It doesn't hurt to be gracious. And letting them think that I'm coming back should give us a little time.'

'What now, then?'

'You eat, we leave.'

'And go where? Is anywhere in this country safe now?'

'I don't know. I need to speak to the man who sent the warning before I can make that judgment. In the meantime, we do what any sensible animal does when danger presses – we go to ground.'

'What sort of ground?'

'The very worst sort. I'm going home, Levin, and you'll be my guest.'

'Moscow is home.'

'No, it's merely where I live. I'm referring to the place I was breached.'

34

Twenty-four hours after KGB Deputy Chairman Semichastny's visit to Ruschestrasse, a *Stasi* team assembled in Bonn. Six men, five of whom were long-time residents of the Federal Republic, travelled separately and booked into four cheap hotels in Nordstadt and Auerberg. They met in a trucker's cafe on the Köln road, at Hersel, and the colleague from Berlin briefed the others. There was quiet amusement when a photograph of the target was circulated with the usual direction to memorize his features – as if anyone might have forgotten their remarkable terrain – but the team leader frowned them into silence.

'This is to make no ripples whatsoever. A quick, smooth, quiet action, the man got into the van without anyone noticing. It's a favour for our cousins, and we don't embarrass Berlin.'

As far as any of them knew, MfS acknowledged only KGB as full *cousins*. One of the others (a thick-set man in his late-forties, wearing factory work-clothes) cleared his throat.

'Do we deliver him to Rolandseck?'

'No. The Russians mustn't be seen to be involved in this, and getting him into the Embassy might be noticed. We're going to use the house at Brühl.'

The others glanced at each other but said nothing. There was a closer safe-house, near Bornheim, but the old, ruinous building in Brühl sat in its own grounds, far from passing ears, and had a substantial cellar that on three previous occasions had been used for interrogations and subsequent disposals beneath its flagged floor. The 'favour' for the Soviets was going to be a full, five-star obligement, apparently.

'The poor bugger looks like he's had his share of luck already.'

'I have no idea what they want him for. We're to deliver the package, not decided what's done with it.'

'Right. Obstacles?'

'None that we know of - no security, no-one who'll miss him the moment he's gone. The Soviets have had one pair of eyes on him, intermittently, for five days now. Obviously, that wasn't serious surveillance; more a guarantee that he was doing what he was sent here for.'

'Sent?'

'He's doing stuff for KGB, so it looks like he's either been outed, turned or squeezed dry.'

The tender conscience shook his head once more but said nothing. The man sitting next to him (a nondescript of medium age, build and complexion), lifted his head slightly and frowned.

'If the Ivans had only one man watching the target, we're not going to have a reliable schedule, are we?'

'We don't have *any* sort of schedule, so we do this on the fly. There's a print shop about thirty metres from his hotel and across the street. The top floor is unoccupied, and reached from a side door. We'll put one man up there and two on the street, east and west of the hotel entrance. When the target emerges we move; as our two begin to follow him the lookout calls the driver – the van will be in a car-park on Kasernenstrasse, about three hundred metres away, so we can be in place almost immediately.'

'Will he be alone?'

'If he isn't, we hold off and follow until they separate or a clear chance presents itself, in which case we put the other fellow down. If it can't be managed, we try again the day after'

'Will five of us be enough to do it quietly?'

'Four – I'll be waiting in the second van a kilometre south of here, the lay-by. There's a gravel space behind the toilet block - we'll transfer him there and abandon the first vehicle, in case anyone witnesses the snatch. He's in his sixties and slightly built, so unless he's studied Turkish wrestling or has concrete in his boots he shouldn't be a problem.'

'How long to Brühl from here?'

'Minutes at most. I've checked - there are no scheduled roadworks on the route.'

There was nothing left to ask. No-one enjoyed extemporary arrangements, but each of them had been involved in far more problematic operations – pealing off abduction targets who had security details, carefully insinuating 'evidence' of criminality where it could destroy careers, and (in the case of the two youngest, most presentable gentlemen present), seducing the secretaries of politicals or civil servants and blackmailing them thereafter. A lone, broken man, manipulated – and now dropped – by KGB, was already on enemy territory and at risk from whatever might notice him. He had no hinterland, no sanctuary from which he'd need to be prised, no hope of rescue. When it happened, the poor bastard probably wouldn't even make a struggle of it - he'd know exactly what was going on, and probably why, too. That sort went limp, usually, and hoped that whatever came next would be quick and mostly painless. *Poor bugger* just about summed him up, though it wouldn't save him.

They broke up at four pm, as the cafe began to fill with teenage boys (probably hoping that some of the more adventurous girls from the Ursuline school nearby had managed to get over the wire). Three of them were staying in the same hotel but didn't acknowledged each other's existence either on the bus back to Auerberg or later than evening during dinner in the hotel restaurant. The others dispersed at the cafe; two drove the vans back to separate hotels in Nordstadt, the third – their leader - made his interim report by public telephone, to a gentlemen who ran a small machine component supplies company in Dortmund, and then walked back to his hotel.

The operation would commence soon after dawn the next day, and if all fell out conveniently the package might be delivered to Brühl and the team dispersing by noon. No-one expected this of course; all of them had been involved in enough snatches to know that one or more – many more – of a thousand minor problems was more likely to occur than not. The target might choose to spend the day in his hotel bed, or order a cab to pick him up at *Landhaus Europa*'s front door, or even – as some targets did – experience some inexplicable premonition of what was about to occur and impersonate a hare. To have achieved the objective by noon the next day would be ideal, but if the thing dragged into the evening or even the next day, they could adapt to cover the unexpected inconvenience.

The men assembled for this task wouldn't have interested the most suspicious police officer. None had a criminal record, nor even a single penalty point on their driving licenses. All were respectable, industrious citizens, the sort who drove the German economic miracle quietly and conscientiously without asking too much credit for it. The five who lived in the Federal Republic voted regularly for one of the two centre-right parties, and to their friends and neighbours expressed neither approval, admiration or pity for the state of things in the German East, much less the further, threatening East. They belonged to various local social societies, paid their taxes uncomplainingly, sent their children into the St Georg, consumed or coveted the same gew-gaws as every other *wessie*, moaned about their football teams, and, in recent summers, had begun to help boost the tourist economies of southern European countries. Even their wives didn't suspect that the brief work trips they were required occasionally to take at very short notice were other than the necessary price of good jobs and better prospects. Preceding and underpinning every skill required to do their work was the necessity of being invisible in the herd.

They knew nothing about the half-faced man they were about to abduct, other than his name, current address and the identity of the Party that wanted him out of the world, and with that each of them – even the Tender Conscience - was perfectly comfortable. The Revolution would come when it came, either by force, stealth or persuasion; their only job was to keep the path swept clean of impediments and tidy the messes that other men sometimes caused. This particular one would be no less neatly erased.

35

Harold Shergold was not to be disturbed. The rest of Broadway took this to mean that, other than to Dickie White, the Prime Minister, Dwight D. Eisenhower and Her Majesty, his office was no less inaccessible than the cave at Makkedah. Voices in *SovBloc* were hushed, pencils ceased to be rhythm sections and only the eternal flight of memoranda, circulars and expenses chits through the building's vacuum tube transit system broke the unfamiliar, museum-like acoustic.

Shergold had cleared his already-neat desk and placed four documents side-by-side across it. Two were originals, the others photocopies of the latter two gifts from their mysterious friends in Moscow (the hard-copies had yet to arrive in London). One – the first – was an English translation of an assessment (probably intended for a very limited circulation among members of the Praesidium) of the risks and benefits of supporting rebels against the American-backed forces of the Congolese Government *du jour*. The second, third and fourth had needed to be translated. Each was a further assessment, or opinion, on foreign affairs matters of the moment; all were dated later than January of that year. What they all had in common, though this may or may not have had a particular relevance, was that they placed an emphasis on American reactions to various Soviet options. One – the first to be received - had no signature attached; the others bore that of someone on the General Staff, one S.A. Zarubin.

The name rang a small, distant bell, but Shergold didn't chase it. Clearly, none of this was of use to SIS. Any competent analyst at Broadway could have prepared assessments on what the Reds thought they could and couldn't get away with, and probably they wouldn't have disagreed much with what he was reading. This exercise had a different purpose, then, and three possibilities occurred.

Firstly, that it was bait. Whoever had sent this material knew that SIS would look carefully at the data before saying anything to CIA, and that revealing the same to Langley would further undermine Washington's faith - such as it was – in Broadway. Second, it might be that this fellow Zarubin was marketing himself to London in the hope of finding a new home, should his future prospects in Moscow seem bleak. Third, someone who wasn't best friends with the General was putting him in a very dangerous place.

Of the three, Shergold liked his first guess the best. Moscow's approach was a cheap, risk-free means of doing serious harm, a slight tug on a pulley that generated serious lift at the other end. He appreciated cleverness, even in an enemy, but given that it was something he might himself have conceived he placed a large question mark next to it. Wishful thinking was not a good means of finding the truth.

The second possibility was less compelling, but not implausible. Would-be turncoats famously over-esteemed their value to a prospective employer. The good ones – like HERO, their current best-in-show – could provide genuine insights and excellent, up-to-the-minute data, but the usual specimen came with limp, historic 'intelligence' that didn't begin to make up for the expense of housing and feeding him until he managed to drink himself to death. Despite his rank, this Zarubin (why was that name familiar?) might be a time-serving nonentity whose loss the Russians could - and would - bear with great fortitude. Only one thing gave Shergold pause in that regard, and that was circulation list on the latter three documents. A man whose opinions were passed to just about every senior member of the Praesidium, including the First Secretary himself, was, or had been, someone whose words carried weight. Whether he could be of use to Broadway was another matter entirely, of course.

The third possibility he didn't quite discount, but it seemed unlikely. Internal Kremlin politics weren't much more familiar to western intelligence agencies than those of the Hittite Empire, and it wasn't beyond reason that one faction or agency might use the stain of treason to extinguish a rival. But was it likely? Since the mid-30s, denunciation had been one of the readier tools in the Soviet back-stabber's arsenal, and Stalin's show trials had sent a generation of awkward political figures to the wall on the flimsiest of charges. Would someone go to the trouble of conscripting SIS, when an implication of wrong-thinking would probably do the trick as readily? Shergold really couldn't make a judgement on that, which was the only reason the possibility remained on the table.

'Eric!'

Less than ten seconds later, a head popped around the door. 'What is it, Shergy?'

'Why does the name Zarubin stir one's memory?'

'Um.' Eric – a pleasant-faced, frail young man - frowned at the floor in front of him for almost a minute. He had an archivist's head for arcane and largely useless information (which made him very useful indeed), and if he couldn't immediately recall a fact, face or circumstance he usually knew which long-untouched pile it lay beneath. He lived with his mother, collected stamps and leaned the Methodist way, all which more or less stood for a pedigree in Shergold's opinion.

'There was a Zarubin who pulled CIA's leg a few years back. He jumped the fence, gave them a lot of information that turned out to be fairly useless and then jumped back again. I don't think we know why he did any of it.'

'Who *was* he?'

'No-one, really - a middle-ranker in MGB, as was. He probably became homesick. You know how the Yanks are with low-level defectors - they squeeze them, give them a dollar-a-day pension and then forget about them until they either jump off a bridge or tell their stories to the gutter Press.'

'When was this?'

'He went back East in '53, just after the death of our beloved Josef. At least, that's when we got word of it.'

'Thank you, Eric.'

It didn't sound like the same man, but one couldn't be certain when it came to Soviet politics. Just as so many high-flying names had fallen burning to earth, mediocrities and once out-of-favour types had emerged from obscurity (and even the gulag) to find a comfortable home in Khrushchev's revisionist administration. If the earlier Zarubin had returned home with sufficient remorse and a stack of confidential CIA papers he might have survived and even flourished. And Shergold reminded himself that the new Zarubin *was* writing about American attitudes and possible reactions, which indicated a level of experience thereof.

Why would someone wish to frame him, though, and who? Hawks in the Kremlin? People whose toes he'd crushed at some point? And again, why go to the trouble of pushing his works towards SIS?

The telephone interrupted Shergold's circular thoughts. His secretary, who had the same orders not to disturb him as had the rest of *SovBloc*, apologized without sounding at all apologetic.

'Sorry too bother you, Sir. It's your wife.'

Bevis *never* called him during work hours, unless …

'Put her through, please, Mary.'

'Hello, Harry, sorry to bother you. I've just had a call. A gentleman asked if he was speaking to Anael, so I thought you'd want to know.'

Another one? 'Thank you, darling. What did he say?'

'He said he needed to talk to you about Otto Fischer. Wasn't that the gentleman who called before?'

'Yes. Did he give a name?'

'Jonas Kleiber. And yes, he sounds very German. *And* a bit upset.'

'Really?'

'At first, yes. But then he collected himself and begged my pardon. He told me that he really, really didn't want to be doing this, but he had a message to pass on.'

'And did he?'

'No. It's long and quite complicated, apparently - and top secret, he said. *Do* people say things are top secret outside of films?'

'Hardly ever. Did you get a number?'

'Yes, but it's a bakery – his landlord, he said. He lives somewhere in Kennington, and would prefer that you came to see him.' She laughed. 'He says he doesn't want to end up in a ditch, or have stuff beaten out of him in a cellar.'

'Oh, Lord.' Shergold took the number, replaced the receiver and sighed. This business had taken up far too much of his time already. He was tempted to ignore the message or send some junior researcher to quiz Herr Kleiber, but the fact that the man had asked for Anael meant that Fischer had at least some confidence in him. If he could cast any light over the present dimness the time might not be wasted.

He spent the next hour clearing the sort of paperwork that, if left untouched, wouldn't be forgotten by those whose lives were lived by the circular. Then, not knowing when an opportunity would next present itself, he ate the sandwich that Bevis had placed into his briefcase that morning and drank half the tea from his thermos flask (Broadway's tea and coffee was fit only to inflict upon interrogatees). While he was doing this a couple of passing heads glanced into his office through the door's small window, so before one of them could conclude that he was now to be disturbed he dialled the number, confirmed that it did indeed belong to a bakery, took down the address and asked that Mr Kleiber be informed that Mr Shergold was on his way and expecting to be with him by 1pm.

Briefly, he considered calling across to Leconfield House and asking MI5 to lend him one of their thugs, but nothing that Bevis had told him about Kleiber roused any of his usually sensitive nerve-ends. A few minutes' careful questioning should allow him to decide whether Otto Fischer's business was something worth pursuing or just a case of Moscow playing games. If the former, he would need to convene an interdepartmental meeting to discuss next steps, and God alone knew what would come of that. If the latter, he would do his very best to ensure that at least two Germans would no longer be welcome on British soil, the message to be reinforced by a robust kicking.

Aware that a rubicon had been forded, Fischer brooded upon it until the exercise became tedious, after which he went to the hotel's reception area, where he ordered a coffee. Both Freddie Holleman and Gerd Branssler had told him that it was a mad, bad idea. He had just made a telephone call to a bakery in Kennington, London, during which a third opinion had been offered, employing some remarkably inventive language (in two languages, no less), that had largely confirmed what he had heard already. None of that changed his own assessment, because as far as he could see here wasn't a possible second option - at least, not one that might keep him in the world.

He was about to betray the betrayers, a very dangerous occupation. When it happened, things would move too quickly for him to influence their trajectory, and of course he had to ensure that everything was in place before he pressed the start button. Almost nothing was, though, and couldn't be. So, he had pressed the button anyway.

A few apt metaphors struck him forcibly. He was a salesman, selling stuff he didn't have. He was a poker player, making his big bet before the dealer dealt. He was – and this one stabbed right to the heart – a parachutist once more, stepping out of the fuselage before performing any of the checks that would prevent him from meeting the ground at a natural velocity. What had Freddie said - that this was no sort of a plan? For once he was being the quiet voice of reason, and he was probably right. The thing relied upon at least five people playing the game exactly as prescribed, and Fischer had no influence upon the intentions and actions of at least two of them.

He had handed the latest package to Mr Broadsmith earlier that morning - the fourth item in just seven days, which, even to a supremely inexpert mind, was pushing things quickly. KGB obviously wanted this finished, which meant that the problem of Otto Fischer might also be wrapped up imminently. He may well have underestimated what time he had remaining, in which case his little plan had failed already.

How much damning intelligence was enough, he wondered. The snare had to be adequately baited, but too much and the whole thing would cease to be credible. KGB would be portraying themselves as idiots, their security a standing joke; and while they might not care about SIS's opinion, that of their true audience was another matter. It would be a fine judgement, but one that he had no way of second-guessing.

He needed a time-table, but it was necessarily arbitrary. The business could hardly drag out for much more than another week, so that was his most optimistic (perhaps wildly so) estimate. The pessimistic case was more problematic, in every sense. If what he had delivered to date was sufficient to the task he might be playing with hours only. He would be their very last piece of housekeeping (being both relatively unimportant and accessible), so he might have a day or two still; but could he use that extra time if his plan was being stifled elsewhere? He had to hope that it wasn't. He had to hope that his sense of things coming to an ugly, deadly head was shared by at least one other person.

A small disturbance made him glance down to his left-hand side. His cup was full once more. By now, he was convinced that Armin could feel an absence of hot beverage before his eyes confirmed the fact, and he hardly needed to half-turn to reassure himself that the man was stood by his side still, coffee pot in hand, like a personal honour-guard. The comradely nod-and-wink of a few days earlier had gradually matured to something that a gauleiter would have recognized in his personal SA bodyguard, though the young bull physique was somewhat lacking.

'Busy day, boss?'

Fischer shook his head. He had practiced the frustrated businessman's persona until he felt almost comfortable in his suit.

'Not really, Armin. I had an errand earlier, but I'm still waiting to hear something definite from our clients. They seem not to want to make up their minds.'

'Tsk. Will you be having lunch with us, then?'

Fischer thought about that for a moment. One of the few ways in which a poor life expectancy could be improved slightly was to deny the would-be executioners an easy shot. If he didn't leave the hotel unless absolutely necessary they would need to improvise, which risked their becoming visible, and he didn't think they'd want an audience. He was waiting – for the next package, for their closing move, for some element of his mad plan to advance itself – and in the meantime had made Holleman and Branssler promise that they would keep well out of sight (which meant more grief for their former colleague's wife). For the moment there was nothing more he could do, and despite his amateur farmer's hatred of idle time he nodded.

'What's on today's menu?'

Armin leaned in confidentially, and though the finger didn't touch the nose there was no mistaking his satisfaction at being offered the opening.

'Whatever you'd like, boss. The chef won't mind.'

Fischer would have been content to leave it up to the man, but that was hardly gracious.

'I don't think I've ever tasted finer sow's stomach than the one you served the other night.'

Pleased, Armin nodded. 'It's his mother's recipe. I'll go and ask.'

The chances of disappointment being slight, Fischer braced himself for a heavier lunch than his own stomach might have wished for. Still, if he was confining himself to the premises it hardly mattered, and with luck (and the help of something from the hotel's tiny library of former guests' abandoned paperback novels) he'd nap away at least a couple of the afternoon's dragging hours. Indolence, at this moment, seemed wholly out of place, but if it could ease his anxieties ...

That pleasant thought faded swiftly as he recalled the further matter on his list. His four meetings with Roger Broadsmith had taken place at the same venue, the café in Münsterplatz. If he'd wanted to make it as easy as possible for KGB to terminate their relationship he couldn't do better than to keep to a set routine. He had no idea when, or even if, the next package would arrive at the *Landhaus Europa*'s reception desk, but he could at least add a little variety to his route from thence to the Englishman. He needed a new meeting place – nearby, very public and with several exit routes available to a prospective target. He would eat his gut-distending lunch, drink just a very little wine and then reconnoitre the options.

The sow's stomach was too substantial, but delicious. The wine he hardly touched, much to Armin's satisfaction (he requisitioned for his own meals the best bottles that customers failed to finish). After that, he gave his digestion the benefit of an hour's truce, during which he read the first five chapters of a forgettable novel of the American Civil War before stepping out to search for his new rendezvous.

As he paused for a moment on the hotel's front step, a man in a high room across the road spoke into his hand-held transceiver, and down on Sternstrasse two loitering pedestrians, positioned equidistantly from Landhaus Europa to the east and west, prised themselves from their walls and waited. When Fischer turned to his left and began to walk towards the market the man in the high room spoke once more. In Kasernenstrasse, two streets away, a grey plumbers' van manoeuvred out of the car park in which it had sat since soon after dawn. Of the three men inside, two hurriedly wiped *würstchen* grease from their hands and checked their automatic pistols, though this was done entirely by instinct and served no useful purpose, the exercise having been performed countless times already that morning.

37

'Incredible!'

General Zarubin looked around. Dust lay thickly upon every surface, painting the few pieces of dark, pre-revolutionary furniture that weren't covered in sheets a ghostly grey. Even in late July the stale air held a chill, confined by the wooden screens over every window. He had opened two to allow in some light, but a venerable accumulation of forest filth had made the glass little more transparent than the bottom of a jar. He sniffed.

'It pulls at heart-strings, certainly. But hardly incredible.'

Levin shook his head. 'I mean, that you grew up less than thirty kilometres from me. You never said.'

'It wasn't on the schedule of my most urgent revelations.'

'But such a coincidence.'

'One has to grow up somewhere, Boris Petrovich. The kitchen's down there, the fourth door on the left, I think. You might get some hot water going – it's a wood-burning stove, I'm afraid.'

'Right.' At the door, Levin paused. 'The sign?'

'Pardon?'

'The sign, at the gates. It said Institute for Statistical Studies.'

'Yes. I had it put up a few years ago, to encourage people to ignore the place. I didn't want anyone coming up the drive, deciding that they like the place and bribing the local Accommodation Committee to declare an ownership annulment in their favour.'

'Someone must have been curious, surely? I mean, you can't just pretend an institution.'

'Why not? I filed its registration papers fifteen years ago, when everything was all still to fuck, and I used an NKGB stamp to discourage curiosity. NKGB became MGB, which became KGB, and along the way so much paperwork was lost that I'd be surprised if anyone could find any mention of this place. It was a middling bourgeois dwelling that once belonged to a hero of the Revolution, and now it's forgotten.'

'A hero?'

'My father.'

'You must be very proud.'

'I never knew him. His ideology was found to be unsound before I was old enough to retain a memory. Now, some tea if you will.'

The property was too far from the nearest town, Pesochnoye, to draw casual attention, but accommodation and agricultural committees were prodded often to deal with housing and arable land shortages. Its conversion to an incomprehensible facility associated (in some opaque way) with foreign intelligence would deter even the most harassed local official from doing more than pushing it into the don't-even-consider-this-one pile. It had taken some time, skill and expenditure upon bribes to achieve its invisibility, and no doubt Levin would regard Zarubin's efforts as evidence of a previously-unsuspected sentimental streak. It was strange how well he understood some aspects of his employer's nature, and missed others by a Roman mile.

It was too far from Pesochnoye, but not so far from the Finnish border that an intentionally weak, short-wave radio signal wouldn't cover the distance comfortably – specifically, to the coastal city of Kotka. The Institute for Statistical Studies possessed a device capable of sending such a signal, a donation that had been made some years earlier. Carefully wrapped in waxed paper and then polythene, the donor (who wished always to remain anonymous) had placed it beneath the former summer sitting-room's floorboards without disturbing their still-impressive lustre, and he was almost certain that no courageous intruder would have discovered it since. *Almost* would be checked and put to bed immediately after tea, because any viable future not involving a KGB cell relied utterly upon the radio being there still.

Using it was not without risk, but Soviet airwaves were jammed with thousands of short-wave signals, so a small number of brief, bland communications were likely to be lost in the general noise. In any case, he had become adept in the clandestine use of transmitters during the early part of the war, when its terrible reverses had hinted at a largely partisan future role for the Red Army. He had laid his ground carefully. The gentleman in Kotka to whom he would speak would know exactly who was calling, and why, and whom he should contact thereafter. At a prearranged time he would receive a further call, and this time he would speak briefly while Zarubin listened. That message would need to be digested and its implications understood, after which the Finn would received his final instructions, to be passed on once more. There would remain only the minor matter of arranging the transportation of a senior (and by now possibly fugitive) Soviet official from a rural location outside St Petersburg to somewhere else entirely, and ensuring he had more than a bullet awaiting him when he arrived. That too, however, had been a work-in-progress for some years now. There were risks – great risks – to be faced, but all that might be done to lessen them had been pushed as far as possible.

Zarubin kept his reassuringly complacent face in place for when Levin returned with their tea. Given the man's extremely sensitive nerves he would be told as late as possible that his present life was effectively over, barring some unimaginable turn of circumstance. He would react in one of two ways, as he always did when presented with bad news: either his mordant stoicism would kick in and anaesthetize the worst of it, or medicinal quantities of vodka would be required to keep his heart beating. The escape option of alternative employment was of course a wraith. Zarubin had lied about the job offer from the State Committee Secretariat to make the man feel a little less like he was tied to a lead buoy, and in fact, there was very little chance that he would survive a successful move against his employer. Victorious parties are never so pleased with themselves that they forget to tie all loose ends.

As for himself, Zarubin was strangely unmoved, and he suspected this was not just a symptom of his innate fatalism. Until he spoke to Kotka he couldn't know the best or worst of it, but something was moving, and he had expected *something* for so long now that another, gentler ending would have been almost unsettling. He had made his preparations as well as the myriad possible eventualities would allow. He possessed no faculty of second sight, and could do no more.

'It's ready, but you'll have to bring it in.'

Levin stood in the doorway, leaning heavily on his stick. In their Kremlin office he jealously guarded a small, four-wheeled trolley that the moral chit of his polio had long since allowed him to commandeer from one of the kitchens. Zarubin recalled that his own mother had possessed something similar – at least, he had a child's memory of a surfeit of sweet pastries burdening a device that glided from room to room – but whether it had survived the intervening decades he couldn't say. So, perhaps he hadn't made *all* his preparations as well as he might.

'I'm sorry, Boris Petrovich. Pull a cover off one of the chairs and rest yourself. I'll be a few moments.'

In the summer sitting-room he knelt and gently prised up a floorboard with his pocket knife. The transmitter was beneath it, the wrapping undisturbed. A second board's removal gave him enough space to lift it out, though his back complained as he took its weight. The car's battery would provide plenty of power (when the world was younger, the house had been marked for electrification, but the Revolution had intervened and Frederic, the estate's general-purpose *wunderkind*, had got himself shot while trying to recruit for the Whites), and one of the ruinous agricultural stores behind the house would make a good, discreet home for it during its very brief working life.

Pleased, he left the transmitter on the floor, found the ancient tea-trolley in a larder and returned to Levin, who was snoring in a chair (into which he had sunk almost to his chest-line). They had flown directly from Tskaltubo to a small military airfield northwest of St Petersburg, where Zarubin's general's uniform had crushed any tentative questions before they could find air. A car – a modest, six-year-old Chaika with Defence Ministry plates – had been arranged in advance by their pilot, who had returned his factory-fresh Ilyushin to Khodynka airfield as soon as its tanks were refilled. A two-hour drive, carefully plotted to avoid areas and installations likely to attract high levels of security, brought them to the house, by which time Levin (who travelled as well as any cripple) had all but climbed to the vehicle's ceiling. Waking him now would be an act of cruelty, and serve no purpose.

Zarubin poured himself some tea and took it to the window. He tried to persuade himself that the visible tree line struck a chord in memory, but he felt nothing. Whatever associations had made this place special to him had been severed before hair first sprouted on his upper lip, the blade having been applied expertly by his uncle, the monster. He had returned, briefly, to bury his mother and close up the estate, but by then he was already broken and reformed, the *paidiskoi* graduated to *eirën*. His uncle had become almost proud of him, which was all that need be said of the wretched process. Any sense of familiarity, belonging or love of anything smaller or less abstract than homeland could hardly have survived it.

My God. I'm feeling sorry for myself. Zarubin laughed, and Levin, mumbling, shifted himself in his sleep. The tree-line shimmered slightly as if a breeze had caught it, and an elk cow and her calf wandered out from it and on to the steppe that the once-English lawn had become. For a few moments the mother paused and stared morosely at the house as if daring it to object, and then set herself to the wild wheat stalks for which she had come visiting.

It wasn't industry as such, but it roused Zarubin from his miserable audit of fled lives. The car's battery had to be brought in and the call made, and putting off the moment was likely to achieve nothing good. Whatever loomed had to be known before it could be avoided, and all he knew for now was that a starting-button had been pressed. If he had any trepidation about taking the first step towards enlightenment, it was that the journey threatened to lead to someone he had sincerely hoped never to meet again.

Freddie Holleman was vaguely aware that a woman nearby was screaming, but his efforts to gouge an eye were distracted him from fully appreciating her efforts. Having only the one full leg he couldn't entirely confine the two that were trying to kick him, though as he toppled he had managed to wrap the entire item around the waist of his assailant (or victim - he could quite recall who had taken the first wound), and one of his hands was keeping the gun from being pointed in a deadly direction. The fingers of the other were trying to find the soft, vulnerable parts of a head that was presently moving violently, and mainly backwards, in an effort to break his nose.

Somewhere off to his left, Gerd Branssler was making a better job of discouraging another young man. He had given no notice of his approach (unlike Holleman, whose shout, meaning to distract, had flagged what was coming), so his first punch had landed squarely on the temple he had aimed for. It did only part of the job, but gave him the space and time to stand back and aim the kick which found most of its intended scrotum. The gun he removed with a second kick, and then pinned his opponent simply by falling upon him.

The third victim, Otto Fischer, sat half-dazed on the ground, looking into the barrel of yet another pistol. It was held steadily, the blow which sent him reeling having had no effect upon the hand. Even in its confused state, his mind had registered the fact that no bullet had yet passed through it, though there seemed to have been time enough for the most careful assassination. It made him a little hopeful, for a reason he couldn't quite locate.

A police siren, growing louder, began to harmonize with the lady, and Holleman's opponent suddenly went limp. Surprised, he couldn't shift his grip to compensate before the man wriggled free, rolled and jumped up. He turned and pointed his gun towards Branssler, who slowly lifted himself from his impromptu mattress and raised his arms. The slightly flattened comrade climbed groggily to his feet and recovered his own weapon. For a moment the three armed men faced their respective opponents, but then they backed away carefully, toward the wide-open rear door of a van parked at the side of the road about ten metres distant. As soon as they climbed inside it moved off, north, towards busy Kölnstrasse.

Branssler, the only upright musketeer, groaned. 'My fucking shoulder!'

From the ground, Holleman extended an arm. 'You shouldn't have punched him with your bad one. Help me up.'

'It's bad *because* I lead with it. Are you alright?'

'My nose – he butted it.'

'Well, who'd notice the damage? Come on.'

Slowly, clumsily, Holleman used Branssler as a wall and dragged himself up. He touched his nose gently and moved it from side to side. When he decided it wasn't broken he grinned.

'That was more fun than I expected.'

'You silly cock!' Branssler turned and looked down at the principal target, whose arse was still warming Bonngasse. 'Are you alright, Otto?'

Fischer attempted to consider the question seriously, but his head was ringing still. The pistol butt had struck him smartly behind his left ear, after which his perception of events had blurred. The scuffling, shouting, oaths, screaming and siren had confused him further, and only slowly was the whole separating out into distinct strands, most of which made at least some sense.

'I told you two to stay out of the city.'

'Do you here that? Ungrateful bastard. You'd have been in the Rhine by now if we hadn't ignored you.'

'Again.'

'Yes, well, you can't look after yourself. Can he, Gerd?'

Branssler shook his head. 'You don't mess with KGB without help, Otto. It's not sensible.'

'MfS.'

'What?'

Holleman pulled a face and gestured towards where the van had been parked. 'They were *Stasi*, probably. Unless the Ivans have learned to curse in German.'

Fischer managed to get to his feet as the patrol car pulled up and two *schupos* emerged. Across Bonngasse, a small clutch of passers-by were comforting the woman whose hysterics had done more to persuade the *Stasi* team to terminate their operation than anything Branssler and Holleman had thrown at them. The policemen, ignoring the three injured men, pushed back the samaritans and began to question her.

'Come on.'

Before they could be pointed out as the cause of her hysterics, the fugitives were around the corner, on Sandkaule. Fischer tugged at Holleman's sleeve, pulling him into the open door of a small supermarket. Branssler gave the street a quick up-and-down and followed. The white-coated manager was serving a lady at the delicatessen counter, and two more waited their turn. The three men stood at the rear of the queue, safe from being asked their business for a few minutes at least.

Holleman stared devoutly at the generous variety of wursts jammed into the cold cabinet, and spoke quietly.

'That was definitely an abduction.'

Branssler nodded. 'They had time to cack all of us. You'd think they'd have done it anyway, once the thing went south.'

Surprised, Fischer realised that he was hungry – a hysterical reaction, probably, to having an unperforated stomach still - and he had to force himself to think about the more immediate problem.

'They were professionals. Killing us publicly would have drawn a lot of attention, in the one city in the Federal Republic where *Stasi* absolutely need to remain entirely invisible. In any case, not killing me gives them another chance at a snatch.'

'We'll have to do something about that.'

'I know.'

'Where were you going, by the way?'

'Ironically, to search out another venue to rendezvous with the Englishman, for if or when I got another package.'

Branssler laughed mirthlessly. 'You won't be getting another package.'

'No. It seems that I've been retired. Did you follow me from the hotel?'

'Yeah. Don't you *ever* look behind you?'

'Not today, obviously. I can't stay with your farmer friend, can I?'

Firmly, Holleman shook his head. 'His wife would leave him. She has her bags packed already.'

'Then we need to go back to the hotel, quickly.'

'Won't they be waiting ...'

'Not yet. They'll need time to polish the alternative plan, now that I've been panicked. We probably have an hour or so.'

'Why the hotel, though?'

'I have to leave a message. I have to leave at *least* a message. Come on.'

'Aren't we going to buy something? I'm starving.'

'Shut up, Freddie.'

Holleman's leg slowed them, but even taking a detour to avoid the *schupos* they were back at *Landhaus Europa* within fifteen minutes. Two-thirds of the establishment's entire complement of staff was at the reception desk; Jeri looked up and smiled at Fischer and the two pious gentlemen she'd seen in her church, but Armin seemed surprised that their longest-serving solitary guest had company.

'Herr Fischer! These are your business associates?'

'Yes, Armin. I'm going to be ...'

'Oh! Before I forget, you had a telephone call - an international number.'

'From London?'

'No, Finland.'

Fischer thought as quickly as his throbbing head allowed. It was the best, and most inconvenient, news he could have heard. It required immediate action, but time – safe time – was vanishing. It also required that a carefully-rehearsed message be modified to accommodate changed circumstances. Half a dozen possibilities occurred to him and were dismissed immediately as being too complex, too hopeful, too wildly unworkable or too utterly idiotic. Only a single, uncomfortable option remained, and that was to be almost truthful.

'Armin, may I burden you with a confidence?'

An ageing, slightly war-damaged spine cracked audibly as its owner stood to textbook attention. 'Of course, Herr Fischer. We'd be honoured.'

The *we* brought Jeri similarly upright. Knowing that if he paused he might say nothing, Fischer blurted it out.

'I wasn't honest wth you, about my work. What I do involves our national security (Freddie Holleman, who'd picked up a fistful of complementary nuts from a table bowl and crammed them into his mouth, coughed violently at this point, spraying the floor liberally), and I may be in trouble. We think that *Stasi* are moving against me, and at the moment I don't have a means of avoiding them. You know this city. Can you think of somewhere I might hide for a while, that won't be discovered?'

Armin nodded vigorously. 'Of course – my home. It's just across the river, in Sankt Augustin.'

Fischer tried not to let his relief show. 'That's very kind. It shouldn't be for more than a night or two.' He turned, and looked pointedly at Holleman and Branssler. 'But I think my friends here would be safer with me. It's an imposition …?'

'I have two spare rooms, so if one of the gentlemen doesn't mind a couch?'

'Thank you, Armin. Do you own a telephone?'

'Naturally.'

'Then may I give the number to the person in Finland? You'll be in no danger, I promise ...'

Armin snorted. 'They don't scare me. I had to surrender my Kar98k to the British, but when I was freed I stole another one with about two hundred rounds of 8mm Mauser and shoved them under the bed. Let the bastards come!'

Jeri nodded firmly, despite her limited understanding of what a Kar98k and 8mm Mauser might be. Armin wrote down his home number, gave it to Fischer and pointed to the desk 'phone.

'Would you like to call him now? There'll be no charge. When you've finished and packed your things I'll get our handyman, Fritz, to bring his van around the back. No-one will know you've gone, and if anyone comes asking we'll say you're out, a business appointment. Won't we, Jeri?'

'Yes! I can make a pie later, and bring it tonight. Is tourtiere alright?'

'No, really, it's too much ...'

'What's that?' Holleman had perked considerably at the word *pie*, which crushed the objection he had been about to make regarding the accommodation.

'It's pork – a French recipe.'

'Oh God, yes. Gerd?'

Reluctantly, Branssler nodded. He was rubbing his shoulder tenderly, distracted by more than the next meal.

'What if ...?'

'What?'

'These calls – what if they don't work?'

Fischer was halfway to the desk 'phone. He paused and turned.

'Then I'll have done all I can. It's not in my hands, is it?'

'But they'll still have reason to hunt you down. You can't spend your life under a bush.'

'I'm beginning to feel comfortable in bushes, Gerd. I can't imagine that they'll spend too much of their budget pushing through rainforests to find me.'

'That's it, though – to be safe you'll need to go somewhere that's not fit for civilized folk. What sort of a life would that be?'

Holleman grunted. 'Like Gerd said the other day, you could defect to the British.'

'And I told you that defectors usually come bearing gifts of intelligence. I don't have anything to give them.'

'You do now. You can tell them that their man in Bonn's probably playing both sides. That'll be worth something.'

'It might be. But what if they *know* he's a double-agent? What if they sent him here to be just that?'

'They'd know at least that he'd been made – and by amateurs, too. A kick up the arse can also be useful, can't it?'

It wasn't an entirely absurd suggestion – God knew, there was little about the wretched, faithless world of intelligence that *could* be entirely absurd – but Fischer doubted that a safe life in England would be offered to him on the back of one thin piece of information, and he had nothing else. He half-shook his head, picked up the hotel telephone and dialled the international operator.

She made the connection and he began to speak into the silence that greeted him, reciting a sequence of paired numbers in four groups. He paused briefly, and then continued.

'Documents are finding their way to London. Nothing interesting, but all bearing the same signature. It would be good to hear what you think about it. I have new contact details ...'

He gave Armin's telephone number, replaced the receiver and checked his watch. Less than twenty-five seconds. He turned to his friends.

'That's it.'

Holleman and Branssler looked doubtfully at him. 'It?'

'Nothing to do now except wait. You can't risk returning to your friend's farm for your things.'

'It's only clothes. And two pistols, obviously.'

'Well, Armin's got his rifle and ammunition. What about your car, though? Can it be …?'

'It was hired, in Frankfurt. Gerd used false papers. We parked it by the river this morning, a covered garage.'

'Good. It can stay there. Well ...'

Fischer turned to Armin, who looked to be immensely satisfied with the way his day was going.

'… we're in your hands now. Could you call your man Fritz, please?'

39

Harold Shergold sat in a deep, shabby armchair, trying to balance a cup on its saucer. Directly in front of him, an equally shabby copy of Constable's *Hay Wain* valiantly sought to distract the eye from the rather hideous wallpaper it sat upon. Beneath both, chipped Delft tiles framed a small fireplace, providing some relief from the general dowdiness. Having been brought up with and among them, Shergold was very fond of Delft tiles.

From the room next door, sounds of frantic rummaging distracted his thoughts slightly but didn't quite remove the smile from his face. He was here on a most serious business, very possibly involving matters of national security, yet he couldn't recall when he found his work quite as distracting as it was at present. For that, he had to thank Jonas Kleiber.

Mr Kleiber was in a State, one that had worsened considerably over the past twenty minutes. Shergold couldn't of course speak to his condition prior to their meeting, but a gentle knock on his door had definitely set him on a path. An introduction had been on acting-Comptroller *Sovbloc*'s lips, and had stayed there.

'I'm not a communist!'

It was an idiosyncratic greeting, but Shergold had merely raised his eyebrows politely. It was always wisest to give someone who needed to talk the space to do so.

'In fact, if anything, I'm Christian Democrat – at least, I would be if I voted. Or if I was a Christian. I'm just passing on a message from a friend.'

'Ah.'

'I know I shouldn't say that, given the circumstances - whatever they are. But he is, a very good one, and I think he's in trouble. I mean, why else would he want me to do this?'

'Well, I ...'

'Oh, sorry. Come in, please.'

A few more minutes' babbling convinced Shergold that Kleiber was no significant threat to the realm. In fact, a heart had never been worn so prominently upon its sleeve. Details of the man's profession, hopes, fears and enthusiastic appreciation of English womanhood spilled out as promiscuously as if one of SIS's best interrogators had rolled up his sleeves and set to. Eventually, the young man drew breath, recalled his manners and offered a cup of coffee. Shergold accepted, if only to allow them both a respite.

The cup was only just in his hands when a thought occurred to Kleiber which seemed to cheer him a little.

'Excuse me for a moment, would you?'

He went into his bedroom, and the rummaging began. Shergold wondered what the thing might be – a certificate, signed by Konrad Adenauer himself, attesting to the bearer's venal instincts; or perhaps membership of a banned National Socialist resurrection cult? Something, at least, to persuade his visitor that he wasn't a deep-cover KGB asset masquerading as an unaccredited hack.

It was a bank-book for a private account, issued by Commerzbank in the name of Jonas Manfred Kleiber, with a rather startling balance. Shergold must have seemed impressed, because the young man smiled for the first time.

'*And* I own a large house in Lichterfelde, which is anything but To-The-Barricades country …'

'I know Lichterfelde quite well.*'*

'You do?'

"I was stationed in Berlin for some years after the war. The Botanical Gardens were one of my favourite off-duty haunts.'

'Were they? Mine, too. Did you know that some old ladies got cacked in the Gardens during the war? Otto solved that one.'

Finally, they had come to the subject. Shergold tipped his teacup slightly in Kleiber's direction.

'Tell me about him.'

For the next fifteen minutes the lives of Otto Fischer were revealed in some detail. Kleiber admitted to gaps in his knowledge, but what he could speak to was quite remarkable. Fallen, smashed nations throw up singular stories, but this one was singularly paradoxical. How a man so bereft of good fortune could have picked his way (or stumbled) through so many minefields and survived - albeit at an all-too visible price and an accumulation of ill-wishers - would make an excellent case-study, or lurid novel. Shergold's first instinct was to hire Fischer, or coerce him into the odd task for which survivors weren't anticipated. First, however, he needed to know why the man was sending a message via his nervous friend, when a quiet word to Roger Broadsmith would have found its way back to Broadway within the hour. With some effort, he allowed Kleiber's biographical epic to reach the present day and then asked the leading question.

'So, he's not an entirely willing carrier-pigeon between Moscow and London?'

'Christ, no! I mean, I don't *think* so. Why would he? All Otto wants is a quiet life.'

'He's not sympathetic to communist ideals? Many Germans are.'

'Ha! He doesn't believe in *anything*. You want to hear his opinion of politicians and dogma, wherever they stand. No, KGB must have something on him, if he's doing this.'

'And what is *this*?'

It had taken a while, but Shergold had manoeuvred Kleiber to the point of their meeting. The young man seemed to realise it also, because his unhealthily pallid complexion drained a little further. He gulped and stretched out a hand and reclaimed his bank book, as if he feared it might be confiscated.

He spoke quickly, giving Shergold the message without adding any opinion, though his expression suggested that he would rather it had come from someone - anyone – else. When he had finished he waited in the manner of an enemy envoy at the court of the Great Khan, while his guest absorbed the bad and the possibly good news. Eventually, Shergold looked up from the dregs in his cup.

'So, we're being played by the Russians?'

'It looks like it.'

'And this Zarubin fellow - how well does Fischer know him?'

'As well as anyone does. They have history.'

'You haven't presented much of a case.'

'It's all he told me to say. He'll know more soon, he thinks.'

'Yes, you told me that. But why didn't he give the message directly to our man in Bonn?'

Kleiber looked blankly at his guest. 'I didn't know you had one, so I couldn't say.'

Shergold thought a little more about what he'd heard. His first, strong reaction was to stand, wish this young man a good day (after the usual warning about absolute discretion and a vague hint of what might happen otherwise) and then walk as quickly and as far away as possible from this whole business. SIS, already reeling, had been set up once more, though the damage this time was likely to be collateral. He knew better than to drag God into Intelligence, but he thanked Him anyway that he'd had the sense to keep it tight – that only himself and Roger Broadsmith were aware of KGB's kind offer. Had he shared the fact of their approach with his peers they would now be enjoying the spectacle of him approaching sharp rocks with both his oars lost. He had done much too well recently not to have generated considerable ill-will.

But the poison had come with something potentially more palatable, though it couldn't yet be assessed accurately. And having listened at length to the excitable Jonas Kleiber he now knew a great deal more about Otto Fischer – certainly more than he'd gleaned from the disappointingly bland observations of Broadsmith (in whose abilities he'd placed a great deal of faith). It wasn't enough to go further, though, not without more information, and for that he would need to wait upon events. He was a patient man, but putting faith in others tested the strongest nerves, particularly in his profession.

He looked up at the nervous young man. 'Did he say how long?'

'He thinks a day, possibly two. He says there *has* to be a reaction, so if he doesn't hear ...'

'We can forget all about it.' Shergold stood up and offered his hand. 'I'm grateful to Herr Fischer for letting me know. Tell him I'll wait for his next word, but for forty-eight hours only.'

'And after that?'

'There *is* no after that.'

In running MfS's Foreign Intelligence Division, Markus Wolf enjoyed an unusual degree of latitude - for which, most days, he was grateful. Its disadvantage, of course, was that when things went badly no-one's else's head was available to be volunteered for the block. And something had gone very badly indeed.

A snatch was an opportunistic business, which is why the best men were chosen to execute them – men who could adjust to the vagaries of weather, a badly-timed glance or a forgotten set of keys, suddenly recalled by the target. They were trained to anticipate ill-fortune, and in doing so make it work for them. They were trained, above all, not to put themselves in a position in which extraction – of the target, themselves or both - became difficult, or impossible.

Which was precisely what had occurred in Bonn. Wolf had stressed that this needed to be done quickly, but they had taken that to mean at the first opportunity, which had turned out not to be anything of the sort. Now, the target was warned and not likely to offer the thinnest chance of a second attempt. A different approach was needed, but what?

That was the operational headache. Much worse were the wider implications. Wolf had taken on this task reluctantly, aware that he was colluding with a man who had misinformed – or at least, not fully informed - the Chairman of KGB. If Semichastny were not widely acknowledged to be Shelepin's anointed successor he would have refused outright, but he hadn't had that exit. Now, Wolf's own boss Mielke would be asking how the fucking mess in Bonn had come about, and why. When he did, there had to be an alternative plan in place, and preferably one that was moving already.

There was only one option, if this thing was to be done in short order (as Semichastny had insisted it must). Wolf picked up his telephone receiver and dialled the extension of Ernst Zeisl, the head of HVA's Abteilung A IX, responsible for the penetration of enemy intelligence services. He asked the man if he might come to his office sometime that morning, which Zeisl took to mean immediately. He was with his Chief within five minutes, which, given that his office was four floors below Wolf's, must have involved a degree of sprinting.

'Ernst, you have an SIS man on your books.'

Zeisl's face fell a little. 'Markus, we had no prior warning that Broadway were sending him to liaise with BfV, otherwise we'd have ...'

'I know. You've been tracking him while he's been in Bonn, naturally.'

'He reports to one of our agents in the Interior Ministry, every other day. Apparently, he believes that nothing will come of the proposed alliance.'

'I'm not surprised. You haven't instructed him to do anything else while he's there?'

Zeisl looked blankly at his boss. 'What would there be for him to *do*? It's in London we'll find a use for him.'

'I assumed you hadn't, but now we need to use him, and it's quite urgent.'

'For what?'

'We were asked by KGB to pick up someone, in Bonn. Our team failed, which must have scared the rabbit. Your SIS fellow … ?'

'Broadsmith.'

'Yes. His contact must have told you that he's also been acting as a conduit for information moving between Moscow and London? The target we missed is the man who's been handing it over. Clearly, therefore, only Broadsmith has a realistic chance of setting up a second attempt for the snatch team.'

'To get the target to a certain place at the right time?'

'Just that.'

'What time do we have?'

'None. I've spoken to the KGB Deputy Chairman. He wasn't very pleased about this, as you can imagine, but I've told him that we'll make a second attempt, tomorrow. You'll speak to our fellow in the Interior Ministry immediately, and have him meet Broadsmith this afternoon to tell him what needs to be done.'

Zeisl looked doubtful. 'A snatch – in Bonn? I wouldn't have thought you'd have agreed to it in the first place, given how many good people we have in place there.'

'I didn't want to, believe me. But this was asked as a personal favour by Semichastny, and doing it ourselves looked to be the lesser of two bad options.'

'KGB wouldn't have taken care not to make a splash, you mean?'

'Precisely - and of course, Gehlen's people will assume that it's us in any case, if it goes so messily as to be visible. I wanted it done subtly, and quietly. We still have a chance to achieve the latter, at least.'

'One more question, if I may?'

'No, Ernst, I can't tell you why KGB have been sending data to SIS. Believe me, you really don't want to know.'

It was a broad hint, but Zeisl's face remained set. As the man responsible for the protection of all MfS's deep-cover agents in the Federal Republic, he detested ripples in what should have been a still pool. Wolf took a deep breath.

'If I tell you that *I've* been told that not even KGB's liaison officer here at Ruschestrasse is to know about this, do you get a better sense of why ignorance is a happy state?'

'Christ. So Semichastny's playing his own ...'

'The Deputy Chairman is what he is, and does what he does. If this business - whatever it is – breaks badly we can say that we did a favour for a man we couldn't very well refuse. Mielke will support us in that – as will Ulbricht, if it comes to plates being thrown. On the other hand, if it's successful we'll not only take credit but *have* credit for when we need something from KGB. Now, get on to Bonn and tell our man to prep Broadsmith.'

'What if the Englishman baulks at it?'

'He agreed to work for us some years ago, yes?'

'Six, I think.'

'And have we pressed him in all that time?'

'Not once.'

'Well then. If he doesn't like it, point out that there's absolutely no loss to us if someone should betray him to his own people. Which I would regard as a certainty.'

'Well, that's it. Your opinion?'

Boris Petrovich Levin started visibly. '*My* opinion? Should I have one?'

'If you think this affects your prospects, of course.'

'My thinking is that I don't *have* any prospects.'

'Everyone has prospects, though some may be thinner than others - mine, for example. You know what this is about?'

Levin nodded. 'You're being manoeuvred, Comrade General.'

Zarubin smiled. 'I'm being *framed*, Levin. That's what the Americans say. The evidence is clear, though anyone who wasn't utterly paranoid would at least pause and question my motives. Unfortunately, no-one in the higher levels of Soviet Government lacks that quality.'

'Couldn't you go back to Moscow, and confront your accusers?'

'Don't be naive. There *are* no accusers – at least, not yet. And when they move, it will be very subtly, from deep cover. At the moment, who would I point to?'

Levin considered this for a moment only. 'Serov? Shelepin?'

'Almost certainly, Serov aches to have his revenge upon me, and for that reason would make a very unconvincing denouncer. Shelepin? I don't know. Given my history he has every reason to want me gone, but … forgive me for saying this, he doesn't *seem* the betraying kind.'

'You despise intuition, usually.'

'I do. But what's *usual*, any more? I have the sense that Shelepin's been quite satisfied with the way things are going – with Khrushchev's increasingly energetic attempts to avoid me and his consistent habit of doing the opposite of what I advise. Why would anyone bother to stir a custard that's thickening nicely?'

'Who else, then?'

Zarubin sighed. 'I've stamped on many toes, if not always intentionally. Besides Shelepin himself, more or less anyone in KGB who has the authority to manipulate the evidence has sufficient cause to do so, but ...'

'But what?'

Motive, opportunity.

'Do you recall that I asked your opinion of Comrade Semichastny, some days ago?'

Levin groaned. 'Oh, God.'

'He's the up-and-coming man, Shelepin's protege, but without any particular triumph on his *curriculum vitae* to make him his patron's undisputed successor. Wouldn't scraping a particularly noisome turd from KGB's boot be just the thing to push his nose clear of the pack? You told me he'd asked for a franked copy of my second Vienna opinion paper.'

'But that was the only time he's shown any interest. The message from Finland mentioned stray *documents*, plural.'

'Yes, but he has access to many franked copies of my work, because his boss is on the senior distribution list. The only one he couldn't put his hands on - at that particular moment - was the one that Shelepin brought with him to the meeting at Khrushchev's dacha. So, he asked you for his own copy.'

'Why would that one in particular be important?'

'Most of my pieces are general position papers on likely American reactions to proposed Soviet initiatives, yes?'

'Most.'

'As fascinating as they may be to the uninformed mind, their loss or further dissemination would represent no great catastrophe to Soviet interests, I imagine.'

'Pfft. Absolutely none.'

Zarubin frowned at his secretary but didn't rise to the bait. 'On the other hand, briefings that pass from the theoretical to the actual – that address situations in which we're directly confronting the Americans – could be regarded as valuable to an enemy.'

'Yes, Comrade General.'

'I'd like to know what else he has.'

'You wrote a couple on the Congo situation, recently.'

'Yes, I did. And three on Cuba, though that isn't quite a looming issue – yet.'

'Put together, it's quite a collection.'

'Enough to get me drained over a hole in the floor. And passing them to the British - that's clever.'

'Why?'

'The CIA are the real enemy, but given my history with the Americans, I could have made a very good argument that I'd be the last person they'd trust to deliver up Soviet Intelligence.'

'Oh. Yes.'

'And Khrushchov likes symmetries. That I could have been betraying us to the British all the while that Blake was betraying them to us – it would appeal to his peasant sense of the melodramatic. I owe my position to him alone, so his being the executioner's hand would close the circle. No doubt he'd shed a fake tear afterwards, and regard himself as Comrade Lear.'

Levin looked worried. 'A straight denial wouldn't move him, you think? I mean, surely he expects KGB to want to nail you to a door?'

'In other times I'd feel more confident of having at least a fair chance. But I've been saying too much lately that he doesn't want to hear, which adds to their case. They'd portray me as the favourite son, who, spurned, turns to his father's enemies. Even if he's never read Shakespeare or Seneca he'll be more than half-convinced before I ever get to open my mouth.'

'And I'm tarred with this.'

'You shouldn't have come to Tskaltubo, Levin. I'm glad that you did, but it puts you firmly in my leaking boat. It's why I asked your opinion about this.'

'Right.' Levin peered gloomily into his standard Red Army mountain ration. This evening's offering was buckwheat kasha flavoured with corned beef, a slight improvement over their breakfast of pea soup and noodles which nevertheless failed to raise his spirits. They sat at a small, circular table, its highly polished surface inlaid with tiny mother-of-pearl tiles. Zarubin's memories of his mother were inseparably linked to the endless games of solitaire she had laid out upon it, her principal distraction (after her husband's death) from the early twentieth-century's brutal progress. To be covered now in iron rations was a desecration of sorts, but her son comforted himself with the certain knowledge that, in seeking to evade the Soviets, he was finally clawing his way up to her expectations of him.

'I'm not sure this has ever met a cow.' Levin had speared a lump and was examining it closely, the thick lenses of his glasses giving one eye a disconcerting prominence. 'You're certain it said corned beef?'

'I don't believe I examined the label. But you were in the war, Boris Petrovich – surely its privations removed any squeamishness about what you eat?'

'I accompanied a General Staff establishment from Moscow to Berlin. Privation was having no cream at breakfast.' The lump fell back into the slop. 'You took care to set up this early-warning arrangement, so I assume you have a plan?'

Zarubin placed his fork down carefully, so as not to mark the table. '*Plan* would be to give it a misleading solidity. It's a resort, and a last, lonely one. You must at least have guessed what it is.'

Levin swallowed. 'I can't leave Mother.'

'When was the last time you saw her?'

'About six months ago.'

'And did she recognize you?'

'That isn't the point ...'

'Of course it isn't. But the pain of leaving will be yours, not hers. You can do nothing to make her remaining time more agreeable. She has helpers, yes?'

Miserably, Levin nodded.

'Well, then. You have provided, as a good son should. Were her head clear, do you think she would want you executed?'

'They'd do that, would they? To me?'

Zarubin laughed. 'As you put it, I'm being *manoeuvred*. Would they spare the one person other than myself who could convince the First Secretary of my innocence? You've seen the recent departmental memos on wastage and good practice - they'll probably tape our heads together to save a bullet.'

'Oh, Christ.'

'It isn't a choice, my friend, so put your mind at rest. I shall send a message, and then we'll know that all is done that can be.'

'That's it? Just send a message?'

'That, and organize every detail of our safe departure, obviously.'

Casa Armin was a substantial villa, its front garden entirely screened from the road by a high, unkempt hedge. There was no drive, so Fritz the handyman dropped Fischer, Holleman and Branssler at the gate. It took a single glance to confirm that their arrival was unnoticed.

The faded grandeur of their temporary home might have surprised them, but Fritz had been a voluble companion on the short drive from Bonn and explained a great deal. Armin had once been *Landhaus Europa*'s owner, having inherited it from his father; but when war came, conscription, the wartime economy and an inconvenient fire-storm on the night of 18 October 1944 had conspired to make the hotel economically unviable to a small proprietor. After the British released him he returned and sold his land-rights to a Bavarian hospitality chain, allowed them to rebuild the place almost exactly as it had been and then applied for the post of manager of the old/new establishment, arguing that his deep understanding of the Bonn hotel market would be an asset to them. He still thought of the place as his own, and gave his life to it accordingly.

The story both raised Fischer's mood and stirred his envy. Armin had made, lost and recovered his niche, and nothing beyond its bounds made him long to expand them. Could there be any purer form of contentment in this world, however many difficult guests a man had to face? He had to force himself to listen to Fritz's list of where things were, who to avoid (an old lady, two doors down, was rumoured to be ex-Norwegian Resistance, such were her powers of knowing how and with whom her German neighbours were misbehaving) and what not to touch (a kettle with loose wiring, and, in Armin's wine-cellar, two bottles of 1950 Chateau Lafleur). When the handyman had surrendered the door key and departed, Fischer did a brief reconnaissance, decided that the place was indefensible (he hadn't expected anything else) and then found the telephone. There were several possible disasters looming, but the device was their sole means of deliverance.

Holleman appointed himself chief forager, went to the kitchen and found a packet of *Kemm* biscuits, half of which he ate before returning to his friends and offering what remained. Branssler devoted himself to the windows – what he could see, what they allowed others to see and possible lines of fire – before drawing-to all the ground-floor curtains excepting those in a small parlour facing the back garden, which was entirely enclosed. Someone targeting them from that direction would first need to get over the high wall, a thought that comforted Branssler for a few moments and then sent him scurrying to find Armin's rifle and ammunition.

A little after 7pm, Jeri arrived bearing two pies – her promised tourtiere and an apple streusel, at which Holleman's ideal of womanhood acquired a new template. She noticed Fischer's slightly preoccupied manner and misinterpreted its cause.

'It's alright - Frau Rehder's already told half of Gartenstrasse that Armin's an old goat and I'm his child-lover. She's used to seeing me come and go.'

Holleman sniffed. 'Old sow.'

'She's a widow, and most of her friends are dead. What other pleasures can she have? Armin says he's staying at the hotel tonight, but that he'll come tomorrow morning. Is there anything you want him to bring?'

'Some amusing anecdotes, if he will. And a helicopter.'

Fischer needed to smile to remove her puzzled frown. 'No, he's done more than enough already. Please tell him that if I need to make telephone calls from here I'll have the operator record their cost.'

'He'll be insulted if you do. I think he's delighted to be involved in something dangerous. He wasn't - during the war, I mean.'

'Then he's the luckiest of men.'

'Are you *really* a spy, Herr Fischer?'

'No, Jeri. Just a fool who couldn't keep away from real spies.'

'I'm sure you aren't ...'

'No, he *is* a fool. Did you know he made us all believe that he was de ...?'

'Freddie, let's not say *too* much, eh?'

'Hmmph.'

Branssler was at the window, peering out. He sighed heavily. 'When it gets dark we won't know who's coming before they've arrived.'

'We weren't followed from Bonn. I was watching, all the way.'

'If they ask questions at the hotel and get nowhere they might suspect your man's helping us. It wouldn't be difficult to get his address.'

'At least we'll have some notice that they're looking. And what will they do – lay siege to the house? They need to be able to sweep me up in a moment, and ...'

The telephone rang. Fischer lifted the receiver but said nothing.

'Herr Fischer?'

'Oh. Yes, Armin?'

'An Englishman, a Mr Broadsmith, has just called the hotel, hoping to speak to you. He says that it's very necessary for you to meet him tomorrow.'

'He didn't give a reason?'

'No. He just asked that you be at the midpoint of the Rheinbrücke at 7am, the northbound side. It's very mysterious.'

'Thank you Armin. Wait … are you there?'

'Of course. You didn't say goodbye.'

"No. Do you know anyone who might lend me a camera, for a few hours only?'

'Go into the garden room. There's a chest there, with a Nikon and some lenses in the lower compartment. The longest is my new 200mm. I assume it's a long lens you need?'

'You're ten steps ahead, as usual. Thank you. I'll be careful with it.'

By the time the receiver went down Branssler was almost climbing Fischer's shoulder. 'What is it?'

'I think you were right, about the Englishman.'

'He's *Stasi*?'

'Unless you believe in striking coincidences. A few hours ago someone tried and failed to abduct me. Tomorrow, early, he wants to meet me where he has a clear view in the only two directions from which any help might arrive. And it couldn't arrive more quickly that a van.'

'A bridge?'

'The one we came over, this afternoon.'

Holleman nodded slowly. 'That was a *long* bridge.'

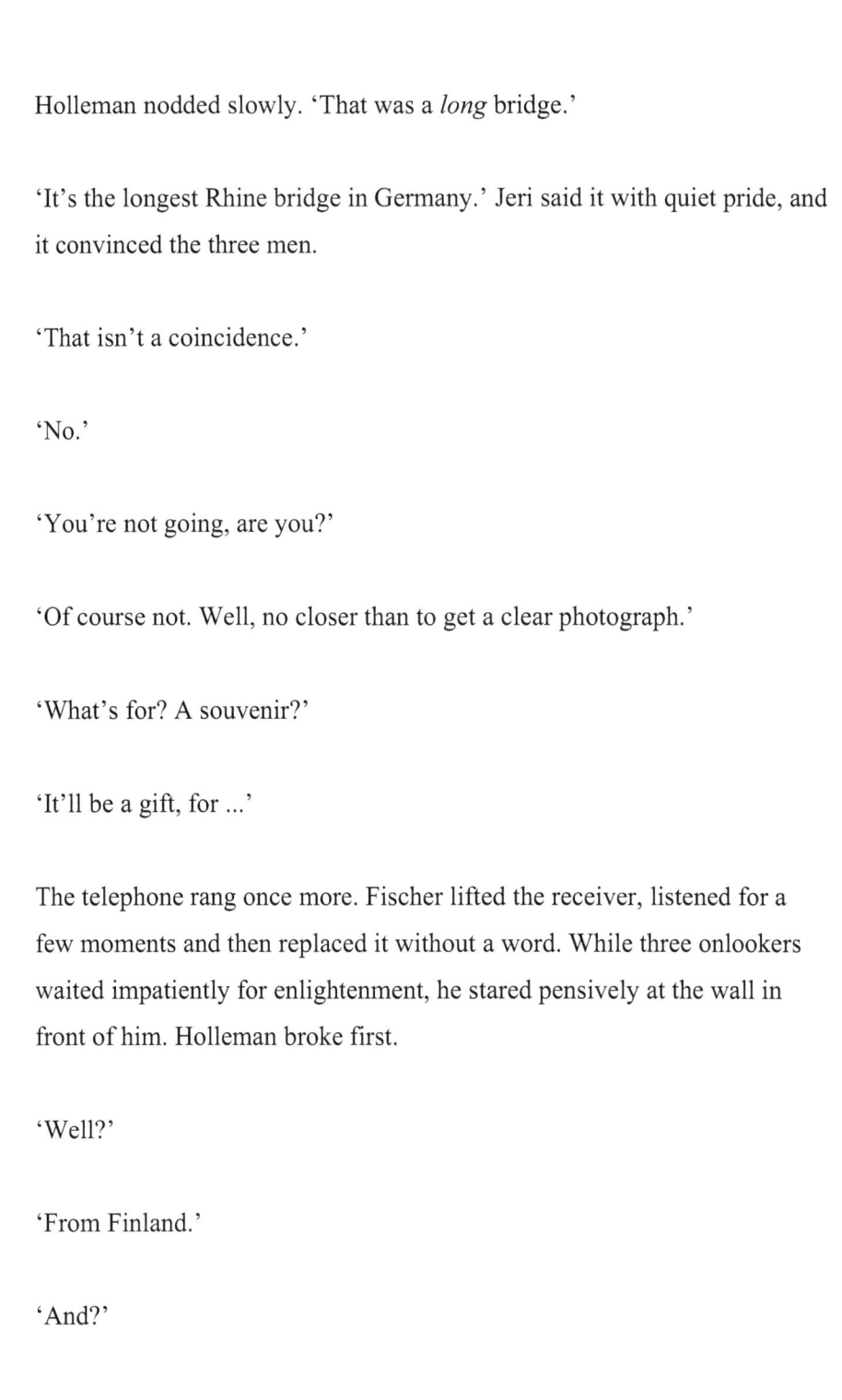

'It's the longest Rhine bridge in Germany.' Jeri said it with quiet pride, and it convinced the three men.

'That isn't a coincidence.'

'No.'

'You're not going, are you?'

'Of course not. Well, no closer than to get a clear photograph.'

'What's for? A souvenir?'

'It'll be a gift, for ...'

The telephone rang once more. Fischer lifted the receiver, listened for a few moments and then replaced it without a word. While three onlookers waited impatiently for enlightenment, he stared pensively at the wall in front of him. Holleman broke first.

'Well?'

'From Finland.'

'And?'

Fischer turned to his friend, a tired smile leavening the frown. 'It seems we're of a mind.'

43

For the first time since his childhood, Vladimir Yefimovich Semichastny felt the once-familiar warnings of an incoming anxiety attack. His heart was accelerating out of the blocks, his head throbbed dully and the fingers of his left hand, supposedly at rest on the desk blotter, shivered like corn stalks caught in a passing downpour. He tried to regulate his breathing and tapped the floor with his foot, a slow, regular tattoo, taking care not to think of the thing that had brought this on.

He had no fear that he was going to die in the dark, or that his father wasn't going to walk in the door at the end of his shift at the Grishino locomotive works, so the worst of it wasn't as bad as he remembered; nevertheless, almost twenty minutes passed before he could bring himself back to the most urgent matter in hand.

How the hell had they failed to take Fischer? The man was a half-cripple, at least sixty years old, and the two passers-by (or accomplices, possibly) who had thwarted the snatch were described as being equally decrepit. A six-man team - the best MfS had, according to Markus Wolf - had been made to look like first-time kidnappers by a *volkssturm* detachment of half their number. He sincerely hoped that someone's arse was being kicked energetically for this.

Given the time-pressures, it would almost certainly be the same team of dolts making the second attempt, which did nothing to ease his symptoms.

And Christ alone knew how his nerves would react to a casual enquiry from Shelepin regarding the neat, quick solution that he had demanded almost a week earlier. Otto Fischer wasn't yet a major concern to the KGB Chairman (not least because he had delegated *concern* to his deputy), but the man didn't forget things. He would ask, soon, and Semichastny wanted to be able to tell him that the matter was closed.

After that he could take his time, wait a day or two and then drop the first of several veiled suggestions that there was a leak somewhere, get KBG's remaining mole at Broadway (a low-level Russian translator) to send confirmation that London was receiving Zarubin's briefing papers and then pounce in the comfortable knowledge that the only existing counter-evidence would be the word of the accused.

First, though, Fischer had to be taken, squeezed and retired, and what had been a confident assumption of success was becoming a nail-chewing vigil. As long as the German wandered in free air he had Semichastny's testicles in his mutilated grip, even if he didn't know his tormentor's name, rank or even true purpose in dragging him from his Portuguese retirement. He had been the prefect choice of weapon – a man with no connections and no chance of refusing what had been offered – and now he was in effect primed, having been made aware of a fate he should never have suspected. Semichastny wished fervently that he had overseen the snatch himself, rather than trust Wolf. And when he thought a little more about it, he also wished that he had conceived an entirely different scheme to drag Zarubin from his perch.

He spent most of the evening dredging through the sort of paperwork one leaves until it begins to fester, knowing that sleep wouldn't come easily. His apartment in the House of Government was rarely used as an office, but he couldn't have remained in the Lubyanka, where anyone or everyone might notice his lack of equilibrium. Wolf would call him here, tomorrow, as soon as he knew that Fischer was taken. In the meantime, he could use his solitude to make a brutally forensic analysis of why he'd allowed admiration for his own genius to override both caution and his habitual thoroughness.

He poured a glass of wine (a rare indulgence) and sat down with a Defence Ministry memorandum on test-failings of the new 8K64. He had just about diagnosed the several problems as being just one (a rushed development schedule) when his doorbell ended all thoughts of ballistic missiles. In the seven months that he'd occupied this apartment, only once – a courteous neighbour, introducing himself on the day he arrived – had anyone called unannounced. The Stalin years weren't so historic that even a deputy chairman of KGB didn't feel his heart's rhythm stagger momentarily, and he struggled to keep his mind clear as he went to the door.

Though not a gregarious man, he could have thought of a hundred faces he would have preferred to confront him. Most pleasing would have been that of his courteous neighbor, come to ask the loan of something. Pioneers raising funds for worthwhile causes would have earned a windfall, his relief inflating the donation spectacularly. He might even have welcomed yet another ear-battering from the semi-retired under-secretary on the second floor, whose one-man residents' committee crusade had most of his fellow tenants praying for eviction. But the good, innocent reason that might have brought the Chairman of KGB to his home on a wet evening entirely escaped him.

Aleksandr Nikolayevich Shelepin, hat in hand, smiled pleasantly at his subordinate, but Semichastny wasn't reassured. Shelepin *did* smiles very well, despite the restraints imposed by the otherwise-lumpy severity of his face. It was a gift, or deflection, that had put at ease many men and women who might better have been served by anxiety, or dread. As his protege and deputy, Semichastny should have learned to parse it more precisely by now, but the man could keep his own counsel very well.

He stepped back and opened the door fully, hoping that his own face wasn't betraying him.

'What a pleasant surprise! Please, come in.'

'You know Comrade Kosygin, of course.'

Semichastny hadn't even noticed the second man, who moved laterally from behind the KGB Chairman and nodded, his face set in its habitual, non-committal cast. It wasn't often that a full member of the Praesidium called upon *anyone* socially, but whether he was delighted or crushed by the occasion wouldn't have been obvious to a sniffer-dog.

The two men entered the apartment, and both failed to resist the contemporary Soviet urge to glance around and measure it precisely in relation to their own accommodations. Semichastny was pleased, suddenly, that he had been allowed no time as yet to put his mark upon the place. It was pleasingly bare, without character, and could excite no envy.

His visitors sat without waiting for the invitation. Kosygin didn't look as if he might start soon, so their host applied himself to his boss, and formally.

'Comrade Shelepin ...'

'Oh, don't be so po-faced, Vladimir Yefimovich. This isn't about anything bad - is it, Andrei?'

The last was a none-too subtle indication of where Shelepin stood in the hierarchy. There couldn't be too many men in the USSR who would dare address Kosygin without deploying the formal patronymic, but the man didn't seem to mind, or even notice. His attention brought back from the window's river view, he turned, half-smiled and shook his head.

Shelepin continued. 'You'll have heard the rumour that I've been considered for membership of the Council of Ministers? Well, the First Secretary's confirmed it. I shall be resigning as KGB Chairman, of course, and that will need to occur before the 21st Praesidium is dissolved and the 22nd appointed, which gives us three months to find my successor.'

The smile this time had a hint of expectancy about it, so Semichastny did his best to seem disinterested (though he was anything but).

'I'm very pleased for you, Aleksandr Nikolayevich. No-one deserves it more than you.'

'That's very kind! In fact, our search shouldn't be too difficult. You must know that you're in with a chance?'

A chance wasn't nearly what Semichastny had been hoping to hear, but he had been practicing feigned surprise for so long now that it managed to cover anything less appropriate. He cleared his throat.

'That's wonderful news, Comrade Chairman. I hadn't really dared to hope that my brief time with KGB would have made a sufficient impression.'

'You're too modest. In fact, I've been discussing your name with several members of the Praesidium, and we think you'd be a very effective Chairman. We would hope, however, that you might answer certain questions regarding how you see the role.'

Semichastny didn't miss the glance that Shelepin and Kosygin exchanged over *questions*' slight emphasis. The role of KGB Chairman was set out in very precise regulations that allowed no latitude of interpretation. What they wanted to know was how far they could trust him, once his rear was warming the seat.

'Please, ask anything.'

Again, the glance. Shelepin scratched his nose (the first hint of a nervous reaction he had ever offered his deputy) and spoke carefully.

'Our system is, of course, one that functions on the principle of collective responsibility. I think we can all agree that we've learned the lesson of allowing a personal perspective to impose itself too strongly?'

It was a delicately bland reference to an era of mass trials and executions, of imperious intrusions into the business of planning military campaigns, and, latterly, of destinies determined by drunken mood-swings. Yes, thought Semichastny, they had definitely learned from that example. He nodded, and Shelepin continued.

'Given that, we must be vigilant to ensure that recidivist tendencies are discouraged, or, if necessary, disarmed. Not that such tendencies are *apparent* at present.'

Kosygin was shaking his head before the last was fully out, but Semichastny wasn't fooled. He was known to be one of the senior Praesidium members most irritated by Khrushchev's habit of having a brilliant idea and then acting on it before informing his colleagues – or, indeed, thinking the thing through. Shelepin had also, if very subtly, indicated his own frustration with recent decision-making processes (or their lacking). Neither man, probably, had allowed the First Secretary's triumph at Vienna to alter their opinions, so what they were asking – what they were *really* asking – was whether Semichastny could be trusted when (not if) it came to making adjustments.

He frowned at the floor for a few moments, giving himself time to think out the correctly-shaded response. It would, of course, be what they wanted to hear, but there was a delicate balance to find. Their successful candidate would be faceless, a conformist loyal to the right cause as determined by a set of circumstances yet to be glimpsed. Yet he would need to convince them also that, if it became necessary, he was prepared to be one of the fingers of the hand that held the gun – perhaps even the one that pulled the trigger.

He had one reservation only, and that was to do with how he had come to be here. Shelepin had long been his patron, but Khrushchev's support had been unstinting also. It had been the First Secretary's idea to bring him back to Moscow earlier that year, to put him in the best position to succeed the present KGB Chairman. And now he was being asked how inconvenient his sense of gratitude might prove to be. Semichastny's nature not entirely without a sentimental strain, but he recognized that quality as being less than ideal both at the present moment and with regard to the job for which he was being interviewed. He looked up and deployed what he hoped was a slightly regretful but firm air of purpose.

'If I were to be chosen for the role, Comrades, I would be fully aware of my duty to the Party, no less than the debt I owe it. Difficult choices come with responsibility, and a man who doesn't understand that has no business seeking it.'

Being specious, hypocritical and a near-affront to anyone whose principles couldn't be discarded at will, he considered his answer to be almost catechismic. Kosygin actually beamed, and Shelepin nodded sagely, the master whose pupil had proved himself fully up to muster. Nothing had been said or even hinted at, yet they all knew what this was about. Nikita Sergeyevich Khrushchev was not likely to change, despite enjoying the same ration of free-will as any other human being. No-one could say how many chances he had remaining, but the patience of the Council of Ministers and General Staff was a finite quality. It might be that his next miscalculation turned out to be his last; it might be that he was as yet several public humiliations from the point at which a mood would shift decisively, and action not only become prudent but unavoidable. When it did, there would consensus on one thing only – that the Soviet Union could afford no more protracted power struggles. Following Stalin's death, almost all those within shooting distance of a chance at replacing him had made the effort, and the man who won had denounced the cult of personality while going his own way just as willfully as his predecessor. It would not happen again. Semichastny had just been invited to be a loyal member of the faceless, collegiate band of apparatchiks who, when the time came, would administer the *coup de grace* collectively and then rule collectively, ready to decapitate any poppy whose head grew even slightly above the median height.

He would feel bad about Khrushchev - but not for long, and not so deeply that he would wish it otherwise. The man who ran the world's largest State Security apparatus served the people, not a single person. In any case, one always had the example of Lavrenty Beria, who tied himself so tightly to Stalin's excesses – and indeed, exceeded them - that the one could hardly survive the other. To be a servant of the masses was to make oneself a difficult target for arrows.

Kosygin and Shelepin had stood. Too late, Semichastny regretted not offering tea or wine, but then it occurred that both men probably wanted to be out of his and each other's company as soon as convenient. At their level, even innocent meetings tended to be misconstrued.

The evening's wretched examination of recent events – of what might or should have been done differently or not at all – had blossomed to one in which new horizons offered themselves lasciviously to Semichastny, and he was eager to be alone with them. Fortunately, his guests seemed to be of the same mind. Kosygin went through the front door without offering any sort of farewell, as was often his way. Shelepin made as if to follow him, but paused at the threshold and turned. His smile, as before, said nothing more than that his face was flexing its cheeks.

'I meant to ask. Where are we with our German problem?'

44

Roger Broadsmith blew on his hands. An early August morning had no right to be so cold, but the river was holding on to the last of the night's mist, and it had found his fingers. He hadn't thought to bring an overcoat from England (why would he, on a summer assignment?), and now he added another regret to his growing collection.

Keep him there for at least ten minutes. Perhaps *Cuttlefish* had a way with an anecdote, or could retain football statistics, but Broadsmith had fretted away half the night wondering what he might do if the conversation died, or – worse – if his reason for summoning Fischer to this place at such an hour wasn't immediately seen for what it was. Would he then need to restrain the man physically? Probably, he could do it. He had more than twenty years and about thirty pounds' advantage, but subduing someone wasn't easy, and doing it quietly required a cosh. And that was something else he hadn't thought to bring from England.

It wasn't hard to fathom the reason for this. Herr Fischer had outlived his usefulness, and whichever player in Moscow was using him had requested *Stasi* to process the retirement plan. It was logical – West German soil was almost home ground for them, and no doubt they had an embarrassment of safe-houses nearby to which the unfortunate gentleman could be taken and dealt with. It was a pity also; their association had been brief, but Fischer had something to him – a lack of artifice, perhaps, or a way of hiding it –

that made him almost pleasant company. Still, not having a choice in the matter made Broadsmith's role in his demise a good deal easier to bear.

He would tell Fischer that he had requested this meeting here, at this time, because he feared that he was being followed, which wasn't implausible. It could very well be that BfV wanted to know more about him, or feared that London was playing games with them. Or Gehlen's lot could be shadowing him in the hope of giving BfV a red face. Anything that was possible could hardly be beyond credibility in their smoke-and-mirrors world. Broadsmith would suggest an alternative location for any future exchanges of Moscow packages, and by then …

What? What if Fischer nodded, turned and walked swiftly away before his *Stasi* taxi arrived? Broadsmith had given that a lot of thought (in lieu of sleep), and arrived at a single, quite clever answer. He had asked himself what it was that a go-between of obscure loyalties might pause to listen to, and one thing recommended itself handsomely – an offer of sanctuary, should it ever become necessary. Obviously, Broadway would have no interest in whether Otto Fischer lived, died or – a halfway house, perhaps - went to live in Wolverhampton, but he couldn't know that. A potential escape route would surely be worth considering, and long enough for even the tardiest assassins to arrive.

It wasn't an admirable strategy, but Broadsmith wanted the thing done quickly and efficiently, the sooner to get his own arse off this damned bridge. He had come here carefully, taking a series of pointless detours, and had noticed no-one who showed an interest, but his experience as a field agent was too limited for him to be certain of that. Remaining here, unmoving, took some effort, particularly as he was visible from both banks of the Rhine. He couldn't help thinking of how a man with a rifle was spoiled for a choice of locations from which to take the shot.

He looked at his watch. Fischer was one minute late for their appointment, which meant nothing yet fired up his nerves once more. A dark green van had just passed by him on the near, southbound lane, and it had slowed just enough to convince him that his East German friends had arrived. He scanned the southern, Bonn-side of the bridge, looking both for its return and the man it would convey to his death.

The van reappeared at 7.34am, crossed the bridge without slowing and disappeared into Bueul-Mitte. Again, Broadsmith scanned the southern extremity of the bridge, and saw no-one. He told himself that there were any number of reasons why a man could be five minutes late, even if his hotel was only ten minutes' brisk walk from his destination. He might have been detained at reception by a talkative clerk; he might have forgotten something and needed to return to his room; he might be finishing breakfast, having failed too noticed he was running late; he might even …

The van appeared once more, coming south, and this time it slowed sufficiently for him to get a clear view of the man who sat in the passenger's seat. A cold, disinterested glance made him feel somehow guilty, as if he weren't playing his part, and the small regret he had for Otto Fischer's looming fate entirely dissipated.

Two hundred metres to the north, in a third-storey room overlooking the river, three men stood at the window. They had broken into the shop below (an auto-parts stockist) before dawn, trusting that, on a Sunday morning, no-one other than an insomniac or drunk could have noticed. They stood just at the level of the bridge road, but the man who waited on it was visible through the superstructure. For a while they had argued about what camera settings would best deliver a sharp, clear photograph in less than perfect light, until one of them – a bald, thick-set former *kriminalkommissar* - had explained the principle of pushing an emulsion during development. Set to under-expose three stops, the Nikon's shutter was working hard.

The gentleman with the artificial leg groaned. 'I'm hungry.'

'We're all hungry, Freddie.'

'How many shots are you going to take? He isn't Hedy fucking Lamarr.'

'I just want to make sure we get at least one sharp one.'

The photographic expert sniffed. 'It's set to 1/250th of a second. You could have a wank and they'd still be sharp.'

'Are you sure?'

'Yeah.'

'Right, then.' The man with the mutilated face rewound the spool, removed the camera back and offered the film canister to the bald man. 'You're sure you know how to do this, Gerd?'

'I checked Armin's chemicals. He's got everything I need.'

'I mean, you won't mess it up?'

'Yes, Otto, I will. Because the one thing that would make half a night's sleep and no breakfast meaningful would be to forget the basics of film development.'

'Sorry, Gerd. I didn't mean … oh, shit!'

Frantically, Fischer pulled another roll of film from his pocket and loaded it into the Nikon. On the bridge the green van was back, and this time it had halted next to the Englishman. He was leaning towards the open window, one hand on the chassis, the other gesticulating, and it didn't need a lip-reader to determine that the conversation was not a happy one. Before he stepped back and the van moved off, Fischer had fired the shutter five more times.

'That's our confession.'

'They might just have stopped to ask directions. It's what anyone looking at a photo would say.'

'They would, Freddie, in the normal world. But someone paid to be paranoid would notice the absence of other traffic and the Bonn skyline beyond, and then they'd look more closely, pick up a magnifying glass, make the face and ask themselves what it was doing there. Of course, we'd already have explained just that, so it would be up to the man on the bridge to try to scrape off the odorous mound of suspicion we'd just dropped on him. Now, let's find some breakfast.'

Broadsmith watched the van until it disappeared in Bonn's old quarter once more. He had done precisely what had been asked of him. He had risked his own anonymity to allow those idiots to put right what they'd failed to do the first time (*Cuttlefish* had been honest enough to explain why it was that he was risking himself), and if they'd failed again he could hardly be blamed for it. So why did he feel the weight of that failure?

They wouldn't be back, so there was no reason for him to linger; but he waited anyway, until after 8am, so he could say that he'd made the effort should anyone question his commitment. It was the first task they had ever charged him with, and ludicrously, he wanted to be seen not to be a poor choice of traitor. There was probably a name for the condition, in the manuals that codified the process of betrayal.

He felt horribly helpless. There wasn't even a prospect of distraction – it was Sunday, and nothing in Germany moved on Sundays. He couldn't go to the Ministry, couldn't drink himself into a better mood, didn't want to be alone with thoughts that would twist a bad situation into something worse. Most of all, he didn't want to begin to address the most urgent question – what had he done or failed to do, that had kept Fischer from his almost-certainly fatal appointment with the gentlemen in the green van?

45

'Are you ready, Boris Petrovich?'

'For what, Comrade General?'

'I meant, are you prepared for our great journey?'

'Not as much as if you'd cared to tell me anything about it.'

'I assumed you wouldn't wish to know more than was sensible, until it became necessary.'

'And now it is?'

'Now'ish. We move tomorrow, before dawn.'

Levin groaned. 'I knew it. A boat.'

'What makes you say that?'

'Why else would we move while it was dark still? You want to be in the water and away from the shore before we're noticed. What is it, a straight lunge across the sea, to Lübeck?'

'Yes, let's do exactly what might be expected of desperate men, and simplify the search enormously. You're aware of how heavily our vessels patrol the eastern Baltic, I expect?'

'I imagined you'd bribe fishermen to take us.'

'Fishing boats are particularly monitored, being intrinsically so much less suspicious than American submarines. No, the water route is far too attractive to consider. We must do this the hard way.'

'Your grateful pilot?'

'No, for all the same reasons plus radar. An internal flight is much easier to arrange and conceal than one that drags its boots through the world's most sensitive tripwires. If we attempted it I doubt the 'plane's wreckage would reach deep water. In any case, Yuri has more than discharged his debt to me. I could hardly ask him to risk his life or live the rest of it in exile.'

'What, then? Horseback?'

'Ha, very good. We'll leave in a manner that no-on would anticipate – slowly, through a great number of checkpoints and across several international borders, making no attempt to conceal ourselves.'

'Be serious.'

'And no false papers or disguises. I shan't even dye my lovely blond hair. We shall go proudly and honestly, as men should. Did I mention that I've brought with me some of those commemorative Soviet Space Triumph postcards I had you buy for me last year?'

'The dreadfully kitsch ones?'

'Delightful, aren't they? At regular intervals upon our westward odyssey I shall address one to A. N. Shelepin, care of the Lubyanka, Dzerzhinsky Square, Moscow. No message, of course, but I'll sign each of them and put it in a field-mail envelope to ensure that it arrives the following day. He'll know where we've been and have a good idea of our next steps. I intend to be a very amenable prey.'

'Forgive me, but are you mad?'

'Consider our situation. We're attempting to defect. By now, the Director of the Defence Ministry establishment at Tskaltubo will be fretting about my non-return to his delightful Spa. So, to ensure that his career isn't hanging in open air he'll have passed the news to the KGB liaison there, who can be expected to have contacted Moscow the moment he found a telephone. Even allowing for slips, oversights and outright indolence, word will have flown to Comrade Shelepin's office. Therefore, we are officially fugitives, even if the Chairman is still wondering who the hell he should tell about this, and when.'

'He'll mobilize everyone, surely, and put out an alert to all ports, airfields and border crossings?'

'He'll *want* to, certainly. But he's a cautious man, and there are complications to consider.'

Bewildered, Levin ran a hand through his sparse hair. 'You mean, whether to shoot you outright or have a pretend-trial beforehand?'

'Among other ordeals, he will need to have an unpleasant interview with the First Secretary. I am, after all, the man's special advisor, so the order to proceed has to come from him. Before he does that, however, Shelepin will be thinking about containment. He can put us both against a tree, deep in the forest, and no-one will ever find our corpses; but the problem of General Zarubin doesn't end with his brains evacuating his skull. There's also the issue of legacy.'

'What you know.'

'And what might not be contained. We believe that our office has been searched how many times in the past five years?'

Levin considered the view towards the former chicken shed. 'Three times, definitely. Five would be a reasonably firm guess.'

'Yet they've found nothing substantial – not even our little safe, with the yellow box. I'm known to be a discreet sort, I believe?'

'You have no friends, no close allies, so what else could you be?'

'And yet even such a profound disadvantage can be useful. They have no idea what I know, and how it might have been preserved. KGB wasn't cleansed with Serov's removal. It has a history – a ripe, full, the Saviour-alone-knows-what-might-yet-emerge history. Shelepin's been in his chair for three years, so as yet he can barely have scratched the scab. He doesn't know what the damage might be, nor who would be splashed, should something cause the crust to burst. Imagine Khrushchev himself being compromised by whatever I know coming out – that is, reaching the ears of those members of the Praesidium whose feelings for him are less than ardent.'

'*Would* he be?'

Zarubin blew out his cheeks. 'Honestly, I couldn't say. During the months immediately following Stalin's death the plotting was so tortuous that everyone or no-one might be stained by it. But actual culpability isn't the point - it's what's feared that matters. So I'm going to ask Shelepin, rhetorically, if he really wants to come after us.'

'Why?'

'To indicate to him that I know too much, and that I'm perfectly aware of it.'

Levin shook his head. 'It's a curious strategy, to make someone believe you'll be better off dead.'

'Oh, I'm sure he's thought *that* for several years now. It's a matter of degree, though – how much does he want or need to see me dead? There's a balance of discomfort in Soviet Politics, and finding it can be difficult. Beria went too far, thinking that other men's fear of him would keep him safe. He didn't see that when fear becomes terror it turns upon itself. His colleagues were paralysed for a while, but eventually they decided to hell with any consequences, because Beria dead was by far the safest option. Serov, for all his brutality, was more measured. He survived his own downfall because other men's fear of what he knew outweighed their fear of his remaining in the world.'

'Ironic, that you helped to bring both of them down, and now you're in the same shit.'

'Yes, isn't it? Of course, I excite neither terror nor excessive loathing – I'm merely a stone in too many boots. I doubt that Shelepin, given the choice, would ever have moved against me. But his deputy has forced *me* to move, and now the Chairman needs to make a choice.'

'You shouldn't provoke him. He might move first and think later.'

'Which is another reason we won't leave by air or boat. Either method would push him to make a quick, decisive decision, and almost certainly it wouldn't be to our advantage. In any case, I mean to remind, not provoke. But you're worried that the blank postcards might be too insolent?'

'I do.'

'Well, then. I meant to send the first from somewhere near Pskov, but I'll let you post it, and it will contain a message - the only message. We'll get Shelepin thinking about more than just me.'

'How?'

'You'll ask a question.'

'What?'

'Why are General Zarubin's briefing papers finding their way from the Lubyanka to British Intelligence?'

'On a postcard?

'Why not? It communicates a message as effectively as a stone tablet. The others will be blank, because *that* message is as important as anything we could write.'

'Not so hard, Gerd.'

Fischer frowned at Branssler, who stooped and lifted the Englishman from the floor to which the back of his hand had sent him. Holleman righted the toppled stand-chair, brushed the seat and stood back.

'He tried to hand you over to *Stasi* assassins. He deserves a few slaps.'

Reseated, Broadsmith felt his forehead carefully. So far, he had managed to maintain a stoic silence which, rather than impress his tormentors, only confirmed that he was as loath as they to attract attention. They currently trespassed in an office in the Federal Interior Ministry building, upon which any amount of succour might have converged, had he chosen to cry out. But he had seen the photographs, and heard what Holleman and Branssler had to say about his meeting in the park, and in between the slaps was trying to work out what options remained to him.

Fischer bent down and placed his mouth close to the Englishman's ear and whispered. 'Don't think about them.'

Broadsmith recoiled slightly but said nothing.

'Choices, I mean. What I'm asking is very simple. You pass on a message to your Mr Shergold in London, asking that he meet me. If he hesitates you urge upon him that it's very much to his advantage to come to Bonn – which it is, by the way. In return, we don't tell him that you're a traitor. Our business will be done, and you can congratulate yourself on avoiding the falling piano.'

The Englishman's head dropped slightly. 'I could do what you want, and you'd tell them anyway.'

'Why? If I'd wanted to bury you I would have sent these photographs directly to him – *and* it would have been a very effective way of proving my sincerity. But if you recommend me and I then betray you, I undermine my own credibility, yes?'

'Then why are you bothering to go through me?'

Fischer looked up, at Holleman and Branssler in turn. It was a question he'd put to himself already, but hadn't tried too hard to answer. Being forced upon him made it a little easier.

'I hope not to sound naive or foolish, Mr Broadsmith, but I want this to be … *ehrlich*?'

'Above board, you mean?'

'Is that what you say? I don't want your Mr Shergold to continue to regard me as a spy, because that's not what I am. This passing of messages, it wasn't something for which I volunteered. I would have no dealings with anyone in Moscow, if I had the choice. I didn't, though. The thing I want you to do now is connected to the other, but I've come to you willingly. I want my word to be believed – by Mr Shergold, of course. What *you* believe is less important.'

'*Is* it to be believed? If I tell him that you're to be trusted and you're not, that's almost as bad for me as if ...'

'I don't want to make an enemy of Mr Shergold. If it helps, you may say to him also that I wish the help of SIS for my own sake, and therefore put myself in his hands.'

Holleman frowned. 'What was that he just said?'

Branssler shook his head. 'I'm not sure. My English isn't good.'

'If he's arranging to die again, I'll kill him. Otto?'

'Yes, Freddie?'

'This fellow speaks perfect German. So why did you just put the scrambler on?'

'Because it's better if every detail of what's happening can't be kicked out of you.'

'That's likely, is it?'

'Probably not, but let's be prudent.'

Holleman sniffed. Branssler went to the door, poked his head into the corridor and checked both ways.

'This place is deserted. They let us in with two questions, tell us where to go rather than march us up here and no-one's checking that we haven't cacked him. This *is* the Interior Ministry, right?'

'They probably don't care about Englishmen - at least, not the ones who talk to the wrong sort of Germans.'

Broadsmith stared at the two men during this exchange but hardly seemed to hear the words. He was passive, waiting, as able to influence a weatherfront as he was his immediate future. Fischer tapped his shoulder.

'So, will you speak to Mr Shergold?'

For a few moments their captive stared at the walls, the thin decor, the door he hadn't thought of trying to reach, and then nodded. 'Not from here. They probably monitor my calls.'

'The main post office on Münsterplatz, then. We'll walk.'

Holleman's leg slowed them a little, but half an hour later they were at Bonn's main post-office. The three Germans took up a loose semi-circular perimeter around the booth from which Broadsmith made his call. He asked the international operator for a London number and then spoke inaudibly for a few minutes. At one point he paused, opened the booth door and beckoned Fischer.

'Where?'

Fischer held the other man's gaze as he thought it through and then gave him Armin's address in Sankt Augustin. The telephone conversation continued for a further minute before the receiver went down. Broadsmith emerged, let the door close and stood with his back pressed against it, as if braced for another slap.

'He'll be here this evening.'

'Shergold? Shergold personally?'

'Yes. He said he's coming alone.'

'You know that if *Stasi* somehow get the address I just gave you …?'

'If they do, I'll have much more to worry about than you three. I'd prefer not to go the way of Blake.'

'Good. You can be on your way, Mr Broadsmith. We won't be speaking further.'

The Englishman managed to withdraw at a casual pace, and didn't look back. Holleman watched him balefully, and sniffed.

'What if that was all crap?'

'All?'

'What he said. He might have phoned his London tailor, and now he's rushing off to find his *Stasi* friends so they can have a third go at you, back at Armin's house.'

Fischer gazed respectfully at his friend. 'I wouldn't have thought of that. But I doubt that he'd risk our having made arrangements already to have the photographs sent to London if anything happened to us. In any case, did you notice anything about our Englishman?'

'His immaculate hair.'

'His air of … what, despondency? We seem to have cornered a half-beaten man.'

'You think he doesn't enjoy kicking the ball both ways?'

'It's hard to imagine that anyone would. To even sleep at night, one would need an iron commitment to a cause, I suppose, or a weakness that could be bought. From the conversations I had with him, I took the impression – and it made me almost like him – that he doesn't really believe in anything.'

'An English Otto, then.'

Fischer nodded. Having seen the back of Broadsmith, both Holleman and Branssler were relaxing visibly. He had been waiting for an opportunity, an unpleasant moment, and he doubted that anything better would present itself.

'You know I'm grateful for what you've done. I couldn't ...'

'Fuck off.'

'What I mean ...'

'What you mean is thanks, lads, but you can go home now. So, fuck off.'

Branssler shook his head slowly. 'We're going nowhere until you can put your head outdoors without it being shot off.'

'The difficult part's done. Now, I need to convince Herr Shergold, and there's nothing that either of you can do to help with that.'

'He might kill you by way of saying no.'

'If you'd met him you wouldn't think that. Even I might be able to deal with him.'

'Then *Stasi* might Off you both – a pain in the arse *and* a top British spy, together. Why wouldn't they?'

'Without Broadsmith's word they can't know, and I can't have you there when I meet him. If he sees a couple of ugly thugs he'll turn and run.'

The ugly thugs looked mildly at each other. 'Are you as hurt by that as I am, Gerd?'

'Ripped open. But I'm staying.'

Holleman turned back to Fischer. 'Alright. We'll go for a walk while you chat to the Englishman. You know where Armin's rifle is. I expect you know how to use it?'

'Better than you or Gerd. I was trained with one, remember?'

Branssler looked curiously at Holleman. 'Luftwaffe didn't show you how to use a rifle?'

'Fighter cockpits tended to be stuffed with instrumentation and pilots, not rifle-racks. Didn't you even *read* about the war, Gerd?'

'Only the deserters' lists. Otto, when this Shergold fellow's been dealt with, will everything be settled?'

'If it goes well, yes. Naturally, I'll need to uphold my side of the arrangement, and you can't help with that.'

'Why not?'

'Because it has to be settled in Berlin, and your wives would kill you if you stepped into that furnace.'

'They wouldn't know.'

'They would, because I'd tell them. Negotiation over.'

47

The moment that Semichastny regarded as heralding the reversal of his promising career was announced by just three words, bad enough in themselves but made infinitely worse by the cold, unfamiliar tone that delivered them.

'My office. Immediately.'

An innocent man might have assumed that a critical situation had arisen in some distant, lose-it-on-a-map shit-hole, or that a senior member of the Praesidium had been found with a CIA-issue fountain pen buried in his neck. Neither possibility occurred to him. Like a schoolboy caught smoking behind the toilet block, he felt the weight of the summons like the Babylonian yoke. A few moments' search for the slightest mitigation confirmed to him that he should have started much earlier, and thought harder.

He told his secretary that he would be with the Chairman for a while (it would take a few minutes at least to arrest and formally charge him), and then gulped down two cups of water at the corridor font in a metaphorical attempt to cool his nerves. Usually, he would have with him a notebook to ensure that no instruction given by Shelepin was overlooked, but it was doubtful that anything said to him today would be fit for posterity, much less the Lubyanka rumour-mill. They would all know soon enough, and it would make for the wrong sort of entertainment for months to come.

He offered a feeble nod to the KGB Chairman's private secretary, knocked once on the inner door and walked into Shelepin's office. His boss was alone, which offered a fleeting half-hope of a break in the storm-front (disgrace was rarely done discreetly in Soviet Politics), but the expression on his patron's face removed that momentary delusion.

'What's this?'

Without looking up from a report he was pretending to read, Shelepin pushed something across his desk. Semichastny leaned forward and picked it up. It was a postcard, bearing a cinematic 'still' of an artificial man, helpfully labelled *Robot!* in lurid script. He flipped it over. It was addressed to Shelepin personally, had a brief heading: *From Pskov*, and bore a short, signed message, framed as a question, that almost freed Semichastny's bowels from their adult restraints.

'It's ...'

Really, nothing came to mind. He had a degree in history and almost the same in chemical engineering (the war had interrupted his studies); had risen seamlessly to lead Komsomol and then shuffled the rats' nest of Azeri politics into a semblance of discipline before being brought to Moscow at Shelepin's personal recommendation. All his endeavours had prospered, and just two days earlier he had been offered – at the ridiculously callow age of thirty-seven – leadership of the world's most powerful and pervasive security service. Years of promiscuous effort and reward, now laid to waste by a brief message, scrawled on the most debased format of communication yet devised by man.

'It's from our friend, General Zarubin.'

Of course it was - the signature said so. Not that Semichastny needed confirmation, given that the rest was a rigid finger, pointing straight at his chest. Shelepin's hand moved, a flicking motion, and two more cards slid across his desk. Both were blank, other than for helpful, one-word declarations of origin and Zarubin's signature. On the display side, one portrayed a cosmonaut (in full spacesuit, naturally) triumphantly holding up the red Hammer and Sickle; the other was a representation of Sputnik soaring high above the Soviet Union; both designs were almost ubiquitous, to be found in any street kiosk from Kaliningrad to Vladivostok, and therefore untraceable.

Shelepin pushed three field envelopes towards him. Semichastny examined the franks. One had been posted, apparently, in Pskov, another in Ostrov, the last in Gavry. He looked up.

'He's heading for Latvia.'

Shelepin rubbed his eyes with a hand. 'Oh, I think he's going a lot further than that. What are we to do, Vladimir Yefimovich?'

'He seems to want to be caught. We stop the train and ...'

'He's travelling by car.'

'How do you know?'

'Because Gavry isn't on a rail line. But that wasn't what I meant by *do*.'

'Then what, Comrade …?'

'About you. What are we going to do with a man who ignores or overrides all KGB command protocols to commence a private war?'

Semichastny swallowed hard. He couldn't recall Shelepin ever having spoken so severely to him - but then, he'd never had cause until now. Saying nothing seemed to be the safest strategy, so he adopted it wholeheartedly. The Chairman leaned forward, reclaimed his cards and shuffled them into a neat pile.

'These are messages, not a taunt. Do you know what they say - I mean, beyond the first one? I think we both understand *that* message.'

'Perhaps he wants to be invited to negotiate?'

'There's no negotiation to be had. If SIS have been receiving his intelligence reports he's for a bullet, personal aide to Khrushchev or not. He isn't a stupid man - he understands this. So, what else?'

'A threat?'

'More likely, yes, but threatening KGB is a dangerous sport. There's a third possibility.'

'Which is?'

'The cards – the second and third cards – are blank. If we receive further installments, I suspect that they, too, will carry nothing but a location and signature. If you wanted to send a particular message, what would blankness indicate?'

Semichastny's mind was equally blank, but the questions seemed to indicate that his opinion was still valued, if only as an echo. He tried, hard, but the only thing that occurred was doltish.

'Nothing?'

Curiously, Shelepin didn't laugh, scowl or tell him to get out. 'In a way, yes. I believe that the General is indicating that he travels with no embarrassments.'

'Embarrassments?'

'To us. Clearly, there's only one place that's safe for him now, and that's anywhere that isn't the Soviet Union or allied territory. He's defecting, and he wants us to know it. He also wants us to know that he presents no further danger, should we be thinking of next steps – as we are, naturally.'

'But … surely, we're going to arrest him?'

Shelepin sat back and regarded his deputy carefully. 'We could do that, yes. He's been set up for a fall, but the act of running is as good as a guilty plea, or so our system presumes. Ridiculously, the consensus would be that an innocent man stays to fight his case, despite all the lessons of the past twenty years that tell us exactly the opposite. Zarubin isn't that sort of fool, though. He has no-one other than the First Secretary to back him, and Khrushchev wouldn't weaken his own position to defend someone he's trying be rid of anyway. The General's only option is escape, and the only factor that would allow it is a reluctance on our part to stop him.'

'It's *Zarubin*! We *want* him dead. KGB has been hoping for a moment like this for years. It's why … '

'It's why you began this game. Believe me, I don't entirely disapprove of the method, just the presumption that you could act independently. I assume you recruited, rather than stumbled upon, this Fischer?'

'Yes.'

'As a former associate of the General he'd give credence to the story you were trying to tell – that he was a trusted go-between to the British?'

'That was my intention. I wanted to give you a triumph.'

'And help yourself into this seat. Which we were going to offer to you in any case.'

Semichastny felt his cheeks warming. There was no way now that his motives could be misinterpreted as being in any way selfless. Shelepin was right, of course – his intention when beginning this bold operation had been to put the Chairman in his debt, to ease himself into the front row of those being considered for the soon-to-be-vacated seat *and* to settle a long-standing score. It had failed, yet the strange thing was that failure had become a success of sorts. He had no idea how Zarubin had discovered the moves against him, but the revelation had set him on the path to his second defection, one that even Khrushchev could never forgive. So why was Shelepin hesitating, now that the beast was in his sights?

As usual, Shelepin seemed to pick up nearby thoughts as if they had spilled like rice.

'This *triumph* may be more elusive than you imagine, Vladimir Yefimovich. I want you to consider the example of my predecessor, if you would.'

'Serov?'

'Now, there's a man who would happily dance on Zarubin's dying body. He intended to do just that, three years ago, but ended up with boot marks on his own spine. Even then, exiled to Khodynka, he's been spoiled for a choice of assassins to finish off his old enemy, yet he hasn't since lifted a finger against Zarubin. Why do you think that is?'

'Perhaps the General has information that would hurt him.'

'Yes, perhaps. And *perhaps* is precisely the problem we share with Serov. We don't know what Zarubin knows. Like Beria and Serov, his two victims, he is by disposition a miner, an extractor, a hoarder of data which other men would prefer to remain buried deeply. Soviet politics leave wounds, mainly in the back, and very few of our leaders are innocent of wielding the blade at some or several points during their ascensions. Which of them could be hurt by their pasts, and how might that pain then be deflected upon us?'

'How can we know?'

'Precisely. If Sergei Aleksandrovich Zarubin could be caught, bottled like a fly and suffocated I should be delighted to give the order, but I fear that a man of his resourceful nature would have long ensured that his secrets can't be bottled with him. If – *if* – we can convince ourselves that he has nothing of current operational significance that he can hand to the British, it would be wiser to take the hint of these blank cards and trust the past to remain where it is. He is, after all, attempting to remove himself from us as decisively as if he'd opened a window at the top of Spasskaya Tower and stepped out into air. Which, I'd remind you, is what we've wanted for almost a decade.'

'But how *can* we convince ourselves?'

'This will be your reward for putting us where we are, my friend. Don't plan to sleep tonight - you're going to be reviewing the circulation lists for every document making mention both of live and legacy operations where our assets might be compromised by Zarubin's mouth. I say *mention*, because as you know we never commit detail to anything that's to be seen by anyone other than the Security Committee and First Secretary. Even lateral references, however, can sometimes point curious noses in a direction we'd wish not to be scrutinized. To counter-check, speak to Shevchenko and ask to see copies of all KGB material – I mean, *everything* - that the First Secretary has passed on to Zarubin over the past three years. We've tried hard to ensure that he doesn't have access to sensitive KGB material, but we need certainty. Whatever dark, personal secrets the General has collected and stored, his departure cannot compromise our work.'

'That will take ...'

'Hours at least, and probably most of tomorrow. So, I won't detain you further. In the meantime, I'll let Karlshorst know that an old friend and comrade is heading in their direction, in case you find anything that makes him too combustible.'

'You think his exit point is Berlin? Why?'

'Because for him it's familiar territory, and Serov told me that he might still have friends there. Because it's what *I* would do, in similar circumstances. But if I'm wrong ...' Shelepin held up his small sheath of outer space postcards; '... I'm sure Zarubin will put me right in the next day or two.'

Despite Fischer's urgings, Holleman and Branssler hadn't quite evacuated the house before Mr Shergold arrived. The three met at Armin's garden gate, in fading light that gave the large Germans an incremental (if undeserved) aura of menace. The visitor paused and took a half-step back.

'Evening, mate.' Holleman winked cheerily, pushed opened the gate he'd just closed and waved a cinema usher's hand towards the house. 'Otto! Your gentleman's here!'

The bellow probably startled homeward commuters down on Wehrfeldstrasse, but it killed any possible concern that this was a carefully planned snatch. The Englishman nodded, offered a *g'n abend* and squeezed himself through the meat gap.

'They're old friends, ex-policemen. They seem to believe that I need looking after. I told them to go away while we spoke.'

In the hallway, Fischer took Shergold's hat and raincoat. On foreign territory, and without his SIS bodyguards, he seemed a little smaller than at their previous meeting – a quite nondescript, indeterminably-aged bureaucratic sort, one might assume. Fischer had only fleeting experience of Westminster, but he imagined that a whole army of similarly grey men passed between and through its buildings of State, hive-busy with the myriad complications of running down an empire. That would probably be an error, but one that men in intelligence work were happy to encourage.

Would you like some tea, Herr Shergold?'

'Yes, thank you.'

In the kitchen, the Englishman sat down at the table and slumped slightly. Fischer played the host, glancing occasionally at his guest while trying to put what he had to say into an order than might convince. He was allowed to do so uninterrupted; it was only when the tea-cup came to rest under the other man's nose that he looked up from the laminated table-cover.

'Thank you.'

'Forgive me, but you look tired. Was the journey difficult?'

Shergold smiled. 'No, it was very convenient. One of our rescue dogs has pupped, so my wife and I haven't been sleeping much lately.'

Fischer relaxed slightly. He liked the sound of dogs, and worried foster parents. It seemed a long way from cold, neat endings.

'Well, thank you for coming.'

'Roger Broadsmith was very persuasive. He seems to think you can be useful.'

'Not me. I'm speaking for an acquaintance who would like to meet you.'

'This would be the gentleman previously mentioned to me by Jonas Kleiber?'

'Yes.'

'And he's something to do with the data we've been receiving from you?'

'It's his signature on almost every document I've handed to Mr Broadsmith.'

'But he wasn't their source?'

'Definitely not. This exercise was intended to implicate him.'

For a few moments Shergold stirred his tea and re-examined the pattern on the table-cloth. The free hand patted his jacket and he looked up. 'May I smoke?'

'Please.'

He filled his pipe while Fischer found an orphaned saucer and placed it on the table. After it was lit he regarded his host through a cloud of smoke

'This acquaintance – his name is Zarubin? - he's being set up by KGB?'

'He's devoted years to making enemies.'

'Why don't they just have him disappear?'

'Because he has friends also – or a friend, at least.'

'This would be a powerful friend, to make KGB move carefully.'

'Probably the *most* powerful friend that any Soviet citizen could have.'

'Ah.' Shergold nodded and drew upon his pipe, as casually as if he'd been offered the sugar bowl. 'And Zarubin's a General, I believe?'

'An honorific. He was an officer in NKGB, a long time ago.'

'Well, NKGB *was* a long time ago. He's not ex-KGB, then?'

'No. But he defected once, to the Americans, and then returned home without punishment. KGB therefore had a reason to dislike him, and as I say, he's teased that sentiment considerably since.'

Shergold looked more engaged now.

'That's very unusual, to suffer no consequences. Perhaps he was *sent* to the United States?'

'I don't believe so.' Fischer rubbed his forehead. 'Mr Shergold, I'm not familiar with all of his career, but I can say a few things with certainty. He came back from America in 1953, with something that allowed Beria to be toppled. Three years ago he was in Berlin briefly, and helped me to escape KGB. This was at a time when Beria's successor, Serov, was moving against him. Just days after that, Serov fell also. Zarubin may be a lucky man, but I think he knows also how to make luck happen.'

'You're being used to try to bring him down, but now you plead a case for him. Is he a friend?'

'No ...' Fischer had never quite found the niche to which Zarubin belonged. At various times they had saved each other's lives, wished heartily that they had never met, tried hard to keep a continent's distance between each other, and, whenever necessary, shamelessly used their relationship. Zarubin was the uncomfortable relative, the embarrassing acquaintance, the indispensable enemy, the ...

'In a way, yes. We have a long history, and not all of it's been unfortunate. I would prefer him to survive this, if the choice presents itself.'

'Then how will you persuade me? You say he isn't KGB, and presumably he's not GRU either. Why would SIS be interested?'

It was a horribly good point. Fischer knew that Zarubin was close to Khrushchev, but precisely what the man did to earn his crust wasn't clear to him. They had last spoken three years earlier, at which time the Russian had asked everything he needed to ask and evaded every straight question put to him. His expertise was in foreign intelligence, but presumably KGB supplied all that the First Secretary and Praesidium needed to hear about the world outside. In any case, would they allow a man they detested to wander anywhere near sensitive data? What else could be spoken of that might tempt Harold Shergold into offering him sanctuary?

Idiot. He was trying to find a way to describe tree-bark, when all he needed to do was point at the forest. Shergold didn't need to be tempted - he'd just heard that this was the man, alone or abetted, who had brought down Beria. That one event had cleared the way for Khrushchev, and whatever role the First Secretary had offered Zarubin in turn had not only allowed him to survive KGB's wrath but topple Serov also. What else need be said of the man?

Shergold was waiting patiently, moving his teacup in a circular motion to agitate its dregs. Fischer tried to apply an open, puzzled expression, but as always his face did what it did, and the result could have said anything.

'Why wouldn't you be interested? This man sits next to Khrushchev himself. He has - had – the power to bring down two KGB Chairmen, and if he doesn't have an intimate understanding of every possible permutation of thrust and counter-thrust that puts - and keeps - men in the Kremlin he's slowed badly in recent years. Think about what you *don't* know about Soviet politics, write it down and present it to him on his first day on English soil. He will enlighten you.'

Shergold leaned forward and replaced the cup in its saucer. 'I'm sure the Foreign Office will be delighted to hear all of that. But I don't report to King Charles Street.'

'You wouldn't want to know the mind of the Russian Premier?'

'I doubt that even General Zarubin can read minds.'

'He can come closer than anyone else you're ever likely to interview. And your Foreign Office would be grateful for such a gift, surely?'

'Does the General have terms?'

'He'll want a roof to keep him dry and a small allowance. He isn't someone who appreciates luxuries – other than wine, I believe.'

'And you? Broadsmith says you want to be part of the arrangement.'

'I have nothing to offer. I hope that KGB's interest in me will die with Zarubin's departure, but I can't be certain of it. If you could put a short-term British visa on my Portuguese passport I'd be very grateful. I don't need money.'

'When will this happen?'

'He's moving already. If he evades KGB he should be in Germany within the next two days.'

'So you're in contact with him?'

'Not now. We agreed some arrangements a few years ago in case things turned for him. It was the price of his financing my new life in exile. I've been able to get messages to him via a Swiss bank and a third party in

Finland, but now he's moving he can't be reached. If he makes it I know where to meet him, and when.'

'May I have those details?'

'Certainly. When you've agreed to bring him in.'

'I've agreed already. It's why I'm asking.'

The weight was only a moral thing, but Fischer felt its passing keenly. When first dragged into this business he would willingly have been the instrument of Zarubin's fall, if it had preserved Zofia. But her murder had hung him out as a bargain-rate Judas, a culpable fool. There wasn't much left to put right, other than this.

He told Shergold what he wanted to know. The Englishman nodded and stood.

'I'm returning to London now. SIS have a safe-house in Charlottenburg that's not too far from your rendezvous.' He removed a pen and envelope from his jacket and wrote quickly. 'Call this number when you have him, say 'Bronwyn', then hang up and wait where you are. They won't be more than a few minutes. We'll get you out through Gatow, the following morning.'

'Thank you.' Fischer folded the paper and looked up. 'Bronwyn?'

Shergold smiled. 'The proud mother whose pups are giving us sleepless nights. Goodbye, Herr Fischer.'

'Is that the last of them?'

Levin moved in the car seat as he asked, but then he moved almost constantly, trying and failing to find some position that would ease his leg. By the time they had stopped each evening he had been twitching like a pigeon on a live wire, and Zarubin had been obliged almost to carry him from the car into the small apartment blocks where, curiously, a vacant, end-of-corridor room was always waiting for them, key in door. Levin had wanted to ask, but, fearing the answer, had stifled his curiosity.

The past few days had felt like scenes from a Kaufman film. They were fleeing across borders, spitting in the face of KGB, yet nothing – literally, nothing – was intruding upon the mundane, dragging act of escape. They drove; they crossed checkpoints at which Zarubin waved a card and guards waved him through; they ate, slept, defecated and recommenced the journey each day as if every one of its predecessors had been a slate, now wiped clean of the events that marked it. They had been challenged only once, at the Polish border the previous day. Passing through unhindered from the Lithuanian side, a young Polish border-guard had taken Zarubin's card and retreated to the command post. A Major emerged and beckoned the General. The two men spoke for longer than Levin's nerves could bear (and then for a considerable while after that), but when the Major returned the card he stepped back and saluted. Even Levin took that to be a good sign.

There had been hardly any conversation as they drove. Zarubin, always preoccupied, never spoke without first being asked a question and answered in as few words as were needed to kill a nascent discussion. He only came to life when they refilled the fuel tank, and then to practise the privileged air of a man who could pass by queues and stop at the small pump that was always kept free for the military and *nomenklatura*. The same card - waved more lazily than when men in uniform asked to see it - had filled the tank each time, no questions asked.

They had spent nights in Pskov, Daugavpils, Augustow, and now, after the longest, most torturing stage, in Poznań. Zarubin had posted his blank cards each evening and then returned to their room, where they would eat whatever food he had found in local shops (or, if he was unsuccessful, one of their dwindling mountain rations). In the mornings, they departed before other residents were stirring, and were seen only once, leaving their Augustow accommodation, when a cleaner looked up from her half-mopped floor, nodded and then returned to her business. Invariably, breakfast was taken at the first road-workers' tea-shed they found (the region's roads being permanently in need of emergency maintenance, they were ubiquitous), where the other fine-diners kept as much to themselves as the most paranoid fugitive might have wished.

Levin told himself repeatedly that a remorseless chase was on, the hunters converging inexorably upon them, but the evidence was lacking. Was Chairman Shelepin really so afraid of what Zarubin might know or reveal that he was holding off? Did he believe that he was being double-bluffed by the postcards, and was searching everywhere *but* along the route they drew? He couldn't believe either possibility, but why else were they not presently sitting in cells, awaiting the arrival of men with needles? They travelled west, day after day, with almost as little hindrance as holiday-makers touring the south of France – it was not supposed to be possible, and though Levin was fervently grateful that he was breathing still, the absurdity felt almost like an affront.

Zarubin, out of uniform, added to the dislocation. He was wearing a dark blue, domestic-quality suit (his beloved Brook Brothers suit was hanging in his Moscow apartment still), a fresh white shirt for each day so far and the same brown tie. Even with the shock of blond-grey hair he looked like a typical Soviet politician, bland and forgettable. Obviously, the card said something else.

'Yes, the last of them. It was my favourite design, so parting was painful.'

'Gagarin, waving at us?'

'That's the one. If Shelepin doesn't know where we're going by now he must be unconscious.'

'I think the postcard from Poznań will remove the last of any doubts he's having.'

The road westward from the city pointed almost like an arrow to the DDR's border-crossing at Frankfurt an der Oder, and from there straight to Berlin. If the border-guards proved to be as obliging as those at Kazlavas-Budzisko they could be there by that evening, after which God alone knew what storm of shit would descend upon them. Levin's hopes had not been rising with proximity, he had seen too many films not to know that denouements always came unexpectedly, and right at the end.

Zarubin was more pensive now, constantly checking his rear mirror and humming to himself. Levin recognized some of the tunes, but their familiarity didn't sooth him. In his experience, the General *never* hummed. At one point he actually began to sing quietly, but, recalling himself, broke off and glanced apologetically at his passenger, who had begun to fear a Rodgers and Hammerstein medley.

'I was distracted, Boris Petrovich. Let me know if I do it again.'

'Are we going all the way to Berlin? I need ...'

'No. We can't arrive until tomorrow, so today's ordeal will be brief. We'll have a pleasant lunch in Frankfurt and find a room there for the night.'

'Have you ever visited the city?'

'Yes, just once.' Zarubin frowned. 'In fact, ...'

The silence endured for so long that Levin assumed his head had moved on to something else, but then he exhaled through pursed lips and half-turned.

'The day after I visited Frankfurt I was obliged to flee, all the way to America.'

'Obliged?' Levin knew of Zarubin's defection, as did most people in the Kremlin; but, enjoying his job, he had never thought to ask too much about the episode. He had assumed it to be an act of will, an ideological decision, later regretted.

'A certain quartermaster-general was about to disembowel me for pushing my face into his rather spectacular black-market activities. I decided to remain whole.'

'Couldn't you have denounced him?'

'Certainly. But he had many friends and business associates with more than enough fire-power to avenge the insult, so I decided to visit Capitalism.'

'It didn't suit?'

'Obviously not. No Russian can be happy in exile. American soil in particular holds nothing to keep a soul close.'

Musicals, and now Dostoevsky. Christ. Levin cleared his throat. 'Mikoyan's secretary told me that he was very impressed by New York City.'

'It's another world, certainly, but a place to visit, not endure. Now, listen ...'

Zarubin slowed, pulled to the hard shoulder and switched off the engine.

'We'll reach the border in about thirty minutes. The German guards there are almost certainly going to give us a harder time than the Poles. Even a Soviet General can't expect to be waved through. So, there'll be some checking, and if there's a problem I may have to put on an act. Do try to look bored rather than terrified, Levin, even if they shout back at me. Remember - I've anticipated this.'

As these words had the precise effect of terrifying Levin, he decided to let the adrenalin work through his system in the hope that it would have exhausted itself by the time they reached the Oder. Consequently, neither man spoke as the remaining Polish kilometres dwindled, and just before eleven am they arrived at the Świecko crossing. On the Polish side, a guard examined the transit visa made out two days earlier and waved them on to his German colleagues. Immediately, an armed Grenzpolizei *gefreiter* stepped out and held up his hand to stop the car (as if the driver might be thinking of accelerating and crashing through the barrier), and then waved it over to a search area. Zarubin parked and waited. The *gefreiter* retreated to the large shed that served as a command post and reappeared with his commander, a *Stabsfeldwebel*, who strolled across to the car with his face set in a mélange of indifference and pre-emptive disbelief which didn't soften when he noticed the car's Soviet plates. He waved a hand at the driver's side-window, and Zarubin passed his card to him.

The *Stabsfeldwebel*'s lips pursed, his eyebrows rose slightly and he looked up, as if trying to locate patience somewhere in the middle distance.

'What is the purpose of your visit to the German Democratic Republic?'

Zarubin smiled pleasantly. 'Matters of State.'

'Please be specific.'

'Be serious. I'm not going to disclose my business with a non-commissioned officer. Have you any reason to doubt my identity? If not, please allow us to pass.'

For a moment, a flicker of self-doubt interrupted the act, but the young man recovered himself. He was a gate-keeper, a sentinel, and not to be cowed by foreigners with impressive credentials (though of course the option of dragging the man from his car and detaining him was not available in this case). He pulled Zarubin's card closely to his chest, though the other man had made no attempt to reclaim it.

'This will need to be checked. With the Ministry.'

'Which Ministry is that? *Grenzpolizei* – or should I say *Grenztruppen* now? - seem to wander between them. Last week it was the Interior Ministry, this week it's National Defence. To whom, precisely, will you speak?'

It was unlikely that any mid-level Soviet *apparatchik* would have know already about the Border Guard's reorganization (God knew, the East German people didn't), and the *Stabsfelwebel*'s iron resolve oxidized considerably. He began to speak, but Zarubin had sensed the backward step and sprang at it.

'Let me assist you, then. If you put through a call directly to my good friend Erich Mielke, I'm sure that he can speak to any reservations you may have.'

There were probably fewer than a dozen people in the DDR – other than his immediate family – who would have considered pestering the Head of *Stasi*, and this young man was definitely not among their number. He paled, and the mouth worked to form words that the brain hadn't begun to arrange.

'Really, I insist. Call him now and settle the matter. We'll wait.'

The *Stabsfeldwebel* continued to process air for a few moments, but he had been given the ugly choice and a reaction was necessary. Still clutching Zarubin's card, he retreated to his shed at far more than a strolling pace and slammed the door behind him.

Aghast, Levin waved at the windscreen. 'But … if he calls Mielke it's finished! We'll spend the rest of our lives – I mean, most of the rest of today – in a *Stasi* cell, waiting for KGB to arrive.'

Zarubin sighed. 'Levin, sometimes I think your cleverness is just a very good disguise. He isn't going to call Mielke, nor anyone else in MfS. He appreciates his job, the money and its perquisites. He doesn't want to be pointed out as the idiot who gave Erich's Russian friend a hard time and now works in a canning factory, gutting fish. Don't worry.'

'So where's he gone?'

'To change his trousers, probably. To give himself time to think of a solution that doesn't make him look even more ridiculous to his men. See ...'

The *gefreiter* who had first halted their car emerged from the shed with Zarubin's card. He walked smartly across to them, handed back the document, saluted and stepped back.

Zarubin smiled. 'Thank you. One more thing?'

'Comrade General?'

'A decent restaurant, in Frankfurt?'

'Umm ...' Clearly, the *gefreiter* was no epicure, but after a moment his brow cleared. 'The *International*, on Am Kleistpark. The best *steak au four* I've tasted.'

Zarubin thanked him and started the engine. As they approached the Oder, Levin shivered.

'Peasant food.'

'Don't be bourgeois - it's good, hearty nourishment. When we're in England you can subsist on quails' eggs and champagne if you wish. Until then, we are of the people.'

'I don't want to go to England. I don't speak the language.'

'How long did you need to learn German?'

'About six months.'

'Well, then. Accept the challenge – you won't have anything to distract you.'

'*Work* will distract me. I'll need a wage.'

'What's in the yellow box is yours, Boris Petrovich, less a thousand francs for my unexpected expenses. No doubt the British will give me an allowance, and accommodation.'

Astonished, Levin gaped at Zarubin. The yellow box was an emergency fund, not a fortune, but it would give a man time to find his feet, and perhaps even buy a small apartment (or whatever they called them in England). And its absence would throw Zarubin entirely upon the mercy of his new employers.

'Why?'

'Because this was not your choice, so take it as my apology.'

'But … thank you, Comrade General.'

'Don't thank me until we've survived the next twenty-four hours. And after that, don't call me Comrade anything. The West has many attractions, but camaraderie isn't one of them. Isn't this bridge pleasant? The last time I was here, it wasn't.'

Zoo Bahnhof.

Carl Ohise must have felt like this, returning to his native Germany after decades on a Pacific island. Fischer had been away from Berlin for just three years, but the strangeness of distance was palpable. Around him, homeward-bound commuters and visitors from the West bustled, oblivious to their surroundings, a thousand preoccupations bouncing off and between each other. He stood still among them, feeling the *Berliner Schnauze* as an alien force, rather than the comfortable absence of lace knickers that it had once been.

He was tired – more so than at any time since he'd last dug out a terrace on a Portuguese hillside. The journey had been an ordeal; Bonn lay 480 straight kilometres from Berlin, but he had changed trains twice – at Cologne and Hanover – in the Federal Republic, and then there had been a long delay at the DDR border (where a half-ruined face, travelling on a Portuguese passport, had raised no alarms), followed by the inevitable crawl across East German territory. In total, almost eleven hours had passed since he had stood on a Bonn platform, enduring bear-hugs from Freddie Holleman and Gerd Branssler and swearing that he would do his very, very best not to get killed.

It was a brave promise, but he was in no position to keep it. The last initiative he'd exercised had been to put the whole thing into motion; after that, all plans, schedules and decisions regarding who should and shouldn't die fell to other men. He had poked KGB with a stick and then compounded his offence by not allowing their *Stasi* friends to lift him from the streets of Bonn. Whatever they might decide regarding the other matter, he had done enough on his own account to earn a face-down swim in the Spree.

But it would have come to that anyway, he told himself. Zarubin disgraced, and either retired or dead, would have left him as a last unwound thread, an insignificant but necessary cauterization. Zarubin's flight had at least diverted KGB's attention, and made Otto Fischer the very least of their irritations. He shouldn't have cared, but if this flipped-coin of a plan succeeded his promise to his friends might be capable of being kept. It was a horrible, painful irony, that by dying Zofia had given him a small chance to live.

It would be done, for good or bad, in the next twenty-four hours, and then he could either mourn her properly or be free of all concerns. But that was a fact, not a choice. He didn't know what scheme Zarubin might have conceived to keep himself alive as far as Berlin, only that the man was sharper than an old whore's tongue. But KGB had clever men, too, and a number of advantages over a lone fugitive – not least, the thousands of agents that could converge upon whatever route he had chosen to take, and another hundred thousand *Stasi* allies waiting at its terminus.

'Will you be moving soon, sir, or shall I get our people to re-direct the human traffic?'

A supervisor had come to check the new statue on her platform. Fischer picked up his bag.

'Sorry.'

The smile, even on that unfortunate face, cleared her frown, and she turned to find some new impediment to her day. He took a first step and then paused. The matter of where to go next had yet to be decided, but one thing struck him forcibly – that this might be his last night on Earth. A man had a right, even in law, to expect some mark of his passing. Didn't the Americans give condemned felons a right to choose their last meal, immediately before frying them? Couldn't Otto Fischer do the same for himself? He had money, and a little time, and an unfamiliar urge to make something of both.

The supervisor, sensing that the statue had re-ossified, turned once more. He gave her the same smile.

'Excuse me – is the Savoy still in business?'

She looked puzzled. 'Of course.'

Of course. It had opened in an age of decadence and then survived National Socialism, British and American bombs and Soviet Artillery almost untouched, He had never stayed there – it wasn't the most expensive hotel in Berlin, but still too fine for the police and Luftwaffe salaries he had once commanded. These days, he could afford a suite at the Adlon, but a night spent only metres from the Line (on this of all nights) would have killed any chance of sleep. Besides, the Savoy had always been fashionable among the more interesting, artistic sort, his business the next day was here in Charlottenburg and the hotel was on Fasanenstrasse, a three-minute walk from where he was presently standing. He thanked the supervisor, and to her palpable satisfaction pointed himself towards the ticket barrier.

The concierge at the Savoy regretted that all his suites were taken, but he could offer a large double room overlooking Fasanenstrasse. Fischer surrendered his passport, booked a table for dinner in the Grill Room and went to the Cigar Bar, where he drank two whiskies in the time it took to read the major stories in that day's *Morgenpost*. After that, an hour in a large, deep bath eased the worst of the day's journey from his joints, while its steam did the same for the creases in his jacket and shirt. By the time he had dressed, his dinner appointment loomed and his appetite was stood pleasingly to attention.

A truffle pasta, followed by rib-eye (carved at the table) and a full bottle of something from high ground to the south of Dijon worked hard to make the world a better place - and, worryingly, harder to depart. He had felt something like this during the weeks following his sale of the farm – the pull of little luxuries and wider horizons, the pleasant glow of possibilities (even if never seized) and the anxiety that the prospect of their loss encouraged. *Money doesn't bring happiness* his mother used to say (he didn't recall that abject poverty had made her dance in the streets either), but there had to be a point, somewhere between destitution and Croesus, where just the right ration of comfort might be found.

That he would never discover it, even if he survived the following day, hardly mattered. He had been a microscopic element of other men's conflicts for so much of his adult life that he hardly wondered whether he might have made a better fist of things. The evening's pleasures were enough in themselves, to the point at which he began to debate whether a second bottle of wine might stifle the last unwelcome murmur of missed opportunities.

I am, after all, dead already. He doubted that Freddie Holleman in particular would ever quite forgive him for that. He's wanted to keep his friends safe, but it had been a stupid, clumsy device, and he deserved a kicking for it. Which, of course, he might well get tomorrow.

He waved over the waiter and lifted the empty bottle. He would have a glass more here, and the rest later, in his wonderful room, when tiredness threatened to reignite his nerves. Between now and them, perhaps a walk down Ku'damm. The Savoy stood just off its most pleasant stretch, where plenty of pre-war buildings stood still - it had been further to the west where Allied ordnance had finally finished Adolf's work by hammering most of the all-male bars and erasing the stain of Weimar decadence. Not that it had stayed erased, of course.

He signed for his dinner, took the almost-full bottle to his room and collected his raincoat. Outside, the street was quiet, but as he turned the corner the Ku'damm buzz struck him like a welcome breeze. Most of his fellow promenaders were late shoppers, or on their way to the theatre or cinema, but it was late enough now for a few of the more optimistic whores to have started their working day. They were out of place here among the new shops and businesses, but like birds they retained a race memory of better, seedier times. As he approached, one detached herself from the wall.

'Hello, handsome.'

He laughed at that. He had almost reached a streetlight, so his ruined face was both visible and rendered even less lovely by the hard, cold illumination. She smiled and shrugged, as if to say that they were both obliged to make the best of things.

'I have a room close by – it's clean, like me.'

She was young, perhaps in her early 20s, and still very pretty. He was old and very ugly, but there was an easy way to bridge that difficulty, and something about a night that threatened to be his last was eating at his resolve. He wanted company, and pride was not a tall barrier.

'How much for an hour of your time?'

'An athlete, eh? A hundred marks.'

He almost laughed again. She'd said it too quickly, trying it on, hoping to make the figure seem less ridiculous than it was. For a hundred marks he could have had the sort of girl who serviced the diplomatic quarter south of Tiergarten (and for the whole night, too), but he had no intention of haggling. He took out his wallet, counted the money and showed her. Her wide eyes gave her away, and hastily she linked her arm in his, securing him.

'It's just around the corner.'

It wasn't, of course, but ten minutes later they came to a surprisingly respectable low block off Uhlandstrasse. She led him in to a ground floor apartment, double-locked the door and immediately began to undo her blouse.

He lifted a hand. 'Can we just sit, and talk?'

She frowned slightly. 'You want me say dirty stuff while you ...?'

'Really, just talk.' He put the money on a table and stepped away from it. 'I'm not a pervert or a missionary, I swear.'

'Talk about what, then?'

'Anything - the weather, the price of beer, football even. I just want to spend an hour chatting. It's something I don't do much.'

'Don't you chat to your wife?'

'She died, a long time ago.'

'Oh. I have schnapps. Would you like some?'

'No, thank you.'

'Tea?'

'That would be good.'

They spoke for almost two hours (she didn't ask for more money, and Fischer didn't think to offer it). He got her Christian name (Gertie) and a brief history, but she was far more adept at the small nudges that open up a customer, and it was he who consumed most of the oxygen between them. The saga of Otto Henry Fischer, its small peaks and abyssal lows, few loves and many complications, dribbled out in heavily censored form while she gave every sign of being interested in what she was hearing (another professional talent, he assumed). Eventually, the monologue died of natural causes; surprised at himself, he looked at his watch, stood and thanked her.

'I don't know why I told you all of that. Perhaps coming back to Berlin has made me think of old times.'

She smiled. 'Your life's been interesting.'

'That's a word for it, I suppose. Good night.'

At the door she put up a hand to his face, the good side. 'You were handsome.'

'Strangely, I was never told that in all the years before the damage arrived.'

'There was no reason to mention it, perhaps. But now the other side of your face makes it obvious. And a shame.'

Curiously, his mood was lifted a little by her words. He found his way back to Ku'Damm and pointed himself eastwards, towards the Savoy. The street was busy still, and an old soldier was trying his luck on a corner, a cap outstretched to catch any tips. A crutch held him upright, doing duty for a leg that had been removed almost at the thigh. When he noticed the ruined face approaching he brightened slightly and waved the cap.

'Evening, Oberst. Got any change for a veteran?'

The coins in Fischer's pocket wouldn't have bought a coffee. He removed his wallet, calculated what his hotel bill would be, added a reasonable amount for contingencies, and put the rest – about seventy marks – into the old soldier's cap. Astonished, the man stared into it.

'But ... don't you need it?'

'Not any more, no.'

'It's ... too much. Really, once you're sober you'll want it back ...'

'I won't. Tomorrow I begin a new life, or perhaps just end the old one. In either case, what I've given you won't matter.'

Carefully, the veteran put the money into his coat pocket. 'Then I wish you luck, *Kamerad*. Though of course, you don't need it.'

'Don't I?'

The other man winked. 'Look at the state of you. No-one comes through that without an angel's hand under each arm.'

Chairman Shelepin was known to be a man who weighed important decisions carefully. He gathered available evidence, tested its strength and weaknesses, allowing no personal preference to dictate what weight he attached to each strand. Inevitably, he had gained a reputation for being cautious, but once set upon a course he acted decisively, and had rarely regretted doing so. No-one was infallible, and not every decision could be the correct one; all, however, had to be sustainable.

In front of him, on his large desk, he had enough evidence to sustain any decision he wished to make, and still he hesitated. He knew what he knew, but he couldn't gauge what he didn't know – or rather, the extent of what couldn't be known. That was troubling, particularly in light of what Semichastny had unearthed and brought to him.

General Zarubin was - had been – First Secretary Khrushchev's principal advisor on the American Political Mind. That, in itself, placed him nowhere near sensitive KGB intelligence, but his employer had a regrettable habit of passing what should have been restricted memoranda between departments, to elicit opinions other than those of the authors. One such document, prepared earlier that year and co-authored by Shelepin, had been a comprehensive analysis of opportunities arising from increasing Soviet assistance to African liberation movements. According to Khrushchev's secretary Shevchenko, the First Secretary had struggled through the first three pages and then passed it to Zarubin, to summarize the remainder and offer his own thoughts on how the Americans might react. More recently, Shelepin had sent a note to the Council of Ministers, urging that counter-intelligence activities in Latin America and Asia be stepped up in order to distract the US (and CIA in particular) immediately prior to the proposed sealing of the internal Berlin border. Again, Shevchenko had been ordered to give a copy to Zarubin. These were current intelligence initiatives, and Shelepin flattered himself that the Africa paper was by far the deepest survey yet attempted upon the Gordian slime of post-colonial prospects. By the same token, its dissemination across the West would undermine any Soviet plans for the region before they climbed off the page.

Zarubin, with his blank postcards, was committing himself to not betraying secrets in his possession, yet the word of a defector could hardly be taken on trust. On the other hand, he held a fistful of other cards close to his chest, and no-one knew what damage could avenge his removal. Something had to be done, yet couldn't be. Whatever was decided, sleep would be lost for months if not years to come.

Being a careful man, Shelepin had made preparations for both eventualities. He had spoken to Markus Wolf – firstly, to apologize for the way he had been dragged into this business, but also to ask him to liaise with his Defence Ministry with regard to a certain gentleman expected to enter the DDR momentarily. Within two hours, Wolf had called back to confirm the event, offer the plates of the vehicle in which Zarubin was travelling and mentioned that he had ordered an *Abteilung X* team to follow it to its destination – presumably, Berlin. Shelepin had been grateful for that, but stressed that a KGB unit would take responsibility for any operation within the city, should it become necessary. He had sensed the relief in Wolf's voice. After two abortive attempts (on disastrously short notice) to snatch Zarubin's German friend in Bonn, *Stasi* were keen for KGB to take charge of their own cock-ups.

Shelepin had spoken also to A.A. Krokhin, Korotkov's acting successor at Karlshorst, priming him for a possible wet job. Krokhin had actually groaned when he heard the news, which was hardly unexpected. He was trying desperately to rebuild the intimate relationship that his predecessor had enjoyed locally with MfS, and also preparing for the inevitable counter-intelligence war that would follow the raising of the Berlin barrier. A successful - that is, discreet - assassination on allied soil, and the clean extraction of his men thereafter, would need a great deal of attention that he had no time or enthusiasm to offer. He agreed readily, as he must, but begged to have the word as soon as any decision was made.

Which brought Shelepin to the First Secretary. He had considered ordering the operation and informing Khrushchev after the event, excusing himself on the basis that a momentary decision had been necessary, if Zarubin were not to fall into the arms of the Allies. As he rehearsed the words he failed to convince even himself, however. The First Secretary's first question would be: why and how had his personal adviser been allowed to get as far as Berlin without KGB being aware that he was running? And if, in fact, they *had* known about it prior to the kill order being given - which would be almost self-evidently the case – what was all this shit about *momentary decisions*?

No, Khrushchev had to give his prior agreement, which meant that Shelepin had a very uncomfortable, and very imminent, interview to plan – *if* he concluded that Zarubin, escaped, was more of a threat than Zarubin dead. And as soon as he had that thought, the worm began to burrow.

After three largely successful years, he was about to hand over the chairmanship of KGB and ascend to the Council of Ministers. Despite the whole universe of trouble that his deputy had dumped on his desk, he intended still to recommend Semichastny as his successor (not least because Khrushchev was also very fond of the young man), knowing that the necessary work of reform would continue under his leadership, *and* that any repercussions regarding Zarubin's flight would certainly be stifled by the man who had caused the debacle. So, Shelepin asked himself, is this really a decision that I need to make?

If Zarubin fled successfully and then decided to tell everything to his new friends, who would be hurt by it? Not Shelepin himself, certainly. Though no KGB Chairman could be regarded as an innocent, the mass denouncements and executions were now mere details of history, and he had used his tenure to rid the organization of men whose reputations had been built upon them. As for his career prior to KGB, he could dare his worst enemies to make something of his war record and time with Komsomol and the World Federation of Democratic Youth. It was other men who would need to fear Zarubin's memory and evidence, and how they might bite their arses.

Other than the matter of history, what else need he worry about? That Zarubin had been forced to flee was known only to Semichastny and himself, and his deputy wasn't the kind of man to admit to past indiscretions over too many vodkas. He was getting what he wanted (which was one less rival for Khrushchev's ear), so it was entirely in his interest that the neatest, least problematic solution be found.

Which was to let the man go. It required no action other than that Shelepin practise a surprised expression for when one of their agents in the West announce that a new defector had presented himself at Broadway or Langley. Someone might question why it was that KGB hadn't known anything about Zarubin's intentions, but that was easily dealt with. The man was a high-ranking special advisor to the First Secretary; absent any reason for suspicion, why *would* he be under surveillance? The red face would be Khrushchev's, given that he had been the defector's only true ally, and Shelepin was very comfortable with that. He genuinely liked the man – he was good company and not prone to vicious tendencies – but as a leader he was disastrously impulsive. If some little wound could dampen his self-confidence and incline him to take more counsel (hell, to take *any* counsel), it was to be welcomed.

Do nothing, then. A strange, uncharacteristic decision, but Shelepin was pleased that he hadn't allowed Semichastny's eagerness to arrest or expunge Zarubin warp his judgement. The decisive solution wasn't always the best one, nor even the most courageous (he told himself). For once, sitting back and letting events flow down their natural channels was probably the most prudent strategy. He …

Markus Wolf. The thought hit him like a clenched fist. Wolf *knew* - not all the story, of course, but certainly that Zarubin was heading west, and that

Shelepin had asked to be kept informed of where he was, and when. So how could he pretend innocence now?

He wondered – but only for the span of a single moment - if the lid might still be held on the pan. Wolf was a good friend to KGB (he was as close to being a Russian as any German could be), but more than that, he had been a good friend to Alexander Korotkov, former KGB Resident at Karlshorst and the man whom Shelepin had hounded into an early grave - so good a friend, in fact, that only a month earlier he had come to Moscow to deliver the eulogy at Korotkov's funeral. Wolf was not a vindictive man, but he would hardly be prepared to forget an episode that would prove his dead friend's nemesis a liar.

Shelepin groaned. He was on record, and so the option of doing nothing wasn't anything of the sort. Sergei Aleksandrovich Zarubin had to be dealt with, and for no other reason than to preserve his reluctant executioner's reputation. He picked up his telephone receiver and dialled a single number.

'Good morning, Andrei Stepanovich, it's Chairman Shelepin. Yes, thank you, very well. I need to see the First Secretary on an urgent matter. No, please don't get your diary. It has to be now, immediately. No, even Comrade Mikoyan must wait, it's really *that* urgent. Thank you.'

Almost an hour later, Shelepin dropped into his chair once more. He was drenched with perspiration, the physical consequence of the string of deflections, half-truths and outright lies he'd just offered to the most powerful man in the Soviet Union. With even that arsenal deployed, he'd only partially convinced Khrushchev of his case. Perhaps KGB had insinuated too much about Zarubin over the past eight years; perhaps the First Secretary simply couldn't believe that a man he'd personally raised up and protected had betrayed his trust (and, of course, he was right about that). Whatever the foundation of his skepticism, it had birthed an ugly, impossible instruction.

Take him alive. I want to know why he's done it.

That couldn't be done, obviously. For KGB (and Shelepin in particular), Zarubin's mouth, moving, was the deadliest weapon imaginable. Still, the order had been given, so anywhere that the man *could* be taken alive was bad ground – which meant that he had to be intercepted where even Khrushchev must accept the inevitability of his death.

Shelepin put through another a call to Karlshorst, and asked for Krokhin.

'Alexei, put on the suppressor circuit. You wanted earliest warning - it's on. Speak to Markus Wolf; his men are following Zarubin towards Berlin, and he'll let you know when he enters the city. Have KGB staff moved now to assist *Grenztruppen* at all east-west border checkpoints this morning. Yes, Zarubin will definitely present himself openly at one of them, rather than try to slip through. Make sure that he's delayed there long enough for your team to get into position to go after him. Into the West, of course. They'll take the shot at the first clear opportunity thereafter. Keep me apprised at every stage of the operation, and give nothing of the details to MfS, or anyone else. On my authority, yes.'

The Kranzler-Eck was a tourist trap, as Americans would say. The western branch of the famous, ancient and bomb-destroyed Kranzler Café, it stood on the corner of Ku'damm and Joachimsthalerstrasse. Itself flattened by the Allies during 1944, it had been rebuilt fourteen years later as a three-storey, rotunda-topped concrete confection of what was, very briefly, the style of the future. Being close to the equally of-the-moment Hansaviertel complex, the café immediately became fashionable, and was almost always crowded.

On a dark night in 1958, Otto Fischer and General Sergei Aleksandrovich Zarubin had stood in a half-ruined, former Jewish school on Augsburgerstrasse, hiding from KGB and discussing a venue for a meeting they hoped would never happen. It had been cold at the time and both men were hungry and very tired, so when a quick, neat solution presented itself they had seized upon it gratefully. After all, the place had just been built (and was likely not to be demolished in the near future, therefore), a man might easily conceal himself among the crowds that were drawn to it each day, and whichever of them arrived first could warm his hands on a hot beverage while he waited for the other.

'Where is it?' Zarubin had asked, and all Fischer had needed to do was lift the plastic sheeting from a broken window and point. Two hundred and fifty metres from their hiding place, the Kranzler-Eck's self-satisfied modernity had stood out from the surrounding half-constructions like a tiara in a dung-pile. Three years later, the dung was gone, but the Kranzler-Eck shone still among the high-rise offices and hotels it serviced.

After a fine breakfast (only partly ruined by too-little sleep and a mild hangover), Fischer had paid his bill at the Savoy and stepped out into a fine August day. He had given Harold Shergold the location and hour of his intended rendezvous, but the latter was necessarily a broad estimate of what would be determined by fate, traffic or any inclination by either KGB or MfS to put themselves between General Zarubin and the Kranzler-Eck. The only thing Fischer could do in that respect was to arrive early, and wait patiently.

He was outside the café a little before 11am. He'd intended to find a seat well away from the windows and in shadow, but the place was all window and no dark corners (modernity, it seemed, required operating theatre-strength illumination to display its charms). The place was very busy, though, and this settled his nerves a little. He queued with other prospective customers for almost ten minutes, until a table became available. At least it was close to a counter, and waitresses passed around it almost constantly. They all seemed pleasant enough, and perfectly capable of blocking a line-of-sight on his behalf.

One of his unwitting human shields brought a menu, which was illustrated with colour photographs of the cakes and pastries on offer (a rather industrial novelty, in his opinion). He ordered a pot of black coffee, opened the copy of *Morgenpost* he had lifted from the Savoy's lobby, put one eye upon the front door and tried to keep his head empty.

Nevertheless, it filled rapidly, with every conceivable bad possibility. He might wait here for hours, for a man whose body was already fertilizing a glade somewhere between Berlin and Moscow. Or, budgets being what they were, KGB might be holding fire until their man met his accomplice and they could gratefully take the two-for-the-price-of-one offer. Harold Shergold may well have revisited his decision, had a change of mind and stood down his men, in which case Fischer and Zarubin would be spending the remainder of their brief lives dashing from one cellar to the next, hoping that their pursuers bored of the chase. An even uglier possibility was that Roger Broadsmith's secret MfS career had been discovered, inclining Shergold to see this whole scheme as a KGB ploy to fill the hole in British Intelligence that George Blake's departure had left. *That* would bring only the one cellar, somewhere beneath Lancaster House, and very little time for regrets.

Testing each of these pleasant fates in turn, he couldn't find anything implausible about any of them. The imperishable truth kept time with the slight throbbing in his head – that this was a situation in which every party assumed that nothing and no-one could be trusted, so they made their plans accordingly and did their very best to disguise them. Otto Fischer was a child in this adult game, wondering where the pieces went, and why.

'More coffee, Sir?'

'Yes, please.'

The waitress had half-turned away when he recalled the due diligence he should have performed already. 'Excuse me? Do you have a telephone that customers can use?'

She pointed to the end of the counter. 'In the back corridor, beside the men's toilet ...'

At least if everything else went well, he could call the number Shergold had given him and have them whisked away to the British safe-house. It was a tiny thing, to please him as it did, and testimony to how distant every other certainty presently stood.

'....but it doesn't work sometimes.'

There was a technique, employed by airborne troops in the moments before they stepped out into blackness, that helped to ease a tormented mind. Fischer took a deep breath, exhaled as much air as his lungs would allow and concentrated upon a small area beneath his rib cage, trying to imagine all his physical sensations and awareness locating there. When he breathed again it was from and to that point; when his coffee arrived he smiled with his belly, not his mouth; and when the front door opened once more his navel told him not to look, because there was nothing to be gained by it.

After a few minutes he was able almost to relax, and he allowed himself to think of the weeks or months ahead, if things went as they should. He had money in his Portuguese bank account still, but it wouldn't eke out indefinitely. Would they allow him to work in England, while he tried to plan a future? He could speak the language well enough, and he was certain that English timepieces needed repairing as much as their European cousins. Perhaps someone would take him on as an assistant, in a small, pretty town that neither the Luftwaffe or Soviet Intelligence had discovered. It was an attractive idea. He would speak to Jonas Kleiber, whose time as a prisoner of war had given him a Baedeker's understanding of English regions hardly seen by foreign eyes (even if it was predominantly of their female attractions).

'Herr Fischer? You're looking well.'

Stupidly, he gaped at a small men, leaning on a stick, who peered down at him through thick glasses.

'It's …. Levin, isn't it?'

'You remember me! How pleasant.'

'But …?'

'You see an unhappy casualty of the General's brilliant thinking. When your messages came it wasn't possible for me to avoid conscription. I'm to be an unwilling Capitalist, it seems.'

'Where is he?'

'Trying to park the car, would you believe?'

'You've *driven* here?'

'Yes. Halfway across Europe, through several border crossings – including this last, the world's most sensitive – and the hardest thing comes at the end. Three times he's pulled in to the side of the road, and three times a policeman has moved us on. The last one directed us to a car park, which is a short distance away, apparently. He dropped me outside, and told me to say that he won't be long. In fact, that's the only thing he's said in the past half-hour that's fit to repeat.'

'A car with Soviet plates? And no-one stopped you?'

'Why should they? The Potsdam Agreement still stands, doesn't it? For the moment, at least?'

'But it applies only to military patrols across the Line.'

'While our papers were being examined at the checkpoint - at some length, actually – he asked a *soldat* to attach a Red Army pennant to the car bonnet. We're quite official.'

'And then you were just … waved through?'

'Yes. Strange, isn't it? I've been quite dazed since we began this journey. It seems we've been moving through a no-man's land between what people would like to do to the General and what they dare attempt.' Carefully, Levin eased a large satchel from his shoulder and pushed it under the table. 'May I sit? And have some tea?'

Zarubin arrived before the waitress. He was as discomposed as Fischer had ever known him to be, his usual, supercilious air submerged beneath a fretting frown and the body language of a mine-clearer. He scanned the room, saw Fischer and allowed his shoulders to slump a half-centimetre.

He sat at the table, and Levin frowned at him. 'Where are our bags?'

'Abandoned, like the car. You have your inheritance – buy new clothes.'

'You didn't find the car park?'

Zarubin rubbed his face. 'Speak German, Levin, it's polite. No, I didn't find the car-park, because I didn't look. Do you imagine that the attendant would have allowed a Soviet military vehicle to enter? I mean, without immediately calling the police, or Army?'

'Where is it then?'

'I drove onto a building site just down the road, got out, smiled at someone holding a brick and walked away. I imagine the thing will be stripped bare within the hour, which might be a metaphor for what our lives have become. You're here, Major - that's very comforting. The British want me, then?'

'They say so. I've been speaking to a man named Shergold.'

'Ah, good. He's one of their best, apparently. What happens now?'

As he asked, Zarubin turned his head and glanced anxiously at the café's other clientele, but no-one seemed to be interested in their table (a diagnosis Fischer had made and re-tested several times in the ninety minutes he had been waiting).

'I telephone the British, and they come for us.'

'Good. I don't want to move again without cover.'

Levin cleared his throat. 'I have to say, General, you seem less relaxed now we've succeeded than you did when nothing was certain.'

'Nothing *is* certain yet. Until half an hour ago, I was Khrushchev's personal advisor, in a world where that mattered. Once through that last checkpoint I became nobody – or worse, somebody who someone needs urgently to become nobody.'

'But you said that Shelepin wouldn't dare to ...'

'I was expressing a fervent hope, perhaps more confidently than the situation deserves. If it were a matter of personal choice, I don't believe he would care if I live or die. But there *are* no personal choices in Soviet politics, and he may well not enjoy any initiative in this. The First Secretary will feel betrayed by my flight, and even if he overcomes that there are plenty of men around him who regard me a slap to their faces. That I survived one defection remains an open wound; a second, unpunished, would be beyond endurance. If they manage to persuade ... well, we can all relax when the British have me in an interrogation room.

Until then, I shall bite some of the few fingernails I was allowed to retain, Major ...' he turned to Fischer; '... if you would make that call now?'

'Yes.' Fischer stood, and paused. 'The telephone here might not be working.'

'Oh, God.'

Two hundred and fifty metres to the south of the Kranzler-Eck, and almost directly above the spot, where, three years earlier, Zarubin and Fischer had chosen their future, unthinkable meeting-place, three window-cleaners went about their business on the fourth floor of a recently completed, mixed-use block. One of them placed duct tape over the mouth of a middle-aged insurance adjuster and gently lowered him to the floor; a second assembled a heavily-customized Armalite A-16 while conducting a quiet yet heated conversation with himself; the third stood slightly back from the window that stretched the length of the room, his binoculars trained on the front entrance to the café.

The one with the weapon spoke through his teeth, to no-one in particular.

'This is fucking ridiculous. No forward planning, no timetable, no back-up for if or when we need to relocate – it's as if they want us to fail.'

'Sshhh, Constantin.'

Constantin waved a hand at the prone insurance adjuster.

'And what if this guy's boss walks in? His secretary? A sandwich vendor? What level of casualties are we allowed to inflict before someone decides it's a fucking disaster and tries – and fails – to pull us out?'

'We've got what we've got. The Resident said it was an emergency. Did you notice that he almost apologized at the briefing? Krokhin? It must be something beyond important. Wait ...'

Constantin finished assembling rifle on the desk. The window was open a few centimetres, and he adjusted the tripod height so that his view through the telescopic sights was clear. He saw immediately what had concerned his spotter.

'Jesus, that's a rough way to look.'

'He's checked the road both ways and down this street too.' The spotter picked up his radio and pressed a button. 'Mother? This is little Kiril. We have a gentleman with a mutilated face leaving the café, possibly of interest. Can you advise?'

In a room in the Lubyanka, Shelepin and Semichastny were listening on speaker to the Berlin Resident, who passed the spotter's question directly to them. Semichastny nodded furiously, but the Chairman shook his head.

'No, Andrei. Ignore him, please.'

'*Why*?'

Shelepin looked sourly at his deputy. 'If we take Zarubin down, Fischer is of no interest or danger to us. If we don't, he's the least of our worries. And how do you imagine a single marksman is going to manage two targets? After the first shot all hell will break forth, and if Fischer survives it he'll dive or throw himself back into the café. If the shooter puts him down he forewarns Zarubin, who won't leave the building until he's got a battalion surrounding him – which he won't need, of course, because our men will have run like hares immediately after the first cartridge ejected itself. I know you haven't been with us long, Vladimir Yefimovich, but try to think these things through. We have one goal, and one target.'

'Got it.' The spotter shook his head. 'Krokhin says ignore the Face.'

Constantin grunted. 'Obviously. He's coming back now.'

The mutilated man paused once more at the café entrance, glanced to either side and entered, followed immediately by two adults and several children. Constantin sighed.

'Messy. Very messy. If you ask me ...'

'We don't. How's our host?'

The third man looked down at the insurance adjuster. 'Still unconscious. I may have hit him too hard.'

'Sad. The corridor?'

'A couple of ladies have walked past. It's quiet.'

'Good. When we're done, we leave quickly. Everything stays here – forensics can't tell them anything they won't know already.'

Constantin groaned. 'I spent weeks tweaking this gun!'

'They'll get you a new one, don't fuss.'

———

'That was quick.'

Fischer sat down at his table. 'There's a 'phone booth about a hundred metres east of here.'

Zarubin leaned in and spoke quietly. 'What did you say?'

'Bronwyn.'

'What?'

'It's the name of Shergold's dog. It tells them that you're here, and alive, and that we'd very much appreciate them coming for us - in force, preferably.'

'And they replied …?'

'Nothing. The person on the other end just disconnected.'

Dissatisfied, Zarubin sat back and drummed the fingers of both hands on the table. Levin looked hopefully at each of the other two men in turn. 'They shouldn't be long, I imagine. Should they?'

Fischer shrugged. 'I can't see any point in them dawdling. You've come a long way; a few more minutes won't matter.'

'Oh, hell. Let's eat something.'

A waitress caught Zarubin's eye, came across to the table and returned to the counter with three orders for coffee and honey cake. The café was full by now, though the human shield seemed not to ease his nerves. He breathed deeply, pursed his lips, gave the establishment another scan and leaned in once more.

'You were able to warn me of this business, so I assume that KGB involved you?'

'They found us, in Portugal. If I did what they wanted, they promised not to hurt Zofia.'

'Ah. And how is she?'

'Dead. She and her new husband were on their way to Mozambique. It was their ship that exploded, killing most of the passengers and crew. It's why I decided to help you.'

'You think KGB were responsible?'

'Who else?'

Zarubin shook his head. 'They wouldn't do that, for very many reasons.'

'Persuade me.'

'Firstly, they needed you to do their business. Why would they wreck that by breaking their promise, at least until it was finished?'

'She ran. They thought she might escape them.'

'If they knew she was on that ship, then obviously she *hadn't* escaped them. But they weren't aware of it, probably, because KGB has no establishment in Portugal and the ship sailed from there, I understand. Second, KGB would never get clearance to create a human disaster, even if they were minded to do it - which they wouldn't be, by the way. Chairman Shelepin is surprisingly human, and very cautious about initiating operations that might go off in his hand. In any case, killing hundreds to get one person would be both disproportionate and inefficient - they could have no way of determining that she wouldn't be one of the survivors. Third, I *know* they didn't do it. It was uncooperative Angolan rebels, taking an easy opportunity to help their comrades around the Horn.'

'You're certain of that?'

'Yes. Apparently, there was a hell of a stink when news reached the Lubyanka, and *everyone* was asked what they knew. It didn't take much effort to get at the truth. But I'm glad that you misjudged the situation, Major. If you hadn't, no doubt I'd be in the Lubyanka myself at this moment. Still, you have my deepest sympathy for your loss.'

Fischer stared at the table. 'If I hadn't misjudged the situation, they would have killed me afterwards, wouldn't they? Once you'd fallen?'

'Definitely. You were the only witness to what they'd done, and even if you had little chance of testifying to anyone that mattered, KGB don't ever leave their bootlaces untied. Your misperception undoubtedly saved us both.' Zarubin glanced around again. 'Or may have. How far have these SIS men to come?'

'Not far, I should think. From Lancaster House, probably.'

Levin brightened. 'Perhaps they're having difficulty parking.'

'Please don't try to be funny.'

Aleksei Alekseevich Krokhin was having the worst day of his Residency so far. Delighted to have been named as Korotkov's acting successor at Karlshorst (it came with a broad hint that the appointment would be made permanent within three months), he had imagined that he might ease himself into the role while handing off the Illegals Directorate to his own successor. Instead, and most unfortunately, his appointment had coincided with Khrushchev finally giving Ulbricht the nod to build his barrier in Berlin, and rather than take time to choose his moment the DDR's Premier was about to bolt from the trap like a greyhound. Everyone at Karlshorst – Red Army and KGB – was consumed by preparations to assist the Germans in getting the thing into place before the Allies could react, knowing that they would have at best a day's notice to move.

And now this. He was directing a delicate operation - hardly planned and horribly rushed - on one telephone while reporting its progress on the other, and if anything went wrong his 'acting' role was likely to last as long as that of a spinal deformation at the Bolshoi. Shelepin's palpable anxiety had wriggled the length of the telephone wire and infected him also; he didn't know why this thing had to happen yet feared its failure as much as if he had conceived it. His ashtray was half-full already, and only a week ago he'd given up …

A voice in his left ear, quiet but urgent, set his heart racing once more.

'It's starting. An F603 Saracen has pulled up directly in front of the entrance. Three men, plain-clothed, have emerged and are entering the building.'

'Is that a problem?'

'Possibly. We're high enough for a head or chest shot as the target leaves, but timing will be extremely tight. Please confirm that we take it, if feasible.'

The final two words were the best thing he'd heard that morning. A last-minute, extemporized operation in enemy territory came with no guarantee of success. That wouldn't necessarily calm Shelepin's ire if it went balls-up, but a spotter's testimony could hardly be dismissed. If the shot was tight, and rushed, and failed to find its target, the KGB Chairman would have to eat his disappointment. This wasn't Stalin's day, when blame *had* to land upon someone with fatal force. Errors weren't tolerated, but insurmountable obstacles to success were just that. By qualifying his question, Kiril the spotter had given Krokhin the means of dampening expectations in advance.

'Wait.'

He flicked the reconnect on the other line and cleared his throat.

'Comrade Chairman, the target is about to leave the building, but a British armoured vehicle is partially blocking access. The shot may be taken, but it will be difficult. The team request authorization to proceed. Please confirm.'

The silence that followed suggested the decision was a difficult one, even for the Head of KGB, but it persisted beyond reason. Krokhin was about to repeat himself when he realised that he could hear nothing – no background conversation, no heavy, anxious breathing, no disconnected tone. They had simply put him on hold, and even though he was presently dancing on eggshells to please the man who would (or wouldn't) make his appointment permanent, he wanted very much to punch him in the face also. What the fuck was Shelepin doing? Did he want this thing done or not? Had he got bored, and wandered off for tea?

He almost slammed the receiver back on to its cradle, but iron self-control was probably listed somewhere in the job description he'd yet to receive. He thumped his desk, picked up the other receiver and flicked the switch.

'Wait.'

KGB's two most senior officers were no longer paying attention to the speaker box. They had stood up and away from Shelepin's desk, and guilt or trepidation had brought them almost to attention in front of the third man, the First Secretary of the Communist Party of the Soviet Union and Chairman of the Council of Ministers. He looked at each of them in turn, hard, and scratched one elbow with his fingernails. It was a nervous habit, well known to those who worked closely with him, and didn't bode well.

'So, a little while ago I was on the telephone.'

Shelepin opened his mouth, which was a mistake. He had nothing useful to say without further information. 'Ah.'

'It seems that Markus Wolf had an urgent conversation with Eric Mielke, who then went to see Walter Ulbricht, who called me – immediately, he said. It seems that our mutual friend crossed the German border yesterday.'

Slowly, Shelepin nodded. 'Yes.'

'Yes. Apparently, Wolf let you know this several minutes after it happened, which was very thoughtful of him. So you've had almost twenty-four hours to pick up our rabbit – I'm sorry, I should have said hare, because he hasn't been veering from side to side as he flees, has he?

Shelepin shook his head. 'No.'

'No. In fact, he couldn't have made it any easier for you if he'd telefaxed his itinerary in advance each morning. Yet you've been holding off. And off. And off. And almost an hour ago I received word that he'd passed through the Invalidenstrasse checkpoint and into West Berlin, which means that he's now beyond the reach of Soviet justice. I should say, beyond the *legal* process.'

This time, Shelepin kept his mouth closed.

Khrushchev stabbed a finger at his chest. 'You're going to kill him, aren't you?'

'I ...'

'Don't deny it! You've had every opportunity to bring him in - since last Monday, in fact. Did I not make it clear that I want him alive?'

'Yes, Comrade Secretary, you did.'

'I knew when I said it that I was talking to the wall. It's why I had our border-guards put me on notice when he reached the Line. I *knew* that you intended to wait until it was too late to snatch him, and then take the only alternative!'

Helplessly, Shelepin ran his fingers through his hair. He had gone to Khrushchev with news of Zarubin's flight specifically to avoid this accusation, yet here it was. How did he know? It wasn't as though …

*Last Monday - t*he day that Zarubin began his epic, preposterous flight. How the hell could the First Secretary know that, if he hadn't been told by KGB? For several moments, Shelepin stared at Semichastny, and wondered if the game he'd played had more than one target. But then a slight noise to his left-side, of something hitting his desk, made him turn. It was a small pile of postcards, slightly scattered by the impact. Each of them carried a Soviet space-programme theme, and looked very familiar.

'He's been sending those to my secretary since he set off on this fucking adventure. On the first one he wrote a brief message, to say that you were getting the same, but the others were blank - obviously, to infer that he wasn't running to the West with secrets. Each morning, Shevchenko and I have had a little bet, on which of these famous cards we'd receive that day. And each day I've waited to hear from *you*, Alexander Nikolayevich, that our good friend had bolted.'

'But ... why didn't you say something when I (Shelepin quashed the *eventually* that almost slipped out) came to see you?'

'What? I should go to the trouble of asking for the truth? Don't I have a right to expect it?'

'No. I mean, yes, of course ...'

'Stop this, now. If it's too late to bring Zarubin home, let him go. He won't be a problem.'

'But what if he *does* talk to the Allies?'

'What can he tell them that they don't know already ? He's had no access to military technical data, or to KGB's illegals operations. Otherwise, the Americans probably know that the Berlin barrier's going up, if not when; they know we're in Africa and Asia, and increasing our work there; they probably know about the problems we've been having with our solid fuel systems. What else can he reveal? That Moscow winters are cold, and strawberries hard to find? Let him go. The only necessary thing is that I don't get any more of his book-length opinions on what you, me and everyone else is wrong about. As to the rest ...' Khrushchev looked pointedly at each man in turn, '... we'll forget that you both ran some sort of operation against one of my advisors without my permission, or even telling me. Now, I expect that you have Krokhin or one of his men on the other end of that 'phone?'

'Yes, Comrade First Secretary.'

'*Tell* him, then.'

The wrong telephone beeped at Krokhin once more. He wanted very much to ignore it, but that wasn't an option. He snatched up the receiver and pressed it to his ear.

'Well?'

'If we don't get the word now, it will be too late. Confirm or abort?'

Krokhin told himself that the decision was not his to make, but that he was being given no choice but to make it. That, in itself, was an exoneration, yet still he needed to make the *correct*, unavoidable decision. For a moment, his instinct urged him to take the least decisive path, and excuse himself later – if necessary – by telling Shelepin that the nature of the task, its complications and the identity of the target required that he give the final word. Unfortunately, the Chairman hadn't hinted at anything resembling discretion, or that there could be any acceptable outcome other than a kill. He didn't know of the complications and couldn't be told until the decision became moot, so the poisoned apple was in Krokhin's hand, inviting him to take a bite.

He sighed, thought about what a wonderful Resident he might have become, and pressed the transmit button.

'Take the shot.'

'I wish ...'

'What?'

Levin looked at Zarubin and shrugged. 'That they were taller. And a little wider.'

The three British gentleman appeared to be typical ex-special services men – wiry, compact, as hard as masonry nails and much the same shape, making them less than effective bullet-hinderers. In rain, they probably didn't get wet. So far, their conversation had been equally sparse. Within a moment of entering the Kranzler-Eck they had made Fischer's face and approached the table. He got a nod from one of them and a slight frown.

'We were told two.' He spoke perfect German, without inflection.

'Well, it will be three.' Fischer extended a hand towards Levin. 'This is ...'

'It doesn't matter. We have a vehicle directly outside. Once in it you'll be safe, but ...' the Englishman half-turned and glanced behind him, '... this isn't ideal. We don't like junctions or tall buildings nearby, so we're going to play safe. Once we get near to the door you'll need to move quickly. Will that be a problem?'

He had noticed Levin's walking stick. The Russian blinked. 'I promise you, when I'm terrified I can be the wind itself.'

The Englishman nodded and turned to Zarubin. 'You'll be the package, then. I'll go out in front of you, these two will be to either side, hands on your shoulders. They may shove, but don't resist. And when the door opens, keep your head down. Is that clear?'

Zarubin nodded. 'Perfectly clear, thank you.'

Fischer lifted a finger and wagged it between himself and Levin. 'We just follow, yes?'

'That's right. It'll be cramped in the vehicle, but we won't have too far to go.'

'To your safe house?'

'No, there's a new plan. We'll take you directly from here to Gatow and put you on to a waiting flight. It's a military 'plane, so again, it won't be very comfortable.'

Fischer nodded. 'I served with the *Fallschirmjäger*. As long as you don't ask me to step out halfway I'll be very happy.'

'Right. We should ...'

'Do you want a table, sir?'

A waitress had noticed the Englishmen and come across from the counter. The dour, serious one who had been doing the talking gave her a brilliant smile.

'No, thank you! We've just come to pick up our friends. Could you bring their bill?'

The moment she turned away he leaned towards Fischer. 'Put money on the table and get up, please.'

As soon as everyone was upright, the Englishmen assumed their triangular formation around Zarubin. Fischer stooped slightly to place a fifty-mark note on the table (which would make the waitress's day, if not week), and straightened. Something heavy hit him somewhere between heart and gut, and the impact made him stagger

'Are you alright, Herr Fischer?

Levin's hand steadied him, but he didn't feel steady. A rush of blood heated his head - he wanted it to be dizziness, but it was something else – a single thought, precise, clear and impassable.

I've had nineteen years that weren't mine. My God ...

'Herr Fischer?'

He turned to Levin. 'Let me go first, will you?'

Levin opened his mouth, closed it and nodded. They followed the other four men, who were almost at the door now. When Zarubin ducked as per orders it left Fischer in clear air, the tallest of the group, emerging into bright daylight. He should have tensed, hesitated, cringed; but the words echoed still, putting a perfect calm where preservation of the self should have been.

The sun was in their faces, and even the SIS men paused for a fraction of a second. Still moving, Fischer barged into the one at Zarubin's left-side, and was pushed back, hard. He extended a foot to brace himself, and it slammed down on another – a deformed, tender item. Levin screamed almost, and thumped his assailant, trying to shift the weight from his tortured foot. Fischer stumbled again, less clumsily, and came up against the door-jamb, which is why the 7.62mm, American-manufactured bullet, which had cleared Zarubin's head by less than a centimetre, missed him also.

But not Levin.

'Oh, stop it. You aren't dying.'

'It's agony.'

''It's a lobe, that's all. You won't notice it's gone unless you try to wear earrings. It was very fortunate.'

Levin, trying not to touch the field dressing, glared at Zarubin. 'It doesn't *feel* fortunate.'

'I meant that it hit you. And not me.'

'Oh, f...'

'You can remove your harnesses now.'

Bernard (he'd introduced himself at Gatow, as the Saracen pulled up behind the RAF transport 'plane) put out a hand and gently moved Levin's head to one side.

'It's stopped bleeding, for the moment. We can brew up some tea, but that's all until Brize Norton, I'm afraid.'

Zarubin glanced around the hold. 'This is a very curious aircraft.' He was speaking English now, in the heavy New York accent he'd acquired in the field, at the turn of the previous decade.

Bernard shrugged. 'It's a Blackburn Beverley. I don't know why they gave us the slowest tub in the fleet.'

'Perhaps to allow us time to change our minds.'

'If you do, we'll push you out the back, so don't. You've visited the States?'

'I lived there, for three years. I'm sure England will be more pleasant.'

Fischer was leaning back against the fuselage, eyes closed, letting the vibrations work through his back muscles. He was wondering how he felt, but getting no reply. He had been ready, perfectly ready, and now he was adrift once more, obliged to look for the path through thorns that had never revealed itself. The bullet had missed him, yet he felt bled-out. He was alive and unhurt, and she was neither; he had pushed a finger up KGB's nose, and it seemed that they were entirely innocent on the matter of her death. They would have killed him, probably, but that wasn't something to hold a grudge about. Perhaps he should write a short note to the Lubyanka, apologizing for the misunderstanding and offering to be more amenable, next time.

They would be in England soon, where he would need to think about yet another course-change. A man had only so many swerves in him, though, and at sixty-three he feared that his allocation was spent. His premature 'death' had lined up too many thoughts of settled matters and closed books for his mind to be where it should be. He had no ideas, no desire to chase them, no heart for the uncertainties of whatever life was coming. *Otto Henry Fischer would like it to be known that he is now retired, from anything that requires an investment in what can't be known beforehand.*

Former General Zarubin beamed at the fretting Levin and an apparently unconscious Fischer. Like a man who had walked away from a burning tank he was finding it hard to quell the euphoria of being unscathed. He had no money, no offer of anything substantial and still needed to find a way to prevent SIS from handing him to the Americans (who doubtless would offer him not-quite-ample accommodation on a very, very long lease); yet a world that had compacted itself to the dimensions of an execution cell had expanded wonderfully once more. He would miss his homeland and, God knew, the perquisites of a system that amply rewarded its elites, but he was breathing still, fairly handsome still, and if he couldn't in short order make the English think him indispensable then they must have sharpened considerably since the war.

He leaned across the hold and tapped two knees. Levin glared at him, but Fischer's gaze was as blank as anything he'd seen in eyes that weren't yet dead. Neither prospect managed to dent his fine mood.

'Do you know, I have a *very* good feeling about this.'

53

Fucking Otto.

Kleiber read it once more, and wondered what he should, or could, do. He wasn't going to contact the English spy again, because he didn't know what the man would do with it, for good or bad. He'd seemed pleasant enough, but then, they said that Heydrich could be a real charmer when he made the effort. The man might use it kindly; he might use it to destroy Otto. Who could ever tell, with those who played at being sphinxes?

Poor Otto.

He couldn't be reached, and nor could Freddie Holleman (his wife had said that he was *away*, and then put down the 'phone rather abruptly). He'd checked out of his hotel in Bonn two days earlier and left no forwarding number, so by now he could be anywhere, not excluding a hole in the ground (*Christ, don't think that*). How the hell could someone who wasn't police track him down?

Kleiber had been fretting for hours now – in fact, since the postman put the thing in his hand and he'd decided to open it. If only he hadn't. Ignorance is a very comfortable state, requiring no great expenditure of perspiration or imagination. His oblivious self might have finished that article on British reactions to the DDR's decision to further limit western traffic to Berlin, if these few lines of scrawl hadn't emptied his mind of everything but Otto bloody Fischer. Why couldn't the man just live as normal people did, decay gracefully on a golf course and leave memories that didn't represent the most exciting passages (in the very worst sense) of his friends' lives?

A thunderous knock on the door interrupted his personal Stations of the Cross. It was trainee-baker Alfred, grinning cheekily.

'Is it a call for me? Let me get my shoes ...'

'It's alright, Jonas. She gave me a message and hung up.'

'She?'

'Bird named Gloria. Says she's sorry, though about what I dunno. Would like to see you again, and how's tonight?'

Kleiber had been relieved to say goodbye to Gloria, but the hint of her still-burning desire for him immediately laid waste to every sensible reason he had to ignore the invitation.

'Did she say where?'

The grin broadened. 'Not as such. She did mention that her parents were in Spain at the moment, and that she was all alone – and lonely - at home.'

A grey afternoon burst into technicolor splendour, and a flood of pertinent considerations – a clean shirt, shave, haircut, bath, flowers, wine, condoms

– crowded out the minor matter of finding Otto Fischer, Kleiber spent the next two hours working through the list and rehearsing ways to apologize for his past sins (whatever they might be, he couldn't say), and it was only as he collected what needed to be stuffed into pockets before departing that he noticed it once more on the kitchen table. This time, reason and logic had a strong following breeze named Gloria to assist them, and he dwelt upon his conundrum for a moment only.

If I can't do anything about it, what can I do?

Still, to reassure himself that he cared he opened it and read it once more, made a silent promise that the matter would get further consideration the following day and let himself out of the flat.

———

Dearest Otto,

I hope this finds you at your friend's address in London. It's all I have for you.

We arrived at the Port of Luanda in good health, but within hours poor Felipe was in great pain, and hardly to be moved. A doctor diagnosed appendicitis, and the operation took place the following morning. It was a success, but we were warned that the city was heavily infected with yellow fever, and that Felipe should be moved, if possible, to where he might convalesce safely.

Fortunately, his brother-in-law owns a plantation at Bom Jesus, and the manager was happy to accommodate us. We spent three weeks there, and it was only when we returned to Luanda to find passage back to Portugal that we heard the dreadful news of the sinking off Mozambique.

What must you have been thinking all this time? Please let me know that you are safe, and quickly! Risk nothing for my sake, and, if you can, come home soon. The world can fight itself without our help, as it always has.

You have my very deepest affection, and I pray that you are well.

Zofia

Author's Note

In October 1961, Aleksander Shelepin was appointed to the Soviet Council of Ministers. His place as KGB Chairman was taken by his long-time protege, Vladimir Semichastny. A few weeks after assuming an interim role as head of KGB at Karlshorst (following the death of the previous Resident, Korotkov), Alexei Krokhin was confirmed in the position, where he served until 1966.

In 1964, both Shelepin and Semichastny played leading roles in bringing down Khrushchev. The process of removing him followed strictly legal forms, but the First Secretary regarded Semichastny's participation in particular as a betrayal. However, it is believed that Semichastny made it a condition of his support that Khrushchev be allowed to retire peacefully and not be sanctioned for his alleged failures in office.

Roger Broadsmith is a fictional character, but Harold Shergold was one of SIS's most effective officers, being responsible for extracting George Blake's confession and running, with representatives from the CIA, the most important Soviet defector of the period, Oleg Penkovsky (whose code-name, referenced several times in the text, was HERO). It has been suggested that Shergold was partly the inspiration for the character George Smiley, though his creator, John le Carré, consistently denied this.

The sinking of the liner/munitions ship MS *Save* with heavy loss of life occurred substantially as described in the text. However, no evidence has ever emerged to suggest that the explosion which destroyed her was other than accidental, and the author's inference that the Angolan liberation movement MPLA was responsible is a fiction.

Printed in Great Britain
by Amazon